THE GEMS OF ELSANA

BOOK ONE: INTO THE WILDBARRENS

CHRISTIAN STERLING

Map Artwork by Daniel Hasenbos

Brusheezy provided vines, corner accents, and main accents for cover art.
Skulls, flowers, swords, and gem were designed by Freepik.

To my mother,
The summers spent under our reading tree gifted me the
imagination to write such a fantasy series.

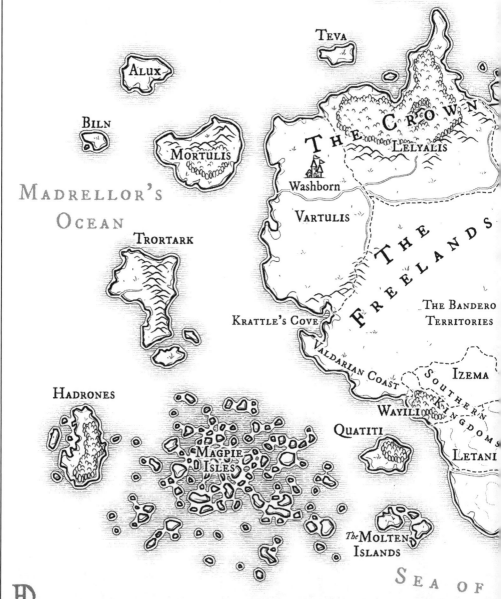

The WORLD of ELSANA

SEA OF

FAERELLEN

TEVA

ALUX

BILN

MORTULIS

THE CROWN

LELYALIS

Washborn

VARTULIS

MADRELLOR'S OCEAN

TRORTARK

THE FREELANDS

THE BANDERO TERRITORIES

KRATTLE'S COVE

VALDARIAN COAST

SOUTHERN KINGDOMS

IZEMA

WAYILI

QUATITI

LETANI

HADRONES

MAGPIE ISLES

The MOLTEN ISLANDS

SEA OF

2019

ETERNAL ICE

SARALYSE

URA

WIZARD
ISLAND

OLIVEL

BORLOCK

TURLEN

OF ELSANA

MYSTICA

RENU

Rendrun
RODRELLAN

Narella

MADRELLOR'S
OCEAN

Rorkshire

THE
OLDWOODS

FIELDS OF DARVA

Ruins of
Darva

WARLOCK
ISLAND

XI

MORTAL MTS.

DRUCULLM

MARROW

SWAMPS

Suntalla

ZUCAN

Monkey
Mountain

VARSA

STONY
VALLEY

TZAL

CADRYL

THE
WILDBARRENS

DRAGOS

ETERNAL FIRE

CHAPTER ONE:
A WIZARD'S CHAMPIONS

Falin inhaled, basking in the perfumed air of Narella's gardens. To the young wizard, the royal palace was a waking dream of enchantment, brimming with flowers so vibrant he could hardly believe they were real. Everywhere his gaze landed, Falin discovered the sight of a new, astounding color. The warm breeze brushed his face from where he stood on the palace turret. He clutched his staff, which resembled a thick branch with a gnarled and bulbous top.

Narella, the capital of Mystica, was a world different from Wizard Island where he'd spent his first twenty years. There, he only knew damp, rainy days and a landscape wrapped with rocky terrain and weeds. It was as if the ancient wizards sacrificed all the beauty of their island when they created the land of Mystica and the sages within it.

Falin heard his mentor, Airo, speak behind him. "I had a feeling you would be up here." Airo strolled beside Falin and looked over the grounds, leaning his own staff against the wall. His plump belly rested against the stone, and wispy grey hair and beard danced in the breeze. "In my five hundred years, I have traveled all over Elsana, and few places are as beautiful as Narella." He spoke slow and confident, as most wizards did. Airo took a deep breath and lifted his face so the sun could shine on it. Despite being five centuries old, he looked no more than a common man would at sixty. "Are you ready for the ceremony?"

"I suppose," Falin answered, nervously twirling his staff. "There is not much I need to do but stand there. It seems like it is more for the Champions than me."

Airo chuckled, soft and sweet. "You are not wrong. This event only comes once a century. More often than not, most experience this once in their lives. It is cause for celebration."

"You're right," Falin replied. He turned to his mentor and leaned against the wall. Airo stared over the gardens with a subtle smile, his hands clasped, hidden beneath baggy robe sleeves. "This tradition lacks sense to me, if I'm being honest," Falin admitted.

"And why is that, my pupil?" Airo asked, peering at a vine of magenta honey flowers.

Falin looked to the four empty slots on the head of his staff. "If it is so important that I gather the Gems of Elsana to come to my full power, why do I only travel with four people? Why not take an army? Why aren't you or any of the other wizards coming with me?"

"Because there would be nothing learned in doing so," Airo explained. "Your journey to gather the Gems is half gaining power here," he said, knocking on the top of Falin's staff, "and half gaining power here," he added, rapping his knuckles to the young wizard's forehead. Airo held his stomach as it jiggled, bellowing at his own joke. "No journey well spent has ever gone without stumbles."

Falin fought a smile, running his fingers on the cool stone wall. "I wish I could've spent time exploring the other nations in the Crown. Everything about Lelyalis sounds amazing. And I want to see the Madorian Lumber Castles in Rendrun, and the Washborn Mountains in Vartulis."

"When you return, I will personally take you to all that you have mentioned and more," Airo promised.

"That's if I return," Falin mumbled. "I know that other wizards have been killed on this journey. We barely have power without the Gems. And it's not like we can be replaced—a wizard is only born every hundred years."

"This is true," Airo replied, "but it is rare for a wizard to perish on this excursion. The last to be killed was twelve hundred years ago, and that was by a warlock who met the full wrath of the wizards."

Falin became a little more anxious than before. "Do you think I'll meet any warlocks?"

"Maybe." Airo shrugged, scratching behind his ear. "You almost certainly will over the course of your life. The ten wizards alive serve the God of Light, and the ten warlocks serve the God of Darkness. You are bound to clash at one point or another. It is more likely you will run into gruns, crags, and augurs, especially if taken too close to the Shadow Kingdoms." Falin scanned the garden beneath, wondering what he'd do if facing a warlock. "Don't be concerned," Airo assured. "I will not lie to you. Your journey will be filled with treacherous challenges, terrible foes, and unforgiving landscapes. Your determination will be shaken, and evils you cannot fathom will present themselves at your most vulnerable." Airo paused a moment before continuing. "But this world is a balance of Light and Dark, and with these troubles, you will make friends the same as you make foes, and you will know victory the same as you find defeat. This is the journey one must take to truly understand what it means to be a wizard in Elsana."

Falin took in everything that was said. "I wonder what my name will be," he thought aloud. "Once I gather all my Gems." The older wizards all carried noble titles from valiant deeds. There was Huran the Giver and Marko the Dragon, then Tani the Wise and Sero the Tide. Falin turned to his mentor, given the name Airo the

Bane. The young wizard found it hard to believe that anyone would consider such a harmonious being a bane.

"That is not of your concern," Airo said. "Spend too much time worrying about how you will be remembered, and you will forget to do anything memorable at all."

Falin peeked at the Gems of red, green, white, and blue in Airo's staff. "Marko once told me that wizards tend to have an affinity for certain Gems. He says that the Fire Gem is where he draws most of his power."

"There is some truth in it, yes," Airo admitted. "I, for instance, feel the most powerful with the Earth Gem."

Falin smirked. "I know. I remember you hurling boulders into the ocean to make me laugh as a child."

Airo chuckled softly, taking another breath of air. "It is time. We must go to the throne room to begin the ceremony."

Falin glanced over the immaculate garden and nodded, collecting his staff to follow his mentor down the turret steps. After navigating the halls of the palace, they arrived at the grand entrance of the throne room—already crowded— where all stood in the audience of Queen Martana, ruler of Mystica, and King Dothmer, ruler of Rodrellan.

A small congregation comprised of sages, madorians, draks, and elves watched in anticipation. This ceremony transpired once a century, and all gathered felt blessed to witness it. Torches of green flame hung from walls of turquoise stone, the meticulous masonry only broken by stained and shimmering glass windows. All were dressed in the noble garb of their people, as an invitation to Queen Martana's court was the highest of honors. Despite being in Mystica, King Dothmer of Rodrellan was given an honorary throne beside the Queen.

Martana, Queen of Sages, was of supreme beauty, her golden, curly hair falling far onto her back, topped with an elegant silver crown. Her air was one of cascading authority and benevolence.

Wearing white linen garb stitched with shiny golden lace, she stood with folded hands.

Beside her, King Dothmer appeared the epitome of a madorian. Standing a foot over Falin, Dothmer's red and golden cloak hid his hulking frame, and his hair was as white as his beard, neatly trimmed so one could still see the gentle smile placed beneath it. Both rulers wore royalty as if tailored to them.

Falin followed Airo through the room, and as he did, all turned their gaze. The queen and king rose in their presence. Airo climbed the steps of the landing to stand beside the thrones where he nodded to the royals, shuffling aside for Falin.

Falin thought it was odd that only two of the four kingdoms within the Crown of Elsana had leaders present for the ceremony. The elves of Lelyalis had no leader, he knew that, but the Drakkish Senate of Vartulis declined attendance citing their elections. Many suspected it was really due to their soured relationship with Rodrellan in the previous two centuries.

Falin scanned the faces in the court. Most stared back at the young sorcerer, eager to learn what this century's wizard would offer.

Draks of Vartulis waited with grim and pale faces, presenting their fanged canines in the few moments they spoke, dressed in either dark grey or black. Their features were mixed of common men and elves, carrying an icy elegance.

Elves of Lelyalis stood beside their drakkish counterparts, small and lean with keen eyes, their skin light, but of a porcelain glow.

On the opposite side of the room, Sages of Mystica wore vibrant garb, their demeanor exuding a pure kindness and magical warmth. They appeared no different than common man.

Finally, Madorians of Rodrellan towered over the rest, all the men with beards, some holding their ceremonial wooden shields and greatswords, each as imposing as the last.

Falin appeared no more than a common man of the Freelands, with scraggly dark hair falling over his forehead and the wisps of a beard beneath his chin. He hoped not to disappoint them. Airo assuringly nudged Falin, smiling.

Queen Martana raised her arms, palms up, and spoke to the audience. Her piercing green eyes met those who listened as if a mother telling her children a story. "In the Beginning, Mother Elsana birthed two sons, the God of Light, and the God of Darkness. The God of Light sought peace and prosperity for his Mother's lands, and sent shepherds: Wizards, faeries, and giants. In the Wars of the Beginning, the faeries and giants were killed by servants of the Dark, but wizards remain to guide us." She paused to scan her audience. "It is but once in a century, Elsana is blessed with a wizard, one of ten in the world. Twenty years ago, The God of Light brought us Falin, and for that, we are thankful."

"We are thankful," the sages in the congregation repeated.

Queen Martana continued. "A wizard's life is that of a thousand years, and in those thousand years they are our guardians, our heroes, and our peacekeepers. They gave life to the sages, and are friends to all creatures sired by the God of Light. Before a wizard may depart into the world as a guiding force, they must collect the four Gems of Elsana to be placed into the head of their staff."

All eyes focused on Falin and his staff with four empty slots. Even now, Falin could feel the magic yearning to be released from his body, hindered by his lack of Gems. The Gems of Airo's staff seemed to sparkle at their mention.

"As is tradition," Queen Martana went on, "one Champion from every kingdom in the Crown of Elsana will accompany our young wizard as he begins his quest. They will pledge their lives to the wizard they accompany, leaving his side only in death, or the completion of his journey. It is my honor to introduce these Champions today. Please allow our first Champion to enter!"

The doors to the throne room opened and in walked Melquin the Healer. She had black, braided hair that fell over her left shoulder. Her skin was darker than most of the other sages present, and she wore a deep purple tunic and pants, carrying a white staff laced with ivy and flowers. Like most sages, Melquin's stride was not one of pomp, nor circumstance, but as if she glided through a garden, her feet meeting the ground so gently it would not damage grass. As she reached the base of the steps, she nodded, then dropped to a knee. Falin sensed magic within her.

King Dothmer stepped forward, removing his greatsword from its sheath with a shimmering ring, placing the flat end of the blade on her head. The sword's hilt sparkled in the ruby gemstones adorning it. In his deep and rich timbre, King Dothmer bellowed, "Do you, Melquin the Healer, Sage of Mystica, pledge your life to Falin during his quest? Leaving his side only by death?"

"I do," Melquin said with her head bent as if in prayer. "I swear it by the God of Light."

"Rise Melquin," Dothmer ordered, "stand with us as a Champion to your people." With a guiding hand, Dothmer gestured to his right for Melquin to stand at his side. Queen Martana's eyes followed Melquin in overwhelming pride.

"May our next Champion enter," Queen Martana announced.

Again, the doors opened, and all eyes turned to Carthon the Warrior. Falin had heard tales of him, a heroic fighter of Vartulis, having defeated the reviled pirate Yelgis in the sieges of the Valdarian Coast.

Despite his legend, Carthon appeared far younger than Falin expected. The drak approached, dressed in a black shirt and pants, with two, single-sided swords draped across his back. His face was the same as all other draks—stoic and brooding—with sharp features on a slender frame. His stride was confident, the chip on his shoulder as evident as his prowess with a blade. Falin noticed elven women crane their necks to better glimpse his suave entry. As Carthon reached the foot of the steps, he fell to a knee.

King Dothmer placed his sword upon Carthon's head of fair hair, proclaiming, "Do you, Carthon, Warrior to the Drakkish Senate of Vartulis, pledge your life to Falin during his quest? Leaving his side only by death?"

"I do," Carthon answered. "I swear it by the God of Light." Falin could not help but notice Carthon's fangs in the few seconds he spoke, shivering at the thought that draks once sustained themselves on human blood.

"Rise Carthon," King Dothmer commanded. "Stand with us a Champion of your people." As Carthon trudged up the steps to stand by Melquin, he denied meeting the gaze of the Madorian King. Though subtle, it was evident to Falin there was a bitterness Carthon harbored for King Dothmer.

"May our next Champion proceed," Queen Martana commanded.

Nym the Assassin entered. The elf came forward, her stride one of playfulness, with mischievous eyes darting the room. She stood no taller than five feet – the average height of an elf – her pointed ears peeking out from her shoulder-length red hair. A small, one-edged sword hung from her waist with a belt of varying sized pouches strapped to it. With a lighthearted grin, she all but pranced forward and dramatically fell to her knee at the foot of the throne where Dothmer placed the sword atop her head. "Do you, Nym the Assassin, Defender of Lelyalis, pledge your life to Falin during his quest? Leaving his side only by death?"

"I do!" Nym exclaimed. "I swear it by the God of Light!"

"Rise Nym!" King Dothmer declared. "And stand with us a Champion of your people!"

Nym leapt over all four steps, nimbly landing beside Carthon and Melquin. She grinned at the other two Champions with her hands clasped behind her back, swaying back in forth in excitement.

Airo elbowed Falin and whispered, "Elves are good at everything, and they won't let you forget it."

"Send us our final Champion," Queen Martana ordered.

The doors opened, and in marched Bossador, Prince of the Madorians, heir to the throne of Rodrellan. He was the spitting image of his father, King Dothmer, but with a dark beard and broad face beneath flowing hair. A greatsword was sheathed by his waist, and a large wooden shield hung from his back. Bossador strode forward with a puffed chest, young and eager to earn his honor before inheriting the Throne of Rodrellan. His imposing frame met the steps, and he knelt, bowing his head so his father could place the ceremonial sword atop.

King Dothmer began. "Do you Bossador, son of Dothmer, Prince of Rodrellan, pledge your life to Falin during his quest? Leaving his side only by—" The king took a steadying breath, one of pride specked with fear. "Leaving his side only by death?"

"I do," Bossador answered in his deep voice. "I swear it by the God of Light." The prince spoke the oath with extreme dutifulness.

"Rise Bossador!" his father said proudly. "Stand with us as a Champion of your people!"

As Bossador climbed the steps to stand with the other three Champions, King Dothmer watched with glistening eyes as his son stood a hero.

"That's a great crew," Airo whispered in Falin's ear. Falin eyed Bossador, Nym, Carthon, and Melquin, feeling a little bit better about being thrust into the world. They were all formidable, confident, and noble.

"We have our Champions," Queen Martana smiled. The crowd applauded, praising those dedicating their lives to the cause. The queen's face fell, and she opened her mouth to speak, then paused as if hesitant. She glanced at Airo, who nodded encouragingly. "Under the guidance of the wizards, we have made some changes to the Tradition of Champions," she said. She again peered at Airo with uncertainty, and once more, he nodded in warm assurance. Falin wasn't sure what was happening, nor did the rest of the audience, but the Champions seemed to pout in the coming news. He looked to Airo in confusion. "The wizards have foreseen the journey will take our heroes into the Wildbarrens."

A flurry of worried murmurs swept through the listeners. The Queen spoke louder. "It has been a rare instance in centuries past to have an individual venture into the Wildbarrens and return. Those who journey there are rarely seen again, and those who are exiled there plead for death." Queen Martana's words hung in the room, silent but for the crackling of green torches.

"By insistence of the wizards, our heroes shall be accompanied by two individuals claiming to have traveled through the Wildbarrens." Falin turned to Airo in surprise, not knowing why he was learning this now. Airo shrugged as the Queen continued. "Please bring them in," she ordered with apprehension.

One final time, the doors to the throne room opened, and to Falin's surprise, the jangle of chains met his ears. Four sage guards escorted two prisoners, each with shackled wrists and feet.

The first, a common man of average height shuffled forward, wearing a wide brim, brown hat of a cattle herder, his dark hair peeking from beneath. With shifty eyes, he rattled to the throne, his gaze darting the crowd before landing on the queen, the king, Airo, then Falin. He was no older than his early thirties, and his sandy face was worn as if he'd experienced a strained life twice that time. His cheeks and neck held faded scars, each with a tale to match. As he shuffled past the crowd, he winked at a group of noble sage women. Attempting to appear appalled by the gesture, they failed and cracked smiles in return.

The next prisoner came into view, and Falin was delighted to see it was a Skully of Quatiti. Falin had only read about skullies, seeing drawings in the faded books he'd been given, but in person, this form of being was astounding.

The skully stood no more than four feet in height, with cracked, deep grey skin, appearing coarse and tough as if made of leathery stone. His head was bald, with bulging eyes and a tiny nose, small ears, and a jaw that protruded outward. He wore nothing but green pants, and his bare grey feet slapped the floor as he walked. The skully innocently examined the crowd that grimaced at his appearance.

Queen Martana peered down her nose at the two who were thrust to the base of the stairs. The man worked at a piece of food stuck in his teeth as the skully twisted his neck in all directions, absorbing the room with a curious demeanor. The skully's gaze fell on Falin, to which he smiled as wide as he could, revealing a set of large pearly teeth. Falin grinned back, sensing magic in the skully the same way he sensed magic in the sages present.

King Dothmer cleared his throat. "It would be wise of you to introduce yourselves in a manner fitting to Queen Martana's court."

The Freelander clicked his tongue, then glanced at the scolding eyes of the queen. "Sure," he answered, with a defiant tone and twang of someone born in the Western Freelands. "I'm Redrick of the Freelands. Y'all can call me Red." Red turned to his skully counterpart and nodded.

"Jimbuah Kah," the skully answered, his voice gravelly and rough as his skin. Despite his tone, his aura was friendly, and he stepped forward with an outstretched hand. As the guards began to point their staves, Jimbuah retracted his misguided gesture, startled.

King Dothmer raised his hand to the guards and descended the steps, standing over the skully. Jimbuah strained his neck to meet the gaze of the king. "Jimbuah," King Dothmer began. "I am King Dothmer, ruler of Rodrellan, Unifier of the Crown of Elsana."

Falin heard Carthon breathe sharply from his nose, and as he turned, saw Prince Bossador scowl at the drak. The two glared at one another in a momentary exchange as the king continued. "It is a pleasure to meet you. I have never been graced with a skully's presence." He outstretched his massive hand and accepted Jimbuah's tiny one.

As the two shook, Jimbuah said, "Takulu lijaki triba."

King Dothmer stared at Jimbuah for a moment before turning to Red. "He said you're tall. Like a tree," Red translated.

The king threw his head back and laughed heartily with his hand to his chest. "Very good, Jimbuah. Very good."

Dothmer climbed the steps and stood beside the queen. Queen Martana, less amused, glanced between the prisoners. "You two were caught stealing from the Duke of Urlen's keep near my border not a month ago."

"We weren't stealin'." Red shook his head and shrugged. "Just passin' through, ma'am."

"They found you in his mead-cellar, half-conscious, wearing the Duchess' jewelry."

Jimbuah laughed, "*Heh-heh-heh-heh,*" in his hoarse voice. Falin heard Airo stifle a chuckle beside him.

"This is considered passing through to you?" the queen pressed.

Red turned up his shackled palms. "What do you want me to say? We were screwin' around and got caught."

The queen took a short breath and continued speaking to maintain some sense of dignity to the ceremony. "You both claim to have traveled into the Wildbarrens. Is this true?"

"Yeah," Red muttered.

"Yekasa," Jimbuah repeated.

The queen turned to Airo. "Do they speak the truth?" Airo examined them, then confidently nodded his head. Falin searched the duo, wishing he had the power that Airo did to discern if someone spoke honestly.

Queen Martana hesitated before continuing. "We offer you freedom in return for your willingness to guide Falin and our Champions through the Wildbarrens. You do not have to remain on this quest for the Gems any further than that. Do you accept?"

Red glanced at Jimbuah, and in that instant, the two shared several thoughts. "What's the alternative?"

Surprised by the question, Queen Martana answered, "Thieves are sentenced to five years of hard labor in the Ice Fields of Drillian, but because it was a transgression against the Duke, it would be ten years."

Red stooped to Jimbuah's level and the two rapidly whispered and gestured, considering their options. Everyone waited in anticipation, bewildered it was even worth a discussion. Queen Martana's brow furrowed as her gaze flitted between the two deliberating her offer.

Red stood and cleared his throat. "We'll take the ten years on the ice fields. Please."

Gasps rippled through the crowd, and the queen's astonished eyes grew wide. "You wish to take punishment rather than be set free?! Are you aware of what life is like on the Ice Fields of Drillian?"

"Well, ya see, your highness," Red explained, "we figure we'll *probably* die going back to the Wildbarrens, but at least we're escaping certain death in the ice fields. See what I'm saying?"

"You are cowards," the queen sneered.

Red angrily pointed a thumb to his chest. "We're survivors."

"Does this man speak for you, *skully*?" the Queen asked in a condescending tone.

Jimbuah pointed to his pants. "Ibati bakulus. *Hijanesa.*"

Queen Martana's glare whipped between the two. "What did he just say?!"

Red raised his eyebrows, hid a gulp, and spoke in a far more polite tone. "He said, 'yes, your highness.'"

Based on the way Airo shifted, Falin could not help but feel only part of the translation was accurate. "Enough," Airo ordered. Though he spoke softly, his voice rumbled through the room like a distant earthquake. The wizard descended the steps and peered between the prisoners, staff in hand. He bent slightly, standing on the step above them. "You two have seen much, I can sense it in you," Airo thought aloud. He tilted his head and examined the arm of Red. Falin followed his gaze and noticed the permanent stain of tiny, inked runes upon the forearm of the prisoner. "I see you were once a prisoner of Cadryl." Red stiffened at the mention of the treacherous place within the Shadow Kingdoms.

Airo waved his staff, and simultaneously, their shackles came unclasped, falling from their wrists and ankles. "Who are we to judge those with less opportunity than us? Why should we ask them to serve a world that has betrayed them?" All listened to the legendary wizard's words intently. Airo sighed and the room became calm, and a once ominous presence became a cloudless day. "Tell us Redrick and Jimbuah, what reward do you seek for returning to the Wildbarrens?"

Red turned to Jimbuah, and this time, they didn't need to converse. "We want a home," the Freelander answered. "A safe one. It doesn't have to be a fancy one. Or anythin' big. Just nice enough to live in and far away from people always tryin' to kill us. We'll take any of the territories in the Crown; preferably not in Vartulis, or anywhere too cold."

Airo turned to Queen Martana. "As a representative of the wizards, I make my formal recommendation that you grant their wish."

The queen scanned the two and nodded. "So be it. You may have a home."

Once again, King Dothmer raised his sword. "Kneel to swear the oath."

Red removed his hat and knelt alongside Jimbuah, and Dothmer placed his sword on the Freelander's head. "Do you, Redrick of the Freelands, pledge your life to Falin until through the Wildbarrens? Leaving his side only by death?"

Red took a thoughtful breath before answering. "Yes."

King Dothmer moved his sword to the skully's head. "And do you, Jimbuah the Skully, pledge your life to Falin until through the Wildbarrens? Leaving his side only by death?"

"Yekasa," Jimbuah answered.

"Rise, Redrick and Jimbuah, and stand with our Champions."

Red replaced his hat and climbed the steps, exchanging an uncertain glance with Jimbuah.

Queen Martana turned to the group. Melquin the Healer, Carthon the Warrior, Nym the Assassin, Bossador the Prince, Redrick of the Freelands, and Jimbuah of Quatiti stood side by side. "May the God of Light be with you in your journey."

Following the exit processional of the ceremony, Falin and Airo returned to the younger wizard's chambers, quietly discussing the events that transpired. Falin slammed the door to his room as Airo took a seat at the edge of the bed. "I don't care that they're prisoners, I care that you didn't tell me I was being given two extra Champions!"

Airo shrugged. "Why does it matter? Not an hour ago you were saying you thought it was silly you didn't travel with more companions as you search for the Gems."

"My whole life, I've been kept on an island of rocks in the middle of a cold sea, and when I'm finally told I can venture into the world on my own, I'm still being kept in the dark. And now I look weak!"

"Settle down," Airo soothed. "You didn't look weak. You must welcome Red and Jimbuah into your life the same way you would your Champions. They offer as much value as anyone else."

Falin shook his head, rubbing his eyes. "How do you know I will be going into the Wildbarrens? Did someone have a vision?"

Airo nodded grimly. "Purla saw it. She said you were in a place that only could've been the Wildbarrens. And that you had six Champions instead of four." The older wizard softened. "I apologize. I should have told you."

Falin leaned against the turquoise wall and pressed his head to the stone. He settled himself. "I like the skully."

Airo grinned and twisted a few strands of his beard. "As did I. They are wonderful creatures, Falin. And as ancient as wizards, if not more."

"I thought they were the same age as wizards?" Falin asked.

Airo shrugged. "No one's really sure. Many believe they were here during the Beginning. We know they were here in the Wars of the Beginning, at least. Them and the stonies. Before the faeries made the elves and the giants made the madorians even."

"You think there'd be a text that has an answer," Falin said.

"If there was ever any evidence, it is long gone," Airo replied, standing from the bed with a grunt. "We shouldn't dally, you must be off soon. Are you packed?"

"Yes," Falin answered, gesturing to a bag by the floor. "I packed light, just like you said."

"Good." Airo nodded. "I have a gift for you. Grab your staff." The mentor wizard reached into his sleeve and retrieved an old scroll, rolled tightly, tied with twine. Falin accepted the parchment and opened it, seeing it was a map of Elsana. "This was the same map I used when I gathered my Gems," Airo said. "Believe it or not, it's still rather accurate to today's borders. I want you to have it."

Falin was touched by the gesture. His eyes scanned the map, wondering what history this document had seen. "Thank you," Falin said quietly.

"Press the head of your staff to the paper," Airo commanded. "Focus your energy."

Falin did as instructed, channeling magic through his staff, and a small blue dot formed atop a depiction of the Mortal Mountains. He gasped in surprise and delight. "Master Rulo told me I would have to use 'Wizard's Instinct' to search for the Gems. I didn't realize I would have a map to them."

Airo shook his head and rolled his eyes. "That is Master Rulo being Master Rulo. What are wizards going to do? Search their entire lives for the Gems? No, this map will guide you in the order you are meant to find them. This blue dot here is likely the Water Gem. After you retrieve it, press your staff to the map again, and the location of the next Gem will appear."

Falin furrowed his brow. "Should I go through the Oldwoods? Or around them?"

Airo shrugged. "Listen to your Wizard's Instinct." His jaw dropped slightly and rubbed his forehead. "I'm turning into Master Rulo."

Falin smiled, and all at once, he was overwhelmed, not wanting to leave his mentor. Part of him wished to return to Wizard Island. "I am going to miss you."

"I'm going to miss you as well," Airo said. "More than you know. But I am sure we will cross paths on your journey. I have work to attend to across Elsana."

Falin cocked his head. "You are not going back to the Island?"

Airo shook his head. "No. Mysterious tidings have arisen. Where they will take me, I do not know."

Falin turned his attention to the map, wondering where Airo would be headed. "Okay. I guess I should be going. I know there's some sort of exit ceremony."

"It's more like a parade from the palace," Airo said. "You'll hate it."

Falin dropped his head and smiled, lingered for a moment, then stepped forward, giving his mentor a hug. "Thank you for every-thing, Airo. I hope to see you soon."

Airo hugged him tightly, patting him on the back. "We shall, my pupil. We shall."

Falin lifted his bag and huffed. "I'm ready."

The two exited the chamber and marched through the palace until reaching the main exit. High wooden doors stood almost thirty feet in height, touching the stone ceiling. Guards lined the walls, and the Champions milled by the doorway.

Airo whispered in Falin's ear. "I'm going to wait on the steps with the king and queen. You should take a moment to meet your Champions." The wizard nodded to the guards, who opened the door enough for him to leave.

In the few seconds the doors opened, Falin could hear the rum-bling of the crowd outside. He turned to the group, still watching him, wishing he had mastered the art of eloquence as Airo had. "Thank you all for embarking on this journey with me."

"Our pleasure!" Nym the elf said.

Carthon the drak nodded without emotion.

"As a sage, it is an honor to serve the wizards," Melquin answered.

Bossador raised his chin and puffed his chest. "Falin, this is my greatest honor. You have my word, as the Prince of Rodrellan, heir to the Madorian Throne, that I will grant you my sword, my — "

"We never got our weapons back," Red spoke over Bossador. Everyone turned to the man. Bossador glared at him. "Sorry, I thought you were done with your whole…" Red motioned his hand in circles, searching for a word. "Monologue."

"I'm not sure that it would be wise to give two *prisoners* any weapons at all," Bossador answered. "We don't know if you are a danger or not."

"Thakutu dujimo," Jimbuah responded in a snooty tone. "Nofato enkamisas."

"Jimmy's right," Red argued. "We're here to guide you through the Wildbarrens. And we can't do that if we're dead. We're not enemies. Scoundrel's oath."

"You can't expect us to trust a pair of thieves," Carthon spoke. All turned to him in surprise. His voice was as cold as his demeanor. "You were in shackles not an hour ago."

"And yet we were given the same honor as you, oh mighty warrior," Red replied.

"We should let Falin decide," Melquin interjected. Her staff rested in the crook of her elbow, and she played at her long black braid. "He's leading us."

The group turned to him in anticipation. Falin did not want to anger the honorable Champions, nor did he want to be responsible for the deaths of Red or Jimbuah. The young wizard lightly tapped his staff on the floor in thought. "I appreciate your concerns," he began, "but Airo placed his trust in them, so I will do the same. It would be a folly to doubt a wizard's instinct, especially one as accomplished as my mentor."

Bossador dropped his eyes and nodded as a disappointed child might. Carthon's gaze flipped between the prisoners and the wizard, nodding so slightly Falin barely noticed.

"Guards," Falin called. "Could you retrieve the belongings of Red and Jimbuah? With haste please." Two guards hustled off to do as told.

"So, it may be my ignorance," Nym began, "but where are we going?"

"That's a valid question," Falin mumbled, opening the map Airo gave him. "Seems like the first Gem is somewhere in the Mortal Mountains. I figured we could make our way to Rorkshire, then through the Oldwoods. Have any of you been to the Oldwoods before?"

Red was the only person to raise his hand. "You don't want to go into the Oldwoods," he started. "Too much strange stuff happens in there."

"Going around will be dangerous," Bossador argued. "We'd be left vulnerable to an assault in open field."

"We'd have coverage," Nym said. "And if we get outnumbered we'd have a better time in the woods than in the field."

Falin nodded. "Yes, I think it's for the best we go through the Oldwoods." Red turned away and grumbled something no one could hear.

"And then once through the Oldwoods, it's straight to the Mortal Mountains?" Melquin asked.

"That's where the first Gem seems to be. Have any of you been to the Mortal Mountains?"

Red and Jimbuah were the only ones who raised their hands. "Yekasa," Jimbuah answered.

Red chuckled. "You Champions ever been anywhere outside the Crown?"

"We all haven't had time to scour the land like you have. Some of us have been busy fighting for our homeland," Carthon said. "Is that something you've ever done?"

Red frowned at the drak. "By the time I was old enough to swing a weapon, there was nothing left of my home to defend." Carthon retracted in his misstep.

Falin scratched his head, unsure they'd make it out of the palace, and in the same instant, the guards reappeared with Red and Jimbuah's weapons and a couple of bags.

Red accepted a short-sword and whip from one of the guards. He tucked the blade onto his belt, then unraveled the whip. "Stupid sages had it wrapped wrong," he muttered.

Falin cocked his head. "Is that an arrowhead at the end of your whip?"

Red nodded and kept his head bent, so his wide-brim hat covered his eyes while coiling the weapon. "Yessir."

Another guard handed Jimbuah a staff, the same height as the skully. Falin examined the item to see it was made of wood, and the top held a bushel of fruit of varying sizes and colors. Some were berries, the largest a yellow fruit the size of a fist. Leaves and vines stuck out from the bunch, and they rattled as the skully accepted the item.

"Is that your weapon?" Bossador asked.

"Yeh," Jimbuah answered, raising the staff proudly.

Nym stepped closer and bent slightly to better view it. "Doesn't the fruit get in the way?"

Melquin approached, running her fingers over the colorful bushel. "They're magic, aren't they?"

Jimbuah beamed, and his large eyes exuded excitement from their interest in his staff. "Tujigo," he demanded, presenting the staff. The two looked at him blankly. "Tujigo," Jimbuah insisted, rattling the bushel.

"He wants you to pluck one of the fruits or berries," Red translated. "Or try to."

Nym grasped the sizable yellow fruit and pulled it; the crop remained firmly attached to the staff by its stem. Furrowing her brow, she tugged again, jostling the staff and Jimbuah's arm. "It won't come off!"

"Heh heh," Jimbuah chuckled. He held the staff out to Melquin.

"Can I pull on any of them?" the sage asked.

"Yekasa," Jimbuah said, shaking the fruits.

Melquin pursed her lips and wrapped her fingers around a red fruit covered in seeds, pulling the same as Nym, twisting with all her might. She stopped and squinted, inspecting the unharmed stem. "Amazing. I've never seen any plant like this."

Jimbuah walked over to Bossador and held out his staff. "Tujigo," he said, craning his neck to meet the eyes of the madorian prince.

"I'd rather not," Bossador said with folded arms.

"Tujigo, tujigo!" Jimbuah demanded, poking Bossador in the ribs with the fruit end of his staff.

"Alright, alright," Bossador relented, snatching the staff from the skully who stood at his stomach. Taking the central part of the staff in one hand, he grabbed a bunch of tiny purple berries by another and pulled. They didn't part. Annoyed, Bossador widened his stance, tugging again so that his neck strained and short gasps escaped his clenched teeth.

Jimbuah laughed openly. Red chuckled, while the surrounding guards watched in amusement. "Gikivi," Jimbuah said, holding out his hand. Bossador huffed and returned the staff to its owner.

Jimbuah beamed at the group and lifted the staff. "Ah?" he said, in his presentation. His little grey fingers gently plucked one of the same purple berries Bossador had struggled with seconds prior. He held it up for all to see the ordinary fruit. Falin watched as his smile turned from cordial to mischievous, glancing first at Red, then to Falin. The skully tossed the berry down the hall of the palace, and the second it hit the floor, *BOOM*, it exploded in a burst of blue flames. Everyone jumped and covered their faces as the fire quickly quelled on the stone floor. Jimbuah doubled over in a fit of laughter.

"What in the name of Elsana was that?!" Carthon exclaimed.

"He's just playin'," Red answered. "You'll be thankful for it when the gruns and crags come about."

Falin eyed the staff of fruit, glancing at his own Gem-less staff, feeling ill-equipped in comparison. A soldier opened the door to the palace and peeked in, bringing the noises of the crowd with him. "We're ready if you are." Falin nodded.

The group lined at the doors. The palace entrance creaked as soldiers pulled them open to the outside courtyard. Sunshine burst through, and they were met with an audience of thousands of sages, elves, madorians, and even some draks.

Falin stepped across the threshold, met with a bevy of applause, and made his way over the stone path through the kingdom's capital. Queen Martana, King Dothmer, and Airo clapped at the top of the steps.

Falin walked along the path as the crowd cheered, the gardens of Narella all around. He felt out of place, having never been around this many people before, let alone receiving an ovation. He tried his best to maintain a confident composure as all standing beside the road examined him. First stood the nobles closest to the palace, then as they continued further, they passed commoners lucky enough to live within the walls of the city. Stone houses covered in ivy and flowers filled the capital, becoming smaller in size the closer the group came to the outer walls.

Behind Falin, Bossador waved to the crowd, accustomed to royal processions. Nym smiled at the onlookers as Melquin nodded to her fellow sages. Red resembled Falin, unsure of how to respond to the adoration of such an audience, especially as he was only a common man.

Finally, Jimbuah bounced along, acknowledging everyone, relishing the outpouring of support. Noticing a group of sage children gawk at him, Jimbuah padded over, smiled, and tapped his staff gently on the stone. A swell of flower petals burst from the head of his staff and fluttered around the children like tiny butterflies. The kids screamed in glee as Jimbuah carried on with the rest of the group.

After walking the path from the castle, Falin reached the gates, already opened for their exit. Soldiers readied horses for the Champions, each prepped with saddles and food. Falin took one final look behind him at the walled city, its endless gardens of ivy and flowers stretching across all he saw. He hoped he could one day return to lay eyes upon the Narella. His Champions waited, already atop their horses. Falin mounted his steed, then led them onto the path towards the Freelands, as it was time they start their search for the Gems of Elsana.

CHAPTER TWO:
ROAD TO RORKSHIRE

The first day of travel came and went with little excitement following the ceremony, and at the end of the second day, Falin and company plodded along at a steady march. Falin kept quiet and listened to Bossador, Melquin, and Nym share their stories with one another. Nym did her best to include Carthon, but the drak spoke little. Red and Jimbuah trailed behind, often muttering between themselves, catching the suspicious glances of Bossador and Carthon.

They approached the border of Mystica for the Freelands, and trees fell scarce as lush fields became common. Much like the capital, Mystica's landscape was serene with babbling brooks and green earth. On occasion, they'd pass a sage heading north, or a tiny farm, but as the Freelands drew near, the road quieted.

Falin scanned the distance and lightly tugged on the reins to slow his horse, falling in line beside Melquin. "Have you ever been to the Freelands before?"

"A couple times," the sage answered. "When I was young, my parents took me to Rorkshire."

"Is it dangerous?" Falin asked.

Melquin shrugged a shoulder. "Anywhere outside the Crown is dangerous. Even the Freelands. Any creature can go anywhere. That's why they're called the Freelands."

"Not anywhere," Bossador said. "I've been on scouting trips by the Rodrellan border to cleanse them of gruns planning to raid Freeland towns."

"How is it you know what the gruns planned?" Carthon called from behind.

Bossador glanced over his shoulder then back to the road. "I've never seen a grun have anything but nefarious intentions."

"You know it's odd now that I think of it," Falin said. "Why is Narella so far south? Wouldn't it be safer to keep Mystica's capital farther from the border?"

"Any kingdom in the Crown would know there was an attack coming across the Freelands long before they got there," Nym answered.

"And even if someone reached the capital, there are plenty of fortresses in the north to fall back to," Melquin added. She thought for a moment, toying at her long, black braid. "You've asked us so many questions about our homes, but you still haven't told us what Wizard Island is like."

"It's rather boring, if I'm being honest," Falin said, playing with the reins of his horse. "A lot of rocks and rain on the coast, but inland is just dreary forests."

Nym rode closer to hear. "You must be able to feel the magic radiate through the land."

"Yes, you can," Falin admitted. "It's an old magic, as if asleep for some time."

"Do all the wizards and wizardesses live there?" Melquin asked.

"For the most part, but they tend to come and go as they please. I've never seen all ten of us on the island at once."

Melquin thought on it. "Have you ever met Tani the Wise? She was a hero of mine when I was little and learning magic."

"Oh yes, I know Tani," Falin said. He was surprised to see how excited Melquin became. "She was more of an eccentric aunt to me than anything. When I was a kid, she would bring me souvenirs from all of her adventures. One time she came back with a turtle hog shell from the Magpie Isles."

"That's amazing," Melquin beamed.

Bossador nudged his horse forward to join their conversation. "Did you do combat training with the other wizards?"

"Yes, that was usually with Marko."

This time, Bossador was the one beaming, his smile lifting his beard. "Amazing! Training with Marko the Dragon! What was that like?"

Falin did his best to remain nonchalant, not wanting to give away how flattered he was by their interest. "I ended those days with many bruises," Falin chuckled. "He knows pretty much every fighting style there is, so he'd replicate all the different races with their weapons. Some days he'd fight with the short-sword of a grun, others the staff of a sage. And I'd have to fend him off with my staff. One time he spent the entire day throwing crag spears at me."

Nym laughed. "Been there."

"And you only fought with your staff?" Bossador asked. "Against swords?"

Falin lifted his dark wooden staff for the group to view it. "No sword will ever break this. It was carved by the wizards."

"That's incredible," Bossador said.

"Can you harness magic without the Gems of Elsana?" Melquin asked.

"Some," Falin answered, dismayed. "My magical capabilities are that of an average sage, so I could hit someone with a blow of magic enough to knock them out, but I'm not really ready to take on an army by myself. The Gems will let me come to my true power. And then some."

"Then some?" Carthon asked. They all turned, surprised to see the drak had ushered his horse closer to be included in the conversation. Nym's pointed ears twitched as she smiled subtly.

"Yes," Falin nodded. "Each of the four Gems represents an essence of Elsana. Land, Air, Water, and Fire. From what they've taught me, I can only manipulate the parts of the world if I have the corresponding Gem. So for instance, if I have the Water Gem, I'll be able to manipulate water. If I get both Water and Earth, then I could control a river."

"Okay." Carthon thought on it. "But you said 'and then some.' What did you mean?"

"Well after I gather all four Gems, I'll have enough power to learn other forms of magic. The magic of old. Become a true wielder of the Light."

"Do wizards ever learn Dark magic? Like the warlocks use?" Melquin asked.

"Some do, but mostly as a means of defense," Falin said. "I don't know that I'll want to do that, though. They use magic based around manipulation, sickness, and necromancy."

"Look," Bossador said, pointing down the road. In the distance, a hundred yards away, rested two boulders of crudely cut blue marble. "We're at the border."

"There are no guards?" Falin asked.

"They're probably patrolling," Melquin said. "The road on this side of the stones is protected with magic. You couldn't feel it?"

Falin thought on it and realized he'd been at ease on the journey thus far, sensing a magic warmth float over them.

The hasty trot of a horse rushed forward, and Jimbuah spoke excitedly. "Ratisu!"

"Yes, we see it," Melquin said. "It's the border."

Jimbuah shook his head and rattled the reins to his horse. "Ratisu?" He asked Melquin. The sage stared at him blankly, prompting him to rattle the reins again. "Ratisu, ratisu."

"He's asking if you want to race," Red called, still distanced from them.

"Oh," Melquin answered, cocking her head to meet the eye of her horse, then fluttered her lips to neigh, which prompted the horse to snort and wag its head. "Leli says she doesn't want to run right now. I'm sorry."

"I'll race you!" Nym said to Jimbuah, snapping her reins. "Let's go!" Her steed kicked into motion, galloping down the road.

Jimbuah beamed. "Boo yattah!" he yelled, taking off in pursuit. "Shyah!" He urged his horse. "Boo yattah!"

"What did he say?" Melquin asked Red. "Boo yattah?"

"It's like their version of cheering," Red replied.

As the elf and skully flew towards the stones, Falin turned to Melquin. "I didn't know you were a beastsayer. How many animals can you speak to?"

Melquin shrugged. "Just common ones. I still have an issue with most bird dialects though…"

"That's incredible," Falin said. "There were so few animals on Wizard Island, I was never able to learn. Could you teach me?"

Melquin nodded proudly. "I'd be honored."

They returned their attention to the race's finish. Nym and Jimbuah stormed past the marble landmarks. As Falin squinted, he saw Nym throw her hands in the air in victory.

"Looks like your skully lost, Red," Bossador called over his shoulder in jest.

"I don't own him," Red responded with contempt. "And he doesn't care at all about winnin' or losin'. He just likes the fun of it."

The group caught up to Nym and Jimbuah who waited at the border, and in the moment Falin crossed the threshold of the two boulders, he felt a sudden anxiousness pass over him. He wasn't sure if it was the magic that guarded the road or his realization that he was no longer in a protected kingdom. At once, the group fell quiet as if experiencing the same hesitations. As they continued on, Bossador, Melquin, Nym, and Carthon all seemed alert, prepared for anything that might hinder their journey. Jimbuah fell beside Red, the two appearing more at ease than the rest.

Falin noticed this, and slowed his horse to stay nearer to the duo to hear what they were saying, but as he did, they stopped talking altogether. The young wizard met Red's eye and said, "I guess this means you're home."

Red snorted. "In a way."

"What part of the Freelands are you from?" Falin asked.

"I'm from out West. The Bandero Territories."

"Like part of one of the towns out there? Or one of the cities?"

"A village, really. It was mostly farmers and herders when it still existed." The man dipped his head so the brim of his hat covered his eyes. "It was destroyed when I was a teen by a horde of crags and gruns. It doesn't exist anymore."

"I'm sorry that happened," Falin muttered.

"That's life in the Freelands," Red sighed.

"And how did you and Jimbuah get together? Did you two meet in the Freelands?"

Jimbuah chuckled as Red shook his head and grinned. "The story of how I met this one needs mead involved."

The skully nodded in agreement, then examined Falin curiously. "Scakuridi?"

Falin furrowed his brow and turned to Red for translation. "He's asking if you're worried."

"No," Falin answered quickly.

Jimbuah snickered, seeing through the lie. "Tukayu," he said in a low tone, nodding to the Champions in front of them, now twenty horse paces away.

Red guided his steed closer to Falin's and spoke softly. "He said they are too. The drak and the elf have seen real action, but I don't know that the prince has fought anything larger than some gruns with a madorian horde at his back. I'm not even sure the sage has seen battle. Not to mention none of 'em have been further than the Freelands. They know what to expect as much as you do."

Falin glanced at his Champions with fresh eyes, feeling less embarrassed of his inexperience in the world, then concerned he didn't have a more seasoned group protecting him. "What about you two? Are you ever scared?"

"We're peachy at the moment," Red answered. "But come time we step foot into the Wildbarrens…" he shook his head. "My pants will be wet more often than not. Scoundrel's oath."

Falin chuckled along with Jimbuah. Red smiled at his own joke, and Falin felt more at ease with the unexpected additions to the group.

The remaining hours of the day carried on as the sun began to dip, causing the skies to glow a soft purple with streaks of red. The fields kept green and the road became hilly as the horses climbed and descended upon the path, with the horizon hidden by the sporadic elevation of the land.

"Ahead," Carthon said, speaking soft, yet harsh. Pointing southeast of the road in the direction they traveled, a faint plume of smoke wafted from the other side of a rocky hill, so far Falin squinted to see it. "There's someone there."

"Likely nomads resting for the night," Melquin answered. "They probably want to keep off the road."

"We should be careful regardless," Bossador responded. "I can ride ahead and look."

"They'll hear you," Carthon answered, dismounting his horse. He handed his reins to Nym. "I'm going to scout," he said. "Wait here and I'll report back." Without a second word from anyone else, Carthon jogged ahead, veering left off the path in the direction of the site. His feet seemed to glide over the grass as if he were running the softest sand in Elsana, and a moment later, he carefully climbed the hill and peeked his head over the opposite side to inspect the source of the smoke. A few seconds after, he turned and began to run back. Falin sensed concern in his haste. Upon reaching them, he breathed as if he had taken a light stroll. "Gruns. Nine of them."

"So close to the border?" Nym asked in surprise.

Bossador dismounted his horse and retrieved his wooden shield from his back. "We should fight."

"We should try and pass them on the road," Melquin argued. "We shouldn't fight if we don't have to."

Bossador shook his head. "And let them attack some other traveler? No, we need to eradicate them. There are four of us and nine of them. Seven if we count Falin and the other two."

Red clicked his tongue, and Jimbuah wagged his pinky finger at Bossador, a gesture Falin could only assume was crude. "Ibati shikiti," Jimbuah said.

"We won't be sitting out on any fights," Red responded. "Your highness."

"The same goes for me," Falin answered. "I appreciate your bravery, but I would rather die at twenty years of age than live a thousand knowing others sacrificed their lives for mine while I stood idle."

Bossador dropped his head and nodded. "So be it."

"We must get moving if we want to surprise them," Nym said. She removed a couple of throwing stars from her belt. "Should we tie the horses?"

"We won't need to," Melquin replied. She neighed, pointing off the road. Each horse walked away to hide behind a boulder. "They're going to wait here for us."

"Come on," Carthon demanded. "We must move quickly."

Falin followed, and as he did, glanced at Red and Jimbuah who shared a knowing look. The group jogged, rarely making a sound as they rushed forward, turning left off the road in the direction of the smoke. Falin grew fearful, unsure of what was to come. As they approached the hill, the smell of a campfire stung their nostrils. In order, Carthon, Nym, Falin, Bossador, and Melquin quietly climbed the rocky knoll, peeking their heads over the top. The other side was a sheer cliff drop to the encampment below.

Falin clutched his staff tightly as he laid eyes on the gruns. The pictures he'd seen in books had not done them justice, as these creatures were truly grotesque. Their skin was a wrinkled grey-blue, with sharp features, their height a little more than the typical elf. When they walked, they did so in jagged movements, as if in the form of a fast waddle, their bodies squat. They spoke the common voice, from sounds deep within the phlegm of their throats and malice underscoring their cackles.

Nine gruns circled a campfire, drinking from skin sacks and feasting on cured meats from burlap bags. Much of their clothing appeared to be dried leather, with fur coverings on their shoulders. Beside each grun were short broadswords, and a couple of bows and quivers with black, feathered arrows.

The onlookers retreated and huddled together at the top of the hill. Falin realized Red and Jimbuah were nowhere in sight, but the others seemed not to notice.

Bossador whispered, "If we rush them, they won't be ready. Nym, can you kill the archers with your throwing stars? The rest a —"

"Good evening, gentlemen!" Red called from the opposite side of the hill. Everyone in the huddle froze, jaws dropped, glancing at one another, hoping their ears deceived them. "It's a beautiful night, ain't it?" Red continued. Falin and company peered over the ledge, this time far less discreet than before. Red and Jimbuah stood to the left of the encampment as a group of startled gruns watched, equally surprised by the brazen appearance of the man and skully. "What's for dinner?" Red asked.

One of the gruns on the opposite side of the fire stood, his short-sword in hand. His frame was larger than the rest, and the manner in which he carried himself indicated he was their leader. He spoke gargled and raspy. "It's looking like man with a side of skully. I've never tasted skully before."

Jimbuah wagged his hips. "Yukari mofami hakusu."

Red chuckled. "Not nice, Jimmy." Adjusting his herder's hat, he removed his short, one-sided blade from his sheath in his left hand, and fingered the handle of his arrow-tipped whip with his right. "Alright." He glanced up at the group watching from above. "Dinner's served."

In one fluid motion, Red and Jimbuah launched for battle. The closest grun reached for his sword, prompting Red to snap his whip. *CRACK.* In a blur, it's spear-tipped end pierced the throat of the grun, who promptly fell, gargling, soaking the grass in blood.

Jimbuah rolled beneath the sword swipe of the next grun, sweep-kicking the adversary off of his feet. The skully brought the bottom end of his staff onto the skull the enemy, killing him.

Red blocked an oncoming blow with his sword, fending off a second grun with a wave of his whip. *CRACK.* Same as the first victim, the grun clutched his throat and fell to die. Red deflected another strike from a grun, quickly plunging his blade into his enemy's stomach before turning to the greater fight.

A couple of archers took up their bows to aim at Red and Jimbuah from across the camp. Jimbuah snatched a few fire-berries from the bushel on his staff and hummed them at the bowmen. The fruit exploded, casting the archers ten feet backward, where their contorted bodies smoldered with blue flame.

Red and the leading grun became entangled in a sword fight, and in the moments they were distant enough from each other, Red would lash his whip. To the Freelander's chagrin, this adversary swatted it away with his sword. The grun lunged at Red who kept on the defensive.

The two remaining foes chased Jimbuah, and he darted for the cliff, climbing the rock as if retreating towards Falin and the Champions. Falin moved to extend his hand over the edge to help, but instead, Jimbuah turned to look at the gruns below him. The skully peeked at his comrades and smiled. A second later, he thrust himself off the wall in a flip, driving the fruit end of his staff to the ground between the two startled gruns. *BOOM*. The hill trembled as both gruns were blown twenty feet away by an explosion of magic, dead.

Metal clashed on metal as Red continued to fight the deceased horde's leader. In a swift and confident motion, Red ducked the swipe of his adversary's sword, dropped his whip, and tossed his blade to his right hand. He parried once more before driving his sword into the chest of the grun. Maroon blood spurted from the grun's chest as he sputtered curses at Red before dying.

Falin and company watched in surprise from above, while Red and Jimbuah casually gazed across the bloodied encampment.

After a hanging silence from those on the hilltop, Bossador yelled, "What in the name of Rodrellan were you thinking?!"

"That was awesome," Nym said. Falin agreed.

Red called to the hilltop. "I didn't want you to get your beard dirty. Your highness."

As Bossador grumbled to himself, the group retreated down and around the hill to find Red and Jimbuah ransacking the belongings of the gruns.

"I did not think scavenging would not be part of this expedition," Carthon said, unamused.

"We're not scavenging," Red explained, dumping out a bag of trinkets. "We're making sure there aren't any human possessions."

"Why?" Melquin asked.

"Because…" Red said, examining an amulet made of black stone. He tossed it over his shoulder, deeming it worthless. "I want to be sure the food we're going to take from them isn't dried villager meat." Melquin turned to the fire and appeared to grow queasy. "If they haven't pillaged any villages lately, or taken anything from travelers, then it's safe to say the food they're eating comes from animals."

Melquin grimaced. "I don't eat meat anyway."

"Your loss," Red answered. He lifted a burlap bag and removed what appeared to be a strip of meat. The Freelander clamped onto the food and yanked a bite off, chewing thoughtfully. "It tastes like belg. Tasty, but tough. Anyone want some?" he asked, holding the sack out to the group." Everyone stared at the bag with uncertainty.

"I've never heard of anyone outside the Shadow Kingdoms eating belg," Nym answered.

"Don't they ride belg?" Falin asked. "Like we ride horses?"

"Yekasa," Jimbuah answered, taking a piece for himself.

Red gnawed with struggle. "Great big bison looking creatures with sharp teeth that'll rip a madorian's arm off in a single bite. They ride 'em, then eat 'em. Try it. It'll put a few more hairs on that wizard chin of yours."

Falin reached into the bag and examined the piece of dark brown meat. Taking a bite, he was surprised to find how savory it was, disappointed upon realizing his teeth might fall out by the time he swallowed. "Tasty, but tough," Falin repeated.

"'Atta boy," Red answered. "We should collect as much of the meat as we can. It stays good for months."

"Not a bad idea," Bossador mumbled. "Good thinking, Red." Red nodded to the prince, awkwardly so from the sudden change in the madorian's attitude toward him.

"Why didn't we just use your berries?" Carthon asked Jimbuah. "Why couldn't we have just thrown the whole bunch down there? Or one of the other fruits you have on your staff. Would that not have been safer?"

Jimbuah shook his head. "Nofa. Thakutu watistu."

"He doesn't like to waste the fruit when he doesn't have to," Red translated. "They only grow back so fast."

"How fast do they grow?" Carthon asked.

"Depends on the fruit. Some a week or two. Some once a year. Some you only get to use once."

The drak peered at the bushel of fruit, intrigued, then turned his attention to the massacre. "We already have camp set up for us. We should move the bodies and rest here for the night."

"I can help you move the corpses," Nym enthusiastically volunteered.

Carthon nodded grimly, and they set to work, dragging the deceased to a pile behind another boulder. Melquin examined the campsite with unease.

"Are you alright?" Falin asked.

"I don't like death," Melquin answered. "Are we to slumber at the gravesite of enemies?"

"Hopefully nights like these are far and few between," Falin replied. "Come, let's get the horses. You can teach me some basic commands." Melquin nodded, and they went on their way.

From there until sunset, the group set to work, settling and feeding the horses, cooking dinner, and gathering wood. The group took the seats of the gruns, staring into the fire, lost in thought. The bread and cheese of Mystica filled their stomachs, and they fell at ease in the company of one another. Carthon sat with his two swords rested on his lap as he slowly ran a whetstone across their black, steel edges to keep them sharp.

Falin looked over the flames at the drak, realizing he had spoken to Carthon least of anyone in the group. "What is Vartulis like?" he asked.

All removed their gaze from the flame and turned to the drak who kept his eyes on his blades. "Grey," he answered. "Grey and overcast in the south. Grey and snowy in the north. All is bleak and the sun struggles to find its place in Vartulis. It is beautiful."

"I've seen some of the stone castles in Southern Vartulis," Nym said. "They are truly amazing."

Melquin spoke next. "What part are you from?"

"Near the southern coast by Krattle's Cove," Carthon answered. "Or that's where I was raised at least. I spent later years studying in the capital up north near the Senate. In Washborn."

"That's what I want to see," Falin said. "The Drakkish Senate. I find Vartulian history fascinating. The draks returning to the Light from Darkness, then declaring independence from the Mortulian Monarchy."

"Not all draks returned to the Light," Carthon reminded him. "There are many draks who roam the land, feasting on the blood of other creatures, living in Darkness, same as they did when the phantoms of old made us from elves."

"Have you ever met a blood drak?" Melquin asked.

"Some," Carthon answered. "Draks guilty of consuming the blood of non-animals are put to death in Vartulis. They are foul and driven mad by their lust for fresh blood."

"How common is it?" Falin asked.

"It is rare within Vartulis," Carthon said. "And even Mortulis nowadays. But during the Drakkish Rebellion a millennium ago, many draks fled into the Freelands and further south, keeping the tradition alive. They tend to live in small packs now, plaguing villages or unsuspecting travelers."

Falin shivered upon the thought of a drak biting him on the neck while he slept.

"Has there been much diplomacy between Vartulis and Mortulis of late?" Bossador asked.

Carthon turned his focus to the flame. "Some," he answered coolly. The drak stood abruptly with his swords. "I'm going to do a round of patrol before we sleep for the night. We should rise early tomorrow to get a start on the day."

"I can come with you," Nym said.

"I'll be fine on my own, thank you." Carthon departed towards the road and left the group in silence.

"I take it he doesn't care for you much," Red said to Bossador.

Bossador scratched his beard and sighed. "I had a feeling he would not. I hope that this journey would be one that could mend madorian and drakkish relations. Carthon is a praised hero within the kingdom of Vartulis."

"Has there been any contact between your father and the Drakkish Senate?" Melquin asked.

"He has sent messengers in recent years, but all have been returned to Rendrun with words of scorn."

"Wija?" Jimbuah inquired.

"I'm assuming he asked 'why?'" Bossador asked. Red nodded. The madorian prince cleared his throat. "I'm not sure if you know this, Jimbuah, but the Crown of Elsana is comprised of the four kingdoms: Rodrellan, Mystica, Lelyalis, and Vartulis. Since Vartulis became members of the Crown at the end of the Drakkish Rebellion, all four kingdoms have maintained an alliance to defend one another against the threat of any foe. This has been so since the War of the Crown a thousand years ago. My ancestor Madrellor, first to navigate the globe, was the first Unifier of the Crown of Elsana. He put an alliance into place that has remained a millennium. One day, my role as ruler of Rodrellan will be to maintain the unification of the Crown."

Red muttered, "Who'd ever want to be a king with that much responsibility?"

Bossador ignored Red and spoke to Jimbuah. "Does that all make sense?"

"Yekasa," Jimbuah answered, listening intently.

"A century ago, my grandfather, Felmer, launched a campaign upon the borders of Drucullm to drive back the scores of gruns, augurs, and crags settling on the Freeland border. The Drakkish Senate was strongly opposed to this crusade, seeing that it wasn't a credible threat to the Crown, and that Rodrellan was tampering with the purpose of the Freelands."

Red scoffed. "The Crown acts like the Freelands exist for their service only. Like some buffer to the Shadow Kingdoms."

Melquin bobbed her head around. "In a way, that's what it's there for."

"I think the millions living within the Freelands would disagree," Red replied. "It's been there longer than the Crown."

Bossador went on. "The Elves of Lelyalis and Sages of Mystica fought alongside us, but the Draks of Vartulis did not. We lost many in that war and had little to show for it. My grandfather King Felmer blamed the draks, claiming if they had joined the cause we could have done more. This was seen as a bitter betrayal to the Rodrellan people and the Crown."

Bossador took a breath before he continued. "Some thirty years ago, when I was but an infant, Vartulis put an embargo on trading with the Trortark, citing they were a pirate state. Mortulis followed suit as did the coast of the Freelands, devastating the Trortark for a time. In the year following, there was a series of Trortarkian raids along the coast of Vartulis in retaliation. My father refused to send reinforcements to the draks, claiming they had incited the violence by placing the embargo. Many draks were killed in the process. We've had little contact with the Senate since."

"Eesh," Jimbuah said.

"Eesh is right," Red continued.

"It's more personal for him than that," Nym said quietly. "Carthon's parents were killed in those raids. He was orphaned because of them."

Bossador's face fell in defeat. "I hadn't known that. It will make mending the relationship all the more difficult."

"How did you know that?" Falin asked. "About his parents? Did he tell you?"

Nym shook her head. "The tale of Carthon is a common one in Vartulis. The elves and draks maintain a strong relationship, so much of our culture is shared. You must remember, draks were once elves corrupted by servants of the Dark. There is much we have in common."

"We will work towards unity as part of our journey, Bossador," Falin said. "I promise it."

"Thank you," Bossador nodded.

"We'd best do as Carthon said and get some sleep," Melquin said. "We should rise early tomorrow."

Falin nodded with heavy eyelids. "Carthon has not yet returned. Leave the fire smoldering so he has light when he returns."

The group stood and went to their own areas of the camp, retrieving sleeping sacks to find slumber. As Falin gazed at the stars, he heard the soft footsteps of Carthon returning to the group, settling for the night. In but a few seconds, he drifted off to the sounds of Jimbuah snoring and Melquin's whispering prayers.

CHAPTER THREE:
RORKSHIRE

Five days came and went since the skirmish with the gruns, and the travelers started to pass tiny villages on the outskirts of Rorkshire. By all that Falin could see, these people lived in squalor, scraping together just enough means to survive for the next day. He pitied them, hoping that once a powerful wizard, he could be of service to common man. As they passed, children ran to the side of the road to watch, as it was a rarity when anyone from the Crown journeyed through their villages; it was an event to see such a mix of individuals. As uncommon as a drak was in this part of the Freelands, Jimbuah the Skully was the clear victor as it came to striking awe.

Falin pulled his horse beside Melquin. "These are all part of Rorkshire, no?"

"They are," Melquin answered.

"Why are members of a kingdom so…" Falin searched for a word so as not to seem offensive.

"Poor?" Melquin finished his sentence.

"Yes. They look like they're barely surviving."

"Many of these people are farmers. The laboring class. They lived generations on the outskirts of the kingdom fighting to stay alive. You will find the same in most kingdoms of the Freelands. Millions of people live this way."

"I can't imagine seeing something like this in Mystica," Falin said.

"Most societies outside the Crown are less fortunate," the sage answered. Melquin extended the head of her staff to a young girl with dirt-stained feet. From the tip of the staff appeared a pink and purple rose. The villager smiled and accepted the flower, holding it as gentle as one might an infant rabbit.

"What is Rorkshire like?" Falin asked. "You said you've been here before."

"I have, a couple times. King Pernicus is a kind man." Melquin lowered her voice. "But it is a whimsical place, Falin. They attempt to present themselves with the same majesty as the Crown, but appear more as a joke than anything. Like something of a children's faerietale."

"We're here!" Bossador bellowed, pointing ahead. On the horizon, the flags of Rorkshire peeked over the road as its walls came into sight.

Red brought his horse trotting beside the prince. "Do you need me to announce your entry into the castle? Shall I beckon the villagers to throw flowers at your feet, your highness?"

Bossador shook his head. "No. But my legs have grown stiff from a day of riding. I will need you to lift me off of my horse and carry me to my chambers."

This evoked a grin from Red. "It shall be an honor to my heart and a death sentence to my back, your highness."

As they approached the walls of Rorkshire, the village houses became less decrepit. Once word spread of the arrival of the company, crowds formed at the side of the road to watch.

Falin turned to his group and spoke so only they could hear him. "Offer them your respect," he asked of his Champions. "This may be the most exciting event in their lifetime." The group did as told, nodding to the commoners. Bossador waved, Nym flashed her charming elven smile, Melquin offered flowers to young girls, and Carthon nodded dutifully to the young men. Falin noticed Red seemed unsure of how to acknowledge the crowd the same way as when they had left Mystica at the start of their journey. Jimbuah, unlike his partner, was delighted, and tossed tiny red berries into the air from his staff, causing them to pop and sparkle above the heads of dazzled children. The dust from the berries rained down and offered a sweet aroma.

Carthon called to Jimbuah. "I thought you didn't like to waste your fruit?"

Jimbuah threw another few over the heads of a group of young men. "Jofayi nekavera watistu."

"He said joy is never wasted," Red translated to Carthon.

Carthon rolled his eyes, then watched as Jimbuah cackled in as a group of children squashed one another in an attempt to smell the berries. For a second, Falin caught the drak smile before returning to his gloomy disposition.

Once at the kingdom walls, they came to a closed, massive wooden door where guards stood atop in chainmail garb. "Who visits the Free Kingdom of Rorkshire?"

Falin trotted to the front of the group and yelled boldly. "I am Falin the Wizard! These are my Champions! We seek the Gems of Elsana! We hoped to find a place of rest at the start of a long journey!"

The guard disappeared for a moment, and the door began to open, stopped, then returned closed. The same soldier peeked his head over the wall. "No one has ever heard of Falin the Wizard. Can you prove you're a wizard?"

"I—" Falin looked at the closed gate in frustration, then heard Jimbuah snicker behind him. "Shut it, Jimmy," he snapped. He didn't know what magic he could perform to prove this.

Bossador hurried forward to assist. "Greetings! I am Prince Bossador of Rodrellan, son to King Dothmer! Our company wishes to hold court with King Pernicus!"

The guard disappeared. After a moment, the door began to open, but yet again, slammed closed. The guard returned. "Can you prove you're a prince?" This time, Red chuckled.

Falin grew angry, hopping off his horse and stomping to the entrance. Putting the head of his staff against the wood, he concentrated, summoning the magic in his being. In a burst of energy, he blasted a hole in the entry ten feet high and ten feet wide. Shards of wood jutted out along its sides and guards on the inside of the walls scattered.

"Come on," Falin said to his group, getting back on his horse. They trotted forward through the closed door, through the entrance Falin had made. Once on the other side, Falin twisted his neck to see the same guard gazing down at him, awestruck. "Believe me now?" Falin asked. He didn't wait for a response.

Inside the walls of Rorkshire, they found rows of stone and wooden homes packed neatly together along dirt streets. Flags of noble houses topped the roofs, and other roads led to business districts where wealthy merchants kept shop. Guards watched, clutching their spears with white knuckles and proper stance, not wanting to agitate the wizard further. The road to the castle winded to the center of the city. Many seemed to watch with intrigue, but with a far more glum attitude than the villagers surrounding the kingdom.

"Is it always so dismal? Even inside the walls?" Falin asked.

"No," Melquin answered in a hushed tone. "The people within the walls are generally vibrant and eager to welcome guests. It may have been your entry that startled them."

"They should have just let me in."

Melquin opened her mouth to speak but then closed it.

"You disagree with how I handled the situation?" Falin asked.

"More tact may have made a better entry. You are a wizard, after all. What would Airo have done?"

Falin sighed. "I suppose you're right. I'll make a formal apology to the king."

Upon reaching the gates of the castle, they came to another drawbridge over a moat, lowered for their entry. A guard halted them with a raised hand, walking to the group. "I can escort you to King Pernicus, but I ask you no longer destroy the king's property."

"My apologies," Falin said, embarrassed, glancing at Melquin. "It will not happen again."

From there, they were guided into the castle, where torches adorned the walls and guards remained posted. Banners honoring past royalty hung proudly, and nobles strolled the halls examining the guests. To Falin, the common men and women of Rorkshire did indeed seem silly as Melquin had described. Men wore ill-fitted pantaloons, and the women wore dresses that fanned out to a ridiculous extent, all vibrantly colored.

There was no magic in Rorkshire, that much was evident to Falin. The stone was cold and spoke of nothing. In Narella, Queen Martana's castle was enchanting, as if every brick had a story to tell, but here, it was a monument to the common man surviving in a world not meant for them. After walking through the grey corridors, they came upon a final set of doors before the throne room.

The guard leading them turned to the visitors, speaking low and hushed. "I should warn you, the king is..." He searched for an explanation that would not send him to the pillory. "...experiencing some personal turmoil. It would be best for you to proceed with caution from here forward."

Falin nodded, uncertain of what was to come in their meeting. The doors to the throne room opened, and they were met with a vast chamber with a sprawling red carpet and stone pillars, and walls decorated with windows of pale stained glass. King Pernicus agonized on his throne with a bent head, crooked crown, and mangled grey hair. The king's beard was unkempt, and his clothes appeared to be wrinkled and ill-fitting. Eight guards stood at the steps in front of his throne, examining the guests.

Falin and company approached, stopping a few feet away from the guards. The wizard glanced at his group as King Pernicus had yet to notice their presence, as instead, the ruler focused on a small painting in his hands with an expression of lament.

"King Pernicus," Falin began. "I am Falin the Wizard. These are my Champions aiding me on my quest for the Gems of Elsana. We seek a place of refuge until we embark on our journey again. We hoped the tales of your graciousness were true."

King Pernicus lifted his head just enough to take note of the group. "Wizard," he said, as if a child recognizing a familiar word.

"Yes," Falin said. "I am a Wizard. These are my Champions."

King Pernicus lifted his head further. "Champions," he repeated, a thought forming.

"You are correct," Falin nodded, unsure of how to proceed. The king scanned them, his eyes more alert than before.

"You are a gift from Elsana herself," King Pernicus said in disbelief. "I have prayed and *prayed* to Mother Elsana. Please send me a savior in my hour of darkness, and she sends me seven! Oh, she is a great and wonderful Mother to us all!"

Falin scratched his head. "What is it that troubles you, your highness?"

The king stood abruptly. "It is my daughter. My sweet Princess Bloom! She was stolen by a dragon but a fortnight ago, and there has been little word of her whereabouts since!"

Melquin muttered, "You've got to be kidding me," under her breath. "See what I mean?" she whispered to Falin. "Faerietale silliness."

"A dragon?" Red said. "Don't you think she's prob—" He flinched as Nym pinched him in the ribs. "Probably..." Red's open-ended sentence hung in the air as he struggled to find an appropriate end.

"She is not dead if that is what you are after," King Pernicus scolded. "She has been spotted in the clutches of the beast near the Ruins of Darva. It must be keeping her there."

"Why would a dragon be keeping her?" Red asked. "Don't they ea—" Nym pinched him harder this time, and he visibly jumped. "Cut it out!" he seethed at the elf.

"Dragons horde what they find valuable," Carthon explained, "and there are more things in this world as valuable as gold. A princess, for one."

"Yes! Yes!" Pernicus exclaimed, pointing at Carthon. "The drak is right. She must be alive! And you are the heroes of Elsana who must be here to save her!"

After an awkward pause, Bossador stepped forward. "King Pernicus, as Prince of Rodrellan, heir to the Rodrellan throne, I pledge we will make every effort to rescue Princess Bloom and slay the vile dragon who has taken her."

The king gasped. "Oh, thank you! Thank you all!"

Red whispered in Falin's ear. "We can't promise that. We have Gems to find. And she's probably a set of charred toothpicks by now."

King Pernicus raised the painting he'd been holding. "This is her," he said, descending the steps, half-stumbling. "Look, so you know her face when you find my daughter."

Princess Bloom's portrait depicted a woman a few years older than Falin, her hair silky brown and poise one of stoic royalty, with a lean frame and fair skin. Her image resembled the quintessential princess of Freeland tales. She posed with her hand upon a horse in a field of multicolored flowers, and her gaze seemed to stare directly from the painting. Princess Bloom embodied royal beauty.

Red lifted the brim of his hat and raised his eyebrows, shoving aside Bossador. "King Pernicus, you have my word, as a Champion of Wizards, citizen of the Freelands, I will do everything in my power to rescue your daughter, Princess Bloom."

"She's probably safer with the dragon," Nym mumbled.

Red put a hand on the king's shoulder. "Do you have any more information about where the dragon could have taken her?"

"No," he answered, staring hopelessly at the painting. "Bloom had taken a group of knights to walk Lake Wilmur a few miles east of here. She requested they give her leave for a moment of peace by the bed of the shores, and before they knew it, she was being carried off." Tears welled in the king's eyes. "I had only just begun to let her leave the castle walls at her insistence. I never should have let her out."

"She had never left the walls of the castle until recently?" Nym asked.

"Yes," King Pernicus answered. "She is all I have since her mother died. I needed to keep her safe and out of harm's way. And now this happens. I have failed as a father."

"You said she's been spotted near the Ruins of Darva, right?" Falin asked. "With the dragon?"

The king nodded. "This is the most recent report we've had. That is where they must be."

"Okay," Falin said, thinking it through. "We are likely to pass the ruins after we make our way through the Oldwoods. We will look for her then."

King Pernicus clutched the painting to his chest. "You are truly a blessing from Mother Elsana! Thank you! I will have rooms made for you all! The court's cook will be at your service until you depart. Thank you!"

In the following hours, they were given lodge by order of the king, decorated rooms meant for guests of royalty. Falin sequestered himself away in his chambers, wondering if his promise to the king was a fool's errand, as the princess may already be dead by the appetite of a dragon.

More so, he didn't know if this search for the Gems of Elsana should be delayed for such an endeavor, as it seemed to be the errand of some shining knight instead of a budding wizard and his company. Appreciative of the castle walls, Falin and his Champions slept soundly that night, each taking to their own chambers.

The following morning, Falin woke to the clinking metal, realizing the sun had risen hours earlier. Rubbing his eyes, he climbed from bed and walked to the window overlooking part of the castle's courtyard. From there, he saw soldiers sparring with one another, some shooting arrows at targets.

Feeling his stomach grumble, he quickly dressed, gathering his staff to depart in search of food. Following his nose, he came upon a dining hall near the kitchen with a lengthy table and candle chandelier above it. The stone walls held candelabras, and a magnificent fireplace sat off to the side. Red sat at the head of the table beside Jimbuah, delving into a morning feast. Plates of eggs, bread, cheeses, bacon, and sausages sat on the tabletop.

"Mornin' wiz," Red managed through a mouth full of food. "Join us."

Falin sat at the table across from Jimbuah and scanned the spread. "Have you two been eating for long?"

Jimbuah patted his bare belly, his green pants straining on waist. "Yeh."

"Mhm," Red said. "The king told the chefs to make us whatever we want. Said they're going to serve us a private feast tonight."

Falin grinned and took a bite of bread. "What'd you ask them for?"

"Jimmy ain't ever had pie before so I told to make the biggest one they could. Ain't that right?"

"Boo yattah," Jimbuah agreed.

"Where's everyone else?" Falin asked. "Didn't they want breakfast?"

Jimbuah nodded with puffed cheeks. Red answered, "They only wanted one course, they already ate. Said they wanted to go outside and do some training."

"Training for what?"

Red shrugged. "Heck if I know. Not like you can train for most of the stuff we'll be seeing on the road."

Falin glanced over his shoulder to ensure they were alone. "You think this princess is still alive? She's worth looking for?"

"If she looks anything like her painting she's definitely worth finding," Red responded. "If we're passing near those ruins anyway, we might as well."

"I suppose," Falin answered. "I think I'll go see what the rest are doing. I'll meet up with you two later."

"More for us," Red said. Jimbuah piled eggs, bacon, and cheese between two pieces of bread, stretching his mouth to bite into his creation. Red watched in awe and said, "That's genius," beginning to replicate his own.

After a couple wrong turns, Falin found the correct exit to the courtyard where the soldiers trained. A wooden fence surrounded a dirt lot where people fought. Nym stood by archers, tossing her throwing stars with pinpoint accuracy into the center of the targets. Bossador held his broadsword and shield, sparring with the far smaller soldiers, guiding them as he did. A brazen young man lurched at the madorian prince, which Bossador sidestepped and tripped him. "Never let the enemy use your momentum against you. Always keep a firm stance."

Falin strolled to the fence beside Carthon and Melquin who watched the events. "You two aren't training today?"

"I'd rather enjoy the sunshine on this side of the fence," Melquin responded, raising her cheeks to the sky.

Falin agreed it was indeed a beautiful day. He noticed Carthon watch Bossador with frustration. "How are you today, Carthon?" he asked, hoping to coax some civility from the drak.

"Fine," Carthon answered, peeling his gaze from the ongoings on the other side of the fence. "How long do you think we'll be here?"

"Not long at all," Falin shook his head. "I figured we would leave tomorrow."

Carthon appeared to respect the answer. "Good. We've just started this journey. I don't want us getting comfortable too early on."

"If I let Red and Jimbuah stay more than a couple days we won't be able to fit them through the doors."

Carthon breathed sharply through his nose. "Agreed. I've come across others like them. They've both gone stretches without food, so when it comes in abundance, they get their fill and then some."

"Were you planning to train with Nym and Bossador, Falin?" Melquin asked.

"No," Falin said. "I am not in the mood to be swinging my staff at others. I want to conserve my energy for the road."

"And for dragons," Melquin added. "Because now we've promised to live out some Freeland child's bedtime story."

Falin shook his head. "I'm still not sure searching for a missing princess takes precedence over finding the Gems. But then again, it is the duty of wizards to care for others. I wish Bossador and Red had consulted me before volunteering wholeheartedly."

"Red's motives lie elsewhere than honor," Carthon said. "And Bossador's promise to the king was nothing more than the foolish oath of a madorian, sticking his nose where it doesn't belong. Look at him," Carthon nodded to the soldiers being walloped by the prince. "He's fueling his ego through the guise of education. I doubt he would do the same were they his size. Or more skilled."

"I am not sure," Falin said, wishing he hadn't agitated his Champion. "I'm sure he meant well."

Carthon didn't respond. "Madorian!" he yelled. Bossador stopped sparring and turned to the drak. "Are you prepared to spar with someone of your own skill set?!"

Surprised, Bossador glanced at Falin and back to Carthon, then nodded. Wishing there was a way to halt the coming fight, Falin sighed to himself. Carthon leapt over the fence as if floating lightly in the air, and upon landing, removed the two single-edged black blades from his back. He swung them in circles, warming his wrists, strutting towards Bossador.

"You might have one less Champion after this," Melquin said to Falin.

"Take your stance," Carthon warned. Bossador took a guarded position with his wooden shield raised beside his greatsword. Carthon held his left sword in a defensive position and the second blade over his head. His left foot extended far in front of his right. They inched toward one another, moving in slow circles.

At a blurring speed, Carthon jumped forward, swinging his swords inward toward Bossador. The madorian prince blocked one with his sword and the other with his shield. He thrust his boot forward and kicked Carthon in the chest, who flew back, sliding on the dirt.

Carthon lunged again, and Bossador swiped at the drak, but Carthon rolled beneath, cutting at the boot of his opponent. Losing his footing, Bossador stumbled, blocking a multitude of attacks upon his shield by Carthon. *CLING. CLING. CLING. CLING.* Carthon railed on the shield, stepping forward and looking for an opening in the madorian's defense. To Falin's surprise, Bossador's wooden shield showed no signs of marking.

Bossador gritted his teeth, leaping back to gain a second of re-cuperation, returning his own series of offensive movements. Carthon swatted away the greatsword with surprising strength de-spite his blades being far smaller. Nym and the archers stopped to watch the fight, as did others passing by this area of the grounds. Falin grew concerned one of them would become unnecessarily in-jured, their distaste for one another more and more evident with every clash of steel.

Carthon refused to slow, as Bossador panted and sweat began to drip from his face. The fight was one of speed versus strength, and neither was willing to admit defeat.

With a mighty swing, Bossador hit Carthon's left sword so hard it flew from his hand. Bossador stepped on the blade before Carthon could retrieve it. The prince attacked again, evoking a drakkish hiss from Carthon, who bared his fanged teeth.

This time, Carthon parried the attack so quickly, he was able to nick Bossador's knuckles with a flick of his blade. Bossador sneered as blood flew from his hand, his next swipe coming close to Carthon's stomach.

Falin had grown tired of spectacle. "That is enough!" he yelled from the fence. They ignored him and continued to fight. Falin became furious they kept on. The young wizard hopped the fence, stomping towards the two who paid attention to none else but each other. As they both prepared vicious blows, Falin pointed the head of his staff at the two, casting a wave of magic upon them. They were tossed in opposite directions into the dirt. Both fell with heavy *thuds*, and Falin slammed his staff to the ground so hard it caused the yard to tremor.

"I said enough!" Falin rumbled. His voice boomed over the training area as he glared at the two lifting themselves. "Am I to journey for the Gems of Elsana with Champions who are lacking limbs?! It seems I am already traveling with two who lack common sense."

Both panted and dropped their gaze with scowls of scolded children. Falin glanced between the two. "Take leave for the day and come to dinner with kinder minds. Go."

Carthon and Bossador glared at one another a final time before stomping off in opposite directions, Bossador for the greater courtyard, Carthon for the castle. Falin returned to the fence where Nym was now perched beside Melquin.

Nym shook her head. "Men."

Falin sighed. "When we began this journey, I was not aware I'd be care-taking for my Champions."

"No?" Melquin asked. The sage balanced her white, ivy staff in the crook of her elbow and played at her long black braid. "I was hoping you could help me fix my hair for the dinner tonight."

Nym snorted. "Is the king joining us for dinner? When I ran into him in the halls today, he asked me eight different ways I would kill a dragon."

"And what did you tell him?" Melquin asked.

"Eight different ways I would do it. Still wasn't enough." She stood up on the top of the fence and walked along it as if it were a tightrope. "How *do* you kill a dragon? I honestly have no idea."

After a pause, Falin said, "Are you asking Melquin or me?"

"Whoever has the answer."

Falin and Melquin looked at one another, realizing neither knew. "I don't know," the wizard replied. "I figured it was like any other creature. Try to cut its head off or stab it in the heart."

Nym moved to do a handstand atop the fence and began to walk along the edge upside down. "Their scales are supposed to be like armor. I have a feeling we'll need magic of some sort. This might be something we want to find a few Gems for. I guess I could always aim for a star in the eye." She hopped off the fence and landed on the dirt with perfect nimbleness.

"You could distract him with somersaults while we sneak up on him," Melquin said.

"What do you have in that belt of yours?" Falin asked, nodding to the utility pouches along the elf's waist. "What is it an elven assassin carries with her?"

Nym unbuttoned one of the flaps and opened it. "Well, I keep my stars for throwing. I use those sparingly because I only have twenty or so at a time. Then I've got explosive dust which can cause a distraction or blind someone." She lifted the top to another pouch. "In here I've got some different kinds of dried poison fruits…and I have some wire in this one to strangle enemies."

Melquin cocked her head. "That's dark."

"I guess." Nym shrugged. "Part of the job, though."

"Who have you killed?" Falin asked.

"Crags are my specialty," Nym answered. "They're so big and stupid, and easy to sneak up on. I'll usually kill ones that are said to be terrorizing villages in the Freelands or encroaching onto the Crown's territory. I've had to kill a few grun leaders before too."

"Who tasks you with these assassinations?" Falin asked. "The elves don't have any kind of leader, so how do you know who to target?"

"Elves just always agree," Nym answered, leaning on the fence. "When we hear about an issue, we're generally on the same page about it, and word spreads of the best initiative. So if there's a problem with a solitary crag, word gets around that an assassin is needed and someone is sent. If there's an army marching towards us to attack, we all gear up and get ready to fight. We don't need leaders. We understand how to live in harmony and move as a group."

"Like fish," Melquin teased.

Nym looked at the sage from the sides of her eyes and half-smiled. "Something like that."

"I'm going to walk the grounds for a bit," Falin said. "I'll meet you all for dinner. If you see the madorian and drak fighting again just beat them over the head until they're asleep."

"Yes, your wizardness," Nym answered.

Falin departed to explore the grounds of the castle, quickly discovering a garden filled with bushes and winding paths. Like all else in Rorkshire, it spoke little of magic, but instead an old history of the kingdom. Crumbling stone seats and fountains decorated the trail, with shrubbery and trees offering homes for birds and squirrels. On occasion, he would pass nobles and greet them, returning to his thoughts upon their leave. Further on the path, he came upon a clearing, and at the center was a man-made pond with pink lily pads floating atop. The pond was surrounded by a small stone wall. A frog jumped from one of the lily pads to another and croaked as Falin approached.

The water was calm, and in the light breeze, little ripples scurried across the surface. Falin took rest upon the stone wall and looked into the murky water, catching a glimpse of his own reflection. He stared in thought, remembering Tani the Wise once telling him reflections were the entryways to other worlds. He still didn't know whether to believe the tale or not.

Falin lifted his staff and placed its head to the water and concentrated, feeling magic within him rise. The water swelled beneath his staff as he carefully lifted it up, only to splash back down again. Little waves cascaded over the pool, and the frogs hopped in a frenzy, surprised their peaceful rest had been disturbed. The young wizard shook the head of his staff off and looked at the empty slots where the Gems would live. He was eager to harness their power to master the essence of Elsana.

Footsteps approached from behind him, and an elderly woman shuffled forward on the path with her head bent. "Hello," Falin offered his respect.

The woman lifted her head, and Falin saw she was blind. "Well, hello," she answered. "Who is it that I am speaking to?"

"My name is Falin," he answered. "And what is yours? Would you like help finding a seat?"

"Delsa. The name is Delsa, dear. And I've walked this path every day for years. I can find my seat just fine, thank you." As she promised, Delsa sat on the wall beside Falin without any assistance.

"Falin is a unique name, one I have never heard in Rorkshire. Are you one of the seven guests of King Pernicus?"

"I am," Falin confirmed. "I am one of the seven."

"Well, let me think," Delsa thought. "You are friendlier than a drak, but less chipper than an elf. You do not carry the presence of a madorian, nor do you speak the tongue of skullies. That means you must be either a sage, a man, or a wizard. Which could it be?"

Falin dropped his head and smiled. "Would you like me to tell you?"

"Bah," Delsa scoffed. "Where would the fun be in that?" She thought some more. "You do not speak like anyone within the Freelands, so I am left with a sage or a wizard, am I right?"

"You are," Falin said, smiling.

As if sensing his smile, Delsa returned one of her own, then, she raised her finger. "Ah! I have it! You're a wizard."

"Impressive," Falin said. "What gave me away?"

Delsa tapped her nose. "Every sage I have ever met smells like flowers. You do not."

Falin laughed openly. "I will remember that next time I bathe."

"But how wonderful, a wizard!" Delsa said. "I hear you are beginning your journey for the Gems of Elsana. So exciting!"

"I am," Falin said. "And it is."

Delsa cocked her head. "I hear doubt in your voice. Why is that Falin?"

Falin took a short breath. "I—there is no one reason. I am anxious to come to my full power with the Gems. I have Champions that bicker like children. I've already been tasked with rescuing a princess. Not to mention following this journey, I'll spend the next thousand years as a guardian to everyone in the world. I've waited all my life to start this quest only to realize it will not be as perfect as I always imagined."

"I see," Delsa said thoughtfully. "All that you feel is valid, my dear. I'm sure every wizard before you has felt the same. Any adventure without trouble along the way is not much of an adventure at all." Falin decided he very much liked Delsa. The elderly woman soaked in the garden's sounds.

"You're right," Falin said. "What is your place here in Rorkshire, Delsa? Have you always been here?"

Delsa reached down and ran her fingertips over the water. "I have not always been the resident blind woman if that is what you are asking. No, I was once Queen of Rorkshire."

A small gasp escaped Falin. "I had no idea. I would have assumed that—that—"

"That what?" Delsa challenged. "I'd be walking around with some entourage to show everyone my forgotten power? No. I lost my husband, then my sight. I will not lose my independence."

"So King Pernicus is your son? And Princess Bloom is your granddaughter?"

"Oh, what a smart wizard," Delsa teased.

Falin relented a grin, but then it faded. "I am sorry about Princess Bloom. I hope that we can find her. I apologize for describing our search for her as a burden."

"It is alright, Falin, you didn't know. I appreciate you appeasing my son in making the promise. Since his wife passed, he has gone a bit... loopy. It was hardest on my Bloom, who not only lost a mother, but in many ways a father. Pernicus tried to control her in every way, and in doing so, she couldn't stand to stay within the castle walls."

"You don't seem worried about her."

Delsa shrugged a shoulder. "Something tells me she's still kicking. She's a tough little thing. You'll see if you meet her."

"I hope I do," Falin said.

"Come, young wizard," Delsa waved her hand. "Walk with me back to the castle. I already ache to lie in my bed. You can tell me of Wizard Island as we walk."

"I'd be happy to," Falin said. The pair stood and strolled through the gardens at a slow pace, less because of Delsa's inability to see, and more for the enjoyment of each other's company. Falin spoke of the wizards and wizardesses and the tales they would share with him.

Upon guiding Delsa into the castle and up the stairs to her lodging, the former Queen stopped at her door and said, "Thank you so much for our talk today Falin. I am sure we will speak again before you depart. Please take the rest of your time in Rorkshire to ease your mind. You will accomplish great things. I know it."

"Thank you, Delsa. It was wonderful meeting you as well."

Falin left for his own room and spent the remainder of the day lounging, studying the map Airo gave him, and at times wandering the halls of the castle. As dinnertime approached, his stomach grumbled, realizing he'd eaten little through the day, having not seen any of the Champions since the events that morning.

Finding his way to the dining room, he came upon Bossador, Nym, and Melquin already waiting for the meal. Bossador's hand was bandaged from his fight with Carthon, but he seemed in better spirits.

A candled chandelier hung above their heads, and a stoked fire kept the high, stone walls warm. They sat around a carved oak table, bare but for the settings, waiting for food.

"How was everyone's day?" Falin asked, sitting beside Melquin.

"Kind of boring," Nym answered. "Mel and I went to the top of the castle to see the view, but we didn't do much else."

Bossador fiddled with his bandage. "After I wrapped my hand I walked the grounds some. I spoke to some of the people living within the kingdom walls. They are very kind and excited to have our company. Are you sure you don't want to stay here longer, Falin?"

"Definitely," Falin said. "I think I'll go crazy if I stay here another day."

They sat in silence for a moment as the smells of meal preparation permeated the swinging door opposite the main entrance. The kitchen entry opened, and to their surprise, Carthon walked through, taking a seat beside Nym and across from Bossador.

"Are you cooking us dinner?" the elf asked.

Carthon folded his hands atop the table and shook his head. "I was making sure meat would be on the menu."

After a pause, Nym asked, "Is it?"

"Very much so," Carthon answered.

Hollering came from the hall and in walked Red, grinning, followed by Jimbuah dressed in the baggy clothes of a nobleman.

"By the God of Light, what is this?" Melquin asked.

"'Tis an ho-nor," Jimbuah said with great struggle in his accent, bowing in a whimsical fashion, then strutting to his chair with a raised chin. He wore ill-fitting, green vestments with gold trimmings and tassels upon his shoulders, and a set of pantaloons to match. Atop his head wobbled a pointed, floppy green hat, bright as could be. The skully was forced to continually adjust the brim so it stopped falling over his eyes. Everyone at the table, even Carthon, could not help but chuckle.

"Jimmy likes to play dress up," Red explained. "I think he pulls off a nobleman rather well. Wouldn't y'all agree?"

"I would be proud to have you in my court of Rendrun, sir," Bossador said.

Jimbuah waved his hand in circles and bowed elegantly. The hat fell over his eyes again.

"When is dinner bein' served?" Red asked. "I'm starvin'."

"I'm pretty sure you ate half this kingdom's food at breakfast," Falin replied. "You're still hungry?"

Red leaned on the table. "There are two things in my life I take seriously: dinner and dessert. Plus, Jimmy told me today he's never had pie before, so we got that comin' for him too."

"Pija!" Jimbuah yelled, slapping his clothed belly.

The sound of approaching footsteps came from the hall, and eight guards marched into the dining room, carrying spears and solemn faces. Behind them, King Pernicus entered and stopped at the far end of the table. "Good evening, my Champions. I hope that you have had a—"

"'Tis an ho-nor," Jimbuah cut him off.

King Pernicus paused and examined Jimbuah in his new attire. "Good evening," he said. "I hope you have all had a day of relaxation. My chefs have prepared a royal feast for you, one I am certain you will enjoy."

"Will you not be joining us?" Falin asked.

"Not tonight, I am afraid," King Pernicus answered. Falin sensed the room let out a silent breath of relief. "My advisors and I are meeting to plan an invasion of the Ruins of Darva should you prove unable to rescue my daughter."

"Alright," Falin said, unsure if the king realized his inadvertent insult. "It will take weeks for us to reach the ruins, however. We must first pass through the Oldwoods."

"I am aware," the king said. "But I'd rather be prepared than not." He tapped his head, causing his crown to become a little more lopsided. "Preparation is key. Perhaps you should revisit Rorkshire after your quest. There is much I could teach you."

"Not humility," Melquin whispered.

"What was that, dear?" Pernicus asked.

Melquin clicked her tongue and raised her eyebrows, surprised he heard her. "Hospitality. You could teach Falin about hospitality, as you've been so gracious to us."

King Pernicus beamed. "Thank you, sage." He clapped his hands together. "Speaking of, here is your meal! I will let you all be. I will see you off in the morning. Have a wonderful night."

As the king and his guards exited, server after server filed from the kitchen bringing endless plates of food to fill the table. Jimbuah bounced in his seat, his pointed green hat wiggling on his head. Cornish hens, freshly baked bread, roasted potatoes, boiled carrots, mashed turnips, buttered corn, cheese wheels, jams, turkey legs, venison, a pot of stew, and biscuits were all placed on the table. Falin caught Carthon lick his lips upon a slab of beef being served. Two young servers rolled in a barrel of wine and mead, eliciting a thrilled gasp from Red.

Once drinks were poured, the head chef stood at the table with his hands clasped behind his back. "Is there anything else you desire before we offer you privacy?"

Jimbuah's eyes scanned the table. "Pija?"

"Pie usually comes with dessert," Red explained. "After all this food."

"Ah," Jimbuah said, nodding in understanding. He turned to the server. *"'Tis an ho-nor."*

"Thank you," the server said, glancing around the table. "We are in the kitchen at your service if you need anything at all." He swiftly departed, leaving the gathering at peace.

Red rubbed his palms together. "I don't know where to begin. Yes I do. Pass the cornish hens please."

Falin could not help but grin, as all at once, everyone began to delve into the meal like hungry children. A sense of knowing what it meant to be a wizard fell upon him, one he had not expected. All gathered were children of the Light. He was born into the world tasked with protecting them. Now, watching them dine together at the start of this journey, he felt like a father watching his family enjoy a special supper. The urge to protect and provide was unlike anything he'd ever experienced, and it brought him immense joy.

He glanced at Bossador and Carthon at opposite sides of the table. To all else they were rival warriors with deep-seated resentment between one another, and for a time Falin felt the same, but now, he saw them as kids; quarreling children he would guide to a better understanding of one another.

"We never had a toast," Falin said.

Bossador ripped a bite off a turkey leg. "I didn't take you to be one for formalities."

Falin stood with a goblet of wine. "I'm not." He raised his cup. "But I want to toast all of you here tonight. My Champions. I had expected four of you, and the God of Light has blessed me with six." Jimbuah beamed and lifted the brim of his oversized hat. "We're still at the beginning of our journey, and we will face many perils, but facing those perils with this company brings me comfort. To my Champions."

"Here, here," Bossador said, as all raised their glass and sipped their mead and wine.

The meal went on, and the more they ate, the more they drank, the more boisterous they became, sharing stories, dreams, aspirations, and insights into each other's lives. At Jimbuah's request, dessert was brought as the rest continued to pick on their main course. The skully reacted so enthusiastically to his first slice of apple pie, he took the entire dessert for himself and ate it in moments.

"And where is it you and Jimbuah envision for your future home?" Bossador asked. "Following our journey through the Wildbarrens, that is."

"We're not sure," Red replied. "Like we said before, somewhere in the Crown, not too cold, preferably not Vartulis. No offense," he said to Carthon.

Carthon glanced at him from the sides of his eyes but seemed to care little. "Most have the predisposition to think Vartulis is nothing but a dreary place. There is incredible beauty there, even to those not born a drak."

"Sell us on it," Red said, pouring another cup of mead.

Carthon bit a tough piece of beef and chewed as if it were cake. "Like the other kingdoms of the Crown, there are diverse landscapes. In the south, bordering the Freelands, are the Forests of Pristima, whose leaves turn every color you can imagine once a year. This area is not cold, but cool."

"I'm intrigued." Red shrugged. "Go on."

"On the coast, where I was raised, there are fishing towns where the food is plenty, and the landscapes are of pure majesty, surely crafted by the hand of Mother Elsana. The earth holds a strong, distinct power in the way the waves crash against the shores." Nym rested her chin in her palm and hung on every word the handsome drak conveyed. "Then there is the north, where half of the nation dwells." He grinned to himself. "All who have never ventured there deem it a place of snowy gloom, grim and bleak, but this is not so. To describe our capital, Washborn, through words alone is a grave injustice, but I will do my best." Carthon wiped his mouth. "Washborn was named after the leader of the Drakkish Rebellion, and our surrounding cities are named after his inner-circle. Djorn, Talon, Fex, Alsi, Relvo, Kiri. All heroes to the cause of Vartulis to gain freedom from Mortulian rule. I digress."

Carthon bit another piece of meat before continuing. "Washborn is a city of immaculacy. Most of the earth is stone, so the snow remains pristine, white and un-muddied. There is little wind, so the chill that often bites in other lands does not hinder you there. There is no fresher air in the world than on the Mountains of Washborn, and every breath is that of untainted Elsana. Stone is in abundance, so homes are too, and drakkish peasants live in houses the people of Rorkshire would consider noble. This is what the Senate offers in Washborn. Fairness for all, and through our Senate, Vartulis maintains a utopia, and we always will."

"Wow," Nym said dreamily.

Red and Jimbuah glanced at one another. "Vartulis might be on the shopping list again. Anyone else tryin' to make a pitch? How about you Nym? I've been to Lelyalis, but I've never been further north than the border."

"I love my home," Nym answered. "The Woods of Juleer is our capital, and that is the heart of our kingdom. The elves live in harmony, and we have no leader, no infighting. There are cave elves that live in the Crystal Halls of Topa, and tree elves that live high in the branches of Olu, where I am from."

"Triba?" Jimbuah asked.

Nym nodded and smiled. "Yes. Entire villages within the branches, connected by ropes and bridges. Great platforms of polished wood sit atop the mighty branches of Oluian trees. One might never think they'd left the ground at all if spending enough time inside. But as I was saying; tree elves, cave elves, the ice elves of the northern coast and southern elves of the Yuni Fields all live in harmony and peace. There will never be a day of worry in your life if residing in Lelyalis."

"Mhm," Red nodded, ingesting her statement. He snapped his finger at Bossador. "You're up, Boss. Dazzle me."

Bossador took a deep swig of mead and placed his pint down, wiping his beard with his sleeve. "If it is solace you seek, Rodrellan is the place for you. We have similar landscapes to most other king-

doms. There are woods and mountains in the north, and the coastline to the east. But…" he raised a finger, "the Forests of Rodrellan
are like none other. The trees stand tall like mountains, some as
wide as a hundred madorian soldiers shoulder to shoulder. These
woods are thick and offer safety from invasions of enemies. The
Lumber Halls we build do not burn, cannot be broken by axe, and
stand as strong as stone, as the trees they are made of are magic,
planted by the giants in the Beginning. My shield is even made from
this wood."

"How do you cut them down then?" Red asked.

"We use a special steel only madorians forge, passed down
through the millennia by the giants before they left this world.
Much like the stone in Vartulis, the trees of Rodrellan are plentiful,
and all are offered a home that they desire. They just have to harvest
it from the soil. There is an old magic within the woods, and it cares
for those who dwell in it. I promise you that," Bossador finished.

"You've seen Mystica," Melquin said. "You've even been familiar with Mystica prisons if I remember correctly."

"Honestly, they're lovelier than some of the nicest homes in the
western Freelands," Red answered.

"Yeh, yeh," Jimbuah agreed.

"Three meals a day, soft beds to sleep on… we didn't even feel
like we were in prison until we had those shackles put on us."

"And what was it you were caught doing again?" Carthon
asked. "Stealing the Duke of Urlen's mead? And his wife's jewelry?
Tell us the story."

"We weren't going to steal the jewelry," Red waved a hand.
"Urlen was holdin' a festival, and most of the castle was empty to
watch a sparring match. We snuck in for some food and came across
the Duke's quarters. As you can see, this one likes to play pretend,"
he said, pointing at Jimbuah, who forced a wide smile. "Jimmy
starts putting on all of her rings, necklaces, tiaras, and prancing
around making these weird noises. Do what you was doin' that
night, Jimmy."

Jimbuah stood up and cleared his throat, then began skipping around the room, making feminine sounds with snooty faces. The room laughed as they watched. "*La la lee! La la lee mola!*"

"What is he saying?" Nym asked through a chuckle, cheeks rosy from the wine.

"Nothin'," Red replied. "That's just how he thinks royalty sounds. It's gibberish," Red said. "So we go down to the mead-cellar, and he refuses to take the jewelry off. Then we start drinkin'. We were only gonna have one, but that turned into one *barrel*." Bossador let a hearty laugh rip as Jimbuah returned to his seat. "There we are, and we're singin' songs, barely able to stand, and I get interrupted midway through singing by a small crew of guards." Melquin covered her mouth and attempted to stifle a snicker, causing her to squeak instead.

"Nofa gukadu," Jimbuah shook his head. "Nofa gukadu."

"Next thing we know, we're gettin' arrested, and interrogated about everything in our lives. That's how they found out we'd been through the Wildbarrens."

Carthon breathed sharply from his nose. "What song were you singing when caught?"

Red turned his attention to Falin and motioned his head. "The ballad about this one's pal. Beast of Burden. About Airo the Bane." Falin became intrigued, having never heard of the song written about his mentor.

"I've never heard it," Carthon said. "Is it a common one?"

"In the south it is. It's about the history of Darva where a certain princess is being kept now," Red answered. "It's a glum tune, but it's beautiful. Have you heard it, Falin?"

"I can't say I have," Falin admitted. "Could you sing it?"

"No, no no," Red waved his hands. "Not enough mead in me."

"Come on!" Nym demanded. "Don't be a flower and just do it!"

"Sikingi! Sikingi!" Jimbuah demanded, slamming his hands to the table.

"Alright, alright!" Red answered. "Just once. Does everyone know the backstory to Darva?"

"I don't, actually," Falin said, surprised he didn't. "Airo had never spoken of it."

Red titled his head. "Really? He never shared it with you?" Falin shook his head and shrugged. Red raised his eyebrows and looked away. "I guess I can understand why. It's how he got his name, Airo the Bane." He took a breath and began to tell the tale.

"Four hundred years ago, Darva was a bustling kingdom, much bigger than Rorkshire. It was during an era when Drucullm's border was much further back, and the concern of the Shadow Kingdoms wasn't as much of an issue. Airo saw it as a place of opportunity for orphans of the Freelands. He oversaw their care and placement in Darva, eventually finding them work when they were old enough. For fifty years, it was a booming city, and Airo loved it. There must've been thousands of orphans he found homes for there and watched them grow whenever he visited. In many ways, they were his children." Red chewed the side of his cheek as if hesitant to continue. "I guess at some point around three hundred and some-odd years ago, a coalition of crags, gruns, and augurs invaded, claiming the kingdom as their own. Those who were unable to flee were killed." Falin let out a short gasp. "Airo had been away at that point, on wizard business I guess. When he heard the news, he went straight there and found what the Shadow Kingdoms had done to the city that had housed the orphans. He razed the kingdom in his fury. He killed every last crag, grun, and augur. An entire kingdom's forces were unable to stop him. This is how he became Airo the Bane." A lull fell over the room upon hearing the dismal tale. "I guess I always liked the song because I was an orphan," Red added. "It was nice to know someone at some time in history cared for orphans too."

Falin felt a little overwhelmed upon learning his mentor had secretly harbored such a tragedy for so long.

"Sikingi," Jimbuah requested, softly this time.

Red nodded and stood, removing his hat and holding it over his chest. He took a deep breath and began singing a melody of haunting beauty and lament.

Warn the crags, augurs, and gruns,
My forgiveness never comes.
I bring you agony, despair,
For taking my beloved.

It's not thunder,
I'm coming for you.

I'm a dragon from the Light,
Your time is burning.
I'm the quiver in the earth,
I'm your beast of burden.

I'm your bane,
I'm your bane,
I'm your beast of burden,
I'm your bane.

The reaper of your reward,
By prize of death, this I swear.
I am your terror in the night,
I am the burden you bear.

Torched earth, wind and rain, wind and rain.
Scorned words, sins, and pain, sins and pain.
It's not thunder,
I'm coming for you.

I'm a dragon from the Light,
Your time is burning.
I'm the quiver in the earth,
I'm your beast of burden.

I'm your bane,
I'm your bane,
I'm your beast of burden,
I'm your bane.

After a moment of silence, Falin took a breath and said, "Wow. That was—so sad, but you sing wonderfully."

Red returned to his seat. "Thank you. It's a bit of a mood killer, hence me being reluctant to sing it."

"I had never heard it, and I am glad I have," Carthon said. "Thank you. Vartulis would be lucky to have a minstrel of your ability."

Red chuckled and cracked a grin. "I should start writing originals then. That's if we decide on Vartulis."

"Why is it you don't want to go back to Quatiti, Jimbuah?" Melquin asked. She realized her error upon his face falling.

"Bakunisha," Jimbuah answered with his head down.

"He was banished," Red translated.

"How could anyone banish you?!" Nym said.

Jimbuah forced a small smile, but his sorrow was evident. Red told the story for him. "Quatiti has strict laws about who they allow on the island. A group of Freeland sailors sought shelter from an oncoming storm, but the skullies didn't trust them, fearing they were Trartorkian pirates in disguise. Jimmy felt strongly they weren't and let them stay hidden in his hut, but they got caught. Long story short, they found Jimmy guilty of harboring unwanted visitors and forced him to leave with the sailors. He hasn't been back since."

"You poor thing," Nym said.

Jimbuah rested his chin in his palm and shrugged sullenly. "Bah."

"Not like we want to go to the Magpie Isles, anyway, do we?" Red said, slapping his back. "What are we gonna do? Find an island and live with lizard people?"

"Lizard people?" Carthon asked. "What are you talking about?"

"There's an island of lizard people in the Magpie Isles," Red explained. "They talk and act like people, but are lizards."

"That's the stupidest thing I've ever heard." Carthon flashed his sharp-toothed grin. "Have you seen these lizards?"

"Well, no. But I met an old sailor in Krattle's Cove who spoke of them once. Swore on his life."

Bossador laughed heartily, smacking the table with his hand so the utensils rattled. "You have been fooled, friend! There is no such thing as lizard people."

Nym giggled and agreed. "He's right. You were fooled by another drunken fool!"

"Lizard people," Carthon shook his head. "If that is not one of the funniest sailor's tales I've ever heard."

"It's real!" Red pressed. "He wasn't lying. I could tell!" Melquin concealed a smile with a covered hand. "I'm tellin' you! You believe me, don't you wiz?"

Falin chuckled. "Maybe. I think it's more likely you were having your leg pulled. But who knows." The young wizard rubbed his eye and looked up at the chandelier, seeing most of the candles were near extinguished from lack of wick. His eyes stung and he yearned for bed. "We have an early start tomorrow. We'd best get some sleep. Has everyone had their fill?" All heads at the table nodded heavily as if becoming tired at the mention of bed. "Good. Thank you all for this evening."

As they stood to leave the room, Bossador said, "May all your dreams be happy ones."

Melquin turned to Red. "Of giant talking lizards." The group laughed as they retired for the night.

The following morning Falin's head felt heavy from the pints of wine and mead. Rays of sun shined through his window and he was eager to depart, growing tired of the magicless kingdom despite its hospitalities. After getting dressed and gathering his belongings, he trekked to the front courtyard of the castle where the rest of his group was already waiting, horses prepared.

"Mornin' wiz," Red said. "You ready?"

"I am," Falin answered. "What are we waiting for?"

"The king wants to see us off." Red nodded behind Falin to the palace entrance. "Speakin' of."

A group of guards ushered the king forward, and behind him, Delsa, the former queen.

"Good morning!" King Pernicus exclaimed. "I am thrilled to see you off on—"

"*'Tis an ho-nor,*" Jimbuah interrupted.

The king glanced at the skully, returned to his usual pant-only attire. The green, pointed hat he wore the night prior stuck out from his pocket. "Hello… " Pernicus returned his focus to the rest of the group. "I am thrilled to see my Champions off on their quest to find my daughter, Princess Bloom."

Falin moved to say they were on actually on a quest to find the Gems of Elsana, but thought better of it. "Thank you."

"I have an item I would like one of you to give my daughter upon finding her," King Pernicus said. "Who would like to carry it for me?" he said, raising a framed painting.

Bossador started to accept the task, but Red shoved him aside and said, "I'll take it, your highness. I will make sure Princess Bloom gets your—" Red took the picture and furrowed his brow. "Small portrait of you riding a horse. Into battle."

"Thank you, Redrick," King Pernicus said. "I am hoping it will inspire her and bring her the courage to make the perilous journey home to Rorkshire."

"You've seen battle?" Melquin asked.

The king raised his chin. "Well, no. The image is meant to inspire her."

"Perfect," Melquin said.

"Oh, and if you could tell her I have tasked all of the kingdom's architects with expanding the walls of the city so she has more room to roam, it would be appreciated."

"Will do," Carthon responded so enthusiastically, the king beamed, failing to register it was sarcasm. Nym snickered, her gaze lingering on Carthon for a moment.

Delsa rolled her blind eyes and shuffled to the Champions. "Where is my friend, Falin?"

"I am here, your highness," Falin said, stepping forward.

Delsa smiled and grasped his arm, turning him away from the rest of the group. "If you find Bloom, tell her I didn't send her anything, because no granddaughter of mine needs anything from anyone."

Falin grinned and nodded. "You have my word, Delsa."

The elderly woman hugged him, patting him on the back. "Be well, Falin. Don't forget to enjoy your journey when you can," she chuckled. "Farewell Champions!"

"We wish you all the luck in Rorkshire!" Pernicus said. "May you find everlasting success on your quest to find Princess Bloom."

"Farewell," Falin said. "We are eternally grateful for your hospitality. I hope that we cross paths again in the near future."

With that, they climbed onto their horses and departed through the southern roads of the walled kingdom, exiting for the surrounding villages. Falin focused on the road ahead, eager to continue his journey.

CHAPTER FOUR:
THE OLDWOODS

The road to the Oldwoods had been dull, with Freeland villages long behind the travelers. Their trek was filled with endless pastures where stone and trees littered the path for five mundane days. On occasion, a weary nomad passed on a rickety wagon, or those seeking shelter headed for Rorkshire. By day the company plodded along on their horses, and by night they camped in fields. Falin grew anxious since their departure of the kingdom, wishing to escape the open road of the Freelands for the cover of the Oldwoods.

Near the end of their fifth day, Bossador pointed forward and exclaimed, "Up ahead!" Falin and company craned their necks, seeing distant trees crawl over the horizon.

"Is it the Oldwoods?" Melquin asked.

"It is," Red answered, trotting his horse forward. "Last chance, Falin. You sure you don't want to go around? You sure you want to go through?"

Something in Falin's gut insisted they pass through the Oldwoods. "Yes," Falin answered. "You have been adamant we go around since we began this journey. What is it you know about the Oldwoods that scares you?"

Red cautiously eyed the looming trees. "It's what I don't know about the Oldwoods that scares me. I've only been in once, and never gone back again."

"What happened?" Falin asked.

Red took a deep breath and began. "I hadn't been in long, and I was in the southwestern corner of the woods. I was hungry, and hunting, and I shot an arrow at what I thought was a full-grown forest-hog. 'Bout this big," Red said, stretching his arms out as wide as he could. He tipped his cap and chuckled softly. "Turns out it was the cub of a craggon bear, and I pissed off its mama *real* bad. Next thing I knew I was runnin' for my life while this big ol' beast is tryin' to hunt me down. Crashing through trees and brush like it was nothing. It stood twice as tall on Bossador on all fours and was three horses long."

Bossador laughed. "We have craggon bears in northern Rodrellan. We hunt them for sport as they are easy to outsmart."

"You didn't let me finish," Red continued. "As I was runnin', I heard a yelp and this horrid crunching noise. I turned around, and the craggon bear was just… gone." The Freelander stared at the ground as he relived the memory. "As I was tryin' to figure out what happened, I hear this crashing in the trees and *BAM*! The bear's decapitated head was tossed from the branches above, and blood started drippin' from the leaves like rain. Somethin' bigger and stronger than a *craggon bear* was livin' in the branches, and yanked it up like I would a fish from a pond."

Falin turned his gaze to the ever approaching Oldwoods. "What'd you do?"

"I left those woods as fast as I could and never went back. 'Til now."

"Okay, you had a bad experience," Nym said. "That's fair. But every race passes through the Oldwoods all the time. And you're forgetting the further we head south the more likely we're going to meet hordes of crags or gruns on the open road. At least we'll have cover in the woods."

"It is for Falin to decide," Carthon interjected. "What do you wish, wizard?"

Falin glanced at the drak and then focused his mind on the Oldwoods. Logic told him to listen to Red. There was too much unknown danger that could cause them to falter, yet something called him to the forest. It was as if the woods itself was speaking to him, beckoning him to enter. "We will pass through the Oldwoods," Falin announced. "We will take turns on watch through the night and stick to the road."

"Alright then," Red muttered.

As the sun began to set, they met the border of the woods where a distinct line was drawn between field and forest. The company stopped a stone's throw from the entrance and wandered off the road, setting camp at the edge of the woods, not wanting to venture in while it was dark. With the last bits of sunlight peeking over the hills, Melquin built a fire, and they took rest from the long day's journey. They gathered in a circle around a fire, though none but Carthon sat with their back to the woods.

"So say we make it through without a problem," Melquin began, "are we setting off straight for Darva to search for this princess? Or do we carry on in our quest?"

"I made a vow," Bossador answered. "As a prince, I need to honor this."

"You also made a vow to Falin," Carthon said, staring into the flames. "Where is it your allegiance lies?"

Bossador sat up straight and raised his chin. "To Elsana. As long as I breathe, I will honor the world in which I was born by doing what is right and just."

Carthon moved to cast mockery at the statement, then glanced at Falin, lowering his gaze to the fire again. "I am here to follow the orders of none other than Falin. I go where he goes. If it is to rescue a Freeland princess, so be it."

"The first Gem is in the Mortal Mountains, right?" Melquin asked. "Do you have any idea where the others will be?"

"No idea," Falin said. "The wizards say at least one will be in the Wildbarrens, hence these two," he said, nodding towards Red and Jimbuah.

"How do they know that?" Nym asked.

"Purla the Lightbringer, one of the wizardesses, has some capabilities of a seer," Falin explained. "She had a vision I would be taken there."

"I didn't know she was clairvoyant," Melquin said. "Not in any legends I've heard of her."

"She's not really clairvoyant," Falin answered. "She'll just get the occasional vision."

"Are any of the wizards truly clairvoyant?" Carthon asked.

"Not living ones," Falin said, "but there have been others in the past. I have heard there is one warlock who is, however. The one born fifty years before me in the cycle, actually. His name is Silas the Clairvoyant." The fire sparked at the mention of the warlock's name. "He's said to be able to know all of the past, present, and future."

"I wouldn't want to know my future," Bossador said. "I'd want a chance to make my own."

"Are we really making our own future, though?" Nym suggested. "Or has Mother Elsana placed us on a path of certain fate no matter what we do?"

Melquin stared into the flames. "There's n—"

The group jumped as a twig snapped at the very edge of the Oldwoods. Everyone reached for their weapons.

"Bibaru!" Jimbuah said with a harsh whisper.

"If that were a bear we'd already hear it charging," Red argued, gripping the handle of his whip.

"Someone approaches," Carthon said, his drak eyes better than theirs in the night.

Bossador put his hand on his hilt, and they stood, ready to fight. Falin sensed a powerful yet familiar energy in the shape that walked towards their light. He was at ease.

"It is wonderful to see such urgency in protecting my pupil," the voice said. At once, Falin smiled, knowing who approached in an instant. The shape of a squat man came into sight, and Airo the Bane entered their camp with his staff in hand. "Greetings to all on this fine evening."

"Airo!" Falin said, hurrying to his mentor. "I did not think I would get to see you so soon!" He hugged the older wizard who seemed to cherish the moment.

"Nor did I," Airo answered. "But it seems fate has brought us together."

"What are you doing here?" Falin asked.

"Wizard business." Airo walked to the circle of Champions surrounding the fire. "Tell me. How has your journey been thus far?"

"Good," Falin answered. "We dealt with some gruns on the second day, but other than that, not much. We spent a couple nights in Rorkshire too. The king's daughter was taken by a dragon weeks ago, and he has asked us to save her."

Airo stroked his white beard and smiled. "A good start indeed. There will be many more adventures within your quest. Cherish them all." As Airo went to sit on a rock by the fire, Falin noticed he had a slight limp, leaning on his staff for support.

"Are you hurt? You are walking as if injured," Falin said.

"Do not worry about me, I am just old," Airo grunted.

"What is it you were doing in the Oldwoods?" Carthon asked. "And how did you pass us on the road without us knowing?"

Airo patted his round belly. "I rolled." After a brief silence, the wizard threw his head back and cackled. Carthon grinned and shook his head. "I am speedier than I look, young drak. That I can assure you."

"What were you doin' in the Oldwoods?" Red pressed. "And why're you comin' back up this way? Is it dangerous?"

Airo tossed his head side to side in deliberation. "Slightly less dangerous than when I entered. I was on a task to rid the woods of unnecessary Darkness." After glancing around the group, his face formed an ominous frown. "Warlocks."

Jimbuah let out a small gasp. "Nofa!"

"Warlocks indeed, Jimbuah. Warlocks indeed."

"Are they gone now?" Falin asked. "Or would it be safer going around the forest? Red seems to think we shouldn't enter."

Airo rubbed his injured leg in thought. "What does your Wizard's Instinct tell you?"

Falin took no time to answer. "The Oldwoods."

"Then listen to that inner-voice. It is a mighty weapon of a wizard." Airo scanned their camp. "I would reconsider taking the horses through. They would attract the hungry mouths of predators and be unable to fend for themselves in such close quarters. Leave some of your food stores with them so they can safely deliver it to the other side of the woods."

Melquin looked at the horses and pouted. "I suppose they'd fare better running in an open field without us on their backs."

"What were the warlocks doing in the Oldwoods?" Bossador asked. "Are they gone now?"

"Yes, I rid the forest of them. There were only two. Nyril the Coercer and Mulgus the Plague," Airo answered in distaste. "But they put up quite a fight. Like wasps refusing to leave a nest." The wizard tapped his staff in consideration. "I did not want to sully Falin's journey with issues of the greater world, but I suppose it is best you all know. The wizards believe these two warlocks were preparing for some form of war. For what, we don't know."

"War where?!" Nym asked. "Against the Crown?"

"We do not know," Airo shrugged. "They did not seem keen on telling me upon my visit to the Oldwoods. If we had to guess, we would assume the Crown. They are servants of the Dark, it makes sense they would be attacking servants of the Light, as history tells us."

"So are they recruiting gruns? And augurs and crags?" Melquin asked. "Are we at war?"

"No, no, nothing of the sort. Sources tell us there is no inkling of war within the Shadow Kingdoms. Drucullm, Varsa, nor Cadryl, which is most curious," Airo responded. Red shifted uncomfortably.

Falin didn't follow. "So then why the suspicion of war?"

"Huran the Giver had been visiting villages in the southwestern Freelands months ago. Ones he had helped settle. To his disappointment, an entire village of men and women were dead. Slaughtered."

"In a raid?" Carthon inquired.

Airo sniffed sharply then spoke so low they had to lean in to hear him. "No. They were all dead by their own hands. They killed each other in a sudden frenzy of violence. A single survivor was left, torn to pieces, the poor thing. When Huran prompted her, she recounted a strange man passing through the village. Shortly after, they were all murdering one another. By her account, we agree it was some Dark magic by the wand of a warlock."

"That's horrible," Bossador shuddered. Everyone ingested the story with contorted faces.

"Indeed it is," Airo agreed. "A warlock would not inflict such evil in the Freelands without purpose. It must have been deemed a worthy endeavor to attract the eyes of the wizards."

Falin felt sick upon picturing the act. "What evil would possess one to do that?"

"It is in their nature," Airo said. "Servants of the Dark don't know any different. As we search for peace, they will always seek violence. It is the balance of the world, and it will always remain this way."

"The two warlocks you fought in the woods," Red began. "You think they were the ones who did this?"

"Between Nyril and Mulgus, it was likely Nyril. He is the Coercer. But even for him, I am sickened." Airo let out a sorrowful sigh. "I wish to slumber, but I do not want my final conversation of this day to be of such wretched matters. Would anyone care to share a tidbit of joy?"

Falin was disappointed to learn his time talking to Airo would be over so soon. Everyone thought for a moment, and Red responded, "Jimmy had his first piece of pie in Rorkshire. Ended up eating an entire pan by himself."

Airo chuckled heartily. "That is delightful. What flavor was it, Jimbuah?"

"Akuple," the skully answered, smiling.

"I do love apple pie too. At the end of your journey, we should share a slice, yes?"

"Yeh, yeh," Jimbuah nodded in agreement.

"Excellent," Airo said. "It is time this old wizard retires, and I imagine you should too. It would be best if you all get an early start on your day tomorrow."

"I'll take first watch," Carthon said. "Red, you take second."

"Yeah, alright," Red agreed.

The group made beds beneath the stars, and Falin felt as though he was at home with Airo in their company. All slept soundly having another wizard in their presence, feeling safe and protected, whether it was the essence of the Light that followed the wizard, or the comfort of knowing an individual so powerful would be ready to fight alongside them. Soon, they were snoring while Carthon took first guard, his gaze to the woods, and at some point in the night, he woke Red to take the second watch. In time, the starry night faded and the sun crept over the world to bring a new dawn.

"Time to wake up," Red prompted the group. Falin's eyes opened, and he felt like he had only just fallen asleep. "Let's see what the Oldwoods has in store."

Bossador sat up and rubbed a knuckle in his eye with grass protruding from his beard. "It is barely light. Should we not sleep a little longer?"

Nym hopped up from the ground and began packing her belongings. "Not if we want to get through the woods within this moon cycle. Let's go."

Red spoke in the exaggerated tongue of an aristocrat. "Doth the Prince wish to slumber further, 'fore I fetch his morning num-nums? Or should I undress thee jammies so we might saddle your strained pony, my liege?"

Falin stretched and yawned, turning to Airo who watched in amusement. "It's been like this for weeks," Falin said.

Airo smiled. "If these are your troubles, then this is good company you keep." The wizard took Falin by the arm and guided him a few paces away, out of earshot of the group who prepared the horses. "You must be careful in the Oldwoods," Airo warned in a low tone. "If you come across any warlocks, do not try and fight them, Falin. They are very powerful and cunning, and would not think twice to kill a young wizard if they believed they could get away with it."

Falin did his best to put on a brave face. "Okay. What should I do if we meet one? Run?"

Airo looked away and thought on it. "Wizard's Instinct. Do what is right in the moment. The God of Light will guide you."

"Alright," Falin said, nodding to himself. "I'll be fine."

"I'm sure you will be," Airo agreed. "And do not dawdle too much on your journey. We will need another wizard of your power if it comes to war. There is no saying what the warlocks are planning."

"There was once a time you were better at putting my mind at ease," Falin grinned.

Airo forced a smile, but Falin could see concern hiding behind his eyes. "Perhaps because my mind was already at ease." The wizard turned to the woods and sighed. "The Oldwoods was once a beautiful place of true beauty and serenity, where woodsfolk gathered and travelers could pass without fear. I admit the wizards have neglected it as of late, providing a home to wretched creatures and other vile activities." Airo raised his eyebrows and looked to Falin. "Hence the warlocks' attraction to it." Falin began to doubt his Wizard's Instinct about passing through. "It is time we part," the mentor said, returning to the Champions. "I thank you all for offering me your welcome within your camp and wish you the safest of journeys. May the God of Light be with you all in times of darkness." The Champions said their goodbyes to him. Airo turned to Falin, hugging him once more. "I'm sure I will see you soon. Be safe, Falin."

"Goodbye, Airo," Falin replied. The old wizard turned to the road, walking at a leisurely pace heading north.

Falin watched for a moment and had his attention recalled by Nym. "Are you ready, Falin?" she asked.

Falin turned to see Melquin petting the horses and whinnying into their ears. They bobbed their heads in understanding and darted west along the tree line to meet the group on the other side of the forest. They watched as the horses took flight, left to carry their belongings.

Falin clutched his staff and started for the trees, feeling as though he entered a mouth that swallowed them whole. Upon stepping into the forest, the air cooled, and a sudden magic tickled his senses. In the shade of the woods, he felt more magic than he had on the road of the Freelands. Far more.

Almost every tree was bulky, holding branches that extended as far as the roots ran deep. The trunks were spaced far apart, so there was plenty of room between them, but the multitude of limbs that hung over their heads created a canopy that hid sunlight. The branches were thick, appearing strong enough for even Bossador to rest upon, and their leaves were the size of Falin's torso. Birds and squirrels rustled in the trees, and on occasion, a rabbit or deer would scurry away as the oncoming troupe embarked deeper into the forest.

The further they went, the more Falin began to sense a subtle dread. It was as if the fringes of the woods still clung to its ancient history as a place of Light, but its core had become rotten, tainted by Darkness. Through their first day, they kept to the path, largely unhindered by roots.

Long after their feet had grown sore, Nym called for them to stop. "Do you hear that?"

"Hear what?" Melquin asked.

Nym's pointed ears twitched as they stuck out from her red hair. "It's water. A brook or stream nearby. We should make rest there for the night and fill our canteens."

"We should be wary of straying too far from the path," Carthon said. He tilted his head. "I cannot hear the brook. It must be far; it would be easy to get lost."

"I can ensure we will not become lost," Melquin replied. "Which way is the brook, Nym?" The elf pointed left off the road.

Melquin abandoned the trail, prompting them to follow. As she stepped over the gnarled roots, moss, and weeds, she lowered the head of her staff to the ground, and tiny, pink flowers sprouted from the earth. Dainty bulbs no bigger than berries budded from the moss, but they were plentiful on the stems they grew from, forming little bright bushels.

Carthon bent over to inspect the plants. "Will these be here in the next day? To find our way back?"

"They will likely be here in the next year," Melquin answered, skimming her staff over the forest floor. "Come. Be careful not to twist your ankles on the roots."

The group did as told, following the sage as they walked over the bumpy terrain. As Melquin led them, a trail of pink foliage guided their feet, and in time, the sound of the brook was heard by all. After the brief hike, they came upon a stream where glistening water tumbled over the rocks and through the woods. Melquin bent by the water, assumed to be drinking, but upon second glance, she was petting a massive rabbit.

"Would you look at him!" Melquin announced. "She lifted the hare with a grunt, and its body stretched the size of a small hound in her arms. Melquin stood with her back bent to maintain hold of the creature. The rabbit seemed to enjoy the company of the sage, hanging leisurely in her arms. "I've heard tales that animals were

bigger in the Oldwoods. I never thought they meant rabbits too."
She made gentle squeaking noises, and the rabbit's elongated ears
perked. It turned its face to her, responding with tiny squeaks of its
own. A melodious laugh escaped Melquin. "He says he's the smallest of three hundred brothers!"

"He looks tasty," Carthon said, examining the animal. "And he
would feed us all for two nights."

Melquin cast a scowl so venomous it made the drak think twice.
She turned her body, holding the rabbit away from him. "He is *not*
for food."

Carthon crossed his arms. "We will have to hunt sometime during this journey. You know this, Melquin."

The sage scrunched her nose and began squeaking at the rabbit
again. The rabbit spoke back, and she listened. "His name roughly
translates to Burlip. Burlip is not on the menu. Is that clear?"

The drak rolled his eyes, turning to prepare a fire. Red furrowed
his brow and looked between Melquin and the rabbit. "I can't tell if
you're magic or nuts."

Melquin hugged the rabbit before placing him gently on the
ground by the stream. The rabbit returned to nibbling on grass. "If
befriending animals is nuts, then I'm the Queen of Crazy."

In little time, they rested in their usual circle as the dusk turned
to night, and the chirps of crickets regaled the woods. The fire crack-
led while pairs of glowing eyes would watch from the outskirts of
their encampment, only to return to the dark.

Their meal consisted of food from Rorkshire; bread, cheese,
dried fruit, and cured meat. Falin felt his eyes tire as he leaned
against a tree covered in soft moss. Melquin held Burlip the Rabbit
who slept in her lap.

Red rubbed the sharpened end of his whip along a whetstone.
"Maybe we'll find the Sword of Elsana while we're in here, Jimmy.
Wonder what kind of a castle that'll get us."

"Bikigi," Jimbuah answered, laying flat on the ground. "Bikigi,"
he repeated.

"The Sword of Elsana is a myth," Carthon replied. "A tale Freeland mothers tell their children."

"I'm not too sure about that." Red shook his head. "Seems to me it's plenty possible."

"I am not familiar with this tale," Nym said. "Tell it before I fall asleep."

Red raveled his whip and tossed his hat to the side. "Everyone here knows about the Wars of the Beginning. It was a mess. Phantoms were turning elves into draks. Warlocks were killing faeries and giants. Wizards ridding the mainland of the phantoms. Anyway, there were three Titans created by the God of Darkness. One of the Land, one of the Sea, and one of the Skies. They were giant beasts who roamed the world, capable of destroying mountains." Jimbuah sat up with crossed legs to better listen. "During the Wars of the Beginning, these Titans were unstoppable… for a time. It was a wizard of old who defeated the Sea Titan in combat. They say he harnessed the Light and killed it. Some say it was a fight that lasted an entire year." Red raised his eyebrows and shook his head as he pictured the battle. "Then, the Sky Titan was the second to go. Do you know which creature of the Beginning killed him?" When no one answered, Red smiled and pointed at Jimbuah. "It was a skully."

"A skully defeated one of these Titans?" Nym asked.

"Indeed he did," Red answered. "Bulo the Skully, if I remember correctly. That right, Jimmy?"

"Yekasa. Bulo," Jimbuah beamed. "Hekaro ini Quatiti."

"But how did Bulo defeat a Titan? I did not think skullies were as powerful as wizards," Bossador asked.

"Sacula," Jimbuah responded in a more serious tone. "Sacula mofasti poturi."

Nym turned to Red for a translation. "He said sacrifice. Bulo sacrificed himself for Quatiti. The skullies believe sacrifice is the most powerful magic there is."

Jimbuah nodded his head in confirmation. "Yeh."

"What does this all have to do with the Sword of Elsana?" Nym pressed.

"Legend has it," Red continued, "that upon seeing the first two Titans fall, the Land Titan retreated to the depths of the earth, to return again one day when summoned by the Darkness. In that time, some wizard got ahold of Bulo's staff, as well as the wizard's staff who defeated the Sea Titan. He crafted their wood into the handle of a great blade to be used when the Land Titan returns. They say that the sword was kept hidden in the Oldwoods for thousands of years. Time has lost it, but not yet forgotten the blade. Prophecies claim a Warrior of the Light will one day be born and slay the Land Titan with the Sword of Elsana."

After a hanging pause, Melquin asked. "Why are prophecies so vague? Why can't they just tell us when, where, and by who? They're always so cryptic."

Falin chuckled. "Where is the fun in that?"

Melquin shook her head, frowning. "Don't like it. Prophecies are just lazy storytelling."

Falin rubbed his eyes, growing tired. "We should all get some sleep now. Who is on watch tonight?"

"Melquin and I will take turns," Bossador asked. "I can take first watch," he said to the sage. "I will wake you when I grow too tired."

Each group member found a bed of moss either against a rock, on the ground, or by a tree, and they quickly fell to sleep by the sounds of crickets and the brook. Bossador sat upon a stump with his great sword unsheathed, ready and alert.

Falin quickly drifted into a heavy slumber, and dreamed of the Oldwoods as a less ominous place than it was now. In his dreams he saw a pair of siblings, a young man and woman, weeping at the base of a colossal tree. They were no older than Falin. Suddenly, the tree's base opened into a door where they cried. The siblings walked in without a second thought, and Falin followed, curious to see what would happen. Spiral steps carved into the earth guided them into a hidden chamber, with ancient tales etched into walls. The roots of the tree hung from the ceiling, and at once, Falin knew this was a sacred place. At the center of the chamber remained a stump of wood, and in it, the Sword of Elsana. As if calling to the siblings, the sword began to glow brighter, prompting the young man to grab the handle and remove it from the stump. In his retrieval of the blade, there was a blinding flash, and Falin awoke to find it was morning.

He bolted upright with a gasp. Melquin turned as she packed her belongings with Burlip following where she walked. "Are you alright?"

Falin took a deep breath and rubbed his head. "I just had the most vivid of dreams. It was like I was there."

"Something from your past?" Melquin asked.

"No," Falin said. "Just a dream. Nothing more."

The group set off in a steady march, and they trudged over the forest path, keeping alert. The deeper they entered, the more Falin became uneasy, and at times, thought he saw movement at a distance. Trees became both larger and older, their gnarly, fat bodies carrying winding branches that intertwined with other trees. Little sunlight shined through the canopy. Burlip followed wherever they went.

During the second day, Bossador noticed there were no deer in this part of the woods, something all agreed was odd for a forest of this size.

On the third night, they sought camp as the sun slinked away, and the hidden stars did little to brighten their surroundings. They veered from the path to a clearing, following a trail of Melquin's flowers. At the center, they created a great campfire and circled it, eager to reprieve their exhausted legs. The area of grass they rested on was spacious, and the glow of the fire reached the ends of the tree line.

"Airo was right about the horses," Melquin thought aloud. "They never would have fared well on this terrain. I hope they're okay." She clutched Burlip tightly imagining their horses' journey around the Oldwoods.

"I'm sure they are fine," Falin assured.

Bossador sat across the fire from Falin, sharpening his sword with a whetstone. "Say all goes according to plan," the prince said. "We save this princess and get her to safety. Maybe we find some travelers to take her home. Then we go to the Mortal Mountains and gather the first Gem of Elsana. What next? Which way do we go if the next Gem is in the Wildbarrens?"

Falin retrieved the map Airo gifted him from his robes and placed his staff's head to it, causing a tiny blue dot to appear in the Mortal Mountains. "I suppose we would have to travel through Suntalla to reach the Wildbarrens."

"The jungles of Suntalla are a dangerous place. We should be wise and go around them," Bossador argued. "It would be in our best interest to go to the Kingdom of Letani. The Crown has kept good relations with the Southern Kingdoms, especially Letani."

Red and Jimbuah exchanged a glance. "I'm not sure that's our best bet. Not the friendliest place to be nowadays."

"Nonsense," Carthon said. "I once sailed the western coast all the way to Letani's capital. It was a beautiful city with kind and brilliant inhabitants. We'd be fools not to take refuge there. You wish to tell me you would prefer the jungles of Suntalla? Kingdom of Beasts?"

Red shrugged. "The jungles are mostly in the southern bits. A lot of it is… not so bad."

"Leaving us open to attack by wild belg, or mole monkeys." Bossador continued caressing his greatsword with the whetstone. "I've always wanted to visit the Southern Kingdoms. I hear the sunsets of Izema are an incredible sight. And the warriors of Wayili are fierce to fight alongside. I've heard their war cries are magnificent, that they can even…"

As Bossador rambled about the warriors of Wayili, Falin blinked hard, then squinted, peering over Bossador's shoulder to the edge of the clearing. At first, he thought his eyes were playing tricks on him, but slowly, the pale face of a sullen drak inched forward into the light.

"Bossador!" Falin yelled, standing and pointing behind the madorian prince. The drak leapt high into the air from the trees with a menacing hiss, fangs bared and eyes locked on Bossador's neck. Bossador turned his blade and pointed it behind him, skewering the airborne assailant by pure luck. The drak hung impaled at the stomach by Bossador's massive sword, his snarl fading with the light in his eyes.

"Blood draks!" Carthon shouted. "Prepare to fight!"

All in the group gathered their weapons in an instant, turning their backs to the fire as twenty pale faces crept from the forest, circling their prey. They wore tattered, mismatched clothing of all different races, likely stolen from victims, with bare feet dirtied from life in the forest. They held their sharpened nails like claws, hissing, baring their canines. Their eyes were bloodshot, with purple bags beneath them.

"Protect your necks," Carthon said. "They move swift and are cunning. Do not let them bite you, for their saliva is poison."

A blood drak among the enemies smirked. "Why not let us have supper, brother? It has been some time since we have feasted on a race of the Crown. We have grown tired of man and grun."

"I am not your brother," Carthon sneered, holding both of his black-bladed swords. "My people have forgotten your barbaric way of life." Falin noted the stark difference in the features of Carthon against the blood draks. Where Carthon's face boasted pale elegance, theirs held an eerie chalkiness. While Carthon had honorable eyes, the blood draks were filled with violent mischief.

"You know what you yearn for," the drak answered. "Pretty and pure as you may be, you were born of the Darkness. Nothing can ever change that."

"Leave, and you shall live," Carthon demanded.

"I shall leave with the blood of your friends in my belly," the drak responded. "Feast!" he ordered his posse.

Draks lunged with throaty growls, swiping at their prey with their talon-like fingernails. Falin blew a drak into the brush with a blast of magic, preparing for another attack.

Bossador lunged and swiped at a drak's head. It dodged and clawed at the prince's stomach, drawing blood from a deep gash. Bossador kicked the enemy away with a powerful thrust.

Nym threw a star across the fire, landing it in the throat of one about to attack Melquin from behind. Melquin twirled her staff and knocked another across the head with blinding force.

Over the hisses of the assailants, Red lashed his whip at approaching draks while fending off others with his sword. *CRACK.* They were severely outnumbered, and the fighting prowess of the draks was far better than any grun. "Jimmy!" Red called over his shoulder. "It's time to go big!"

Jimbuah ignored him and bashed an attacker in the jaw, then rolled beneath the legs of another, hitting him in the groin. "Nofa!" he yelled back. "Watistu!"

Bossador growled and swung his blade, cleanly decapitating a drak whose head still sneered in death. Carthon fended off numerous assailants who resented his renouncement of his ancestry. He cut the hand off one, and then a nose off another, causing them to retreat into the woods.

"Jimmy!" Red yelled, now with a gash dripping down his cheek. "GO BIG!"

"NOFA!" Jimbuah shouted back from the other side of the clearing. "Watistu!" He threw a handful of fire-berries at approaching draks. They burst into flames, darting from the clearing while patting themselves.

Falin spun his staff with all his might, casting a burst of magic at an attacker. From behind, a drak sunk his nails into Falin's arm and shoulder. It stung like tiny knives in his flesh, and he yelped. Falin could feel hot breath on his neck as the drak prepared to bite him.

Before he could brace for the poisonous teeth to break flesh, the drak's hands released and he turned, seeing a throwing star embedded into the eye of the enemy. Nym nodded to Falin and continued fighting with her sword.

What seemed like an eternity really lasted minutes, and the draks began to dwindle as they retreated or were killed. Falin turned to the center of the encampment after driving the bottom of his staff into the skull of a drak.

Five enemies remained, carefully seeking a chance to taste blood. One lurched at Bossador, and he grabbed it by the throat, tossing it back to the woods like a doll. The group fought them off with careful swipes of their weapons, until finally, they were left alone to the crackling of the flames, now bloodied by claw marks.

"Is everyone alright?" Falin asked. He wiped his forehead of blood.

"Yekasa," Jimbuah said by the clearing edge, cleaning drak residue from his staff. A rattling of leaves came from the branches above, and they jumped as the same drak that taunted Carthon fell from a branch, snatching Jimbuah by the arms. He sank his teeth into the skully's shoulder and slurped.

Jimbuah yelped as the drak released, retreating to the center of the clearing. The bloodsucker backed to the tree line and laughed with purple blood dripping down his chin.

"I've always wanted to taste skully!" he howled, licking his lips in victory. All looked on in horror, except for Red and Jimbuah. "It is a shame you won't let me have more while he is fresh! If you could leave his bod—" The drak blinked rapidly, then swayed, stumbling back and catching himself on a tree.

Jimbuah clutched his shoulder and began to chuckle, "He-he-he-he-he," in his raspy laugh.

The blood drak stared at the forest floor struggling to see, clutching his chest and panting. "What is happe—why—wha?" Baffled, he looked to the group as if they would offer an answer to his sudden discomfort.

Jimbuah buckled over while his shoulder poured blood, his up-roarious laughter echoing through the woods. He pointed at the drak in mockery. "Poi—poi—" He was unable to speak from laughing so hard. "Poitasona! Poitasona! Dujimo-fujiko! Poitasona!" The skully held his bare belly as it jiggled.

As the drak fell against a tree, shocked and confused, a violet foam began to spurt from his mouth.

"Skully blood is poisonous to consume," Red chuckled. "But I guess this stupid drak wouldn't know that."

The blood drak convulsed, gaping at Jimbuah in horror. In but a few seconds, he grew still with heavy eyelids.

"But will their poison hurt him?" Melquin asked, rushing to Jimbuah to examine his wound.

"Nofa," Jimbuah answered. He plucked a green leaf from his staff and gnawed on it, spit it back out, and rubbed it to his shoulder's bite mark.

"Does that cure poisons?" Melquin asked. "Is it magic?"

"Yeh," Jimbuah smiled, patting the bite mark. A wind of relief flew through the group. Falin leaned on his staff and nodded. To lose a Champion would be torment.

Carthon scanned the corpses and body parts of the draks. "We should stay awake two at a time from here on out."

"Let me help heal some of our wounds before we sleep," Melquin said, examining the gash on Bossador's stomach. The sage muttered incantations, rubbing the cut. Its bleeding slowed within seconds.

Nym began collecting her throwing stars from the bodies of fall-en enemies. "What was it you were saying to Jimbuah during the fight?" she asked Red. "Go big?"

Red began to ravel his whip. "Yeah. Just a surefire way to win a fight when we're outnumbered. Jimmy doesn't like usin' it because the fruit takes months to grow back. Nofa watistu."

"Amazing!" Bossador yelled, looking at his stomach. "The wound appears to be a day old. Sages never fail to amaze me."

"Be lucky it wasn't deeper," Melquin said, turning her attention to Falin. "There are some wounds I cannot heal." She pressed her thumbs over a cut on Falin's arm and began mumbling. As she worked at the punctures, Falin scanned the clearing of the drakkish massacre, realizing the sudden graveyard could have been comprised of his party.

CHAPTER FIVE:
SONGS AND SPIRITS

Four nights passed since the attack of the blood draks and all in the group were on edge. Falin sat cross-legged within a dried riverbed beside his Champions, examining his arm. The drak's scratch appeared weeks old after being treated by the tender hand of Melquin, no more than a faded scar of a distant altercation.

Night began to fall, and they decided on a late start the following day, taking refuge in the former river. Walls of dirt sheltered them with roots poking out from their sides. The earth was covered in smooth rocks, and the trees above seemed taller than ever. Bits of starlight winked through gaps in the leaves, but most branches shrouded the riverbed.

"I'm so tired of walking," Nym groaned, falling to the ground. She unlatched her utility belt and tossed it aside. "I miss riding our horses. They better be on the other side of this woods."

"They will be," Melquin assured. "They are horses bred of Mystica. They are smarter and faster than any steeds in Elsana."

"Horses only get so smart," Red retorted. "I figure a smart horse and a dumb grun are about the same."

Melquin cast a scowl at Red. "Same as an average man," she added. The sage lifted Burlip the Rabbit and stroked his head, making gentle squeaking noises.

"Is that rabbit a new Champion now?" Red asked. "He gonna protect us if the draks come back?"

Before Melquin could answer, Carthon said, "He looks like dinner once our rations start getting low."

Melquin turned the rabbit away from Carthon. "I will pluck your fangs and jam them in your eye sockets the second you move to eat him, Carthon. Try it."

A hearty chuckle escaped Bossador. "A wicked threat for a sage."

Melquin stroked Burlip's ear. "Bloodlust is not absent in those who forgo eating meat. It is merely redirected to those who unnecessarily harm animals."

"How much food do we have left?" Carthon asked. "That will sustain us, at least? We should begin a hunt soon."

Red dug through a couple of satchels. "We still got a lot of the jerky we took from those gruns near the border of Mystica. And we have about a quarter of the food left from Rorkshire, so yeah, we'll need to get hunting soon enough."

"And foraging," Melquin corrected.

"How much longer do you think we'll be in the woods, Falin?" Nym asked. "Is there anything on your map that indicates where we are?"

Falin had been wondering the same question on a daily basis. "No. I have no idea. I hadn't expected it take more than a week to pass through, but now I don't know. Perhaps tomorrow you can climb one of the trees and see if there's an end in sight."

"I pray to the God of Light I find one," Nym said, resting her head on the ground and staring up at the sky.

Jimbuah walked to Melquin and outstretched his arms to take the rabbit. "Gikivi," he demanded. Melquin transferred ownership of their pet, and Jimbuah stumbled as he tried to clutch the weighty animal in his small frame. His rear plopped to the rocks as he hugged Burlip, burying his face in its soft fur.

"Who is on first watch tonight?" Falin asked. "Do we feel we need two at a time tonight?"

"Not here," Bossador said. He scanned the lip of the riverbed on each side of their heads. We are well hidden."

"I'll take first watch, if you take second," Red volunteered.

"That I can do," Bossador agreed.

Falin tucked his knees to his chest and stared at their meager fire, wishing he knew where they were. He glanced at his staff with the four empty slots in the head, knowing he'd feel better about their journey once possessing a Gem or two. There was a helplessness that taunted him. It perturbed Falin knowing these people had already come close to death in protection of him. If he had more power, he could be the one protecting them.

Within a few hours, their subtle snores and the glow of the fire were the only indicators of their presence. Night was far from dawn and a full moon hung in the sky, gandering through the leaves at the sleeping travelers. It was then, well into their slumber, that Falin was awakened by some beautiful sound.

As Falin lifted his head, he scanned the camp with heavy eyelids, seeing that Bossador, Jimbuah, and Carthon had woken as well. Red stood tip-toed with his gaze over the wall of the riverbed. They listened intently. Nym and Melquin did not stir.

A woman's ethereal voice sang far in the woods, a sweet ballad of unending notes that floated over branches and atop moss like a perfect breeze. Falin knew not what she sang, but it didn't matter, because such incredible warmth resonated through him.

"It must be Mother Elsana herself," Carthon said, rubbing his eyes. "My ears have never been graced with such magnificence."

"Bujiti," Jimbuah agreed.

"We have to find her," Red proclaimed, his stare unmoved from the direction of the sound. He climbed the riverbed, and those awake followed, concentrating on every syllable sung. Falin was the last to depart, noticing Burlip peek awake atop Melquin. Nym rolled over to her other side, but did not wake in their exit.

Leaves crunched under their lumbering feet, drowsy and hypnotized by the voice so alluring, they dared not speak for fear she would cease. Falin wondered if she was some forest nymph or spirit who would offer them shelter and food. Perhaps Carthon was correct to say it was Mother Elsana.

Falin absorbed the Oldwoods as they passed, with scrawnier trees appearing decayed and closer together. Wooden vines swayed on crooked limbs. The air became muskier, and a slight fog rose from the forest floor. Still, they pursued the shimmery voice beckoning them.

At an area of the woods far from their camp, they stumbled into a small clearing of mossy earth. In the center, a woman of golden hair rested upon a tree stump, singing in some tongue of old by a fire. She smiled at the group, continuing her song. Dumbstruck, they stared on, as her melody matched her face, an aura of gorgeous charm too elegant for this world. She wore loosely hanging white linen, and a veil of light seemed to surround her. She was surely some relative of Mother Elsana.

They ambled forward, Red with his mouth agape, Bossador and Carthon in vacant stares, blessed to witness this being. They, along with Jimbuah and Falin sat on the lush moss and listened. The woman's gaze met each of their eyes with tender compassion. Heat from her fire warmed them the same way her voice did, and they hoped she would never stop singing.

Swaying to her song, they failed to notice the vines creeping from the branches, reaching around their arms and legs, first gently, moving so slowly that the listeners never noticed the plants caressing them. In minutes, so much vine was weaved around them, they were stuck sitting on the ground. She sang more for a time, ensuring they were at ease. Finally, her ballad came to an end.

Falin blinked, and everything changed about the woman; everything but her smile. Much happened in an instant, and confusion clobbered them all. They were no longer staring at a beautiful singer of the forest, but a creature in the form of a woman with green skin and black eyes, and hair that resembled ivy. Seeing this, they panicked, but the vines clutching them denied any chance of escape.

"It was a spell!" Falin yelled, looking to his left, hoping one of them had broken free. "She's a siren!" Bossador, Red, Carthon, and Jimbuah remained in the same predicament as him, tangled in vines.

A raspy snicker came from the siren. "What spirited youth I have captured tonight. Your flesh will sustain me for years to come." She was hideous, her green skin appearing that of a decayed leaf, with soulless eyes and scraggly hair, and veiny hands wielding sharp black claws.

Bossador strained under the vines with gritted teeth to no avail. "Foul evil! I thought sirens were a creature of the sea!"

The siren shrieked with ear-piercing force and darted for Bossador. She grasped his face, her claws tested the strength of his skin. "I am no siren of the seas! I am Rila! Siren of the Oldwoods! My might is not limited to the waters of Elsana!" She opened her mouth to reveal a set of yellow razor-like teeth, wet with strings of mucusy saliva, moving towards Bossador's throat.

Falin sought to delay their fate, desperately so. "How did you come here? Why did you leave the ocean?"

Rila closed her mouth and curiously turned to the young wizard. "What interest is it to you, boy?" She slinked to Falin and examined his face.

"I am a wizard," he explained. "And as a wizard, all beings of Elsana interest me."

"A wizard!" Rila beamed, licking her lips. "My beauty will know no bounds after consuming you." Her lengthy tongue licked his face, and she took a longing breath. Falin turned his head, wishing he could wipe the saliva that stung his cheek. "I was born of a warlock and a siren many years before any of you existed," she explained. "And have been gifted by great magic. I hold the blood of a warlock, unlike the powerless temptresses of sailors you speak of."

"If you have warlock blood, what other magic can you perform?" Falin asked. "Do you only sing and manipulate vines?"

Rila stood tall and bared her teeth. "What other magic does one need?! I have a wizard in my grasp, do I not?!" She swung her arms, and as she did, the vines around the clearing whipped in the same instant. "Arrogance is the recurring trait of the Light! Every man of the Light I take plead with honor and goodness. It is vain pride!"

Falin considered how best to calm her, but keep her occupied until one of them discovered an exit. "I see you are fierce, yes," Falin said. "Why have tales not been told of your power?"

Wicked contempt seeped from Rila as she glared at Falin, shrieking again. They cringed as it stabbed their ears. "What survivors have left my path? None! Are you fool enough to think any could leave my grasp? Merciless I must be to serve the Darkness!"

From the opposite edge of the clearing, movement caught Falin's eye. He saw it was Burlip the Rabbit. "Great Rila, may I ask you one more question?" Falin asked.

"Hurry wizard," Rila answered. "I yearn for flesh." She eyed Carthon with a starved gaze.

For whatever reason, his Wizard's Instinct urged him to provoke her, and smirking, he did so. "Are you fool enough to think there were none others in our company?"

Rila tilted her head in confusion, in part from hearing there were other travelers, second in this wizard's audacity. As she did, a throwing star flew from the woods, embedding deep in her collarbone. She hollered, and again, they winced as it brought their ears much distress.

Nym swung from a vine, flinging another star which Rila narrowly dodged.

Melquin ran from the trees and began tugging at the vines that held Falin. "They're knotted tight and she is magic," Falin explained. Melquin put the head of her staff to the binding plants and they started to smolder. When a strand broke, she yanked it and began on the next part.

Nym fought Rila in an acrobatic fashion, flipping, leaping, and dodging the vines that attempted to snag her. The siren swiped at the elf with taloned hands. Their shadows danced as they flitted in circles, parrying one another's attacks, lunging when they saw a chance to strike.

Nym lashed at Rila with her short-sword, seizing the opportunity to reach into her belt of items. She threw powdery black dust in the siren's face. Shrieks flooded the forest as Rila thrashed, pawing at her eyes, causing the vines around them to flail wildly. A vine whipped Nym across the cheek, and she fell, rolling backward before leaping onto a branch.

Melquin was able to free Falin's upper-half, and he wiggled, still stuck. Burlip gnawed at Carthon's vines in an attempt to liberate the drak, breaking strand by strand as fast as his bucked teeth could. Regaining her eyesight, Rila wailed so loudly Melquin paused to cover her ears. It was as if Rila's screech stabbed their souls.

Nym almost lost her footing on the branch, leaping from tree to tree as she evaded the vines snapping at her ankles. The siren's attacks always seemed just a hair too late. Nym launched from a tree and rolled underneath another vine, throwing a berry-sized object from her belt. At once, a red, misty fog filled the clearing, making it impossible for all to see past an arm's length.

The siren's howls continued as she fended off the elf within the scarlet fog. Falin wriggled free of the vines and began to tug at the plants holding Jimbuah. Melquin turned focus to Bossador as Burlip kept chewing at the vines that clutched Carthon.

Falin glanced over his shoulder as the mist began to settle and noticed the outlines of the tiny elf and siren embroiled in battle. He watched in horror as a vine clasped Nym's ankle and yanked her off of her feet. Rila jumped onto Nym with teeth eager to shred, but in a final second of defense, Nym lifted her blade and shoved it into Rila's chest, through the siren's back.

A final hoarse scream blared through the woods. The siren contorted atop Nym, the foliage she controlled flailing. A burst of energy blew through the clearing, and those free of vines were thrown. The siren's body slumped, and Nym shoved the creature off of her, removing her sword from the heart of her enemy. The vines fell still. Falin and the Champions watched in the misty crimson clearing as Nym the Assassin stood over her slain foe, Rila, Siren of the Oldwoods.

Panting, Nym asked, "Is everyone alive?" She limped to the stump, falling where Rila once sat.

"We're all here," Carthon answered. He twisted from the vines and hurried to her, kneeled, and inspected her face, covered in cuts, as was her body. "Are you alright?" He took her hand and examined a gash.

Nym's eyes fluttered in surprise, glancing between Carthon holding her hand and his face of concern. "I am. I will be."

Bossador and Jimbuah pulled themselves from the vines leaving only Red to be freed. "How did you know where to find us?" Bossador asked. "We traveled far into the woods."

"Burlip saw which way you went," Melquin answered. She lifted the rabbit and walked towards Carthon, thrusting it into his confused arms. "Remember, the rabbit you wanted to eat? He's the one who saved you. He's even the one who chewed through your vines."

Carthon looked between Melquin and Burlip. "I suppose I owe Burlip an apology." Melquin nodded. "Sorry, Burlip," he mumbled. The rabbit squeaked approval, leaping back to the ground.

"We heard her awful singing," Nym said, "and followed her voice."

Carthon shook his head, not understanding. "To us, it sounded enchanting."

Nym smiled at the drak. "Lore tells a siren's call will only affect a male ear. To us, it sounded like a cow giving birth."

Red, still trapped, wriggled in the vines, and yelled at them, "What'd I say about the Oldwoods?! We could already be around the other side having ridden our horses! But did anyone listen?! No! Instead, I almost got eaten by some ego-ridden spawn of a warlock!" He seethed and shook his head. "Is anyone gonna cut me out?! Or am I going to have to gnaw my way free?!"

"I'll cut you out," Nym said tiredly. "Mel, do you want to get their weapons?"

"You brought our weapons too?" Bossador asked.

"Yes," Nym answered, slicing the vines that held Red. "We didn't know if you'd have to fight, so we grabbed them all. We had to leave everything else at the camp, though." After freeing her comrade, she began to retrieve her throwing stars around the clearing.

Melquin returned with Bossador and Carthon's swords, and Falin and Jimbuah's staves. "Thakuni," Jimbuah said, accepting his weapon.

"We should rest here and travel back to the camp come sunlight," Carthon said. "Melquin, can you tend to Nym's wounds?"

"Yes, I planned on it," Melquin answered, walking to the elf to whisper incantations. Carthon watched with a deep focus.

"I'll take guard for the rest of the night, as it was almost my turn when we woke," Bossador announced.

Following the treatment of Nym's wounds, they laid to sleep in utter fatigue. Bossador took a seat on the stump with a diligent eye. They slept heavily, for the evil aura that once held the clearing had vanished but for the decaying corpse of the siren.

Soon, daylight snuck through the leaves, and they woke again to the sounds of birds. Falin breathed the morning air and sat up, feeling as though he'd only been asleep for a moment. His head pounded, wishing the light would remain at bay until his eyes knew true rest.

"Wake, friends," Bossador announced. "We must return to camp before the animals feast on our rations."

The group stood and stretched, ready for their trek back. Melquin headed for one side of the clearing and Nym to the other. "Where are you two going?" Red asked.

They turned to one another in confusion and simultaneously said, "Camp is this way."

Falin's heart dropped. "Tell me one of you is about to realize you were wrong."

"We entered on that side of the clearing," Nym insisted. "So we could get a good angle on the siren, remember? Camp is in this direction."

Melquin shook her head defiantly. "We came upon the clearing here," she answered. "And walked around to where you swung in by the vine."

Nym bit her lip and thought on it. "No, I'm certain camp is this way."

Jimbuah rubbed his forehead in concern and sighed. "Obah."

Melquin turned to the larger group. "Does anyone remember which way you wandered into the camp?"

"Can't imagine any of us do," Red answered. "Considerin' we were all under a spell and it was night."

"Ask the rabbit," Bossador suggested. "He got you here, maybe he remembers the way back."

"That's a good idea," Melquin agreed. She lifted Burlip and began to squeak. He turned his head in all directions, squeaked back, and her face fell, dismayed. "He says it was too dark. He has no idea."

"Let us decide before it is nightfall again," Falin said. "Our backs were to the entry point when we were tied," he remembered, motioning to the cut vines. "We will head in that general direction and hope for the best."

"Fair enough," Nym said. Melquin nodded and they set off. They trudged through the forest and over the roots and mossy ground, coming upon tiny hills and divots in the earth as they went. None of it seemed familiar to any of them, whether it be from the blinding of spells or nighttime. They doubled back upon deciding it was the wrong direction, trying another route until realizing it was the incorrect way again, changing course three times until giving up.

Falin drove his staff to the ground. "We are lost," announcing what none others wanted to admit. "We have no choice but to relinquish our belongings at the camp and continue south until we exit the woods. Does anyone have any issue with this? Were there any valuables aside from food in the camp?" All kept silent.

"We have our weapons," Carthon responded. "And the clothes on our backs. We need not much more."

"So be it," Falin said. He peered through the trees. "I cannot tell which way the sun falls as these leaves cover the sky. Perhaps one of us can climb one of these trees so we can be sure we travel south?"

After a beat of silence, Red sighed and said, "I'll do it."

"I can start to forage for some food," Nym said. "At least to get us through the day."

"You're hurt," Carthon said. "Let me go with you."

As Red began to climb a tree, Nym walked from the path, and Carthon followed. Nym easily ducked through the brush, sliding by prickly branches with Carthon not far behind. The thicket became dense with leaves, so much so they were unable to see a few feet ahead of them. As Carthon was about to suggest they turn back, Nym stopped abruptly and said, "Do you hear that?"

Carthon listened intently, pushing a branch away from his face. "Sounds like buzzing."

Nym crept forward, and they shoved through a wall of branches. They entered a small clearing and gasped at the sight. A single tree sat at the center, covered in multicolored, dazzling leaves. Giant hives hung on the prismatic branches, from which tiny colorful bugs flew on and off. So much of the woods had been dull and dreary, it was shocking to see such a tree.

"It's incredible," Carthon said. "What is it?"

"It's a rupela tree," Nym replied. "We have them in Lelyalis, though they are rare."

She took a step forward, but Carthon grabbed her by the wrist. "What about those hives? Are the bugs not dangerous?"

The elf grinned. "Not in the slightest. The tree has turned that color because of them. They are rupelas. And we are lucky to find them." She removed her sword and cut the lowest hanging hive, then shook it. Carthon recoiled expecting them to swarm, but instead, the bugs fled up into the trees. Nym cut into the hive and cracked it open, revealing tiny combs. A dark brown liquid slowly oozed from the crevices, to which Nym scooped a bit with her finger and ate it. She laughed upon seeing Carthon scrunch his nose in disgust. "Try it," she insisted.

Carthon did the same, carefully putting the nectar to his tongue, raising his eyebrows in surprise. "That is quite sweet. What is it?"

Nym took another swipe. "Rupela nectar. It's a delicacy in Lelyalis. The nectar inside should be able to sustain us for days, it is so nutrient rich."

Carthon tasted it again, this time with a bigger scoop, thoroughly enjoying the snack.

Nym returned her attention to the tree, but Carthon kept his eyes on her, entranced. "You fight with the prowess of legendary beauty. You are truly a daughter of faeries."

Surprised by his remark, Nym laughed softly. "I do not know that killing a siren is something you can make beautiful."

"Yet it is a feat you accomplished."

They stared at one another, in a splendid peace and sudden solitude. Carthon brushed a strand of her red hair aside from her face, letting his hand graze her cut cheek, basking in the elegance that was her elven face. Nym took a heavy breath and focused on his normally icy gaze, now alive with fire. Carthon glanced to her lips and tilted his head, leaning forward. Suddenly, the branches beside them shook, and he retracted. They both reached for their weapons.

Jimbuah popped through the brush, spitting a leaf from his mouth. "Dujimo triba. Peh." Another leaf was stuck behind his grey ear, and he swatted it away. "Ah!" he exclaimed, seeing the magnificence of the rupela tree. "Prekati! Prekati triba!"

Nym hid a frustrated sigh. "Yes, Jimmy. The tree is very pretty."

Jimbuah glanced between the elf and drak, not understanding why they stared at him with aggravation. "Wakutu?"

Carthon rubbed his eyes and chuckled softly. "Do you see those hives, Jimmy?"

Jimbuah examined them. "Yekasa."

"Nym tells me the nectar inside will sustain us for days. Help us carry them back."

The skully turned to them excitedly. "Boo yattah!"

The group cut the hives from the tree and shook them free of bugs, collecting enough so each member of their group would have one. Nym smiled at Carthon and followed Jimbuah through the thicket.

Once returned to the main clearing, Red climbed back down from the tree. "I didn't realize how dense the air was down here until breathing fresh air."

"Which way is south?" Bossador asked.

Red pointed in the direction. "I saw the Fields of Darva in the distance. A little more than a day's hike at most." He grabbed Jimbuah by the shoulders and rattled him. "We're almost out of here buddy."

"What are those?" Melquin asked, suspiciously inspecting the hives.

"They're filled with rupela nectar," Nym replied. "They should last us the next couple of days."

"Good enough for me," Bossador said. "We should eat."

"Let's not delay too much," Falin said. "We are not free of the woods yet."

After their break to eat the nectar, they departed south, moving slowly in their off-trail hike. On occasion, a branch would scratch a face, or catch someone's clothes, but they trekked on, eager to exit the woods. Night fell again, and they took rest on an area of moss.

"I will take first watch tonight," Falin volunteered. "I feel at peace in this part of the woods, for reasons I do not know."

"There is a better aura here," Melquin agreed. "I do not sense a Dark presence as I had before. It seems to be at our backs."

"You would think the southern part of the woods would have more issues," Nym said. "It is so close to Drucullm."

"One would think," Falin pondered. "Take rest. If we are lucky, we will be able to breathe the fresh air again tomorrow."

Nym sighed. "Then to fighting a dragon for a princess."

"Beard of a warlock," Falin cursed. "I forgot about this princess. I do not know that we should risk our lives to serve King Pernicus. At least not until I have a few Gems."

"Well hold on a minute," Bossador argued. "I swore to Pernicus I would try to save her. My honor depends on it."

Carthon stood and scoffed. "How many oaths do you intend to take before this journey ends?"

"Do you have something to say, *drak*?" Bossador spat, standing aggressively.

Carthon took a step forward. "I fear that you jeopardize all of our lives because you are too busy playing the honorable fool like every other madorian. We're not living out some faerietale."

Bossador snarled, "What would a drak know about honor? You are orphans of the Light."

Carthon hissed angrily at the insult. Before he could reply, their wizard interjected.

"Enough," Falin growled, slamming his staff to the forest floor, causing the trees to quiver. Loosened leaves twirled in their descent to the earth. "I cannot think when you bicker like children." Falin took a deep breath as Carthon and Bossador returned to their seats with scowls. "I will decide upon our exit of the woods. Everyone sleep as I take watch."

Jimbuah removed his pointed green Rorkshire hat from his pocket, draping it over his eyes. The sun started to set, and in their exhaustion, they came to sleep while it was still light.

Falin mulled over the continuation of their journey upon exit of the Oldwoods. He had looked at the map Airo gave him so many times he did not need to retrieve it from his robes, as its image was burned to his memory. His Champions slept soundly, exhausted from the hike through the unforgiving terrain and nights of fighting, and he looked on as if a father watching his children slumber. His decisions would impact their lives, and he knew not how to grapple with the responsibility.

A rustle came from behind one of the trees to Falin's right, and startled, he grabbed his staff in preparation to fight and alert the others. A jackalope peeked at the camp and hopped towards Falin, examining him, then his staff.

It wore light gray fur and the body of a jackrabbit, with the antlers of a small deer. Antlers included, the animal stood about half Falin's height. Unsure of how to communicate with the animal, the wizard presented his hand to its nose as one might with a hound.

The jackalope looked at his hand, then Falin. "What are you doing?" it asked.

Falin jumped and retracted, shocked to hear the animal speak. "Y—you— you can speak?"

The jackalope sighed. "Follow me. There is someone you need to meet." The jackalope hopped away from the camp. Processing what had happened, Falin debated what was best to do at the moment. Was this another trap of the woods? As if reading his mind, the jackalope reappeared. "Come on," it urged. "Your friends are safe in this part of the forest. I promise."

Falin took another second to examine the group sleeping soundly. He sensed no evil within this animal. He hurriedly followed the jackalope across the root-ridden earth, at times losing his way in the thicket. Golden streams of light cut through spaces in the leaves as the sun made its dusky descent. Falin came upon the jackalope waiting at the mouth of a cave.

"Where are you taking me?" Falin asked. "Who are you?"

"I am Solton, messenger to Boschi, Spirit of the Oldwoods. He is waiting for you, Falin." Again, without further explanation, Solton departed into the cave. Falin bumped the end of his staff to the ground causing its head to glow, letting him see in the darkened tunnel. He carefully stepped over the stones and roots that reached through the space, stooping in the instances the roof of the cavern jutted out. Bits of light peeked through a partial opening to the opposite side. Solton pushed his way through the vine-covered exit. Falin did the same and gasped.

He looked over a pristine woodland valley, so large he could hardly see the other end. The sky above donned hues of purple and pink as the final rays of sunlight cascaded over the treetops. Cliff faces covered in ivy surrounded the valley, and the trees of Oldwoods towered above this hidden realm. Animals of all sorts scurried about the grassy area, some parts with little thickets of woods, others floating about tiny ponds. Awestruck, Falin followed Solton in wonderment, basking in the beauty of the hidden domain. "What is this place?" Falin asked.

"It is a hidden realm of the Oldwoods," Solton answered. "The last remnant of what this forest once was thousands of years ago." Falin trailed the jackalope across the lush valley. To his left, a waterfall poured into a lake where otterfox floated atop nests of moss, pawing at the fish with playful red paws. A craggon bear drank at the lip of the lake with its cubs—a mountain of a beast—jarring in such a serene environment. A turtle the size of Bossador waded into the shallow part of the water, to which several tiny beaver pups climbed atop his back to take a ride.

Jackalope scampered by their path, usually in small packs, their running not in fear, but of playfulness. In a wooded area to Falin's right, a family of eight owls sat upon a single tree branch and watched as they passed. Tree badgers burrowed in hollowed earth beneath trees, and moon skunks hung upside down on branches by their tails. A family of striped deer settled for the night beneath a tree filled with honey birds. Constant chatters and squeaks of animals were sounds of peace within the valley, underscored by the gentle sway of trees and running water.

Finally, at the center of the valley, Falin came upon a spring where crystal water trickled over rocks to a large pond. At the opposite side was another cave with moss covering its mouth. White and pink flowers speckled the earth where the moss grew, and varying animals lounged around the pond. Many rested on giant lily pads drifting in leisure. At the center of the pool were tiny stone pillars creating a path to the cave.

"Watch your footing," Solton cautioned as he hopped across the stones.

Falin followed, careful so as not to slip. Fish of every color meandered between, some tiny, others as large as Falin. He quickly realized the pond was far deeper upon second glance, but the water was so clear he could see the bottom, more than three times his height in depth. A lily cat with webbed feet and spotted yellow fur swam to the surface to examine Falin, shaking itself dry to rest in a nest of grass. Once across, Falin came upon the moss at the mouth of the cave, gripping his staff in preparation. There was only Light in this place, he knew that.

A shape formed in the cave, and out walked a magnificent beast resembling a common wolf, but this animal outsized even the craggon bear. Its fur was a mix of black, grey, and red, with paws the size of Falin's torso.

"Greetings, Falin," the wolf said in a voice of all-knowing wisdom. "I am Boschi, Spirit of the Oldwoods. I welcome you to my home."

Falin nodded, taking in the animal's size, never mind the fact it spoke. "Thank you. I am honored to be in your presence. I did not know the Oldwoods had a spirit such as yourself."

"Little do, aside from the ten wizards," Boschi answered. "Please, sit with me," Boschi said, motioning his head to a rock. The wolf took a seat, and Falin moved as directed. "Tell me, wizard, how goes your journey for the Gems of Elsana?"

Falin looked at the head of his staff. "I do not have much to show for it yet. I hope to find the first in the Mortal Mountains."

"I have no doubt you will, young wizard. Airo speaks very highly of you."

Falin's jaw dropped a little in surprise. "You know Airo?"

"I have known Airo for many years, yes," Boschi confirmed. "I saw him most recently in his search for two warlocks within my woods. He told me to look out for you."

"He says he fought them off," Falin said. "He was headed up north when I saw him last."

Boschi nodded knowingly. "I could feel their presence leave. And then again a night ago, I felt another weight of Darkness lifted. Would you know why?"

Falin thought on it and answered, "An elf in my group killed Rila the Siren in battle." The creatures around the pond spoke of the news to each other in thrilled squeaks and chirps.

"This is good tidings," Boschi said. "She has plagued us for many centuries." The forest spirit took a breath in thought. "Tell me, Falin, how has your journey of the Oldwoods been thus far?"

Falin debated whether honesty or politeness was the best option. "It has been difficult; more than I had expected. We were ambushed by blood draks a few nights ago, then again we were almost eaten by Rila. We often felt evil eyes on our backs for much of the journey, and were disappointed to find the forest was not the place of Light it was said to be centuries ago."

Boschi nodded. "This is exactly why I have brought you here tonight. Darkness has crept into my home, and I have struggled to keep it at bay." Boschi turned to the greater valley. "This place is one I created, where creatures of the woods can find solace if they choose. It is invisible to the eyes of Darkness, and the only thing preserving the memory of what the Oldwoods once was."

"It is a perfect place," Falin said. "And I hope that it is what the afterlife is like."

Boschi chuckled softly. "A high compliment from a wizard. There was once a time when the entirety of the Oldwoods resembled what you see before you. Harmony and serenity knew no bounds. And then the Darkness came."

"What happened?" Falin asked.

"I had a brother who guarded this woods with me," Boschi explained. "A warlock of old killed him in the Wars of the Beginning."

"I am sorry to hear that," Falin said. He was surprised to learn how old this being was.

Boschi continued. "Since, over thousands of years, I have done all that I can to keep the Dark away. But I have been overwhelmed in centuries past. There is little I can do on my own, and have failed the creatures of my woods."

"Why haven't the wizards helped you?" Falin asked. "This is their duty, is it not? To bring balance?"

"They have been preoccupied with more pressing matters. For this, I cannot blame them. I have not requested a wizard aid me. Until now."

Falin listened intently. "You asked Airo to help you?"

Boschi shook his head and smiled. "No, Falin. It is *you* Airo said should be helping me. He said you have a pure heart, and that if someone were to instill Light into the Oldwoods again, it would be you."

It took a moment for Falin to respond, as he was taken back by the faith placed upon him. "Are you sure? It may be some years before I can even begin my work."

Boschi chuckled softly. "Yes, Falin. I have lived countless centuries, a few more years will not cause too much ire."

"Okay." Falin thought on it. "I would be honored to make this my first task after becoming a full wizard. I sense old magic here, much like the woods on Wizard Island."

"The Oldwoods has been a place to many important events in years past," Boschi added. "And there are many more to come. It is imperative you succeed."

"What do you mean in the years to come?" Falin asked. "Are you a seer?"

"Look," Boschi said, standing and walking to the pond. Falin followed and peered into the water. The wolf ran his paw along the top, and a ripple caused an image to appear. Falin bent close to ascertain what he was seeing. A silhouette formed, holding a sword of glowing light.

"I've seen that sword," Falin whispered. "From a dream during my first night here."

"A vision," Boschi corrected. "The Warrior of Light will be born of the Oldwoods. And they are going to lead a great many to prosperity within your lifetime. This will not come to pass if the Oldwoods are not cleansed."

The ripples in the water settled and again, Falin stared at fish in the pond. "When will this happen? When will this hero be born?"

"That, I do not know," Boschi answered. "You must understand this is a revelation of the Light. When you or I see a vision of good things to come, it is the possibility of a world in which Light succeeds. Those serving the Dark see a vision far different from ours, where we meet our demise and they reign."

Falin turned back to the water. "So these visions are not absolute? It is what is possible, not what is destined?"

"Precisely," Boschi answered. He padded back to the mouth of the cave and sat again. "Which is why we must continue to serve the Light at every turn in the road. These are images of hope we must yearn for, not depend on."

Falin sat on the rock of moss again. The lily cat from earlier strolled over to Falin and laid beside him, to which the young wiz-

ard stroked its head. "The entire forest was really once like this valley?"

"Yes," Boschi responded. "And it was one of the most perfect
places in Elsana. I yearn for those days again."

Falin thought on it. "You spoke of experiencing the Beginning.
You must be one of the oldest creatures in the world."

"I am. But there are others like me. More than you would
think."

"Incredible. Did you know any faeries or giants in your time?"

"Well I knew many of them!" Boschi said fondly. "I knew the
faeries when they created elves, and I knew the giants when they
created the madorians. It was a wonderful time, and I am blessed to
have experienced it."

Shaking his head, Falin gazed across the pond and said, "It is a
shame the faeries and giants were all killed by the hands of the
Dark."

Boschi kept silent for a moment, then answered, "So it is."

Falin smiled as the lily cat he pet purred. "There is a sage in my
group who is a beastsayer." He thought a moment and turned to the
Solton the jackalope who beckoned him to the valley. "Why is it I
could understand Solton?"

"Solton is a special friend who I have gifted the tongue of non-
animals."

Solton rubbed his nose. "You wouldn't believe some of the
things I've heard travelers in the Oldwoods say. It's a mess out
there."

"You said your friend will teach you the tongue of animals?"
Boschi asked.

"Yes," Falin said. "I hope that I might learn quickly enough." He
pet the lily cat on the stomach. "I've always been fond of all creatures."

"Perhaps I can help you," Boschi offered. "As a gift of thanks for
your readiness to save my home." Before Falin could react, the wolf
placed his enormous paw on Falin's head, lifting his muzzle to

howl, echoing over the valley. A tingly jolt of energy rushed through Falin, and in an instant, a flurry of voices met his ears.

Falin looked around in all directions as Boschi and Solton laughed.

The lily cat Falin pet moaned as he rubbed its belly. "Oh yes, a little lower."

Falin's eyes bulged, retracting his hand, turning to the pond where an otterfox drifted on its back. "That fish is dinner if it nibbles my tail again," it said with closed eyes.

Birds flew overhead and dove for trees chirping, "Sleep, sleep, sleep, sleep."

He turned to the lily cat. "Can you understand me?"

The lily cat twisted its neck and stretched its webbed paws in surprise. "This one can talk like me!" It rolled so that it stood. "You must be special."

"He is, and will continue to be," Boschi affirmed. The sun almost completed setting and dusk cast a light grey sky over the valley. "It is time you must leave Falin. It grows dark, and you should be there with your friends. I will have Solton escort you back. I wish you everlasting luck on your journey."

"Thank you," Falin said. "It will not be long before we meet again. Goodbye, Boschi."

"Goodbye, Falin."

Falin followed the jackalope across the pond and through the valley, where most of the animals began their slumber or were already well into it. Exiting through the cave, they traipsed through the Oldwoods, dismal in comparison to Boschi's Valley. They came upon his sleeping Champions as he had left them.

"Thank you, Solton," Falin said. "I hope to see you soon."

"You will," Solton answered. "Be well." The jackalope hopped away to return home.

Falin reflected in the darkened woods, keeping his staff lit to see. His eyes were tired, but he had too much to ponder following his meeting with Boschi. The idea of waking someone to take watch crossed his mind, but he preferred they sleep to their heart's content. The night passed, a great moon rising and fading, until morning rays of sunshine poured through the trees and the group stirred upon mounds of dewy moss.

"Good morning," Falin said to them all.

Red rubbed his eye with a knuckle. "You take watch the whole night, wiz?"

"I did," Falin said. "I wasn't tired, so I thought to let you sleep."

"You should've let one of us take guard," Melquin yawned. Burlip the Rabbit sat on her lap and yawned himself.

"Did you sleep well, Burlip?" Falin asked, hoping to test his new skill.

Everyone, including Burlip, looked at Falin with wide eyes. "Yes," Burlip squeaked. "Thank you for watching over us."

"It was my pleasure." Falin smirked as the group gaped at him. "What?"

"Did you just talk to the rabbit?" Carthon asked with a furrowed brow.

Falin shrugged. "Just a little something I've been working on. I think Melquin's talents are rubbing off on me."

"Beastsaying took me years to learn." Melquin squinted. "There is something you hide from us."

Falin stood and stretched. "A wizard must keep his secrets safe. Are we ready to get out of these woods?"

Jimbuah leapt to his feet and nodded. "Boo yattah! Gofo!"

Without delay, the Champions and Falin began their trek south. The promise of exiting the woods gave them hope, and their legs the encouragement they needed to press on. Suddenly, Nym stopped and pointed forward.

"Look!" Nym exclaimed. They halted, and through the trees, could see a more considerable amount of light.

"By Madrellor's sails, we have made it!" Bossador yelled.

They hurried, and soon, the trees cleared, and they stepped onto a field of grass. A burst of sun shined on their exit of the Oldwoods.

Red walked into the tall grass and fell to his back, basking in the open Freelands. "We're out. We're out, Jimmy!"

Melquin stood at the tree line and pouted at Burlip. "I guess this is where we part." She lifted the rabbit and hugged him as he squeaked back. "I'll miss you too," she answered, watching him scurry back into the forest.

Falin gazed across the field. "I wonder where the horses are."

Melquin walked ahead, scanned the horizon, cupped her hands to her mouth and whinnied so loudly, Bossador covered an ear. The call carried for miles. She stood still, listening intently, then cocked her head upon hearing something. The thuds of horseshoes met their ears, and over the hills sprinted their steeds.

"We left food with them, did we not?" Bossador asked.

Nym nodded, walking towards the oncoming horses excitedly. "We did!" She pet them as they approached, kissing each on the muzzle, then examined one who walked with a slight limp.

Falin saw a gash across the leg of another. "What happened?" he asked the horse.

The horse looked to Falin, surprised to hear him speak. "Gruns," it answered. "Arrow hit me. We ran, but I'm okay."

Falin pet the horse's muzzle. "You did well. All of you."

Red sighed. "Now we have two of them neighing."

They accepted each of their horses, patting them, thrilled to have their companions back after days of walking across rough terrain. After raiding the food supplies left with the steeds, they made camp a safe distance from the woods. As the sun set, Falin gazed across the Fields of Darva in thought.

Red asked what was pressing all of their minds. "So which is it, Falin? Do I get to meet Princess Bloom and slay a dragon? Or are we going to the Mortal Mountains?"

Falin looked to the curious Champions and scanned them with a sly expression, letting his Wizard's Instinct speak for him. "We have a dragon to visit."

CHAPTER SIX:
A FIERY WELCOME

The Fields of Darva were rather unlike the fields prior to the Oldwoods. Where the landscapes of the north held a serene beauty of diverse terrains, the Darvan Fields resembled the same burnt yellow grass as far as their eyes could see. A solitary road led them south, and they kept a constant state of alertness, feeling exposed. It was the sixth day since their escape of the Oldwoods, and despite a sense of vulnerability, the travelers remained in better spirits.

On their fifth morning, Melquin had discovered field potatoes, and Nym killed a deer later that day, gifting them an abundance of food.

"At what point should we move off the road?" Falin asked Red. "We are close to Drucullm and Varsa. I fear we will capture the attention of gruns or crags. Do augurs come this far north?"

Red frowned. "Not augurs, but we should keep alert for gruns and crags. The augurs mostly keep to Cadryl."

"We must be getting to Darva soon," Falin said. "Have you been to the ruins before?"

"At a distance," Red answered. "But I have never ventured inside. It's a broken city and I had no reason to view your mentor's handiwork."

Falin scanned the empty miles surrounding them. "There's not a soul in sight. Are the western Freelands as devoid of people as this?"

Red shook his head. "No, the Freelands out west is filled with all sorts of settlements. Villages, cities, and even some small kingdoms. Millions of people, actually. More than the Crown and Shadow Kingdoms combined."

Melquin trotted beside them. "The horses are growing tired. They could use a good night's sleep. We have given them little rest when there is light."

"You are right," Falin said. "Let us see if there is a good place to rest nearby."

"Waka!" Jimbuah yelled, pointing southwest over the fields.

Red turned, where faint shapes of bushes sprouted from flattened earth. "Could be. Jimmy says there might be water there. It'd be a good place to stop and refill our canteens."

They veered off the path into the fields for the shrubbery. Nym squinted, facing south as they did. "I think I can just make out the ruins. It should be a short ride there tomorrow."

Carthon craned his neck. "Your elven eyes are a gift from Elsana. You are right. I can see them now."

Nym fought a beaming smile and settled for a grin. They came upon a creek and stopped by its bed, giving their steeds a break for the day. The sun set as they made camp.

Falin splashed his face, cleaning it of sweat. "I can feel the weather getting warmer the further south we travel."

Red chuckled. "Well if we keep traveling south, wait until we reach the jungles of Suntalla."

"We would not be in Suntalla long at all, let alone its jungles," Bossador corrected. "Why must we keep reminding you we have set course for Letani if we are taken to the Wildbarrens after the Mortal Mountains?"

Red lifted his hat and wiped perspiration from his forehead, glancing at Jimbuah. "Just figure it makes more sense is all. We should probably figure out how best to proceed depending on what the situation is. The second Gem might not lead us that way at all."

"Yekasa," Jimbuah agreed wholeheartedly.

Carthon sat at the bank of the creek and slipped his boots off. "That's if we make it past this dragon." The drak still opposed their plan before finding the first Gem. "We may find Princess Bloom in the form of smoldering bones upon our arrival. For all we know, we are merely giving this dragon a taste of the Crown."

"I made an oath," Bossador said. "I will die by it."

"Yeah," Red agreed. "We made an oath to save this princess. My honor depends on it."

"Right, Red, " Melquin said, rolling her eyes. "For your honor."

"And yet, I still have not heard a formidable plan to kill this dragon. Are we to charge like barbaric fiends?" Carthon posed.

"Why don't you show him your great big teeth," Red said, making fangs with his fingers. "Bet he'll be runnin' to his dragon mama when he sees your drakky chompers."

Jimbuah laughed and pointed, causing Carthon to glare at him. "Well," Carthon began, "maybe we can feed Jimbuah to the dragon since we know skully blood is poison. Problem solved."

Jimbuah's face fell, clearly hurt by the suggestion. He kicked at the dirt and shrugged, muttering, "Nofati fujino." He turned on his heel and began strolling south along the creek in dejection.

"Real nice, snaggletooth," Red growled.

"Jimmy," Carthon called apologetically, but the skully ignored him. The drak scanned the group who watched in disapproval. "Oh please, it was a joke."

"Yes, but it's mean when it's about Jimbuah," Melquin said.

"You should go apologize," Nym pressed. She nodded where Jimbuah kept on walking.

Carthon sighed, "Alright," and began jogging down the bank to catch the skully.

Falin rubbed his forehead and took a breath. "So aside from biting the dragon and feeding it Jimbuah, does anyone have any real ideas? I've read dragon scales are near impenetrable, but I am wondering if Nym can catch it in the eye with a throwing star, we might have a chance. Or maybe Jimmy has a special fruit we can use." Falin glanced down the creek as Carthon gestured to Jimbuah in explanation.

"I think that's the way to go," Bossador said. "We don't need to kill it. We need to save the princess. If we can blind it and save her, that's all that matters. It won't be able to chase us if it can't see."

"Think you can land a star in a dragon's eye?" Falin asked Nym.

Nym bobbed her head in thought. "Probably. No promises."

"I think it's our best plan for now," Falin said. Again, he peeked past the group. Carthon stopped talking, to which Jimbuah nodded and hugged the drak tightly. Carthon returned the hug with as much affection as a drak could offer. The two returned to the main group.

Once settled, night took hold of day and the sky became dark, prompting them to build a fire. Red splashed his face in the creek as the rest leisured by the flames, eating their stores of food under a multitude of stars.

"How many dragons are in the world right now? Does anyone know?" Bossador asked.

"There can't be more than a few dozen," Nym answered. "I'm sure there's some in the Wildbarrens. Maybe a few in the Magpie Isles. Some have been known to travel in packs."

"My ancestor Madrellor claimed most are hidden in the mapped world. When he explored parts unknown a thousand years ago, before the War of the Crown, he came across none."

"He mapped out much of the Crown," Melquin started. "Why was he not mapping the parts unknown? Across the oceans?"

Bossador chuckled. "Because he was more often than not trying to stay alive with his crew. He wrote of many foul beasts in his journeys, with scorn directed to more than dragons."

"I've always wanted to see the Island of Dragos," Carthon said. "There must be great magic in the birthplace of dragons."

"That's if you don't burn your feet off," Nym answered. "They say the ground smolders like an oven."

Melquin cleared her throat and called the group's attention to Red, who wet his hair with creek water, then splashed his armpits.

Falin smirked. "What're you doing there, buddy?"

Red returned his hat to his dripping head. "Nothin', just cleanin' a bit."

"He's dolling up for the princess," Bossador chuckled.

Jimbuah snickered, tossing a tiny red berry from his staff at Red, causing it to poof into dust. "Smekali."

Red swatted the dissipating vapors. "I didn't need that." A fruity aroma followed him.

"Well now you smell wonderful, " Melquin sniffed. "Are you ready to ask King Pernicus for his daughter's hand?"

Red scowled. "You kn—"

A startling roar in the direction of the Ruins of Darva caused them all to jump, and as they turned south, a burst of fire exploded into the air like a beacon. As quickly as they appeared, the flames vanished, and the group was left to the sounds of crickets and the creek. They sat in nervous silence, listening intently.

Falin sighed. "At least we know the dragon is still alive."

"And well," Carthon added.

"Let's get sleep," Falin directed. "We'll need it for tomorrow."

They slumbered as Nym took first watch, Jimbuah taking second. The stream babbled on, and the warm air let them sleep with comfort. Every so often, the grass would rattle as a breeze flurried by, but all else kept quiet. As morning broke, they rose, unable to sleep further as they were anxious to face the Dragon of Darva.

"Watiku! Watiku frekenda!" Jimbuah urged Bossador who remained asleep. He poked the prince's beard with the end of his staff. "Watiku."

Bossador bolted upright and scanned the camp, heavy-lidded. "Is it morning already?"

"Yekasa," Jimbuah confirmed.

Falin gazed across the field, unable to see the ruins as Nym could. "Nym, how long will our ride be?"

"Not long at all," she answered, peering across the dawn sky. "Your eyes will see the ruins in little time."

"Let us go," Falin said, climbing onto his horse. He thumbed his reins, anxious as they departed, while Carthon's hesitations echoed in his mind. He had no Gems, yet here he was, performing the deeds of an empowered wizard.

Soon, the broken kingdom's remnants crawled over the horizon. Bossador rode beside Falin and stared at their destination with an intensity. The rest trailed a short distance behind. "Are you alright, Bossador?" Falin said softly, as if the dragon could hear.

"I am," Bossador answered. He opened his mouth to speak further, but closed it again.

Falin could sense there were more than dragons troubling his mind. "What is it?"

Bossador glanced to Falin, and after a few seconds of consideration, said, "I am nervous."

"I think we all are," Falin muttered. "We'd be fools not to be. Perhaps we are fools for coming here."

The madorian prince kept his gaze forward. "I am not nervous about fighting the dragon. I am nervous I might fail. I have yet to perform any great deeds as my forefathers. I wish not to be remembered as the lame prince of Rodrellan."

"The journey is early yet," Falin said. "There are many valiant deeds you could accomplish."

"And there are many I could squander," Bossador grumbled. "Madorian royalty is a line of endless heroes. Starting with Rodrellor who founded our kingdom and his sons Thadmir and Madrellor. My grandfather Felmer killed the barbarian King Ulguth in his youth, and my father Dothmer once strangled a crag general with his bare hands. Every prince of Rodrellan feels the need to prove his worth to the throne. My father calls it the Madorian Burden."

Falin thought on his encounter with King Dothmer at the ceremony for Champions, surprised such a gentle soul could kill a crag in such a brutal manner. "Your father was a kind man, for the little time I met him."

"My father is all that I aspire to be," Bossador admitted. "Kind and just, strong and willful. He embodies the line of Rodrellan."

"An aspiration well within your grasp," Falin encouraged.

The ruins came into sight, the city surrounded by a massive white wall. The fields turned to dirt, and for miles, there was naught to be seen. Red softly trotted forward. "We should leave the horses here," he said. "They will be too noisy for us to keep quiet."

"You are right," Falin nodded. He climbed from his horse and spoke to it. "Take rest here, off of the road. If we do not return, make for Mystica."

"Be safe," his horse answered. The horses did as told, venturing off to wait for their return.

Falin clutched his staff and nodded to the rest, speaking low as they began their walk. "Keep your wits about you at all times. We do not know what this dragon can do. Take cover for yourselves first."

"I can distract the beast while Nym tries to put a star in its eye," Red offered. "Maybe that's when Jimbuah can go for hitting him with one of his berries." The Freelander turned to the skully. "Do you think now is a good time to go big?"

"Nofa," Jimbuah shook his head. "Watistu."

"I don't know when else would be a more worthy time," Red muttered.

As they came upon the Ruins of Darva, the dwindling walls of the city towered over their heads, thirty times the height of

Bossador. All remained fortified except a gaping hole that was once a gate, with broken stone covered in burn marks from Airo the Bane's wrath centuries prior. The rest of the wall was covered in moss and dirt, forgotten by centuries. Upon passing through the broken wall, they came upon a dismal sight.

Everything was in shambles, destroyed first by Airo, second by time. To a keen eye, the remains of a once incredible kingdom could be seen, but at first glance, there was only decay. Scorched stone lay in pieces, and former dwellings were shattered. Pillars that once upheld mighty buildings were cut like a straw sliced by a sickle, with structures lying in rubble as often as they were not. The debris stood tall, like buildings of their own, high above the heads of the visitors.

Within the rubble, bones of Airo's enemies were scattered throughout, the multitude of skeletal pieces indicating a vast number were killed by the wizard's hand. His need to avenge the city of orphans was evident.

At the center of the kingdom was its castle, one of the few monuments left intact by Airo. With the walls of the city blocking the wind, all was silent. No birds, no people, no rodents. Nothing. It was a dead city. Falin now understood why his mentor earned his title 'The Bane.'

They stared at the abysmal ruins at its entrance. It was so quiet, that upon Falin's first step, the crunch of his shoe sounded like shattering glass. Carthon placed his hand on Falin's shoulder, pointing to a castle tower on the left side of the structure. Its stones were blackened and burnt, recently so, by what could be none other than a dragon. Falin nodded in understanding.

The Champions and Falin kept their weapons at the ready, half-crouching as they hurried through the city. The patter of footsteps seemed like thunder in their attempts to go unnoticed. Reaching the castle, they came upon an archway once holding a great door, now lost to history.

Falin led their entry to a lengthy hall of grey stone. A musty odor set upon their nostrils as they continued, fearfully vigilant. They moved carefully to minimize the echoes of their feet, passing chambers emptied long ago, with deteriorated banners fallen limp on the floor, artwork faded.

Coming to the end of the corridor, they discovered a set of spiral staircases heading towards the targeted tower. They climbed in single file, gaining balance by grabbing the cool stone wall. Round and round the spiral stairs they went, ascending the tower, passing tiny windows where Falin could not help but peek outside at the ruins. Nearing the top, the smell of charred brick wafted down, signaling they neared the enemy.

Falin squeezed his staff and slowed his pace, glancing behind to ensure all was good with his Champions. They looked to him with determined faces, ready for battle. He could not ask for a better crew to fight a dragon with.

He came to a landing at the top of the stairs, with a doorway leading to a great room. Raising his hand to halt his group, Falin peeked around the corner of the opening.

Had there not been a sleeping dragon present, Falin would have gasped. He quickly returned his head behind the wall to hide. It took Falin a moment to register he saw a dragon. A real dragon. The same as those depicted in the tales he read during his childhood. He stared blankly, processing what he just saw. A living, fire-breathing dragon.

Again, with more reservations, he crept around the corner to assess the slumbering foe. To Falin's surprise, the dragon was smaller than expected, head to tail no more than the length of five horses. With its tail curled to its head, the dragon slept by the broken opening of the tower, its scales a dark purple, his underbelly a pale yellow. Its scales were individually the size of Falin's fist, covering its body like a suit of armor. Razor-like, yellow teeth poked from its snout. The dragon's head rested atop clawed feet as big as Bossador's torso. Little, bony horns protruded atop the dragon's head, forming a spiky spine down its back to its tail. Folded wings rested like a blanket on the beast, and its body took heavy breaths, but made no sound. Each time it exhaled, Falin felt a wave of heat caress his face.

Retreating behind the wall again, Falin looked to his group, and they became bleak upon sensing his blatant fear. Falin motioned his eyes to the room, gripping his staff with white-knuckled hands he tried to keep from trembling. They crowded the foyer, pressed to the wall around the door, waiting for Falin's signal. Falin peeked around again, waiting for the dragon to exhale, thinking it might give them an extra second before the monster could inhale and breathe flame. Falin raised his hand, getting a sense for the dragon's pace of breathing, then gestured they charge.

All at once, they stormed the room and circled, causing the dragon to wake and jump to its feet, startled. Nym flung a star at its eye to which the dragon batted it away with a wing. In the same instant, Jimbuah tossed fireberries towards its face. The dragon swatted them with its spiny tail, unharmed by the flames. Standing tall with wings spread, the beast appeared a threatening foe. Falin braced as the dragon inhaled, hoping a burst of his magic could subdue the fire and protect his Champions. To his surprise, the dragon did not exhale flame, but yelled instead.

"Not all dragons are bad! Not all dragons are bad!" the dragon shouted. It flared its nostrils as his eyes darted around the room. "Not all dragons are bad," he stated again, stomping a foot.

"Where's the princess?!" Red yelled, cracking his whip.

The dragon flinched at the sound. "The princess is safe. You have nothing to fear."

"You must unhand her!" Bossador demanded, clutching his sword. "Or face our wrath, foul beast!"

The dragon rolled his eyes. "Bloom!" he yelled. "Bloom! Get up!" Moving aside, the dragon revealed a wooden door he had been sleeping in front of. He tapped his tail to the wood. "Get up! You have company." It glanced at Bossador and Red. "Ease your arms and lower your weapons. If I wanted, I would eat you both for breakfast, then use your sword as a toothpick and your whip as my floss."

The group looked between one another with surprise. Falin shrugged at Melquin. Slowly, they lowered their weapons, keeping them tightly in hand. The dragon rolled his claws on the floor as they waited, tapping the door with his tail again, louder this time. "Bloom! Wake up!"

"I'm coming!" the princess called from the other side of the door, sounding annoyed.

The dragon sighed and shook his head at the group. "Princesses."

The door whipped open and Princess Bloom stood in a pale blue dress, tattered and wrinkled, her brunette hair in disarray from a night's sleep. Red let out a small gasp, clearly infatuated in her raw beauty. Bloom examined the newcomers with a furrowed brow, then turned to the dragon. "Who are they, Bjorgun? Do you know them?"

"No," Bjorgun the Dragon answered. "But clearly they know you."

"Princess Bloom," Bossador said, "I am Bossador, Prince of Rodrellan. We a—"

Red snapped himself to attention and crossed in front of Bossador. "And I am Redrick of the Freelands. You can call me Red. We made an oath to your father to rescue you from the dragon. Are you alright?"

Unamused and ignoring Red's question, Princess Bloom scanned her rescuers. "Is that a skully?"

Jimbuah smiled and bowed. "'Tis an ho-nor."

Wishing to take control of the situation, Falin spoke next. "Princess Bloom. My name is Falin, I am a wizard on my quest for the Gems of Elsana. These are my Champions. At the beginning of our journey, your father, King Pernicus, told us of your kidnapping by, uh..." he glanced at the dragon. "Bjorgun." He continued as the dragon snorted hot air. "My Champions and I promised we would make every effort to rescue you. So here we are."

The princess looked to the dragon, and in an instant, they began to laugh. "It is very kind of you to come here, wizard," she said through their mocking snickers.

Princess Bloom strolled to the center of the room, and her face fell, annoyed again. She crossed her arms. "I did not get *kidnapped*. I discovered Bjorgun during an excursion from Rorkshire and convinced him to take me away. I left Rorkshire because I *chose* to leave."

After her explanation hung in the air, Melquin asked, "Why?"

Bloom sighed. "Do you have any idea what it's like to be under the thumb of someone like my father?" She looked around expecting someone to answer, but none of them did. "I was not allowed to leave the castle until I was twelve. It wasn't until my eighteenth birthday I left the city, and that was within sight of the walls. Then there I was, a woman of twenty-five years of age, forcibly under guard day and night no matter where I went. I was imprisoned every step I took."

Bossador eyed the dragon cautiously. "And you choose to live with a dragon instead?"

"Yes," Bloom snapped. "Because unlike my father, *he* offers me freedom."

"Easy," Red demanded with his hands up. "We were just tryin' to do the chivalrous thing and rescue you."

Princess Bloom strolled in front of Red, wearing a scowl, leaning into his face. "Has it ever occurred to you that perhaps the princess doesn't need rescuing? That she doesn't want a dashing hero," Bloom said, flicking his hat askew, "or some prince charming," she added, dismissively gesturing to Bossador. "Did it ever cross your mind that perhaps it was not the *dragon* who stole the princess away, but it was the *princess* who demanded the dragon take her elsewhere? Spare your chivalry, *sir*, as it is wasted on this princess."

Red adjusted his hat and leaned his head back from Princess Bloom. "You have clearly had some time to think about this."

Carthon spoke next, to the dragon. "And why do you, Bjorgun, concern yourself with the demands of a princess?"

Bjorgun examined the drak from the corners of his eyes. "Is it impossible to believe a dragon would perform a deed solely for the good of his heart?"

"A little," Carthon answered. "We've all heard the tales of dragons."

"Time has been unflattering to my kind," Bjorgun retorted. "And I have heard many stories regarding blood-thirsty draks. Should I warn Bloom to protect her neck from your fangs?"

Carthon glanced away from the dragon. "No."

Bjorgun nodded. "Only a fool demeans the character of an entire race based on the reputation of its minority."

"Oh come on," Red spat. "We've been told our whole lives about the story of the princess and the dragon. You can't be offended we assumed things were sour."

"Take it as a lesson," Bloom answered. "Citing old norms blinds those in changed times."

Falin leaned heavily on his staff. "I have to admit, I am relieved. I've grown tired of fighting."

"You are on your quest for the Gems of Elsana?" Bjorgun asked. He craned his elongated neck and peeked into the head of Falin's staff. "It does not seem to be going well, young wizard."

"The first is in the Mortal Mountains," Falin responded. "We are getting close."

Bjorgun thought for a moment and turned to Bloom. "We should offer them shelter here. Perhaps I can find a stray sheep from a village up north for us to eat today."

Bloom mulled it over. "As long as they promise not to try and take me back to Rorkshire."

"You have our word," Melquin promised on behalf of the group.

Bjorgun moved to the broken tower opening, turning to the Champions and Falin. "I have offered you all kindness today. Disrespect the princess and I will rescind it in the form of flame." Without further warning, he leapt from the tower and took flight over the Ruins of Darva. The flaps of his wings washed over the city in his departure. *FWOOM. FWOOM. FWOOM.* They faded as he flew through the morning skies.

An awkward lull held the room until Red cleared his throat. "Your, uh—your father asked me to give this to you." He dug to the back of his pants and presented a small painting from his waist. Red stepped forward and handed it to the princess.

She accepted it, scrunching her nose in confusion. "Is this a painting of my father riding into battle?"

Red rubbed the back of his neck and sighed. "Yeah—he said it was supposed to inspire you to make the perilous journey home."

"Right." Bloom shook her head. She carelessly tossed the painting aside.

"Your grandmother, Queen Delsa, also entrusted me with a message," Falin added. Bloom was at once intrigued. "You do? How is she? Is she alright? She isn't too worried about me, is she?"

"Not at all," Falin answered. "She told me to tell you she didn't send you anything, because no granddaughter of her's needs anything from anyone."

The princess beamed and her eyes glistened. "I miss her."

"She misses you," Falin responded.

Bloom longingly gazed out of the tower opening before regaining her impatient air. "Come on," she said, waving them to the stairs. "Let me show you where you can set up camp." The group exchanged a bevy of uncertain glances as they followed the princess down the spiral tower stairs. "I'm assuming you'll want your own rooms, so I'll take you to what I think was the noble quarters."

Bloom led them through a corridor and opened a wooden door to a courtyard at the center of the castle. "This is my favorite place here," Bloom gestured. Grass covered the space and ivy swarmed every inch of the walls. Ten or so old statues worn from weather stood with missing pieces, and benches crumbled throughout. She put her hands on her hips with a subtle smile. Turning to the guests, she asked, "Why are there so many in your company? I thought the tradition only entailed a wizard and four Champions?"

"That was the plan," Falin replied. "Until the wizards decided we should be accompanied by people who have made it through the Wildbarrens. That's how we ended up with Red and Jimbuah."

"You've been into the Wildbarrens?" Bloom asked the duo, examining them with curiosity.

"Yekasa," Jimbuah confirmed.

"Tell me of it," she said. "What was that like?"

Red bit his upper lip in consideration. "It ain't really a fun place. Lots of rocky deserts, lots of big things that are trying to eat you, and lots of servants of the Dark trying to kill you."

"Why did you go there in the first place?"

Before Red could answer, Jimbuah said, "Rujino."

Falin cocked his head. "Did he say you were running?"

Red cast Jimbuah a tight-lipped scowl causing the skully to glance at the Champions and Falin. "We were working with some traders from Letani. They wanted us running goods to a Wildbarrens outpost." Falin sensed this was untrue, but let it go.

Bloom stared at Red for a moment then turned, walking through the courtyard. "I've always wanted to see the Wildbarrens. I've asked Bjorgun many times now, but he won't let me."

Instead of letting her lead them, Red walked beside her. "It's not a place you want to go."

"You don't think I could hold my own in the Wildbarrens?" she snapped.

"Maybe if you took the dragon," Red responded.

Bloom breathed sharply from her nose. "Bjorgun seems to care little for adventure. But I'm sure I could convince him." They came to the end of the courtyard and walked through another door leading to a great hall. A row of wooden doors were kept closed. "You will find chambers in each of these rooms. I fear they are old and dirty, but they will keep you safe for as long as you stay here."

"Thank you," Falin said.

"The horses!" Melquin exclaimed. "I forgot about the horses! We need to go back and get them. We left them in the fields."

Falin nodded. "I'll go with you. The rest of you can stay here and get settled." Melquin and Falin hurried off to leave the kingdom and retrieve their steeds.

Bloom held her hands behind her back and examined the remaining Champions. "Red, come wait with me in the courtyard for Bjorgun. That is normally where he brings our food."

"Sure," Red nodded, glancing behind as he followed. He glared at Jimbuah, who wiggled his eyebrows and wagged his hips.

Once returned to the courtyard, Bloom fell to a stone bench, patting the seat beside her. "Sit with me," she said. "I want to hear more about how a Freelander became a Champion of Wizards."

Red scratched under his hat. "Pure luck, if I'm bein' honest. Jimbuah and I were passing through Mystica, and they found out we'd been to the Wildbarrens."

"And you volunteered yourselves as guides?"

Red bobbed his head around in consideration. "More or less."

"And where in the territories are you from?" Bloom asked. "Your voice is that of a westerner."

"I'm from the Bandero Territories. Part of a cattle village that's no longer around."

Bloom thought about it. "I see."

Red looked up to the sky and squinted at the morning sun. "Why is Bjorgun watching you? What's in it for him? Lecture me all you want, but you and I both know it's an odd thing, you two."

"It is, I will give you that," Bloom admitted.

"Then what is it?" Red pressed. "You promise him gold or somethin'?"

Bloom sneered. "Not all dragons are obsessed with gold."

Red raised his hands. "Alright, alright. I was just asking."

"When I came upon Bjorgun, he was at a lakeside in the woods, moaning and wailing. For whatever reason, I walked up to him and asked what was wrong." Bloom smiled at the memory. "He startled so easily, he nearly took flight until he saw it was just me. I asked him again what was wrong, and he had this horrible pain in his mouth. He'd accidentally eaten a needle-fish from the lake, and got a dozen or so quills stuck in his gums." She shook her head. "I offered to remove the needles since I could get my hands in his mouth."

"You stuck your hands in a dragon's mouth?"

Bloom grinned. "I did. And it was the best decision I've ever made. He was so grateful, he offered me anything I wanted to repay me. I asked him to take me somewhere very far from Rorkshire, and he granted that wish."

Red shook his head in amazement. "But why does he keep watch over you?"

"We're friends," Bloom shrugged. "As a princess, there aren't many who are my friend for more than their own benefit. And I am sure Bjorgun was hard pressed to find a friend who would readily stick their hands into his mouth. We trust one another, and for our kind, that is rare."

"Huh." Red thought on it. "So then what's the plan? You ever goin' back home?"

Bloom grimaced. "Not if I have any say about it."

Red frowned at the young woman for a moment. "I get that your father is a pain in the rear, but he's beside himself." Bloom looked away in guilt. "You have to face the music sometime, Bloom."

"One day, I will," she said. "Though I'm not ready yet." After a hanging pause, Bloom said, "I wish to see the world."

"Which parts?" Red asked.

"All of it."

"You don't want to see all of it."

Bloom raised her eyebrows, glowering. "And how do you know what it is I want? You do not know what it is like to spend your life imprisoned."

Red took an agitated breath and lifted his arm, presenting the tattoo of runes. "Do you know what this is?" Bloom shook her head. "This is what a group of augurs inked on me as a teenager as they shipped me off to Cadryl. I spent four years of my life a slave in the worst place in Elsana. I know what it means to be imprisoned. So trust me when I tell you, there are parts of this world you don't want to see. Scoundrel's oath."

Bloom dropped her gaze. "I'm sorry that happened to you."

"That's how it goes. Don't ever get too comfortable, because life's going to kick you back down when you least expect it."

The princess opened her mouth to speak, hesitating at first. "What was Cadryl like?"

A vacant gaze came over Red, and he stared in the grass. "I'd rather spend a thousand lifetimes in the Wildbarrens than go back to Cadryl. It is a horrid place where they do wicked things to creatures not of the Darkness." He shook himself from his memories. "Why did you pull me aside to talk? You have every race from the Crown and a skully, but you want to hear an average man's tale?"

Bloom shrugged. "Races of the Crown are born into great stories. It is almost expected of them. But here you are, a man born of cattle herders now a wizard's Champion. You were born of the ordinary and became part of the extraordinary. I envy you."

Red snorted. "Well fancy that. A lovely princess like yourself, jealous of a rascal like me."

She laughed sweetly and said, "And how is it you came upon Jimbuah?"

The Freelander smiled and thought back on it. "It's a bit of a long story, but we met in Krattle's Cove on the western coast awhile back. We were..." he mulled over his words. "Mutually in trouble, and were able to finesse our way out of it together. Been partners ever since."

A breeze brushed by and Bloom sniffed. "Do you smell something fruity?" She leaned forward and sniffed Red's clothes. "Oh! It's you! You smell wonderful."

Red tried to subdue a beaming grin. "A high compliment from royalty." They stared at one another for a moment, until the sound of flapping wings came from over the castle walls. Bloom stood, shielding her eyes from the sun. *FWOOM. FWOOM. FWOOM. FWOOM.*

Bjorgun circled above, descending with an animal in his grasp. The flutter of his wings caused the grass to whoosh and Red's hat to fall from his head. He dropped a large cow onto the earth with a *thud*. "I found her astray," Bjorgun said. "It should feed you all."

"Is that enough for you to split with us?" Red asked the dragon.

"I ate my fill a couple of days ago, and do not need to feed for some time longer."

Bloom examined the dead heifer. "How should we cook it? The sheep have been much easier to prepare."

Red furrowed his brow. "You've never skinned a cow before?"

"What part about 'sheltered princess' aren't you getting?!" she yelled.

"Alright!" Red answered defensively. "I'll show you then." He reached into his pocket and removed a small knife that opened on a hinge. "I hope you're okay with getting your hands dirty."

Soon, Falin and Melquin returned with the horses. Red spent the next few hours teaching Bloom how to skin and gut the cow, and in little time, they were covered in smiles and blood. Melquin chose to keep to her chambers as they did this, but the rest lounged in the Darvan sun.

Bossador and Falin stretched in the grass beside Bjorgun who watched Bloom wield the carving blade. As Bossador ran a whetstone across his greatsword, he said, "Tell me, Bjorgun. Could I have pierced your scales with my blade if I chose?"

Bjorgun eyed the weapon. "I doubt it."

"But this is madorian steel," Bossador urged.

"Try it," Bjorgun offered. "Do your worst, prince."

Debating whether not to accept the challenge, Bossador tossed his whetstone to the grass and scanned the scales of the dragon. After a few seconds of deliberation, he half-heartedly swung his blade at the ribcage of the beast. It bounced off with a tiny *clink*.

Bjorgun appeared amused. "Nothing. I assumed a madorian of your stature could hit harder than that." More determined than before, Bossador raised his greatsword over his head, landing a blow across the side of the dragon. He sought a reaction on Bjorgun's face. "Do I feel a breeze at my back?" Bjorgun teased. Falin chuckled at the comment. "Try again, madorian."

Bossador clenched his teeth and frustratedly hit the dragon with his greatsword a multitude of times. *CLINK. CLINK. CLINK. CLINK.* Bjorgun yawned in jest.

"You will tire yourself out for the rest of our journey," Falin warned.

Panting, Bossador abruptly changed his tactic and stabbed Bjorgun with the tip of his blade instead.

Bjorgun screamed, rolling belly-up on the grass, grasping at his side with a claw. "AH!" he roared in pain. "By Mother Elsana! What have you done?! What have you done to me?!"

"I am sorry!" Bossador yelled. He looked to Falin for help. "I did not mean to! I am sorry!"

Bjorgun dropped his paw and revealed unbroken scales, his expression of agony transforming to one of mischief. "I play. It is what a blade of grass would be to your skin, madorian."

Bossador gulped a huge breath of relief. "Thank the Light."

Falin smiled. "And how would one slay a dragon, Bjorgun? Say we come across one of your kin who is not so keen on friendship."

"Magic will do the trick, young wizard," Bjorgun responded. "Magic will succeed where the blade fails."

Falin thought on the answer. "Most of us were holding weapons that would not harm you when we attacked earlier," he said. "Why is it you were so intent on halting our assault?"

"I feared for you," Bjorgun answered. "I sensed the Light upon all of you, and did not want you harmed from a simple misunderstanding."

"That is mighty honorable of you," Bossador said.

Bjorgun rested his head atop his front feet. "I suppose."

Falin glanced at Bloom, covered in cow's blood. Red wagged an intestine at the princess and she screamed, reaching into the cow and throwing an organ in the Freelander's face. They began to fight with the innards of the animal in flirtatious delight. He turned to Bjorgun. "How many dragons are there in the world?"

Bjorgun thought on it, rolling his claws. "It is difficult to say. Most tend to keep to themselves for their lives unless seeking a mate. But some travel in small packs. If I had to guess, thirty, maybe forty."

"You'd think their sightings would be more common," Falin said.

"Some tend to find islands in the oceans of uncharted Elsana. It is there they can live in paradise for their lives, starting a family and what not."

"I thought all dragons were born on Dragos?" Bossador asked.

Bjorgun shook his head. "A common misconception. Legend tells of the *first* dragons being born there. Some still inhabit the isles, but dragons can be born of any land, like every other race."

Falin twirled his staff in his hand as he listened. "Dragons have lifespans longer than all other beings from what I've read. Is this true?"

"It is," Bjorgun answered. "Twice that of wizards. More often than not, we roam for two thousand years."

Bossador whistled. "That is a long while to spend on this earth."

"It is. But I will tell you this: even in the thousand years of my existence, it still feels like the blink of an eye. Cherish every moment." Bjorgun watched Bloom lay in the grass beside Red. "Friends come and go quicker than a gust of wind. When they do come along, I find myself holding tight."

"A thousand years," Bossador repeated. "Who have you come across in those years?"

"That would interest you?" Bjorgun tapped his claw in the dirt in thought. "I hardly remember it, but I was present when your ancestor Madrellor sailed the globe."

Bossador's jaw dropped. "Incredible! Where was this?!"

The dragon grinned. "It was on the island of my birth, one that had no name. I was merely a hatchling at the time, and my father offered Madrellor and his company safe harbor until they were ready to journey again. They spent weeks with me, my sister, mother, and father."

The madorian prince thought hard on what he was told. "I have read the tales of Madrellor a hundred times in my upbringing. Not once did I even hear of him meeting a dragon."

"Then he is a man of his word," Bjorgun said. "In return for my father's hospitality, Madrellor promised my father he would never speak of the location of the island."

"For your family's safety?" Falin asked.

The dragon scanned the wizard as if he had more to tell, but answered, "Something like that."

Falin thought back to his conversation with Airo before entering the Oldwoods. "Have you ever come across any warlocks?"

"Four or five. Which are four or five more than I care to admit." Bjorgun lay his head back in the grass. "They bother me little now, as I am a lost cause to them."

"Why?" Falin asked. "What do you mean?"

"Dragons are neutral creatures, the same as the common man, skullies, and stonies. We have a choice between Light and Dark. Warlocks will often try to sway a dragon for their own use, but their promises of power or riches never interested me. They stopped pestering me long ago."

"We were warned of two causing trouble in the Freelands recently," Falin began. "Nyril the Coercer and Mulgus the Plague.

They are said to have caused a village of Freelanders to murder one another."

"Nyril," the dragon spat. "A vile being."

"You have met him?"

"Once." Bjorgun thought back to his encounter with the warlock and breathed deeply, causing a stream of smoke to escape his nostrils. "I will admit, in all the attempts of a warlock to seduce me to the Dark, he came the closest. He has earned his name as the Coercer. You say he forced Freelanders to kill one another?"

"Something of the sort," Falin said. "My mentor Airo the Bane told me of it. Have you met him?"

"I know of Airo, but we have never crossed paths," Bjorgun admitted. "But I feel as though I should thank him for the home," he gestured to the ruins around them.

"He fears Nyril and Mulgus are planning for war against the Crown," Falin said, "but has no evidence of this from the Shadow Kingdoms."

"Very curious," Bjorgun thought. "Very curious indeed."

Falin watched as Red and Bloom began assembling a fire pit to cook the cow. Bloom turned to them and said, "Think you can spare a little fire, Bjorgun?"

CHAPTER SEVEN:
HIDE AND SNEAK

Falin woke on the floor of the Darvan castle chambers and stretched. His back ached from a night spent on chilly stone. He would have missed the soft moss of the Oldwoods had it not been for the constant threat of predators.

It was their fourth day in Darva, and the wizard was growing restless. After donning his robes, he departed into the castle hall where all was silent, wondering who else had risen. The faint sound of metal on metal met his ears, and he headed for the courtyard where they often congregated. Opening the door to the central section of the palace, he came upon Bloom and Red swinging swords at one another while Jimbuah, Melquin, and Bjorgun lazed in the grass.

Falin strolled to the onlookers and sat beside them, rubbing his eyes. "Good morning all."

"Hekalo," Jimbuah answered.

Melquin worked at rebraiding her dark hair. "Did you sleep well?"

Falin stretched. "Can't complain. What's the plan today?"

"I believe the others are still asleep, but Nym and Carthon said they wanted to explore the ruins."

"I may join them," Falin said. He turned to the dragon. "Do you spend much time outside of the castle?"

Bjorgun shook his head as he watched Red parry a blow from Bloom. "Not unless I need to for food or Bloom wants to explore surrounding areas. I enjoy the comfort of these walls."

Red smacked away Bloom's swipe with ease. "You need to learn how to fight people bigger than you," he explained. "This isn't a fencing class in Rorkshire. You're trying to out-muscle me..." He grabbed her sword-wielding arm and pushed her to the ground. "And it ain't gonna happen. Fight smarter, not harder."

Bloom scrunched her nose and stood without wiping the dirt off. "How?"

Red shrugged a shoulder. "That's for you to figure out. Fight dirty if you got to. Jimbuah," he called the skully. "C'mere and show Bloom how you fight."

Jimbuah hopped up and squared against Red, holding his staff as Bloom moved away to watch. Red swung his blade at Jimbuah, and the skully blocked the blow with ease. They kept in defensive positions, taking conservative stabs at one another in search of an opening.

Red lurched in his next blow, prompting Jimbuah to roll underneath the sword and slam his staff into Red's ankle. As Red worked to recover his footing, Jimbuah caught him in the stomach, knocking his partner to the ground. Jimbuah held his staff to Red's nose and smiled. The skully retracted his weapon, clasping Red's hand to lift him.

"See what he did?" Red asked, as Jimbuah plopped to the grass. "He wasn't going to beat me in strength, so he took out my balance and used it against me."

Bloom blew hair from her face and thought on it. She looked at Jimbuah's staff, then the staves of Falin and Melquin. "What should I do if I'm fighting magic?"

"Hurt their hands," Red answered. "They can't do magic so good without their hands."

"What is it like to fight with magic?" Bloom asked them. "I saw a sage do it once when I was a child. He knocked one of our knights right off his horse with nothing but a staff."

Melquin finished her braid and stood with her white, ivy-covered staff. "It's sort of like a burst of energy you can channel through your body." She put the head of her weapon to Bloom's stomach and nudged it. Bloom stumbled backward and caught her footing.

Bloom held herself and looked at her untorn clothing. "Incredible. It felt like you punched me. How strong can you push something?"

"It depends on how much power you have, and energy," Falin answered. "You can only swing a blade so many times. We can only use magic so many times before we fatigue. I could try and knock a castle wall down in one strong blow, but then I'd having nothing left until I recovered."

"So it's like magic endurance?"

Melquin nodded. "Exactly."

Bloom strolled to Falin's staff, examining the empty slots where the Gems of Elsana belonged. "And the Gems will give you extra power?"

"Yes," Falin confirmed. "It will give me command over the essence of Elsana. The wind, the earth, fire, and water. And once I collect all four, I will be a true wielder of the Light. The first is in the Mortal Mountains."

"That is still a ways away," Bloom said. She pondered it a second and turned to Bjorgun. "Do you think you could fly them there so they don't have to travel near the border of Drucullm and Suntalla?"

Bjorgun clicked his tongue. "Do I look like one of their steeds?" he asked, gesturing his head to the horses in the corner of the courtyard.

"No, but they have been good company. I thought offering them travel would be something kind we could do."

The dragon shook his head. "To carry all of them would be too tiring, even for me. It would take days for us to reach the Mortal Mountains. Not to mention it's harder to manage a party of people on your back if one falls from the sky..."

Jimbuah twisted his face and shook his head. "Nofa gukadu."

"Don't fret over our travels," Falin told Bloom. "Our horses have been of good service to us. We do not mind riding them to the Mortal Mountains."

Unsatisfied, Bloom chewed her lip before debating with Bjorgun further. "You and I should go to the Wildbarrens and help them through."

"This isn't even a discussion I will entertain," the dragon replied.

"We'll see," Bloom muttered.

Nym and Carthon exited the castle, milling through the courtyard at a leisurely pace.

Melquin took note of their weapons and said, "Are you two headed out?"

"We thought we might explore the ruins today," Nym answered. "We've felt cooped up here."

"Where is Bossador?" Falin asked. "Is he still asleep?"

Carthon nodded. "There is no other race but a madorian that snores loud enough to be heard through stone."

Falin raised his face to the sun. "I think I'll join you as you explore the ruins." As he stated this, he noticed both Carthon and Nym appeared dismayed, for a reason unknown to him. "If I am not intruding?"

Both shook their heads unconvincingly. "Not at all," Nym answered.

Falin stood and wiped the grass from his robes. "We shouldn't be long. Don't let Bossador sleep too late," he said to Melquin. "It is difficult enough to wake him on the road."

Falin, Nym, and Carthon departed the courtyard for the entrance of the castle, speaking little, and upon coming to the front doors, they scanned the ruins. "Which part did you have in mind?" Falin asked.

"I was looking out from one of the towers yesterday," Carthon started, "and the western end of the kingdom looks to be the most intact in comparison to the rest. I couldn't see much more than decay on the eastern front."

"West it is," Falin answered.

They set off, turning left onto the road that led to the western portion of the city. As Carthon claimed, sections remained, albeit crumbling.

With an entire day at their disposal, they dawdled, entering whatever building met their fancy. The group inspected structures once belonging to inns, taverns, smiths, and more, rummaging through the items left behind in old pots and chests to understand what life was like in Darva. Much of the ruins had already been raided, and items belonging to gruns and crags from their time ruling the city were among those of the Darvans. Having spent hours exploring, they left a blacksmith shop for a city square.

"It is incredible to see so much of this city untouched," Carthon said. "I assumed the Shadow Kingdoms would have pillaged it all. That or Airo would've destroyed it."

"There may have been too much to go around for the Dark forces that raided," Nym responded. "It is a large city."

"And I do not think it would be Airo's way to destroy what is not necessary," Falin said. He scanned the square and thought on Airo's past lament in seeing one of his greatest works destroyed, sympathetic to his fellow wizard's turmoil. "What is this?" Falin said, pointing across the city plaza to one of the largest buildings they'd come across.

The structure stood half as tall as the walls to the city, with massive columns holding it in place. One column lay broken atop the flight of steps leading to its magnificent entrance.

"It appears to be a temple," Carthon answered. "Let us see."

Falin examined the triangle molding above its entrance, exhibiting rays of marble sunlight. The group climbed the steps, walking around the fallen pillar. Falin brushed his hand along the marble, wondering what lengths the Darvans went through to get such a massive slab of rock to this city, as it stood taller than them even as it lay flat.

Inside, streams of light flooded a colossal marble room through open windows and birds fluttered in the corners of the ceiling. Rotting wooden benches lay overturned on the floor, and a fine layer of dirt covered all.

"It is beautiful," Nym said. "It's a temple dedicated to Mother Elsana."

Falin twisted his neck in all directions, soaking in the monument. "I did not know the common Freelanders were capable of such feats." Their footsteps echoed as they walked through the space.

"Look at the artwork," Carthon said, pointing directly left of the entrance. A station of marble carvings depicted Mother Elsana's creation of the world. "It is the Beginning." He gestured to a section of wall a few steps away, which presented Mother Elsana bringing life to her sons, the God of Light and the God of Darkness. Nym ran her fingers over the stone imagery. "This rivals the work of elves. It is cut so clean and elegantly."

The trio strolled along the wall, stopping to examine the detailing of each milestone from the Beginning. First was Mother Elsana creating her sons, the Gods of Light and Darkness, then the God of Light making the wizards, faeries, and giants. The next section showed the wizards bringing life to the sages, faeries creating the elves, and giants conceiving the madorians.

On the opposite side of the temple showed the God of Darkness producing warlocks, phantoms, and the Titans, and in turn, the warlocks spawning their own servants, and phantoms corrupting creatures of Light to Darkness.

These images followed their world's history through the slaying of the Sea and Air Titans, and the destruction of the faeries and giants.

The artwork came together at the front of the temple, depicting an immense carving of the beginning of the Freelands and common man in the image of Mother Elsana, born with free will to choose between Light and Dark.

They stared in awe at the artistry, towering over their heads. "Amazing," Carthon whispered. "I hope to never forget this image."

Nym's eyes searched every inch of the picture. "Everything is so perfectly intertwined. The creation of the Freelands, then the Crown, the draks returning to the Light. It is perfect."

Falin was overwhelmed as well, now understanding the tragedy that happened here centuries ago. A race of peaceful beings capable of so much was destroyed by unruly hands. It tore at him, and his purpose of being a wizard reared its head, hoping to one day be part of ushering a city such as this to the world.

Taking a final glimpse at the temple, they turned for the exit in silence. They stood atop the steps, overlooking the metropolis. Nym climbed the fallen column, shielding the sun with her eyes. It was then that Falin was overcome by a sudden dread.

For reasons he did not know, he clutched his staff with an instinct to fight. Darkness approached. A terrible and evil Darkness. "Nym," he said with harsh concern. "Get down from there."

Carthon and Nym sobered upon sensing his urgency. Nym leapt down, and he pulled them behind the overturned pillar, crouching, listening. Nym's ears twitched, and she cocked her head in surprise. A few seconds later, Falin and Carthon could hear it as well.

Two voices approached, not belonging to anyone in their company. The newcomers entered the square where the temple resided, and it was then the group could hear clearly. A chill crept over the air.

"It is as I told you. There is nothing for us here," the first voice said, speaking rich and confident. "It was foolish for us to waste our valuable time."

"There has been much death in this city," the second answered, gravely and high, sounding that of a crotchety old man. "There could have been great value for me had Airo the Bane not been such a brute. It is foolish to say this trip was a waste, Nyril."

Like a blow to the gut, Falin realized it was Nyril the Coercer and Mulgus the Plague. The trio's eyes grew wide in sheer terror. The longer the warlocks lingered, the more dread settled into the group. To Falin, it felt as though any bit of joy he had known fled into the air.

"Watch your tone with me, Mulgus," Nyril warned. "You forget, I am your elder."

"By no more than a century," Mulgus replied. "If this is so daunting, then we may leave. I have already admitted there is nothing worthy of my time here."

"As it stands, yes," Nyril agreed. "But you may very well be able to perform that level of necromancy following our journey to Hadrones."

"I intend to," Mulgus answered.

Falin felt the urge to peek over the wall but did not want to risk revealing their presence. He looked to Nym and Carthon, who appeared suffocated by the appearance of such Darkness.

"Let us make our leave," Nyril said. "Sila—"

"Be quiet," Mulgus snapped. "I sense Light. There are creatures of the Light present."

Falin's heart began pounding. He clutched his staff, and Nym and Carthon carefully began reaching for their own weapons. He could see both of their hands were trembling. An overwhelming urge to protect his children of the Light beckoned him.

"It is the stain of Airo," Nyril responded. "This city is drenched in it. Are you just sensing this now?"

"No," Mulgus argued. "I can feel them."

The trio stood so still, holding their breaths in fear they'd be found.

Nyril sighed. "Perhaps a sage is holed away somewhere, we haven't the time to sniff them out. Silas is waiting for us in Suntalla. We are already late."

"So be it," Mulgus conceded. They turned and began to walk away. "Shouldn't Silas know exactly when we'll be arriving in Suntalla? He is clairvoyant after all."

The warlocks' voices faded, headed for the city's western gates. Falin, Nym, and Carthon remained motionless for as long as they could. After a few moments, Falin nodded, sensing the warlocks' Dark aura was gone.

Carthon took a massive breath of relief. "I have never felt such evil." He placed his hand on Nym's arm as she quivered openly. "Are you alright?"

She nodded feebly. "That was terrible. They were so — so — "

"Dark," Falin answered. His skin still crawled as their conversation echoed in his ears. "We have to hurry back to the castle and warn the others."

Without further delay, the trio hurried through the streets of Darva, keeping vigilant for any sign of the warlocks. In little time they were returned to the castle courtyard.

Their comrades lounged around a fire, eating lunch, oblivious to the nearby warlocks. They spoke loudly to one another, Red pointing at Bloom and laughing. "Hush," Falin called. All turned in confusion. "Warlocks," he said. "They are in Darva."

Bjorgun sat upright and readied his wings. "Are they coming here?"

"No," Falin answered. "We sensed their presence and hid. We heard them say they were headed for Suntalla."

"What should we do?" Melquin asked. "Is there anything we can do?"

Falin thought on it. "We should keep quiet and stay put. And we should also put the fire out. The smoke may signal them if it burns too large." Red immediately began to stomp the flames. "It was Nyril and Mulgus," he said to Bjorgun. "We heard them speak each other's names."

A low growl rumbled from the dragon. "What is it they were doing here? Passing through?"

Falin held his forehead and thought back to the conversation. "No. I don't think so. They were speaking of necromancy. But they said the city was of no use because it was bits of bone. Then they mentioned the island of Hadrones and Silas the Clairvoyant."

Bjorgun thought on it for a long moment. "These are strange tidings."

"What do we do, wiz?" Red asked. "Should we hide out here longer?"

Falin shook his head. "Just the opposite. We've stayed too long. I need to find the first Gem. Based on what Airo told us and what we heard, they're clearly planning something. We leave tomorrow at first light." Red and Bloom shared a dismayed glance, but neither argued.

"I think that is wise of you," Bjorgun agreed. "Let us all take comfort in the fact they have left."

The remainder of the day was kept sedated, and Falin found himself alone, pondering the overheard exchange between the warlocks. He wished Airo was present so he could share the news and perhaps gain further insight as to what the warlocks conspired. He feared for the safety of the Crown and all that would come in the months to follow.

Falin strolled the castle, his head bent in focus. After walking all of the corridors twice, he came upon a tower that overlooked Darva. It was there he sat against a wall to watch the sun set, eager for the following day, and as dusk turned to night, he slipped into slumber.

It was not until he heard Melquin's voice calling him did he wake again, seeing the morning rays of sunshine flood over the sill. He hopped up and shook himself, feeling as though he had just blinked. Melquin shouted again, and he climbed down the tower stairs. "I am here!" he answered.

Melquin turned a corner and sighed. "We are ready to leave. We saw your room was empty and grew nervous when we couldn't find you."

Falin fixed his robes and ran fingers through his hair. "I fell asleep in the tower last night. No need to worry. Is everyone ready?"

"Yes, they're all waiting out front for us now."

Falin and Melquin hurried to the front entrance of the castle. All waited by their horses and turned. "We were worried you went on a hunt for warlocks," Bossador said.

"That would be foolish," Falin answered.

"Dujimo," Jimbuah agreed.

The wizard turned to Bloom and Bjorgun. "I cannot express how grateful we are for your hospitality these past days. I am sad to say goodbye so soon."

"As are we," Bloom said. She glanced to Red then dropped her gaze.

"I wish you all safe travels," Bjorgun announced. "Welcome the Light and beware of the Dark."

As Falin climbed on his horse, the rest followed suit, aside from Red.

Red hesitated, looking to the group, then back to Bloom. He reached into his pocket and removed the knife he taught her to skin cows with. "It ain't much," he muttered. "But I want you to have it."

Bloom smiled and accepted the blood-stained knife, then stepped forward to kiss him on the cheek. "Until we meet again, Red."

Red tipped his cap and grinned, turning to climb atop his horse.

"Farewell to you both," Falin said. He snapped his reins, and they dashed away into the sunrise for the Mortal Mountains, having made friends of the dragon and the princess.

CHAPTER EIGHT:
UNDER AN OCEAN

For three days, Falin and his Champions traveled west from the Ruins of Darva, taking wide berth around the Suntalla border for the Mortal Mountains. The fields quickly turned to woods again, but sparse and of little bushes. The trees stood tall and thin, easily moved by the whistling wind, creaking as they swayed. Crows squawked in their passing, and from what Falin could hear, they were surprised to see guests of the Crown. Pine needles covered their path, and the moments they could see through the tops of the foliage, the first peak of the Mortal Mountains loomed ahead. Falin could sense the first Gem was close, and he was eager to obtain it in light of the recent encounter with the warlocks Nyril and Mulgus.

"These woods are eerie, even in the morning," Bossador said, examining the trees. "I feel a chill at my skin despite this warm weather."

"It is so quiet," Nym agreed. "I can hear little but the occasional bird. It is odd so few animals are here next to Suntalla, Kingdom of Beasts."

Falin stared at the Mortal Mountains towering over them. "They say this land was once cursed by phantoms of the Beginning. And that many of the creatures who reside here live in the mountains to roam the night."

Nym nodded in confirmation. "It is where the phantoms first corrupted the cave elves of Isetta into draks. Isetta is now a city lost to history."

Bossador examined the forest. "Is this not the land where the tale of the lycan started? Half-man, half-wolf? They were said to be born here, hunting unsuspecting travelers."

Jimbuah gasped. "Nofa!"

"Yes," Bossador insisted. "My grandfather claims to have seen a lycan in this area in his youth. A horrible beast of a wolf's body, running on two feet. His party could hear the creature howling at the moon every nightfall."

"A myth," Carthon asserted. "Absurd as Red's claim of lizard people in the Magpie Isles. There have been no documented accounts of it. Your grandfather likely saw a bear on two legs in the dark of the night."

"My grandfather was not one to be uncertain of what he spoke," Bossador growled. "Yo—"

"Guys," Falin cut him off, drawing their attention to a split in the road as well as halting the oncoming spat. "The road forks here." He trotted his horse forward to the division. A stone as tall as the horses rested in between the two paths, with crudely carved arrows offering directions. "Left is the Mortal Caves," Falin announced. "And right is the Mortal Peaks." Like a punch to the chest, Falin realized he did not know whether the Gem was on top of the mountains or below it.

As Melquin, Carthon, and Jimbuah moved for the right trail leading to the Mortal Peaks, Bossador, Red, and Nym moved for the caves. They looked between each other, then Falin.

"I assumed the Gem would be on top of the mountains," Carthon said. "Is it not?"

Bossador furrowed his brow. "I am certain it makes more sense they are beneath, not on top of them."

"How would we ever find a Gem underneath a mountain?" Melquin fired back. "Are we to dig with our hands?"

"In the caves, Mel," Red responded condescendingly. "Are we going to fly to the top of the mountain?"

Nym smirked. "Perhaps some sage spell that could give us flowery wings."

"Klikimo, dujimo-fujikos," Jimbuah sneered, motioning they climb with an added insult.

Red pointed a warning finger at his partner. "Watch it, Jimmy!"

"What did he call us?" Nym asked.

"He called us dumb-f—"

"Enough," Falin snapped. "I am trying to think." He motioned his horse to stand at the trail's division. He could not sense which path, only forward. The Champions watched intently. Falin began to absent-mindedly twirl his staff in his palm, and each second he loosened his grip on the weapon, something felt odd to his fingers. It was as if it was being gently nudged by an invisible hand.

Falin held the staff parallel to the ground with an open palm, and its head slowly moved to point left for the Mortal Caves. With his free hand, he moved it to point in the other direction, only to have the staff's head swing gently back to the left. "It seems to me we are headed to the Mortal Caves."

Antagonistic chuckles rippled from Bossador, Red, and Nym as they made their way for the left path. As they rode forward, Falin examined his staff, glad to know it would help guide them to the Gem. He tucked it into the crook of his arm and they continued through the woods. The path began to slope downwards, the terrain rockier. In a few instances, the horses stumbled but managed to keep their balance.

Falin squinted a distance down the trail, now at the base of the mountain. "It is as if the path disappears into nothing." He thought it may be some trick of the forest, shrouding the route in some dark abyss.

Nym leaned forward on her horse to get a better glimpse. "Because it does."

In but a few moments, they came upon the mouth of a cave embedded into the first of the Mortal Mountains. They stood at the entry, gaping at the sheer size of it, towering over their heads so high they had to crane their necks to see the top. The opening stood ten times the height of any tree within the woods. Upon coming to grips with the enormity of the cave, they realized sunlight was lost inside within a stone's throw.

"You first," Red said to Bossador.

"We cannot take the horses in here," Melquin announced, looking to the uneven and rock covered terrain. "They will break their ankles within moments."

"What do we do with them?" Carthon asked. "We do not know which part of the mountains we will come out of."

Falin thought on it and spoke to his horse. "Do you know the way to Mystica?"

The horse nodded. "We do."

"We should send them home," Falin said. "They know the route. We can ask the Kingdom of Letani to supply us with new means of travel when we get there."

"I don't know that we can count on that," Red argued. "We're not certain we'll be headed in Letani's direction anyway."

"They are the closest allies we have in this part of the world. We should take refuge there no matter what," Bossador stated.

Falin climbed off of his steed, speaking to the horses. "You have served us well. We thank all of you for your service. Make haste across the Freelands and return home. Tell the sages you left us well and eager to find the first Gem of our journey."

The Champions said goodbye to their individual horses, the animals wished them all well, though none but Falin and Melquin could understand. "Be safe, Falin," his horse said. "Come," he called to the others. They began to walk the way in which they came.

Melquin watched for a moment, as a mother might a child departing on a journey. Red patted her shoulder. "They'll be alright, Mel. They're smart. Smarter than most horses. And most madorians for that matter."

"Watch it," Bossador warned.

Falin scanned the cave. The air was foul, not by smell, but by aura. "We must take care to move quietly," Falin said. "The Mortal Mountains are said to be infested by gruns and crags."

"It is their second home," Carthon answered. "And the first home to many other Dark creatures."

"Let us begin," Falin said. He took the lead, entering the cave, swallowed whole as they filed in. At the edge of light, Falin bumped the bottom of his staff to the earth and a soft glow emitted from its head, lighting their way. Melquin did the same, her light a whiter shade than Falin's. Jimbuah, trailing behind everyone, shook his staff and muttered a spell, causing his fruit to emit an orange glow.

They carried on, careful of their footing on the path of rocks, the trail sloping inwards to the earth. The further they went, the closer the ceiling of the cave dropped. Falin glanced behind him and saw that the entrance was no more than a tiny dot of light. The shadow-ridden faces of his company were gloomy.

"How are we supposed to know if it's day or night?" Bossador asked. "Are we just going to rest when we feel tired?" His voice echoed off the cavern walls.

"Yes," Falin answered. "It would be wise of us to keep guard two at a time while we sleep. One of whom should always be able to conjure light."

The stony path winded, and Falin would wave his staff to view the walls of the cave, thinning with every step. Water trickled along the rocks, causing the ground to become slippery. In a couple of hours, the tunnel became rather small; so small, that Red was forced to remove his hat, and Bossador to stoop and shuffle.

Eventually, the walls held tight, and with great difficulty, Bossador said, "Are you sure we are going in the right direction? Did we miss a turn somewhere?"

"No," Melquin answered. "I have been searching for alternate routes. This is the only way forward."

"Then I fear I will be forced to retreat if the mountain continues to swallow us," Bossador replied, hunching.

Even Jimbuah, who stood less than two-thirds the height of the madorian, ducked his head. He encouragingly poked Bossador in the butt with his glowing staff in motivation. "Nibado yuka. Nofa quijito."

They continued on as such for hours, the cave closing in at a sneaking pace. Falin extended his staff hoping the path expanded again. As he pulled it back, he thought he saw a sparkle of light ahead. He paused and felt Nym bump him.

"Why'd you stop?" the elf asked.

"I thought I saw something." Falin squinted, waiting silently to the stifled breathing of his Champions. Again, he saw a glimmer. "There is something creating light ahead of us. For a second at a time."

"Does the cave get bigger?" Bossador asked, resting on his knee.

"I hope so," Falin said, continuing on. Before long, they were crawling in single file, their possessions scraping the suffocating stone.

Bossador struggled most of all, his stomach pressed to the ground as the shield slung to his back thudded against rock. "Perhaps we could rest for a moment," he said. Falin twisted his neck to find the madorian appearing truly disheveled, taking the brunt of their cumbersome mode of transport. Scrapes covered his face and his attire was tattered. "I imagine everyone else's knees must ache as mine do."

Carthon shook his head. "It must be midday outside," he called behind him. "We will spend an eternity under this mountain if we are to rest every time you bump a rock."

Bossador took an agitated breath. "I have only asked that we rest for a moment. Not make camp." After a silence, he asked Carthon, "Does this suit your wishes, *drak*?"

The faintest hiss escaped Carthon, "I have a name, prince. Use it when you address me."

Ignoring them, Falin caught another little shimmer of light ahead, realizing it was the end of the tunnel. "We're at an end!" he said. "It opens back up!" A short distance further, Falin slithered through an opening, astonished at what he found.

The wizard stood at a ledge, and above him, an endless cavern ceiling pulsed a deep blue glow. Sections of light waxed and waned, prompting areas to flare cerulean warmth before fading to black again. It appeared a body of mystical water.

Beneath the blue ceiling was an abyss, where tiny roaming dots glistened in open air. One of these lights flew to Falin and landed on his staff, throbbing a soft, white glow. He examined it, discovering a bug whose abdomen shined on and off. The cavern appeared a midnight ocean flipped upside down, the ceiling water, the chasm of bugs a bustling starry sky.

One by one, the Champions squirmed from the opening, gasping as they witnessed the cavern. Finally, Bossador yanked himself through, and Jimbuah followed, lining at the ledge, gaping.

Carthon spoke first, softly. "Where are we? It's incredible."

Melquin gawked in wonder. "I have read about this place. It is known as the Earthly Ocean. Many say it was Mother Elsana's first attempt at creating a sea."

Jimbuah tilted his head so he could view the cavern upside down. "Boo yattah," he whispered.

"It's amazing," Red agreed. A bug landed on the brim of his hat which he moved to knock away, letting it rest instead.

Falin saw no end to the void. "How deep do you think it is?"

"Hmm." Jimbuah plucked a berry from his staff and muttered into his palm, causing the fruit to glare so bright they squinted.

Cocking his arm, the skully grunted and tossed the berry as far as he could.

The light flew, and flew, and flew, and flew, and flew, and flew, and flew, and flew, and flew, and flew, and flew, and flew, and flew downward, less visible every second. They watched in awe. Finally, the berry disappeared, extinguished by never-ending darkness. They stood in silence, coming to grips with the depth of the void. "Vekari dibapa," Jimbuah said.

Red sighed. "In case you didn't understand, Jimmy says it's very deep."

"Thank you, Jimmy," Falin answered. He breathed heavily. Despite being underground, there was something fresh about the air. He peered right, discovering the ledge continued on a path until no longer visible. "Are we ready to press on?"

All voiced agreement and they turned right, navigating the ledge that jutted from the cavern wall. The path was wide enough for them to move comfortably in single file, but they were routinely forced to slow their pace as it narrowed to a frightening degree. Same as the cave prior, water trickled from the walls, sometimes forming tiny streams across their path. The ledge winded along with the wall, keeping at an even level.

For Falin, it was difficult to watch his footing, as his gaze was often drawn to the Earthly Ocean. The sheer size amazed him. He wondered what the lights on the ceiling were made of, and why they pulsed blue. For hours they marched, the scuffs of their feet the only sound to echo. In order, Falin, Melquin, Nym, Carthon, Bossador, Red and Jimbuah carried on, plodding along. Eventually, the ledge grew thin, and they shuffled so as not to slip.

Falin carefully stepped over a small stream that trickled from the wall, using his staff for balance. Melquin followed suit, as did Nym. Carthon, who had glanced to view the Earthly Ocean, did not see the stream, slipping upon the water. He fell from the ledge.

In his gasp, the group turned in shock; all but Bossador. Bossador moved into action. As if on instinct, the prince dove off the edge for Carthon and managed grab hold of the drak's ankle. The madorian prince snagged the ledge with his other hand, grunting with white-knuckled strain.

Nym, Red, and Jimbuah, jumped to grab hold of Bossador's arm, but they struggled to lift both.

"Hang on!" Falin yelled, terrified. "Pull Bossador! Carthon, grab my staff!" Falin lowered his weapon to Carthon who swung in the sparkling void, his swords close to falling from his back. He snatched the head of Falin's staff, and the wizard pulled. In an instant, Bossador had an elbow over the ledge, and Carthon was raised so he grasped the rock with both hands, teeth clenched. The Champions were then able to assist their comrades up. Once all were to safety, they fell to the cavern wall, huffing and puffing.

They sat in silence for a moment. Carthon held a blank stare, focused on the endless cavern. He mustered the words, "Thank you. Thank you, Bossador. You should not have done that. Thank you."

Bossador nodded, blinkless as the drak, wiping sweat from his forehead. "If it's alright with you, I'd like to take a moment's rest."

"Yes," Carthon agreed immediately. "By all means. A rest sounds excellent right now."

Everyone pressed their heads to the cool stone at their backs, gazing across the Earthly Ocean, once so beautiful, now a fearsome sight in its representation of certain death. Subtly so, Carthon clasped Nym's hand, but none took notice. They recessed for a time, lost in thought. Falin clutched his staff and felt a tug. They were nearing the first Gem.

"We shouldn't stay here long," Falin said. "We should try and make it to the end if we can. Is everyone ready?"

"Yekasa," Jimbuah announced. They carefully stood.

"Be cautious and watch your step," Falin guided, leading the way, making a mental note to announce potentially hazardous footings.

Hours more they trekked, and Falin grew concerned they would spend days on this ledge, like some overturned coastline without end. The path began to widen, slowly so, but in time, it stretched, and they came to an end of the cavern. Eager to be reprieved of the cliff, they hurried to a spacious landing. Five tunnel openings presented them with differing paths.

"Which one are we to take?" Melquin asked.

Falin raised his staff horizontally. It turned to the tunnel on the far right. "Right it is. We should sleep here for the night. We have space, and do not know how long those tunnels are."

The Champions dropped their possessions and fell, eager for a pardon from hiking and crawling over rock.

Red stretched and yawned. "It's gotta be nighttime out there, right?"

"I'd imagine it is," Nym answered. "It is strange, becoming tired without seeing sunset."

"Our sleep patterns will probably get a little weird if we're inside the mountains for too long," Red responded. "Best thing we can do is listen to our bodies."

Carthon lay against a rock with his swords beside him. "You speak as if from experience."

Red looked to the drak from the sides of his eyes. He rubbed his head under his hat. "When I was a slave in Cadryl, the augurs didn't take too kindly to…" he pursed his lips as he searched for the right words. "Back-talk. When I spoke out of turn, they would put me in a cell with no windows, no light, nothing. Once a day I would get fed a meal and see the smallest bit of firelight through the crack in the door, but that was it. Scoundrel's oath, I'd be more hungry for light than I was for meals."

"How long would they keep you in there?" Nym asked.

Red shrugged. "Depended on the sentence. No more than a month at a time, 'cause I was always of more value working than wasting in a cell."

Carthon thought for a moment. "How was it you escaped?"

Red looked to the drak with emotional fatigue. "Patience."

None spoke following his answer, until Falin said, "We should sleep. Melquin, will you take first watch with Bossador? I will take second with Carthon so that we can keep our company alight."

"I will," Melquin agreed. She raised her staff to better examine the five, shadowy tunnels, but said nothing more.

Soon, they were asleep, and the waves of the Earthly Ocean pulsed over their tired heads. It was a deep sleep Falin came upon. Perhaps because he was in the dark, or it was the overwhelming silence, but he felt as though he was adrift in the void. No dreams came to him. Instead, he knew sound slumber for some time; that was until Melquin's voice woke him.

"Everyone wake up," she demanded.

Their heads groggily lifted, their hands pawing for their weapons. Melquin and Bossador faced the tunnel second to the left, prepared to fight.

Falin squinted to where they focused. "What is it?"

Bossador held his sword. "Something lurks in the shadows," he muttered.

All rose, anticipating an attack. A disjointed shuffling of bare feet on rock came from the tunnel, and from the shadows, the shape of a two-legged being approached. It came to the light, and they were stunned by a grotesque image. Red warned them, "A ghoul! It's a ghoul!"

The ghoul approached, appearing that of a common man with sickly grey skin, his arms contorting and writhing spastically. It shuffled forward to the light, walking as if its ankles were broken, unable to move fluidly. Deep, guttural sounds emanated from its mouth as if trying to speak, but unable to communicate. Its eyes did not seem to look at any of the travelers directly, instead, haphazardly darting across the landing. A thick string of drool fell from the ghoul's slack-jawed mouth as its glottal moans echoed the walls.

The hair on Falin's neck stood. It appeared so close to human, yet was so far from it. Its elongated fingers curled, and feet were barely able to keep its balance, yet gracefully sidestepping every stone it should have tripped on. Its face held beady eyes, a crooked nose, and a lipless mouth.

"They are far stronger than they look," Carthon cautioned. "Keep it at a distance."

"What does it want?" Melquin asked.

"Food," Red answered. The Freelander lashed his whip at the monster. To all of their shock, the whip did not crack, but instead, the ghoul caught its end tightly in his palm. Before Red could release his weapon, the ghoul half-groaned, half-bellowed, tossing the whip and Red into the cave wall.

Falin forced a blow of magic at the ghoul, and what would have knocked Bossador clean off his feet made this creature stumble. Nym threw a star that it swatted with the back of its hand to clang off the rocks. Bossador launched and swung his blade. The ghoul ducked, then shoved him in the stomach so hard the madorian nearly tumbled off the ledge into the abyss.

Carthon leapt high in the air hoping to drive his swords into the throat of the monster, but it sidestepped, grabbing his ankle and slamming him to the stone. Melquin smacked her staff against the back of its head. The ghoul screamed with a stretched mouth of rotted teeth and flailing saliva. It grabbed ahold of her waist and threw the sage over his shoulder, retreating to the cave where it came from. Melquin fruitlessly beat her capturer with her staff as it disappeared into the tunnel, her wails and its moans clashing in horrid harmony.

"Melquin!" Falin yelled, taking chase. The Champions followed, running through the rocky downward-sloping tunnel, often tripping as they ran. Red grabbed the nearest bag of rations as they took pursuit. Falin and Jimbuah's light guided them, and they hurried as fast as they could, their harsh breaths clattering against the darkened walls. Falin listened intently, realizing Melquin's shouts quickly faded. He darted forward, slipping on a rock that sent him tumbling into an opening. Upon examining their surroundings, they panicked.

They stood in a circle cavern with a flat floor and nine tunnel exits. The ghoul could have taken Melquin into any one of them. Falin twisted his neck in all directions, his light casting bewildered shadows.

"Which way did it go?!" Bossador yelled.

Nym raised her hand. "Be quiet! I am trying to listen." Her pointed ears twitched, and she stalked the entry of every tunnel, becoming increasingly concerned each she passed. "I cannot hear them. They are gone."

Falin felt short of breath, having failed one of his Champions. He desperately sought a clue as to which way she was taken, finding no solution.

"We should split up," Carthon said, "and search for her that way."

Red shook his head as he panted. "We could get lost. Then we'd all die. We need to stay together."

"We could search each path and retreat," Bossador suggested. "But it might take too long."

Carthon considered it. "She will be…" he shook his head. "We need to act."

Jimbuah raised his staff, and curiously crept to a tunnel entry on their right. He crouched, lifting a tiny, pink flower from behind a rock. "Ah!" He held the flower for them all to see.

Falin stepped forward, and hope nudged him. "Melquin has left us a trail! This is a flower from her staff!"

"Let's go!" Nym directed.

With a lead to follow, they sprinted through the tunnels, Falin holding his light low to the rocks. On occasion, they would pass a pink flower, a message from Melquin to keep pursuing. Again, they came upon another cavern, and this time it held seven new tunnels. They examined each entry, and by the passage that was third from the left, Bossador found another flower. "This way!"

For near an hour, they hastened deeper into the mountain by guide of Melquin's petals, coming upon a dozen more caverns, each with a new winding tunnel. The once cool air became warm and muggy, and their breaths grew labored as sweat poured from their faces. Their knees ached and their shins were torn by the jutted rocks from their path.

In a tunnel of jagged stone, Falin's heart skipped upon hearing the familiar sound of the moaning ghoul ahead. Raising his staff, they slowed their pace, creeping so as not to startle the monster. To Falin's relief, he heard Melquin struggle in her captivity, then, she was suddenly silenced.

Falin and Champions rushed in, fearful they'd arrived a second too late. They found the ghoul's den, and in the center, Melquin lying unconscious. The ghoul was nowhere to be seen.

Bossador knelt to lift her bruised face. "Melquin, we are here. Are you alright?"

The sage muttered a word that they could not hear. She lay among bones and the clothing of victims from decades past. A vile stench wafted to their nostrils as they searched for the ghoul.

"Where did it go?" Red asked. They scanned the room, ready for action.

Carthon pointed a sword to a tunnel, opposite the one they entered. "There is another path leading deeper. It must've run into the bowels of the mountains when it heard us coming."

Bossador gently shook the sage. "Can you wake, Melquin?"

Melquin's eyes fluttered to vague consciousness. "Up," she muttered.

Bossador furrowed his brow. "You would like me to carry you?"

"Up," she said forcefully, coming to.

It was then that Falin felt a hot, wet goo dribble across his right ear. He looked up, and saw the ghoul clinging upside down to the rock ceiling, drooling. Before he could call for warning, it thrust itself from above with an appalling wail, swiping at Jimbuah, sending the skully flying. Bossador lifted Melquin and carried her to safety, guarding her with his greatsword drawn. The rest surrounded the ghoul with raised weapons.

"We need to attack all at once," Falin commanded, "and over-whelm it." The ghoul opened its mouth and half-gurgled, half-growled at Falin as if understanding. "Nym, blind it! Red, ensnare its feet!" After another second of positioning, Falin yelled, "Now!"

Nym threw a tiny green ball from her utility belt. The ghoul swiped, and it burst into a green powder, causing the creature to claw at its burning eyes.

Red capitalized, wrapping his whip around the monster's ankle, yanking with all of his strength. Upon seeing it stumble, Falin hit the ghoul with a burst of magic. It writhed and howled as it fell to its back. Carthon jumped and thrust both ends of his swords into its throat, causing it to flail, hissing, squirming, before falling still. The ghoul of the Mortal Mountains lay slain before them.

Jimbuah picked himself up and hobbled forward. "Dekada?"

Carthon inspected its contorted face before removing his swords. "Seems dead to me."

They hurried to Melquin. Falin knelt beside her. "Are you hurt?" He placed his hand to her bruised cheek, but could find no other wounds.

"I am," she nodded, shaken. "Thank you for not leaving me."

Red and Bossador lifted her from the ground, and Nym dusted her off. "How could we ever?" Nym said. "We are on this journey together."

"Fakumilo," Jimbuah added. He plucked a small red piece of fruit from his staff and bit the skin off with his teeth, rubbing the juice to soothe the wound on Melquin's cheek.

"He's right, Mel," Red said. "We're family now."

Falin watched as his Champions cared for their hurt comrade, harboring a sudden flare of love for these children of the Light. He hoped it was an image for what the Crown and Freelands could be in the years he served Elsana.

"We should return to the Earthly Ocean," Carthon said. "We can follow Melquin's flowers all the way back."

"Good thinkin' on that by the way, Mel," Red added.

Nym smiled. "We were sure we had lost you."

Grimly, Melquin nodded. "I was sure I was lost."

The group moved to the exit, but something stopped Falin. He held his staff open in his palm, and it quickly swung in the direction of the tunnel opposite to the one they entered, further into the mountain. "Wait," Falin called. The group turned and saw his staff pointing the opposite way. "We must travel deeper still."

CHAPTER NINE:
OBAH

After taking a break in the ghoul's den, the travelers quickly grew sick of the smell, departing into the tunnel further into the mountain. When coming upon a split in their path, Falin's staff offered him guidance, and with each step, he felt the first Gem of Elsana nearer. The tunnels often rose so steeply they were forced to climb rather than hike, and other times began a descent so rapid they resigned to crawling backwards for fear of falling. Taking minimal breaks, they kept on, no longer aware of what time it was, nor what level of the mountain they were in. All they knew was rocky earth by the light of the magic staves of Falin, Melquin, and Jimbuah. When Falin began to grow concerned they may never escape the maze of caves, he stepped into an opening far different from all else they'd seen in the mountains.

He was surprised to find a hall of brown stone, with walls carved into elven figures in large lifelike depictions. They stood three times the height of Falin, wearing robes of stony cloth, so finely carved one would assume a gust of wind would cause them to flutter. Dry fountains adorned the base of the walls, and ancient elven carvings told stories of tales past.

While the Champions exited the cave and looked on the hall, Falin realized he was able to see it in its entirety, far past the light cast from his staff. Upon further inspection, the high ceiling emitted a soft yellow glow from crystals, similar to the pulsating Earthly Ocean.

"What is this place?" Bossador asked.

Nym examined with eyes of wonder. "It is a hall of the first cave elves. Those who ventured from Lelyalis in the Beginning."

Running his hand along the cool wall, Carthon examined one of the great elf statues. "They look as though they might walk from the stone."

Falin was thrilled to have his eyes reprieved of the dismal tunnels with such rare beauty. "What was the purpose of this place? Was it a gathering place?"

Red looked at the tunnel they came in from, broken and cracked. "My guess is our entry wasn't always here." He pointed to both ends of the hall, one covered in rubble, the other a small passage topped with an archway. "We probably need to go that way," he said, pointing left to the arch.

Falin felt his staff twitch. "Agreed." They walked the hall, scanning the artwork, all wishing they could dally to ingest the discovery if not for the urgency of finding the first Gem.

They came to a rock tunnel where two elven statues stood on either side, welcoming them into the smaller passage. Falin felt the air change as he marched through, and they were presented with a cavern of grandeur.

They stood atop a grand stairway, and below them, a city of stone carved beneath the mountain. It was as if the structures sprouted like plants from the rock, creating an impeccable sight of endless, perfect architecture. It waited dormant, comprised of homes both proud and humble, some with towers, others with smokestacks. Crystals on the ceiling and upper walls pulsed a golden hue, high above their heads. All was lit by a soft shine.

Falin could barely see the opposite side of the rock city. It was as wide as it was long, with roads set on a grid, separating the buildings.

Nym wiped a tear from her eye. "It is the lost city of Isetta. I cannot believe I am here."

"It has been nothing more than legend to the madorians," Bossador said. "I am thrilled to find it real."

Melquin searched the space. "It is so intact. What happened?"

"This is where Dark servants of centuries past corrupted the elves." Nym dropped her tone. "Turned them into draks." Carthon looked away as if in guilt.

"Warlocks?" Red asked.

Nym shook her head. "Phantoms." A chill fled through them as she mentioned their name.

Falin turned to the elf. "If we are able, perhaps we can take rest here after we find the Gem. It will give us time to explore the city."

"I would love that," Nym said. "Thank you, Falin."

He scanned the marvel before taking his first step of descent to the stairs, and as he did, he paused. "Do you feel that?"

Carthon raised his chin. "It is wind. There should be no wind in these caves."

Falin waited for its return, and sure enough, he felt the brush of air coming from the left side of the city. "There must be an exit there," he said, glad to know they were no longer buried. "We should search for it after finding the first Gem. But let's keep moving while we have the energy." His body was sore, but his ambition to find the Gem made him impatient.

Descending the stairs, they took the central road for the opposite wall. Their steps were soft, to respect the memory of the former inhabitants and escape the eyes of hidden evil. They gazed upon the homes which stood as if built only years prior.

Ancient elvish text reminiscent of the modern alphabet indicated the purpose of the structures. Some were residences, others were blacksmiths, bakers, tailors, and food services. It saddened Falin to see a place where such civility and order was accomplished to be destroyed by the chaotic Darkness.

"Wait," Carthon whispered harshly.

He titled his head and knelt by the corner of a building, lifting an object to the light of Melquin's staff. The flat, metal item was the length of his forearm. It held a dull sheen and was crudely made, with a broken strap around the center. "It is a shin guard."

Red stepped forward and examined it. "That ain't elf armor. It's a grun's."

"How old is it?" Falin asked. "Can you tell?"

Carthon squinted. "There is hardly dust on it. And I can still smell the stench of grun. They must travel this city for their own halls. We must be careful."

"You don't think they're living here?" Red whispered.

The drak shook his head. "They do not wish to dwell in a place created by elves. To them, it is tainted with the Light, and they would prefer to live here as we would prefer to spend our time in a place built from Darkness."

"Yet they use it as their roads," Nym scoffed.

"We should keep going," Melquin said. "We do not want to alert a horde of them when we are so close to the Gem."

"She is right," Falin said. "Let's go."

They hurried through the earthy metropolis, vigilant for signs of gruns. Without any trouble, they climbed another set of stairs that allowed them to look over the city yet again. Nym peered over her shoulder to gaze upon Isetta.

The group entered another hall akin to the first they came upon. This one held three other doors. Falin raised his staff, and it directed them to their left.

Next was a grand, circular room, and at the center a large round stage with steps leading onto it. The ceiling was shaped to that of a shallow dome, with moldings of fanciful characters. "It is a theater," Nym said. She walked the central platform and climbed one of the four short sets of stairs to stand atop. They gathered on the stage at the center of the room and looked around the circular hall. "The room's shape lets everyone hear what the performers spoke or sang. I wish I could have seen the works they put on."

The Champions stood on the platform and examined the artwork. Jimbuah inhaled to begin singing, but Red slapped a hand over his mouth. "Do you think the gruns will be asking for an encore?" Jimbuah glanced away then shrugged. Red flinched and retracted his hand. *"Don't bite me."* Jimbuah chuckled and clacked his teeth together.

Falin examined the round theater. There were four exits, and it was perfectly symmetrical, making it easy for him to lose sense of which door they entered. Continuing on, they descended from the stage and headed into another dividing hall, entering a door to their right, this time into a temple.

Stone seating aligned a middle passage to an altar, where a statue of Mother Elsana ten times the height of Bossador stood. She wore a crown of crystals that glowed yellow, and her hand was raised as if welcoming them. Large individual crystals jutted from the wall as a candle might in a modern place of prayer.

A statue of the God of Light rested over the heads at the entrance, depicted as a young, male elf with open arms. To Falin, it was not so different from the place of worship he explored in Darva. The only difference was the lack of Dark history represented by artwork—only tales of Light were here, mostly pertaining to the elves.

"Which way do we go?" Melquin asked. "There is only one opening, and it is the one we entered."

Falin raised his staff and it swayed in the direction of Mother Elsana. "It points to the statue."

Bossador rubbed his beard. "Is this Gem somewhere in the statue?"

"I'm not sure," Falin responded, strolling forward. Standing at her feet, he craned his neck to examine their creator's face. Holding his staff flat yet again, it pointed past her. Following the instructions of his weapon, he walked to the backside of the statue, revealing a hidden alcove. A slab of rock covered a doorway. "Over here," Falin called. Markings of ancient elvish were etched on the stone.

Carthon tilted his head. "What does it say?"

Falin racked his brain, wishing he had paid more attention when Rulo the Peacemaker forced him to learn ancient elvish in his youth. Falin spoke rather slowly. "May Light find thorns wormy who vulture across the Bride of Isetta to the Fools of En−En−Enlightenment?"

"Close," Nym said, as an encouraging mother might to a slow child. She reread the text with far more ease than the wizard. "May Light find those worthy who venture across the Bridge of Isetta to the Pools of Enlightenment."

Falin nodded. "Yeah. That makes more sense." He stepped back and examined the flat rock blocking their way. "How do we open it?"

Bossador rolled his shoulders. "I'd imagine the old fashion way. It's not too big for us to slide. Red, Carthon, Nym, and I can shove this side," he said, standing on the left of the stone. "When we push, the rest of you can give it a big hit of magic with your staves. That should be more than enough."

Carthon shrugged and mumbled. "Not a bad plan."

The group took their positions, all piled atop one another for space. "On the count of three," Bossador declared. "One... two... three..." All at once, they shoved, and luckily, the rock slid, opening to a small precipice. Their tiny, joyful moment of camaraderie was quickly bashed by the sudden sense of Darkness.

Harsh voices of gruns and crags spoke in the distance, and they froze, listening intently in an effort to discern how close they were. Falin peeked through the entry and saw a thin rock bridge stretched across the top of a vast cavern. Flickering shadows clashed on the ceiling above. They crept forward and looked over the landing connected to the bridge.

Beneath was an immense cavern, home to at least a thousand gruns and crags. Crude tents, huts, and fires filled the space as they blathered on between one another, taking no notice of the group high above their heads.

Having seen the grey, squat, and ugly gruns before, Falin's eyes were quickly drawn to the crags peppered in the encampment. They were the size of Bossador, with wide, muscular bodies and flat heads, and hardly any neck. Their skin was a slight shade of green, and each wore one large tooth that curled from its mouth in a random spot. Their arms dangled to their knees, with powerful fists clutching spears and clubs. They wore loose fitting pants and baggy shirts, many wearing piercings on their brows, noses, or lips, and when the crags spoke, they did so in ferocious growls, without any subtlety.

The gruns outnumbered the crags four to one, yet the crags were twice the size of their Dark counterparts. Gruns sat in circles and ate the bones of what Falin hoped was hunted animal and not man, drinking deeply from barrels filled with thick, brown liquid. Some sparred, and others slept, and few told tall tales of their Dark deeds, laughing, arguing, fighting, and boasting. Their putrid smell wafted up the cavern along with the smoke from their fires.

Slowly, Falin's group backed away into the temple. As they did, Falin looked to the other side of the bridge, where he saw another tunnel. He knew it was where the first Gem of Elsana hid.

"What do we do?" Melquin whispered. "We can't let them see us cross the bridge."

"It is so high up," Nym answered. "I doubt they will notice us if we tread carefully."

Bossador shook his head, unconvinced. "Perhaps not the crags for they are dumb, but there are many gruns with keen eyes. We will have to move discreetly so as not to arouse suspicion."

"Why do they not have guards up here?" Falin asked. "Patrolling, if it is so close to their home?"

"They likely see no need," Carthon responded. "They must only use Isetta as a means for passage. They would have no desire to enter a temple of Light. It would cause them great discomfort. The cavern below must be one separate from the elven kingdom."

Falin tapped his staff on the ground in thought. "We cannot go back. The Gem is this way. We must continue on."

Red examined the rock bridge. "It's narrow. We'll have to crawl so they don't see us. We'll be grun-stew the moment we fall."

"Then it's decided," Falin said. "We move forward." He turned again to the opening and breathed deeply, walking to the bridge's edge, dropping to his knees. Pressing his belly to the ground, he dragged himself across the rock overpass, taking care to keep out of sight.

His Champions followed, and they slithered above the gruns and crags, occasionally peeking over the lip of the bridge to view the camp below. Falin wondered what this group of Dark servants was purposed for, as there were no families, or at least not anything that resembled women and children. Instead, it all appeared to be soldiers of Drucullm and Varsa present. The grumbles below were constant, and the voices echoed over the cavern ceiling making it seem as though the enemies taunted from above.

After what felt like an eternity, they came to the opposite side, and Falin kept crawling until coming to a corridor of carved rock. He stood, turning to see his group join him. Last to enter was Bossador, who wiped the dust from his vestments, stooped his head so as not bump the top of the newest tunnel. Falin raised his finger to his lips to signal they remain quiet, continuing through the corridor. They hurried, and the voices of the crags and gruns quickly dissipated behind them.

"That was a command post," Carthon said in a low voice. "Did you see there were only soldiers?"

Bossador nodded as they walked. "We must be close to an exit in the mountain. I am sure they are there to perform raids on Freeland villages."

Falin half-listened to their conversation, squeezing his staff. An excitement bombarded him; they were close. For a few miles they plodded on, their path alight by glowing crystals on the walls. The air became refreshing as if atop a mountain. There was no Dark here.

It was then that Falin heard the running of water, but unlike a river. "Ahead!" he announced. "Can you hear it?"

"I can," Nym confirmed. They hurried through the corridor and Falin saw that it came to an opening. He had to keep himself from running, so elated he sensed the first Gem.

Upon exiting the passage, they found a towering, hall-like cavern. At the opposite end, a gentle waterfall spilled from the ceiling high above their heads. Its water fell into a sizable pool, surrounded by a short, semi-circle stone barrier.

The walls of the cavern were covered in multicolored glowing crystals, pulsating a vibrant display as if a slumbering rainbow. Falin walked to the edge of the clear water, its ripples reflecting the kaleidoscopic walls.

Behind the waterfall, the pool extended into a cave, and in the water, a faint blue shimmer caught Falin's eye. Wasting no time, he stepped into the pool.

The water was nourishment to his aching bones. He felt an overwhelming warmth, the comfort of being wrapped in a blanket amid a blizzard. It was a bath of healing, blessed by the God of Light.

Standing chest deep, he waded forward. His Champions watched in anticipation. He bent his head as he passed through the waterfall and let the stream run over his hair and down his neck. He felt his soul cleansed of the horrors he'd encountered on the journey thus far.

Continuing into the cave, the crystal walls brightened as if welcoming his presence, and underneath the water, he saw a glowing blue item. He bent under the surface, feeling a surge through his body upon clasping the object.

Falin lifted the Gem from the pool and held it up, blinking through droplets to better view its cerulean sparkle. It was small, fitting in the palm of his hand. His staff beckoned for its placement. Taking no more time, Falin dropped the Water Gem into one of the four free slots of his staff, and it locked into place, now immovable. The lights within the cavern brightened further, and the water glistened as if covered in diamonds.

He was overwhelmed. In an instant, Falin felt one with the water, as if an extension of his being, and it was his to control. He turned, wishing to exit the cave, and as he waded beneath the waterfall, he raised his staff, dividing the water so that he passed unhindered. His Champions watched in awe, standing by the edge of the pool. Their eyes fell to the Gem on his staff.

A smile spread across Nym's lips and she began to laugh. "We have done it! We found the first Gem!"

Melquin beamed. "We have."

Falin stood in the pool, and scanned his surrounding Champions. They waited for him to relay profound wisdom in his newly enlightened power. Love shrouded Falin as he watched these Children of Light. They were his to protect, and his to bring joy. He smiled, wanting nothing more than for them to share the moment with him. Falin swung his staff over the water, commanding it leap from the pool and pour over the Champions in a sudden splash.

They stood drenched, faces dripping, surprised by his action. Falin chuckled mightily. "Am I to keep the Pools of Enlightenment to myself? Join me!"

Needing no encouragement, Jimbuah yelled, "Boo yattah!" and leapt into the water.

Nym unclasped her utility belt and tossed aside her sword, diving in herself, followed by Melquin, Red, Bossador, and finally Carthon. The dirt that covered them seemed to instantly disappear in the ripples. They splashed and swam, laughing in the pristine pool, a bath of untainted Light.

Jimbuah floated on his back in serenity, and Bossador soaked his beard in the water. Melquin stole Red's hat as he chased her, splashing her with cupped hands as children in a pond might. To keep her head above the water, Nym wrapped her arms around Carthon's neck, and he took the opportunity to carry her underneath the waterfall, evoking a shout of sudden delight. Falin watched them all in unbridled joy.

"Come on, Falin," Red urged. "Show us what you can do."

Unsure of the extent of his newfound powers, Falin looked to the waterfall and raised his staff, guiding the water away from the pool and causing a stream to float through the air. They watched in wonder as the waterfall twisted and turned, making fanciful designs through the cavern by the young wizard's hand, until he gently guided it back to the pool.

"Incredible!" Bossador exclaimed.

Jimbuah clung to the pool wall and shrugged as if unimpressed, teasing Falin. "Beh."

Bossador shook his head at Jimbuah beside him. "And what skully magic do you know that is better?"

Jimbuah thought for a moment, then dipped his lips, filling his cheeks with liquid. He then held one nostril closed, strained, then sprayed water all over Bossador from his other nostril. Jimbuah fell into a fit of hysterics, barely clinging to the wall of the pool. Bossador swatted his face of the skully-tainted water.

Nym put a hand on her head in disbelief. "You just shot sacred water through your nose!"

The skully laughed so hard he made little noise, instead shaking, a huge smile fixated on his grey face.

In retaliation, Bossador snatched Jimbuah by the waist, and with a mighty grunt, tossed his comrade high into the air. No longer amused, Jimbuah shrieked until landing on his butt, splashing them all. After a second of being underwater, he sprang through the surface and shook the drops from his face having enjoyed the toss. "Boo yattah! Upa! Upa!" Jimbuah demanded he be tossed again.

Bossador chuckled and provided the service of flinging his friend through the air thrice more for the skully's enjoyment.

They lounged for hours until growing tired, eventually climbing from the pool, sitting in a circle. They did not miss the flames, however, as the cavern offered them an unmatched warmth. In high spirits, they jested with one another, telling tales of their youth, and their aspirations following the journey, nibbling on the rations of food Red snagged before their pursuit of the ghoul.

When the images of the warlocks Nyril and Mulgus crossed Falin's mind, they were quickly tossed away, as this place was of too much Light to consider such Darkness. The shimmering cavern walls and its plentiful colors made them know true peace.

Carthon sat cross-legged, resting his wrists on his knees. He turned to Falin in thought. "It has just dawned on me. We do not yet know where the next Gem is."

"I completely forgot to look," Falin replied, surprised with himself. He reached into his robes where the map Airo gave him was kept. He shook the parchment, surprised and relieved to find it was unharmed by his time spent in the water. Upon pressing his staff to the map and focusing, a small white dot appeared on the bottom of the paper at the southern coast of the Wildbarrens. There was no indication as to any landmarks around the site.

Red cleared his throat, prompting Falin to look up. His Champions waited in anticipation. Falin breathed deeply and announced, "We are headed to the southern tip of the Wildbarrens." A moment of acceptance swept through them as they came to terms with the next stage of their journey.

Melquin thought on it. "It seems as though Purla the Lightbringer's vision was correct."

"And it is a good thing we ended up bringing these two," Bossador said of Jimbuah and Red.

"We are lucky to have them, Wildbarrens or not," Nym added.

Red dropped his head so that none could see his eyes beneath his brimmed hat. Jimbuah smiled wide. "Hakupo tuka," he agreed.

"So south it is then," Carthon thought aloud. "We should make for the Kingdom of Letani once we exit these mountains. We will find shelter there, and good rest for as long as we need. They have always been friends of the Crown."

Red glanced at Jimbuah. "We could head for the Stony Valley as well. The stonies are a kind people, from the few I've met, and would give us the same shelter as Letani. They know the Wildbarrens better than most as well."

Carthon shook his head. "The stonies will not provide us with the hospitality Letani will. Perhaps Letani may even lend us a ship to sail the coast rather than travel through the Wildbarrens on foot."

"I hadn't thought of that," Falin said. "Carthon's right, we should go to Letani."

Falin sensed a fear within Red and Jimbuah regarding Letani, but resisted pressing them. "Perhaps Jimbuah can don the garb of the Letani nobles the same as he did in Rorkshire. I hear Letanis are a stylish bunch."

Jimbuah grinned and shrugged, playing with his pointed green Rorkshire hat poking out of his pocket. "Matibi."

Melquin placed the head of her staff into her palm, and a large pink flower grew from it. She tucked it behind Jimbuah's ear and laughed. "You would make a wonderful sage with enough flowers."

Red chuckled as Jimbuah presented his new earpiece to the group. "Don't tempt him. He'll get all dolled up and start playing in no time."

A sudden sleepiness hit Falin, and his eyelids grew heavy. "We should rest," he told the group. "Sleep as long as you'd like. We will head back to Isetta tomorrow to find an exit from the mountains."

Everyone nodded and laid to sleep, their ears nuzzled by the waterfall pattering the Pools of Enlightenment. It was the best night's sleep they'd received since the start of their journey. There was no worry of a Dark invasion; no reason to keep guard through the night. They were in the presence of Light, and they could bask in its glory to their heart's content. After hours of slumber, they began to stir, and one by one, they rose for their trek back. Jimbuah was the last to wake, and Falin went to him, gently nudging the softly snoring skully.

"Jimbuah," he called.

Jimbuah rolled over, his eyes fluttering, the flower from Melquin still tucked behind his ear. He smiled sweetly. "Hekalo."

"Good morning," Falin said. "Or evening. I'm not quite sure what time of day it is. We are getting ready to leave."

The company departed the cavern of the Water Gem, taking a final moment to soak in the vibrant walls. Feeling unhurried in their exit, they walked through the corridor leading to the Bridge of Isetta. In truth, they'd forgotten about the massive horde of gruns and crags they were to pass over. The further they carried on, the more reality settled into their minds, and all grew serious as it came time to return to the harsh world outside the Pools of Enlightenment.

For miles they walked, and in time, the noises of enemies struck their ears. They came to the end of the corridor overlooking the Bridge of Isetta and peeked over the edge of the ledge to view the horde below. It was the same as last they came through, if not rowdier than before.

Falin motioned for his comrades to begin crawling over the bridge to keep out of sight. Nym began, then Carthon, Red, Bossador, Melquin, Jimbuah, and finally Falin. They scraped along the rock. Falin focused on keeping his staff and clothing out of sight over the ledge. Smoke wafted on either side of them from campfires carrying the stench of gruns and crags with it.

Halfway across, Falin noticed Melquin's flower still set upon Jimbuah's ear. Even worse, it began to loosen from being jostled. "Jimmy," he whispered. The skully did not hear him. The flower wiggled looser. "Jimmy," he called, slightly louder. The skully kept crawling, unaware he was being beckoned, doubly unaware the flower clung to his ear by a petal. Falin grew increasingly anxious. "Jimmy," he said a third time, poking the skully in the foot with his staff.

Startled, Jimbuah quickly turned his head around, and in that instant, the flower drifted from his ear, off the bridge before either could grab it. The Champions ahead heard their stifled gasps, and all turned to watch as the flower slowly spun in its descent upon the cavern.

They gawked as it twirled in the windless air, teeth clenched and wide-eyed as it floated below. Falin's heart pounded in his ears, hoping it would land unnoticed, to be crushed by the clumsy foot of a crag. To his chagrin, the flower dropped in the center of a grun circle. It startled them, and one lifted the blossom by a petal as if it were a rancid object, sniffing it in disgust. They looked up, shocked to see the seven faces staring down at them.

Jimbuah sighed and shook his head. "Obah."

A grun jumped up and pointed, screaming in his gurgly voice, "Intruders! Intruders on the bridge!"

A thousand gruns and crags looked up. Falin and his Champions gaped back. There was a moment of shocked silence between all parties. The first to speak was Red, who yelled, "RUN!"

Falin and company leapt up to sprint across the remainder of the bridge as arrows whizzed by their heads. In that same instant, gruns and crags scrambled for tunnels that would lead them to the elven city above. The Champions came to the temple of Light, and Falin could already hear enemies swarming Isetta in their pursuit. They ran through the temple, drawing their weapons.

Approaching enemy footsteps and shrieks clashed through the walls, but they were not yet seen. They exited the temple and came to the hall with four exits. "Which way?!" Bossador yelled. "Do we go back to the city?!"

"We may be able to hide there," Falin huffed. "Or find an exit."

"The gruns will be swarming the city," Carthon argued. Stampedes echoed through every chamber, making it impossible to discern which direction their enemy came from.

"It is the only way we know," Falin replied. "Come!" They ran through the hall for the theater they passed through, and Falin glanced behind him to see the shadows of gruns approaching in the opposite corridor.

They entered the round theater and sprinted up the steps of the large circular stage, making for the opposite hall that would lead them to the city. As Falin hit the first step descending the other side of the platform, he saw the shadows of enemies running through their targeted hall. "Go back!" he yelled, nearly tumbling down the stairs.

They returned to the stage, and at every entrance, the clamor of gruns and crags came near. Forming a huddle on the circular platform, they readied for action.

Nym clutched her sword in one hand and a throwing star in another. "We must protect Falin at all costs. Guard the steps to the platform. Falin, if you see a chance to run, take it."

Falin couldn't fathom leaving his Champions to die in the mountain. "We should charge one of the halls before they are all here."

"Too late," Carthon said.

Gruns poured through each entry, flinging themselves at the stage. They swung their short-swords while screaming. A crag ran through an entry with a club in its hand, to which Nym quickly flung a star into its throat. It clutched its windpipe, stumbled, and fell.

As two gruns ran up the steps, Bossador swung his broadsword, cutting one of their heads clean off, partially impaling the second in the same blow. Carthon hissed at a group of gruns scrambled up the wall of the stage, prompting a flurry from his swords, cutting their arms.

A giant spear thrown by a crag narrowly missed Red, and he answered with a crack of his sharpened whip. "JIMMY!" he yelled to the skully at the other side of the stage. "JIMMY! GO BIG!"

Jimbuah tossed a fireberry at an approaching crag, lighting its face in blue flame. "YEH!" he ardently agreed, seeing the enemies flood the theater. He ran to the center of their group for protection, and plucked the largest fruit of his staff, sitting cross-legged, biting into its yellow skin.

The Champions stood at a slight strategic advantage on the platform, though the sheer number of enemies entering would soon overwhelm them. Falin blew back three gruns running up the steps, and Melquin swung her staff to knock a couple whizzing arrows off course. Falin glanced behind him to see Jimbuah at the center of their circle, frantically devouring the fruit, juice sloshing across his lips and over his grey fingers.

"JIMMY!" Red yelled again, looking behind him. "ANY DAY NOW BUDDY!" He blocked the blow of a grun who had made it onto the platform, cutting its throat with his blade. Falin glanced behind him. Jimmy neared completion of the fruit, and Falin prayed whatever magic it offered would deem helpful.

Gruns began to make it onto the stage as others waited their chance to climb on. The Champions were near overwhelmed, fighting for their lives. The clashes of their weapons on enemy blades echoed on the walls. Falin caught a glimpse of Jimbuah convulsing on the floor, doubled over and clutching his stomach.

A spear flew by, narrowly missing Falin's throat, instead nipping Bossador's arm. Falin hit a crag in the eye with magic, causing it to fall to its back. There were a dozen gruns below him as more entered, and he feared his group was soon to be killed. It was then Falin heard a mighty roar, and the lights from the crystals above were suddenly shadowed.

The wizard turned, shocked to see a hulking creature resembling Jimbuah at the center of the stage. He stood twice the height of Bossador, his body bulging muscle. His massive fist gripped a staff, grown proportional to his size. The Champions stared with dropped jaws. Crags and gruns alike paused their assault, stunned by the sudden appearance of the skully behemoth. All fell silent in awe. Red grinned.

Giant Jimbuah chuckled with his same gravely tone, this time octaves deeper. He scanned the room of enemies now dwarfing him, speaking in a voice deeper than Falin had ever heard. "Boo yattah."

Without delay, Jimbuah took a gargantuan step to one side of the stage by Falin, crowded by gruns at its base. He swiped his hand, knocking half of them across the theater into the wall. The remaining few swung their swords, but his muscular paw knocked their blades away like the butter-knives of children. Moving with surprising speed for his size, he leapt from the stage, waving his tree-sized staff. He bashed a couple of crags across their skulls and kicked at gruns as if fleas that nipped his ankles. As he fought, he roared, partly in anger, partly in delight.

"Gofo!" he beckoned his group to follow as he made his way for the city of Isetta.

Reinvigorated, they ran from the stage and continued behind him, fighting through the remaining mess of enemies he mostly cleared a path of. Bossador and Red took the rear, blocking attacks from behind.

Jimbuah ducked through the exit of the theater and swatted his staff at the surprised gruns and crags who backed away in terror. Jimbuah plucked an oversized fireberry and chucked it into the doorway. It exploded in a huge burst of flames, deterring following enemies from passing through.

Falin blocked a swipe of a sword by a grun, but its blade still sliced part of his forearm. He yelped in pain, seeking to retaliate, but before he could, Jimbuah lifted the grun like a doll, flinging it into the stone wall. It hit the rock with a gruesome *splat*.

They ran for the corridor leading to the stairway that over-looked Isetta. Jimbuah lagged behind to fend off the approaching enemies, but gruns and crags still took chase. At the top of the stairs, Falin looked over the site.

Nym pointed to their right at the far end of the city. "There is light! An exit!"

Their eyes followed her direction, and a faint glimmer of sun-light rested on the side of the city. It was the same direction they felt the wind from on their first entry, and Falin realized it must have been night at the time.

Needing no encouragement, they fled down the stairs onto Isetta roads as scores of enemies kept pursuit. Jimbuah threw a bulky fireberry to ward them off, but gruns continued to trickle from every corner.

They turned right to head for the direction of the light, currently invisible behind the stone buildings that towered over their heads. Arrows fell from the sky and landed in the earth and rock around them, narrowly missing their targets, whistling as they poured from above. Falin glanced behind him to see the pursuers were close, hollering in enmity at the members of the Light in their domain.

The company's ragged breaths strained as they were exhausted from fighting and fleeing, but finally, they came to the city's edge.

An underground lake prevented their passage, a broken stone bridge in pieces atop. The sunlight doused exit rested atop another set of stairs on the opposite side of the lake. Gruns and crags drew nearer on their heels, and the rumbling of their charging feet startled them all.

The group stopped at the lip of the body of water. Before they could decide whether or not to swim, Falin breathed deeply and felt the lake as an extension of himself. He raised his staff, and the water parted, giving them a path to retreat. As they ran, Falin struggled to both run and keep the water separated. His arm trembled from the weight of the water, testing his new powers. They sprinted between the watery walls, their assailants too afraid to follow. Once across, Falin released the water, and it slammed together, sloshing within the lake.

The horde of enemies stood on the opposite side, some beginning to wade into the shallows to continue the hunt. Others ran around the edge to keep attacking.

All but Falin climbed the steps to the exit. The young wizard stood at the edge of the water as gruns and crags rushed around the lake. He knew the enemies would not halt upon his group's exit of the Mortal Mountains.

"Falin!" Melquin called from above at the cave's entrance. "Falin!"

As the horde circled, he swept his staff, forcing an enormous wave to crash across every edge of the lake. Falin slammed it onto their heads, cleansing the bank of their enemies. Gruns and crags were thrown into stone, others sucked into the water, struggling to keep their heads above the wavy surface. The remaining faction stood on the opposite side of the lake, and Falin swooped his staff, lifting the entirety of the body of water. It caused him much strain, but he cared not, for he was protecting his Champions.

He cast the lake at their chasers, flooding Isetta with a tide of massive proportions. The enemies were swept away, sent barreling over the stone, slamming into the rock buildings of ancient elves. Those lucky enough to survive the aquarian assault fled, desperate to be reprieved of Falin's wrath. Falin turned, running up the steps to his Champions.

They ran through the tunnel, quickly finding themselves outside of the Mortal Mountains, squinting in the overwhelming sunlight. They blinked and rubbed their watery eyes, panting, falling to the ground in exhaustion. Giant Jimbuah took guard at the cave's mouth, but there would be no need to fight further. Falin's arm was covered in blood, and he looked to the rest to see they all held comparable wounds.

"Is everyone alright?" he asked. His Champions nodded in dishevelment, gasping. Melquin went to Red, wasting no time to begin mending a gash on his leg.

Falin examined the landscape, finding a forest like nothing he'd seen before. The trees were gnarly, and the hoots of birds and other animals spoke in strange accents he struggled to understand. Branches were long and wiry, hanging like vines. The ground was damp, covered in moss. "Where are we?" he asked.

Red rubbed his wound that Melquin mended. He lifted his hat to better scan the space. "These are the Marrow Swamps. We are in Suntalla, Kingdom of Beasts."

CHAPTER TEN:
DISMAL DELAYS

Falin and company trudged the mucky terrain for a fifth day, on guard in Suntalla's unforgiving Marrow Swamps. Their paths were limited, often mere trails of mud straddled by murky water brimming with dangerous wildlife. Vines of oily leaves hung above, the trees making home in the water, with twisted roots covering the earth. Thumb-sized bugs sought to feast on their skin, quickly swatted away in their buzzing approach. The swamp often belched air bubbles, signifying creatures lurking beneath the surface.

They stopped at a patch of dry land bordered by stagnant water, and Bossador said, "May we take a moment's rest? This air is a struggle to breathe."

Falin was weary as well. "Yes. Everyone take a moment to sit and eat our rations. What is left of them."

Bossador sat on a jagged stump bordering the water and removed his boots. He wiggled his blister-covered toes. "I envy Princess Bloom. What a lovely thing it must be to have a dragon fly at your command."

"I don't know that Bjorgun would let anyone ride on his back," Red muttered. He scratched the scruff on his face. "She is special. Bjorgun sees that."

Melquin struggled to re-braid her hair, as it was abnormally frizzy from the muggy weather. "It seems that more than Bjorgun finds her special."

Red peered at the sage from underneath his brim. "Nothin' came of it."

"Nothing came of it *yet*," Nym corrected. "Something tells me you two will cross paths again."

Carthon chuckled. "When Red happens to make a trip to the Ruins of Darva on a whim."

Jimbuah clasped his hands to his cheek like a faerie-tale princess and batted his eyelashes. "Oh, Red! Red! 'Tis an ho-nor! Tra la la!"

Red grinned at his partner's impersonation of the princess. "You're a master of mimicry."

"It would be a wonderful love story," Bossador thought aloud. "An outlaw Freelander made prince to the princess of a Freeland Kingdom. You didn't even have to fight a dragon! Just befriend him!"

Amused at the thought, Red cocked an eyebrow and shook his head. "I'm not sure King Pernicus will want me as the next King of Rorkshire, even if Bloom's runnin' the show. Not sure she'd want that either, come to think of it."

"You never know," Melquin argued in a sing-song tone. "She seemed quite eager to spend time with you in Darva. I've never seen a girl so thrilled to skin a cow."

"King Redrick!" Nym exclaimed. "Ruler of Rorkshire. Enemies cower by the crack of his royal whip!"

Bossador laughed heartily, slapping his knee. "And King Redrick shall cower at the crack of Bloom's!" They snickered at Red's expense.

Falin noticed the water bubble behind Bossador. Sensing something large about to break the surface, the wizard yelled, "Bossador! Look out!"

Bossador jumped barefoot from the stump and raised his sword. A gargantuan snake sprang from the swamp and towered over them, hissing with fangs bared. It stood as high as the trees, with a torso wider than their trunks, fixated on Bossador, swaying its head seeking an opportunity to strike. Falin moved to thrust it away by commanding the water, but instead, a second explosion of swamp muck drenched the shores.

A gator of comparable size jumped from the depths and snapped its massive jaws around the serpent's body. The snake violently hissed, turning its attention to the gator. The beasts thrashed, the gator refusing to let go of the snake, the snake spiraling its body around the foe. The group ran further into the swamp, uninterested in the quarrel's outcome.

As the commotion died off with its loser, they paused to rest. Bossador carried his sword in one hand and his boots in another. His shield slung loosely from his back as he gulped air. "I would've killed the snake if the gator gave me a chance."

Red rested with palms upon his knees, curling his lip. "Maybe if it choked on you." Exasperated laughs escaped Carthon and Bossador at the comment.

They moved on, startled each instance the water bubbled. As the sun began to descend to the hidden horizon, they made camp in a clearing distant from the swamp waters. Gathering enough dry firewood proved tasking, but in time, they huddled by the flames, eating fish Jimbuah caught barehanded and roots foraged by Melquin.

"These fish taste like mud," Nym sighed. "We haven't had a real meal since Darva. I hope we can find something better soon."

Red picked a scale from his teeth. "It ain't that bad. But if we're lucky, we'll come across a village in these swamps. If they're nice, they might give us some grub."

"There are villages here? In Suntalla?" Falin asked. "I assumed none inhabited the place. Hence the name, Kingdom of Beasts."

Red shrugged. "Animals still live in kingdoms of people. It's just that in these parts, beasts are runnin' the show. Jimmy and I have come across a few tribes southeast of here who are mostly friendly."

Carthon swatted a bug on his neck. "I am very much ready to be in Letani. Or any kingdom free of swarming insects."

"We should begin heading southwest as we can," Bossador said. "Is their capital not closer to the coast?"

"It is," Carthon confirmed. "And if the charts I've read in the past are correct, we should come to easier terrain if we head southwest. More open plains."

"What is southeast?" Melquin asked.

"Jujinglos," Jimbuah replied softly.

"Jungles," Red translated with his head down.

Falin noticed a change in their air, but did not know why. He sensed their hesitancy in Letani's mention, as they'd been outspoken about avoiding the kingdom.

"I am ready for a fine bed and warm meal," Bossador continued. "And if Letani food is half as good as what I've been told, we may need more than one horse to carry me through the Wildbarrens."

"I'm going to take a bath every night," Nym dreamed. "And soak the guck of this swamp off of me."

Red appeared sick, and Jimbuah frowned in fear. "We can't go to Letani," Red announced suddenly.

Carthon shook his head, not understanding. "And why not? Why are you so resistant to the kingdom?"

Red took a deep breath and glanced at Jimbuah with dismay. "We're fugitives of Letani. We're wanted by their king." Jimbuah's eyes scanned the group in fear of their reactions.

A dismal tone struck them. Melquin frowned, subduing her temper. "You are joking."

"No," Red said somberly, shaking his head. "I wish we were. It's why we were forced to travel into the Wildbarrens. We were chased there by Letani soldiers."

Bossador scoffed and threw his remaining piece of fish to the ground in disgust. "And you wait until *now* to tell us this?!"

"We didn't think it mattered until now. Which it didn't. So we waited until the time was right."

Nym crossed her arms. "Of course it mattered. We would have been able to prepare better if we're not going to safety."

Falin was disappointed in the duo, but kept silent, letting the Champions work through the problem themselves.

Red nodded respectfully. "I understand, but—"

"I *don't* think you do understand," Melquin scolded. "This journey is not one of survival for *you*. Or us. It is one of survival for him," she said, pointing at Falin. "And because you lied about Letani, you have jeopardized the potential balance of the Light for all of Elsana!" Her statement hung in the air a moment.

Bossador waved a bug away from his ear and glowered. "Now what? We are supposed to gleefully traipse into the jungles of Suntalla?"

Jimbuah looked to Bossador and spoke meekly. "Safari."

Bossador's eyes bulged and he growled, "You think *now* is a time to jest?!"

Red came to Jimbuah's defense as the skully retracted. "He said he was sorry. Safari means 'I'm sorry' in Skully." He paused. "We're sorry. We are."

Jimbuah repeated the sentiment. "Safari."

Carthon sneered. "Is there a part of this world you two have not been dregs to society?" Jimbuah bent his head in shame. Red scowled at the drak but kept silent.

"Alright," Falin said. He leaned on his staff to stand. "They have admitted their wrongdoing. There is no need for added insult." He paused for a moment, pitying Red and Jimbuah. He remembered Airo's words in the ceremony of Champions. They were two individuals mistreated by the world, doing all they could to survive. "We will travel into the jungle around Letani. They have been there before, they will guide us."

Carthon looked away and mumbled, "We should make them face their judgment in Letani."

Bossador nodded in agreement. "It is the honorable thing to do."

This struck a nerve with Falin, and he stomped to the drak and madorian, pounding his staff to the ground. The earth around them rattled, causing swamp waves to lap at root-filled shores. "You disappoint me," he said through clenched teeth. Carthon and Bossador leaned back in the imposing presence of the young wizard, who suddenly loomed taller than before, carrying a voice akin to distant thunder. "All of you," he said to the Champions of the Crown. "You forget, we accepted these two as prisoners, who asked for nothing more than a *home*. They could have fled on any given night in search of safety, yet where do they sit? By our side. I saw no hesitation when they faced blood draks in the Oldwoods." He turned to Melquin. "Nor did they hesitate to run to the depths of the earth to save you from a ghoul. Nor do I remember any complaints when Jimbuah saved us from a horde of gruns and crags in Isetta!" He continued scolding them. "Yet the moment you are robbed of a soft bed and warm meal by their past mistakes, you are eager to abandon them! You should be ashamed."

The Champions of the Crown hung their heads, realizing the misstep in their frustration. Bossador guiltily looked to Red and Jimbuah, considering his following words. "Safari."

"We apologize," Carthon agreed. "We spoke from anger."

Red nodded and replied softly. "It's alright. I get it."

Melquin glanced between Falin and the Letani outlaws, unsure if she should ask the question pressing her. "What did you two do? To become fugitives?" Falin sat back down to hear the response.

Red cleared his throat, speaking gently. "Well, Jimbuah and I were in a pretty desperate time. We had just hitched a ride down the coast into Letani by a few merchants. So we get into Letani's capital, and there's all these shops and food stands, and traders of all sorts of goods. At this point, we're looking for handouts or for work that can get us some scraps." He sighed. "Anyway, we come across this back-alley merchant who needs us to run some livestock to the southern border. Anyone here ever seen a hipobara?" Red asked.

Nym shook her head. "I've never even heard of that."

He stretched his arms into a circle. "It's this giant fat rodent. Got to be the size of a cow, but it's a rare animal to come by, so it's largely considered a delicacy there. And we had the fattest of the fat hipobaras, didn't we Jimmy?"

"Yekasa," Jimbuah confirmed sadly.

"This thing was huge," Red said. "We had it tucked into a wagon covered on all sides, with holes so it could breathe. Well, as it turns out, this hipobara was being sold on the black market."

"Is it illegal to eat hipobaras in Letani?" Falin asked.

"Nofa," Jimbuah answered.

"But this one was," Red explained. "As we're leaving the capital, we notice all the wagons are getting stopped and searched by soldiers." He shook his head and stared at the fire, replaying the memory in his mind. "Turns out this thing was stolen from the royal grounds, and was the personal favorite pet of the Yopa, King of Letani."

Carthon rubbed his eyes, groaning, "By Washborn's blade, tell me you weren't caught."

"Oh yeah," Red replied. "By the time we figured out what was going on, we're surrounded by soldiers and knee deep in trouble. We were able to unhitch the wagon, and Jimmy tossed a couple fireberries to scare off the soldiers. Then we took off. They chased us all the way to the Wildbarrens for transgressions against the King. Last we've heard, we're still wanted."

Falin closed his eyes, then began to laugh, shaking his head. "Over a hipobara."

Red pursed his lips and nodded. "A hipobara. One extra fat, extra royal hipobara. Sent us into one of the worst places in this world."

"Alright," Falin said. "We will turn our course for the jungles of Suntalla tomorrow. Everyone sleep."

"I can take first watch," Red offered. "Jimmy'll take second."

"Thank you," Falin answered.

The night went without event, and aside from the occasional splash in the swamp, they slept soundly. Come morning, the group took course southeast, headed for the jungles. They were quiet, as they were tired and hungry from their hike, and there remained an awkwardness from the previous night's confrontation.

Falin wished to exit the swamp as soon as they could, sensing a dark aura within it. It was not a happy place, but one of glum atmosphere by nature. He thought of the Oldwoods and his aspirations to cleanse it. The Marrow Swamps did not seem to be a place ready to be purged. In time, solid earth became more abundant than water, allowing them to move freely.

Red stopped abruptly on their path, gazing up at a tree. Falin followed his eye but could see nothing. "What is it, Red?" the wizard asked.

The Freelander pointed to a low branch, and Falin saw wooden chimes camouflaged by its color. "We are near a village," Red replied. He turned to the group. "Do not draw your weapons. They will take it as a sign to fight. Be kind and soft-spoken. If we speak their tongue, it will be easier. If not, we must be very sensitive in how we gesture and carry ourselves."

They continued on the path, keeping a cautious eye to the surrounding brush, and soon the trail opened, and forty or so wooden huts were scattered in a clearing. Red stopped at the edge of the site and placed his hand to the handle of his whip.

"I thought you said no weapons," Carthon muttered.

Red scanned the horizon with concern. "I did. But something isn't right. It's too quiet."

Melquin stepped forward and examined the village. "There was death here. Can you sense it?" she asked Falin.

Falin nodded. It was evident. The turmoil resonated into his being. A dark tinge covered the space, and sadness crept over him. There had been pain here recently. "We should proceed with caution."

Their footsteps softened as they approached. An eerie vibe set upon them. Even the animals were quieter in this part of the swamp. Falin examined the first group of huts. One to his left held a dried, smeared handprint of blood. Broken wooden spears were scattered on the ground, also stained by violence. There had been a massacre in this place.

"Where are the bodies?" Nym whispered.

Falin shook his head. "They are gone. Could animals have eaten them?"

Red crouched and picked up a broken piece of pottery, examining the dried blood. "This is hardly a day old." He turned to the group. "Why were they fighting with broken bits of jars?"

"Maybe they were attacked? From a neighboring village?" Bossador proposed.

"But then where are the bodies?" Carthon asked.

The Freelander took a deep breath and stood. "Maybe the attacking village has some sort of ritual with the enemy's dead. The rest are taken prisoner. I've seen weirder things happen."

Falin was unconvinced. He walked further into the encampment, and they found more signs of bloodshed, parts of huts broken from attacking hands. He looked at the dirt and saw no indication of bodies being dragged away. There were only footsteps from a scuffle. "It is strange." A chill ran through him despite the humid air. "I don't wish to linger here longer than we have to. Search some of the nearby huts for food, then let's make our way out." The Champions did as told, filling their bags with the stores of the missing villagers. Falin made a mental note to offer thanks to those who provided them food in their absence.

As Falin waited for the group to finish their search, a black bird landed on the edge of one of the huts. It cocked his head to examine the wizard. Falin wondered if he would be able to communicate with the exotic bird. "Have you come here before?"

"Yes," the bird squawked in a strange accent.

Falin grew nervous. "Where are all the people?"

"Dead."

He twirled his staff in thought. "Who killed them?"

"They did."

"Who is they?" Falin asked.

"Them," it answered.

Anxiousness spilled over the wizard upon learning an un-known, murder-hungry enemy lurked in the swamp. "And they took the dead with them?"

"No."

Falin grew confused. "Then where are the bodies?"

"Dead." The bird took flight over the trees before it could offer Falin any further explanation.

An unsettling fear shrouded Falin, and he turned, jumping in fright as he saw Jimbuah standing behind him unexpectedly. Falin held his thumping heart. "Jimmy! Oh, you scared the Light out of me!"

"Safari," Jimbuah apologized, holding up his hand, offering some dried, red berries he'd found. "Ibata?"

Falin was unsure what the mysterious food would do to him, but he was too hungry to care. He took a couple and tossed them into his mouth, wincing at the sour taste. "You like these?"

Jimbuah shrugged, shoving the remaining fruit past his lips and chewing. "Beh."

"Over here!" they heard Bossador yell from a hut. They darted in his direction, and he stood at the threshold with his hands raised. Falin turned to the corner where a young woman no older than himself held a sharp stick in defense, backed to the wall of her home. "It's alright. We're not here to hurt you," Bossador promised.

Despite his assurances, the young woman remained frightened, more so as the group gathered at the door of the hut. "Babaka! Babaka!" she threatened.

The tribeswoman was of tan skin, slightly darker than Melquin's, her black hair in disarray and matted with blood. She wore garb torn at her stomach, and a bloody cut covered her forearm. Her hand quivered so much, she was barely able to hold her makeshift weapon.

Melquin nudged past Bossador and raised her hands to show she meant no harm. Still, the woman held her stick at the ready. "Babaka! Babaka kutilmo!"

The sage slowly stepped forward into the hut, not breaking eye contact with the frantic young woman. "It's alright," she assured. The tribal survivor began to calm in Melquin's presence. Carefully, Melquin reached for the woman's arm. The woman yanked her hand away and pressed herself to the wall. With a confident, gentle motion, Melquin pulled the injured arm back. She muttered an incantation, and the wound began to close.

"Can you speak our tongue?" Melquin asked. "Do you know our language?"

The woman looked to Melquin, not understanding, her eyes welling in fear. Melquin put her arm around the woman. She began to shake and sob, clutching Melquin like a child. "I know," the sage soothed. "I know. I am sorry for what happened here."

Melquin stroked the woman's back, resting her chin atop her head. For a while, the woman wailed. The Champions watched in respectful silence, until finally, her sobbing slowed. She sniffed and looked to Melquin with pleading eyes, as if asking for what she witnessed to be undone.

Melquin took the woman's hand and pressed it to her chest. "Melquin. Melquin," she said. The sage then took the woman's hand then pressed it to her, but she didn't respond. Melquin took the woman's palm and pressed it to herself again, saying, "Melquin," then returned the tribeswoman's hand to her own chest.

The woman's chin trembled, and she timidly answered, "Tula."

"Tula," Melquin nodded, offering an assuring smile. "Tula," she repeated.

Tula glanced nervously at the group, staring at her from the hut door. Melquin turned to them. "We need to take her from this place. I don't know where we'll go, but she can't stay here."

Nobody argued. Falin pitied Tula, and hoped they could offer her safe passage to another welcoming village. Carthon eyed the villager, then said, "I walked the perimeter after searching for food. It is odd. I saw no signs of anyone attacking from outside."

"They are definitely dead," Falin said. "A bird just told me."

Bossador thought on it. "Did it say who killed them?"

Falin shook his head. "He said it was 'them' whoever that is." Tula listened to what they spoke, wondering what it meant for her. "Did everyone find food that will get us through the next few days?" All nodded. "Good. Let's leave. I feel sick in this place."

Melquin placed a hand around Tula's shoulders. "Come," she said in as docile a tone as possible. "Come with us."

Falin and company walked ahead of them, offering Tula and Melquin space, and slowly, Tula exited the village with Melquin's arm around her. She took a final look behind, weeping once more. Melquin continued to comfort the woman, and they moved on.

For the remainder of the day, they hiked through the swamps without indication of a hidden enemy. Their pace was lethargic, as they were wary, vigilant, and eager to find a space where they could make safe camp. In time, they observed a patch of land that seemed promising. Their mood was dismal, and they spoke little, in part not to alienate the woman new to their group.

"What happens if we can't find a tribe to leave her with?" Carthon asked in a low tone. He stared into the flames of their campfire in thought. "We cannot take her with us. It is too dangerous."

Red nibbled a piece of dried meat from their stores. "Chances are we'll come across another one. Or signs of one. Worst case scenario we'll leave her with the stonies."

"Even if we find another tribe, how do we know they will speak her language?" Nym asked. The elf sat cross-legged on the ground. "They seem so isolated from one another."

"From past experience, I think they're just speaking different dialects. If we find a nearby tribe, she'll be fine," Red replied.

Tula sat closest to Melquin, near clinging to the sage through their day of travel. She listened to them speak, but said nothing. Falin could see the constant fear in her eyes, with underlying heartache from whatever massacre she witnessed. Each time a twig snapped or some swamp water would splash, her head would jerk in the direction of the noise, terrified it would be some mysterious enemy skulking in the night.

Melquin insisted Tula take a few pieces of dried fruit to eat. "Eat," she pressed. "They are from your people."

Tula cautiously looked to the little purple berries and accepted them, chewing in somber silence. Falin examined the gash on her forearm, still bright red even after Melquin's healing. "That must've been a deep wound to still look so bad," Falin said.

"It was deep," the sage answered. "It will likely scar."

Tula's eyes struggled to stay open, exhausted from being on guard since the attack on her village. Melquin shuffled closer to her, placing her arm around the woman. "Sleep," she said. Tula did not understand and looked to her, heavy-lidded. Melquin placed a bag upon her lap, motioning the woman rest her head there. "Sleep," she said again. Tula nervously gazed around the fire, resigning to slumber. The villager laid down, and after a few blinks, quickly drifted off. They kept silent for a few moments to ensure she was deep in rest.

Melquin peered down at Tula. "This poor thing," she whispered. "I cannot imagine what she witnessed."

"Some horrendous and barbaric villainy, no doubt," Bossador said. "We should be careful as we proceed through these swamps. It must have been a fearsome enemy to accomplish such a horrid feat in that village." He turned to Jimbuah, his eyes landing on the skully's staff. "I assume you will not be able to grow large as you had before."

Jimbuah shook his head. "Nofa. Grofa tijami."

"It's going to take some time to grow back," Red translated. "His fireberries grow back pretty quick, but that fruit... What do you call it, Jimmy?"

"Wumbapo."

"That just fits," Red thought aloud. "Anyway, the wumbapo fruit will take at least a few months to grow."

Falin examined the bushel and wondered what magic hid inside. "Is that the most powerful one you have?"

The skully looked to his staff and considered it. "Nofa."

Soon, the group became as tired as Tula, and slept with Nym volunteering for first watch. Come morning, they returned to traveling through the swamps.

For four days they trekked, and little by little, the swamp lessened, and solid ground came in abundance. Tula became comfortable within their group, unafraid in their presence. When in search of food, the tribeswoman would opt to depart with Melquin, showing great skill in foraging for edible items to sustain them in their journey.

Following one of their excursions, she returned to the camp, and Falin noticed a change in Tula's demeanor. She displayed the tiniest bit of happiness, not showcased in the form of a smile, but her lack of frown. Tula and Melquin returned from the brush, each with an arm full of small red-orange fruits, the size of plums.

"Look what Tula found," Melquin announced. They approached, and Melquin lifted her arm of produce. "They're delicious."

Tula walked to Falin and gestured he take one. Falin was unsure what constituted a ripe version of the mysterious fruit, so he picked one at random. To his surprise, it was incredibly sweet, like a candied good made by the hands of a sage. A small grin peeked on Tula's face upon seeing his reaction. Falin nodded and smiled. "It is very good, very good."

Tula insisted the rest partake. Soon, all devoured the delectable treat, Tula included. "They're so sweet," Nym said.

Carthon nodded in agreement. "Almost as good as meat."

Nym smirked as a juice trickled down her chin. "That's saying a lot, coming from you."

The drak grinned and wiped the juice from her face with a flick of his finger. Nym hid a bashful smile and looked away. Hungry from their day of hiking, they quickly delved into the foraged meal, ending with a pile of pits.

"What are these called?" Melquin asked, holding up a pit and pointing. Tula furrowed her brow, not understanding. Melquin gestured to herself. "Melquin." She pointed to Tula. "Tula." Next, she pointed to the fruit and waited.

An expression of recognition crossed Tula's face. "Cheppa."

Melquin turned to the pit and examined it, nibbling a piece that hung off. "Cheppa," she repeated. "Candy of the Marrow Swamps."

Falin lifted his head to look through the leaves of the tree, seeing the sun indicate it was only early afternoon. He breathed deeply and said, "As much as I would love to laze, we should keep going. We're nearing the end of the swamp by the looks of it." He turned to Red for confirmation.

"Yeah," Red said, scanning the trees. "It ain't gonna happen all at once, but before we know it, we'll be in the jungle. Maybe another day or two of traveling."

"What's safer, the swamp or the jungle?" Bossador asked.

Red squinted an eye and thought on it. "What's safer, a giant snake or a giant gator?"

Bossador breathed sharply from his nose. "Fair point."

They departed southeast, eager to change the scenery. Dusk took hold of the day, cooling the air and greying the sky. As the air chilled, a fog set upon the edge of the swamp, making it challenging to see farther than a stone's throw.

They halted at a clearing, its earth solid, and in the center, a large overturned tree. "We should camp here," Falin said. "The fog will make it too difficult to travel as it becomes dark."

Sitting around their fire, Falin readjusted the way he rested on the hardened ground, once again missing the soft moss of the Oldwoods. He thought of Boschi, Spirit of the Oldwoods, wondering if there was a similar spirit of the Marrow Swamps. Likely a glum, dismal creature, Falin thought. He imagined returning to the Oldwoods as Boschi had asked of him, remembering the prophecy pertaining to the Warrior of the Light. He was eager to set out on this task, but felt so far from it having only gathered one of the Gems.

His attention was drawn from thought as a whisper crossed their camp. He raised his head and scanned the group, all in their own focus. "Did someone say something?"

Red lifted his head and frowned, shaking his head. "I didn't hear anything. Might've been Bossador. He mutters to himself when he gets tired."

Bossador furrowed his brow. "If I am tired, it's because I've been walking through this bug infested swamp to amble into a bug infested jungle." He cast Red a stink-eye.

It was then Falin heard the whisper again, but before he could speak, Red did. "Do you have something you want to say to me, your highness?"

"It has been said plenty," Carthon sneered. "We are stuck walking through the depths of Suntalla because of you and your skully's idiocy."

Red leapt up. "You'd best watch the way you're talking to us, blood-sipper."

Bossador stood, placing his hand on the hilt of his sword. "It'd be best for you to sit down, Freelander. You are acting as an aggressor to a member of the Crown."

Carthon curled his lip. "I don't need your intervention, madorian. Know your place."

Falin moved to settle them, shocked to find them so quickly aggressive, but Bossador's voice boomed instead. "I am sick of your insolence, drak! I am the prince of Rodrellan! You will respect me, or I will beat it from your lips."

Carthon hissed. He removed his swords in preparation to fight, and Bossador retrieved his greatsword, each blade making a shimmering sound of violence. Nym stood and held a star. "You will find your throat bloody the moment you lay your crag-fingers on him."

Falin stood and raised his hands. "Enough!" he hollered. They ignored him.

"Shut that little mouth of yours and stay out of it, Nym," Red demanded. "Before I close it for you."

Carthon hissed louder this time and repositioned his stance to better face both Red and Bossador. "I will empty your guts the second you move towards her, thief."

Jimbuah stood and spoke with malice previously unseen on the amicable skully. "Smakushu yukari fatisu!" he snarled.

"You are scaring, Tula!" Melquin exclaimed. Falin turned to see the villager hiding behind Melquin. The sage stood with her staff in protection.

"She is no more a pet to you than was the rabbit of the Old-woods," Nym replied.

"Do not blame me we came across her," Melquin answered. "Blame Red and Jimbuah for making us come this way in the swamp!"

"She's right," Bossador agreed. "We should have at least left Red with Princess Bloom. This way, it would be her disappointed with his company instead of us."

Red raised his whip, smoldering. "Speaking of her like that again and die."

Bossador readied his sword. "Fitting a peasant would die for a peasant princess."

As all prepared moved to take their first blow, Falin swept his staff, and in a wave of magic, knocked them to the ground. All groaned from hitting the rocky earth, and Falin struggled to comprehend why they suddenly became so savage with one another. It was then he sensed the overwhelming dread he experienced once before in the Ruins of Darva; a dread signaling the presence of his antithesis. He became furious.

"Show yourselves!" Falin demanded, twisting his neck to all sides of the foggy clearing. His Champions did the same, rubbing their heads as if waking from unconsciousness.

From each side of the mist-ridden edges of the clearing, three warlocks glided into the camp. Two appeared older and of white hair, but the third seemed not much older than Falin. They wore robes that were billowy and black.

Before the Champions and Falin could fight, the younger warlock raised a wand of bone and tossed the weapons from their hands.

One of the elder warlocks spoke in a high, crotchety voice, and Falin recognized him as Mulgus. "How lucky are we to stumble upon a young wizard," Mulgus taunted. He strode to Falin, his long, stringy white hair floating in the air. Even beneath the black robes, one could see his frame was scrawny and emaciated. His yellow smile sat above a pointy, crooked chin. "You are Falin, I presume? I am Mulgus the Plague."

Falin did not speak, but instead glanced at his Champions to ensure they were alright. They trembled in the presence of the Dark servants. Mulgus squinted and stood so close to Falin their noses nearly touched. He sniffed. "Were you in the Ruins of Darva recently?"

Falin thought on it, and seeing no need to lie, admitted, "Yes. We heard you as we explored one of Darva's temples."

Mulgus turned swiftly to the other, older warlock. "I told you, Nyril! I told you I sensed them!"

Nyril the Coercer raised his chin, his white hair and beard fuller than his counterpart, pruned and clean. Despite being older than Mulgus, he appeared younger, his skin less cracked and his posture and broad frame impeccable. His voice was low, with a rich timbre. "What of it? We have them now."

Mulgus refocused on Falin, scanning the young wizard's face with contempt. "We should kill him. All of them. They should suffer. They are of the Light."

Nyril placed his hands behind his back and examined the group with indifference. "Killing them may antagonize the wizard swine. We have greater plans to attend to."

Mulgus' lip twitched in subdued revulsion. "One less wizard helps our plan."

"What plan?" Falin asked.

A gurgling hiss escaped Mulgus, and he clasped Falin's chin, pressing his wand of bone against the wizard's throat. "You mind your place wizard. I will offer you a thousand years of torment if I wish."

The younger warlock stepped forward, his hair sandy brown, near hanging over his eyes. His pale face showed no emotion. "You cannot kill him. You must let him continue with his quest."

"Why, Silas?!" Mulgus rasped through clenched teeth. Saliva spat from his lips. "You never give me reasons."

Silas' eyes closed and his lips trembled for a moment, his mind gone elsewhere. His eyelids fluttered, and he slowly turning to Falin. "His survival will bring your plan to success. It is what I have seen."

Mulgus' gaze flipped between Silas and Falin, still unconvinced. "You never tell me *what* you see in your clairvoyance. What is it? How could letting him live provide any use to me?"

"Us," Nyril corrected. "Silas has steered us right for some time now. We must trust his judgment."

Mulgus looked over his shoulder at Nyril and then to Silas, still pressing his wand to Falin's neck. "And what about them?" he motioned his head to the Champions. "Can we kill his animals?"

Silas shook his head. "Leave the Champions be." His head tilted slowly, and his gaze fell to Tula. "Who is the villager?" His eyes shifted to Falin.

In the instant their eyes locked, Falin felt a significant purpose in meeting Silas. "She is a woman we have taken in. Her people were attacked by another village. She was the sole survivor."

Mulgus looked to Tula then back to Falin, his chuckle forming into an unnerving cackle. He released Falin and backed away. "I see. Did you hear, Nyril? A tale of warring villages."

Nyril, appearing less amused than Mulgus, stepped forward. His stature was imposing, and he showed little interest in games. "I have heard whispers Airo the Bane is your mentor, Falin. Is this true?" Falin nodded, raising his chin to show he was unafraid despite the fear that gripped him. "Mulgus and I had a run-in with Airo in the Oldwoods."

"He told us," Falin said. "We crossed paths on the road south."

Nyril nodded in thought. "I hate wizards, Falin, as you feel the innate need to hate us. But I have always respected Airo the Bane. He is of a great power."

"He is," Falin agreed. The sense of dread he felt seemed to dissolve. Nyril held a hidden kindness to him. His voice was deep and crisp, soothing as warm honey.

"I always thought the tradition of the wizards and their Champions was a silly one," Nyril thought aloud. "Aren't wizards supposed to protect members of the Light? Not thrust them into danger?"

Falin thought on it. "There is symbolism in it. A harmony between the creatures of the Light and the wizards."

"I suppose," Nyril considered. "Do you feel they are like your children? These people here?"

"I do," Falin admitted. "I love them all. And I am and honored to have them with me on this journey."

Nyril showed a smile of genuine altruism, one akin to Airo's. "It is a wonderful thing to see a creature of Elsana true to their own kind. After all, we are all one with Elsana, whether it be Light or Dark. Are we not Falin?"

"We are," Falin agreed. He'd never thought of it that way.

Nyril stroked his silky beard and scanned the Champions. "Though it is odd. I do not remember any legends of a Freelander and a skully acting as Champions."

Silas spoke for Falin. "They were chosen as guides," he explained. "I saw them part of Falin's group in a dream once."

"And where did you see them?" Nyril asked.

"The Wildbarrens."

"Ah!" Nyril said, raising his eyebrows and crossing his arms. "You go to the Wildbarrens? You must take good care of your Champions there Falin. It is a dangerous place, especially for those of the Light."

Falin nodded obediently. "I will."

Nyril looked to the group again. "But the Wildbarrens are no place for a villager of the Marrow Swamps," he stated of Tula. "And no other tribe will take her in."

"We thought we could leave her in the Stony Valley. With the stonies."

Nyril let out a small gasp. "Well I should hope not! She would certainly perish there! So far from her element and peoples."

It made sense to Falin. "Then what do you recommend I do with her?"

Turning Falin away with a gentle arm, the warlock spoke in a low tone so that the Champions could not hear, offering his counsel. "Falin, there are times in any wizard's or warlock's life where he must make difficult decisions. Do you care for your Champions?"

"Of course," Falin answered. "Like my children."

"Then you must see this tribeswoman is a burden on your children. Sharing food, leaving you vulnerable to attack. You can see this, right?"

"I can," Falin nodded.

"Then you must do what is right by your children. You must put this woman from her misery. Not because you want to, but it is because you wish to do what is right for your Champions." Nyril waved his wand of sharpened bone, and Falin's staff flew into his hand. "Here," he said, handing Falin his weapon. "So she doesn't suffer."

"Thank you," Falin replied, gripping his staff and looking to Tula. She cowered by Melquin and peered at the wizard with frightened eyes. He stepped forward, then a boulder of logic smacked him. He shook his head. "Wait, I will not kill this woman!" Falin pointed his staff at the warlock. "Your Dark magic will not work on me!"

Nyril chuckled and glanced at the head of Falin's staff. "Lower your weapon. You are three Gems and several centuries short of practice from being a threat to me." He paced away from Falin and took a deep breath. "I have coerced common men and women, madorians, draks, sages, and elves. Skullies, stonies, and even a couple dragons. I have yet to ever coerce a wizard, however, but tonight, I came close. Honestly, you shocked me, Falin. I didn't think I would get as far as I did."

"You would have this woman killed for the mere trophy of coercing a wizard?" Falin asked, appalled.

Nyril looked to Tula, and a subtle expression of disdain crossed his face. "She is the sole representation of messy work on my part," the warlock replied.

Falin cocked his head, not understanding at first, then realizing what Nyril meant. "You killed the village we found Tula in," he accused.

Clicking his tongue, Nyril considered it. "Yes and no. I prompted them, as I prompted your friends here to fight moments ago. I willed them to kill one another, but never raised a finger."

"Blood on the hands of a servant stains the palms of a master," Falin retorted.

Nyril smirked and breathed sharply from his nose. "You are wise, young wizard."

"But why?" Falin asked. "Why do something to such innocent people? They are not even of the Light. They are Elsana's children."

"Much like a blade, the powers of magic must be kept sharp, and much like the wielder of said blade, magic's wielder must be kept practiced."

Falin felt winded hearing the village was killed for mere practice. "And what of the bodies? Why were there no bodies?"

Nyril raised an eyebrow, turning to his counterpart. "Care to show them?"

Mulgus beamed hideously and waved his wand in the air. In less than a moment, the noises of awkward footsteps crashing through the brush met their ears. At the edge of the fog, the shapes of people limped into the site, eighty or so individuals circling the group. Tula screamed, clutching her heart.

Falin's blood turned cold. At first glance in the dim lighting, one could see that these people were villagers akin to Tula, with similar features, now with blank faces and drooping eyelids. Upon closer inspection, to his stunned horror, Falin saw that they were dead.

Their lips were blue, and skin drawn. All had some form of mortal wound, whether it be their throats slashed, a knife in their back, or a spearhead in their stomach. Their arms hung limp and they stared straight ahead. Falin and the Champions sickened as Tula wailed. Melquin struggled between comforting the woman and staring at the dead with ghastly awe.

Falin became short of breath. "What is this?"

Mulgus the Plague cackled. "You innocent creature of Light, have you never heard of necromancy?"

Tula shrieked in seeing her loved ones in such a state. Falin gulped and examined the soulless eyes of the villagers, their mouths slightly agape. "Y—you control the dead?"

"I can," Mulgus confirmed. He rolled his eyes at the wailing Tula. "Though it seems my set is incomplete." With a quick flick of his wand, Tula's body jerked and she fell limp to the ground.

Melquin screamed, lunging for Tula's body. "No!" The sage pawed at Tula, finding no signs of life. She muttered incantations between sobbing gasps, but they did nothing. Gently, Bossador pried Melquin from Tula's corpse and held her.

Like a dog being served a meal, Mulgus stalked to the body and licked his lips, twirling his wand with unblinking, wide eyes. Tula's fingers twitched, and her eyes fluttered. Slowly, the dead villager stood, half-lidded and emotionless. She hobbled to file in rank with her tribe. Melquin wept, burying her head into Bossador's chest.

It ached Falin's soul to know such evil existed in this world. He felt as though he was finally coming to understand the tasks ahead of him in his life as a wizard. "Why?" Falin asked. "Why do this?"

"Because young wizard," Mulgus explained, "controlling the living is as much fun as controlling the dead."

Falin shook his head. "I still don't understand. *Why?*"

Mulgus looked to Falin as if he were stupid. "Life is merely half of our existence. And a short bit of it. Death is the other half, yet eternal." Mulgus swished his wand, and all the corpses knelt, bowing their heads. "The dead are obedient. They are for my control." Falin's eyes glanced to the opposite side of the clearing, where a small group of corpses remained standing. Mulgus turned to see where he was looking, waving his wand again so they fell to their knees with the rest.

Falin turned to Nyril. "And what is it you get from this?" He could tell in their short time together, Nyril was a higher caliber of warlock than Mulgus. He would not partner with such a grimy magician had he not seen some benefit for himself.

Nyril smirked. "I intend to control the living." After a hanging silence, Nyril said, "We have overstayed here. Come Mulgus, Silas. It is time we go. We have other business to attend to before we depart to Hadrones."

"I wish to stay here a little longer," Silas said. "I will meet with you when it is time again."

Nyril examined Silas and nodded. "So be it. Come Mulgus. Bring your pets."

Mulgus hesitated, clearly agitated. "Are we to leave this wizard and his Champions unharmed? If we may not kill them, can we at least detain them? Or maim them?"

Nyril looked to Silas for an answer. The young warlock shook his head. "Leave them be."

A bitter gurgle came from Mulgus. He sneered at Falin. "May it be in your best interest I do not find you alone, wizard." He turned with a swish of his black robes, twirling his wand. The corpses followed, often stumbling on the terrain. Melquin whimpered as Tula followed obediently.

"Farewell, Falin," Nyril called. "Give Airo my best should you cross paths."

The sounds of the dead and warlocks quickly disappeared into the swamp. The group sat in silence for a moment. Silas walked to the center, sitting upon the decaying tree to examine the group. His eyes were cold, and that of the Dark. "I wish to speak to Falin alone," he announced. Silas raised his wand, and quite suddenly the Champions' eyes became tired and they fell to the earth.

Falin leapt up and pointed his staff, but Silas did not react. "What did you do to them?!"

"I put them to sleep. They will wake well rested in the morning," Silas replied.

Falin examined his Champions who breathed deeply, seeing no evidence the young warlock lied. "Why do you want to speak to me alone?"

Silas lifted his head. "You and I are, in many ways, counterparts."

"I suppose," Falin said. "You were born in the fifty years prior to me, were you not?"

"I was," Silas confirmed. Despite being seventy years of age, Silas seemed no more than a few years older than Falin. "Have you been told of the tale regarding the Warrior of the Light?"

Falin tilted his head, thinking back to the prophecy seen in Boschi's pool in the Oldwoods. "I have. Why is that tale of interest to you?"

"Prophecies of Light have just as much impact on the Dark, do they not?"

"I suppose," Falin admitted. "If you are clairvoyant, can you see if they are true or not?"

Silas turned his gaze to the ground, unblinking. "I know it is a tale of truth, but not much more than that. What I can see of the future is akin to your memories. The farther away, the more difficult it is to know every detail. But…" Silas closed his eyes for a moment, and his lids fluttered until opened again. "I can see glimpses. And I can tell you they are real Falin."

Falin did not know how to make sense of this cryptic conversation. Instead, he asked, "Why are you aiding Nyril and Mulgus?"

"Is that not what servants of the Dark are supposed to do? Aid one another?"

"I have been taught that selflessness was not a trait of the Dark. And in my few experiences in this world, it remains to be true."

For the first time in their encounter, Silas showed emotion, with a slight crack of a grin. "I serve Nyril and Mulgus for my own purposes. For reasons I do not have time to share."

"So they have just been roaming Elsana? Nyril gets people to turn on each other then Mulgus takes the rest?"

Silas nodded. "More or less."

Falin remembered Airo's account of the village in the Freelands, facing the same fate as the swamp villagers. "I was told they did the same thing to a Freeland village north of Suntalla. Where were those people? Why did Mulgus not keep them?"

"Like you and I and every other being of magic, their powers are limited," Silas explained. "You have the Water Gem, yes? You may be able to manipulate a river, but you will never wield an ocean. Necromancy is a rather difficult form of magic, and controlling as many people as Mulgus can has taken him centuries. He can only maintain so many."

Falin remembered the few corpses who didn't kneel when commanded by Mulgus' wand. "He seems to want a greater power."

Silas searched the ground, deliberating whether or not to answer, speaking anyway. "Mulgus and Nyril both seek to enhance their abilities."

"Alright," Falin said, thinking through what he was told. "And then by what means does Nyril hope to control the living? Coercion?"

"Coercion and force," Silas answered.

"They have set their eyes on the Crown of Elsana," Falin asserted. "Have they not?"

Silas kept his mouth sealed, his gaze turning to the slumbering Champions. He tilted his head. "Have you enjoyed the company of the skully?"

"Jimbuah," Falin said. "Yes. They are wonderful creatures."

Silas waved his wand, and Jimbuah's staff flew into his free hand. He took the item and examined it. "We speak of tales of the future, I assume you know tales of the past. Do you know the story of the Titans?"

"Yes," Falin replied. "There were three Titans born by the God of Darkness to serve him in the Beginning. One of Land, Sea, and Air. The Sea Titan was killed by a Wizard, and the Air Titan was killed by a skully. The Titan of the Land is said to sleep in the depths of the earth."

"So it is said," Silas responded, his eyes still on Jimbuah's staff. "It is also said the staves of the Titan-slaying wizard and skully have been repurposed for use by the Warrior of the Light in the form of a sword." Silas thumbed through the bushel of fruit. "It is funny that a creature as insignificant as a skully would be so powerful as to kill a Titan. One must wonder how it was accomplished." Buried in the fruit were two, tiny golden berries that seemed to glow. They were no larger than the tip of Falin's pinky finger, but radiated light. Silas stooped his head to examine them, clasping one to tug at it. The berries sparkled, and he jerked his hand away in pain.

"I do not know what those berries do," Falin said, "but I do not believe they are for your use."

"No," Silas agreed, massaging his hand. He carelessly tossed aside the staff towards Jimbuah.

They sat in silence for a moment until Falin spoke. "What bone is your wand made from?"

Silas lifted his wand and looked to it. "Warlock." He spun the wand, and at once, Falin became sleepy. "Farewell, Falin. We shall meet again."

Falin fell to the ground into a deep slumber, his mind plagued by nightmares of living dead, titans, warlocks and every other evil creature imaginable. He dreamed of the Oldwoods burning, its inhabitants dying a horrible death. Then, images of his Champions perishing by hideous hands crawled through his mind. It was as if his sleep was poisoned, and there was no antidote to waking him. It was then, finally, he yanked himself from slumber and bolted upright. He squinted in the bright sunlight, grabbing his staff. The Champions remained asleep beside him.

"Wake up!" he called. He bent over Bossador and shook his shoulder, causing the madorian to stir. Falin moved to shake the rest. "Wake up!" he ordered. Falin scanned the clearing to ensure they were alone. The edge of the Marrow Swamps was without fog, returned to its previous muggy state of insects and strange animal noises.

Red lifted himself and held his head. "My head is pounding. Wha—warlocks?! Where are the warlocks?!" he exclaimed, remembering what happened.

"They are gone," Falin assured. "They left last night."

Melquin stood and searched the clearing. "Tula," she whimpered. The sage held her heart, and tears welled in her eyes. She turned to Falin. "Please tell me that was a nightmare! Please tell me what I saw was not real!" A dispirited Falin shook his head.

Nym, with her hair sticking at all angles, hurried to hug Melquin. "I am sorry. We all are. Tula was a sweet being who did not deserve such a fate."

Carthon remained seated on the ground with his forearms resting on his knees. "I have seen many atrocities in my time, but none so repulsive as necromancy."

"What could we do to stop them?" Bossador asked.

Falin looked to the south, where leagues of travel separated them from their destination. "We need to find the rest of the Gems. Let us not waste any more time here." Doing as told, the Champions gathered their belongings, taking flight for the jungles of Suntalla.

CHAPTER ELEVEN:
COLORFUL GREETINGS

The Champions craned their necks to view the jungle canopy, watching a horse-sized sloth climb from one branch to another. Mid tree-transition, the sloth peered down, examined the group, then continued on to disappear into the foliage. Shrieks, squawks, hollers, hoots, howls, hisses, and grunts were all they had heard in this energetic jungle. Vines draped from limbs, and every step involved some form of shrubbery or another. The air boiled and sweat gleaned on their foreheads on their eighth day trekking through Suntalla's jungles. Their skin was covered in bug bites, and half the plants they touched seemed to evoke a rash.

Nym kicked at shrubbery in agitation. "Is there not a path in this forsaken jungle?" The height-challenged elf struggled to move freely. "Every bit of earth is covered by some plant."

"The beasts of Suntalla have no need for paths," Red answered, leading them. "We ju—" He stopped in his tracks, appearing to inspect thin air.

"What is it, Red?" Carthon asked.

Red slowly shuffled back, then tore a leaf from a shrub. He crumpled and tossed it in the direction they walked. The leaf seemed to hang in mid-air, jostling about, and it was then Falin could make out the strings of a spider's web. From around a tree, a gangly, black and yellow arachnid the size of Falin's torso scurried onto its web, disappointed to find the lack of a meaty meal.

Bossador lurched backward in disgust. "By the beard of my father! What is that monster?!"

Red calmly removed his sword and stabbed the spider's head. Its feet contorted and pincers thrashed until it fell still. Red jimmied it off of his blade, slicing through the web. "A shrouded pincer," Red replied. Falin's hair stood on his neck, staring at the bug's corpse. It was hideous.

Bossador's shivered at the thought of being bitten. "Well by the grace of Elsana, why does something so monstrous exist?"

Red kicked aside the dead spider. "You ain't gonna like the Wildbarrens, your highness."

Melquin hurried to walk beside Falin, her black hair still frizzy from the humidity. "Do you think there will be any more warlocks we need to worry about in Suntalla? There are seven more lurking throughout Elsana aside from those we met."

Falin thought on it and shook his head. "I don't think so. From everything Airo taught me, warlocks are not as unified as wizards. They tend to scour the earth spreading their own mischief. The fact we found three together is an oddity."

"I suppose," Melquin said. "But there have been other times in history that they have come together in the name of Darkness. The last time during the War of the Crown."

"You're right, you're right," Falin admitted. He recalled their encounter with the warlocks, then his private conversation with Silas the Clairvoyant after.

"Even in Nyril and Mulgus' unity, they still seem to be working for their own personal gain though," Falin thought aloud. "Maybe they plan to share the Crown."

Melquin swatted at a bug near her ear and scowled. "I have never wanted any living thing to suffer until I met them." Despair flashed across her face. "What they did to Tula…"

"I know," Falin agreed. "It was a glimpse into the purest form of evil." He shook his head, forcing away the image of living corpses.

"What does Silas want out of it though?" Melquin pressed. "Did he tell you?"

Falin took a breath. "No. He did indicate he had his own intentions. But they did not seem as imminent as Nyril and Mulgus'. I fear for what they might do when they are ready to turn their attention to the Crown."

"Do you think it will be soon?" the sage pressed. "Should we be returning north to warn them?"

"I considered it," Falin admitted. "But they said they had other business to attend to before Mulgus and Nyril were to depart to the Hadrones. I'd imagine their travels will take a little while longer. And you forget, Airo has been investigating their movements. He may already be privy to more knowledge than we are. We need to focus on finding the next Gem."

"What is that?" Carthon announced, pointing through the thicket to their left.

The group's gaze followed where he directed, viewing what appeared to be a small wall of sticks tucked away. "Nekasta!" Jimbuah yelled, darting in that direction.

"Be careful, Jimmy!" Nym warned.

They chased, hopping over shrubs and batting vines from their faces. Once to the object, Falin saw it was a large pile of dried branches, tightly packed in the shape of a circle, standing as tall as Bossador.

"What is it?" Melquin asked.

Jimbuah began to excitedly climb the wall. "Nekasta!" he repeated.

"It's the nest of a thunderbird," Red translated. "Thunderbirds live on Quatiti with the skullies. The skullies ride them."

Jimbuah stood atop the nest lip, beckoning his comrades. "Klikimo!" He leapt from the edge into the center out of sight. Waiting no further, they began to climb, finding solid footing among the intertwined branches of the thunderbird's home.

Once atop, Falin saw the spacious opening. Eggshells the size of Jimbuah lay broken aside faded yellow feathers, but there were no signs of any recent lodgings. Jimbuah stood at the center and beamed with his hand on his hips.

Falin climbed into the nest and examined it. "It's huge. How big are thunderbirds?"

Jimbuah stretched his arms as wide as he could. "Vekari."

"This is like a little piece of home for Jimmy," Red added. "Too bad the thunderbird livin' here wasn't still around. We could've ridden it right over the Wildbarrens."

Jimbuah chuckled. "Yeh."

Falin sat in the den, surprised to see how comfortable it felt. The interior was layered with the enormous jungle leaves. "We could make this our camp for the night," Falin suggested. "I know it's still early, but we've traveled far."

"This heat makes it difficult to breathe," Carthon added. "I do not think we will need a fire tonight."

Nym shook her head. "No. And I cannot stand to see all the eyes we attract with our flames another night. They watch us unblinking. It is unnerving."

Melquin ran her hand over the bottom of the nest. "They say a thunderbird can summon a storm, commanding lightning as it wishes. Is that true?"

"Yeh," Jimbuah replied. He flapped his arms like a bird. "Wikingis thujindero."

Red removed his hat and leaned against the edge of the nest. "When a bunch of full-sized thunderbirds take flight, it can sound like thunder, hence their name. Not sure how they go about conjurin' lightning though."

Falin considered the power one must feel controlling a storm. He looked to the head of his staff, realizing water would be half of what he needed to manage the feat. "So we've been in this jungle for over a week now. How close are we to Stony Valley?"

"Should be gettin' close," Red replied. "We'll have to pass Monkey Mountain first."

Bossador furrowed his brow. "What's on Monkey Mountain?"

After staring at Bossador blankly, Red responded in a condescending tone. "What the grun do you think is on Monkey Mountain?"

Bossador scrunched his nose. "We have the Hills of Giants, and there are no longer giants there anymore!" he retorted.

"Will there be any trouble with Monkey Mountain?" Carthon asked. "You speak as if you've been there before."

Red nodded. "Jimmy and I passed once prior, but we've made good with the monkeys. It shouldn't be an issue."

Nym scanned the nest. "We really are in a Kingdom of Beasts. Has there ever been a ruler in Elsana's history?"

"Not in anything I've ever read," Falin answered.

"What would there be to rule?" Carthon asked. "Most of these creatures bow to none but their will to survive."

Bossador tremored. "Who would wish to rule a land where spiders as large as my shield are?" He removed his boots and wiggled his toes. "Perhaps some madman, one day."

Nym rested her head to the wall of the nest. "I am tired. And I miss home."

All nodded in agreement, but for Red and Carthon. "There are some nights I even miss Wizard Island," Falin replied.

"Did you not like it there?" Melquin asked.

The wizard shrugged a shoulder. "I did not dislike it. But it was all I knew for my entire life. I was not allowed to leave and kept under watch to learn."

"And then they set you free, little bird," Melquin teased.

Falin turned to Nym. "What is it you miss most about Lelyalis?"

Nym took little time to consider it. "My family. I miss my parents and all my siblings."

"You've spoken little of your family," Bossador said. "How many children are there in your house?"

"Thirteen."

A booming laugh escaped the madorian prince. "That is a massive family! Even by elven standards!"

Nym grinned. "I can hardly remember a time my mother did not have an infant in her arms."

"My goodness," Melquin smiled. "My parents were hardly able to handle me, and I was an only child."

A smirk crept across Red's face. "I can't imagine you were much of a troublemaker. You're the best behaved of everyone here."

Melquin raised her eyebrows and shook her head. "My father would call me his little wildflower. It seemed every other week he'd be mending a wound from me climbing a tree too high or petting an animal too unfriendly."

Nym laughed softly. "Was your father a healer too?"

"He was," Melquin replied. "One of the best in Mystica. He taught me everything I know. It's how I ended up in Queen Martana's court."

They sat in reflective silence for a few seconds before Falin asked, "You are the only male heir to the Rodrellan throne, are you not, Bossador?"

"I am," Bossador confirmed. "I have two sisters, who admittedly, would do just as fine a job ruling as I could, but traditions of old maintain the eldest male will take his father's place."

"King Bossador," Melquin said. "It has a ring to it. Are you ready to rule?"

Bossador scratched his beard. "I hope not for a long time. My father is as much a friend to me as he was a parent. I love him greatly, and hope he may rule for decades to come." Carthon shifted and struggled to mask a scowl. Instead of ignoring his fellow Champion's discomfort, Bossador said, "I am sorry, Carthon."

"It's alright," Carthon said softly, not looking at the prince. "You may speak of your father. It is your right."

"No, you misunderstand," Bossador corrected. "I am sorry for my kingdom's decision to not aid Vartulis during the Trortarkian Raids. It was a judgment that was wrong, and one I can tell you my father regrets." Carthon stared at Bossador with surprise, his lips tight and eyes wide. "I cannot offer you anything that will fix the struggle you endured, but I can offer you this: when the day comes I sit on the Rodrellan Throne, there will never be a second's hesitation to aid Vartulis, no matter the circumstances."

Carthon gazed away and whispered, "Thank you."

Falin basked in the exchange, proud of Bossador's readiness to mend the wound between Rodrellan and Vartulis. Even more, Carthon's willingness to accept the apology without lashing out gave him hope.

Somewhat abruptly, Carthon said, "My mother sang like a faerie." All turned to hear what he had to say. "Not that anyone knows what a faerie would sing like, but it is what my father claimed. And I believe it to be true. There were few nights as a child I fell asleep without her singing." He paused a moment and toyed with a freed stick from the nest. "I still hear her sing when I fall asleep at night."

Nym sat beside him, and great sorrow passed across her porcelain face. "I am sure your mother sings to you from the afterlife."

"Perhaps," Carthon answered. He tossed away the stick from the nest.

"I once saw my mother punch a bull in the face," Red announced.

Bossador snorted. "Go on."

"Ain't much to it. I was eleven or twelve, and this fat ol' bull kept droppin' dookie in front of our cabin. One day she stepped in it and got so mad, she planted a few knuckles into its mouth and it stormed off. Never dropped poo near our house again."

"How old were you when..." Carthon began, then looked to Red who shared similar unfortunate circumstances to their upbringing.

Red took a deep breath. "Thirteen. A grun raid came through." Red steadied himself and shook his head. "I'd been out riding that day when it happened, but I saw smoke and returned. When I rushed back, I was taken by gruns, and they sold me off to the augurs to make me a slave in Cadryl. What about you?"

"I was young," Carthon answered. "No more than seven or eight. When my parents saw the Trortarkians coming, they put me on a horse and sent it running north." He thought for a moment. "There is no higher honor than a parent sacrificing themselves for their child's wellbeing." Wishing to finish speaking of his family, Carthon said, "And what about you Jimbuah? What of your family? What was your father like?"

"Fakutu," Jimbuah said, gesturing a round belly and his father's size.

"And your mother?" Falin asked.

Jimbuah gently caressed the nest floor. "Rijadi bucas."

"She rode thunderbirds," Red translated.

"Very impressive," Falin said.

Soon, the sun fell beyond the horizon, and the jungle bugs chirped so loudly they could hardly hear each other. Opting not to build a fire, they curled into their own corners and quickly fell asleep in the warm, dense air. On occasion, an animal rustled in the brush, other times in the branches above, quickly leaving to prowl elsewhere in the night.

As dawn came about, they woke one by one, until Bossador was the only remaining Champion asleep. He lay sprawled on his back, snoring, his legs and arms outstretched. Jimbuah looked to the madorian and chuckled softly, as a mischievous expression crept across his grey face. The skully tugged a bunch of interwoven sticks from the nest and fidgeted with their ends, so eight twigs stuck out farther than the rest. Carefully, he tiptoed to Bossador and placed the bundle on the prince's stomach. The twigs slowly rose and fell in time with Bossador's breathing.

As all watched in confusion, Jimbuah turned to Red and whispered, "Yekala spijadu."

Red beamed and covered his mouth to avoid laughing and wake the madorian. He steadied himself, glanced at the rest of the Champions, then shouted, "Bossador! Bossador! Wake up! There's a spider on you! Bossador! Spider!"

Bossador's eyes flew open, and his hands moved to his stomach, feeling the sticks before his eyes could adjust to the morning light. He hollered and tossed aside the bundle, leaping up, swatting at his belly. "By giant's stones!"

The onlookers fell into hysterics at his expense. In confusion, Bossador squinted and saw that it was not at all a spider. Jimbuah rolled on the nest floor and held his gut, kicking his legs and trembling. Bossador clutched his chest. "By the God of Light, my heart nearly leapt from my body." After a moment to steady himself, a grin peeked across his face. "And whose idea was this?"

Melquin nodded to Jimbuah, still laughing. "Who do you think?"

The prince smirked. "Well done, Jimbuah. But now I must get my revenge."

Jimbuah sat up and crossed his legs. "Ah?"

Bossador nodded, his serious expression specked with playfulness. "You and I have entered a game of tricks. Be prepared to suffer my antics."

Dutifully, Jimbuah stood and walked to Bossador, outstretching his hand. "'Tis an honor."

Falin attempted to view the morning sun through the canopy, but was unable. "We should get going. If we're lucky, we will reach Monkey Mountain before sundown. Do you think that's feasible, Red?"

Red shrugged. "We've been in these jungles long enough. We've got to be there soon."

Leaving the nest behind, they continued their hike, swatting at bugs and keeping attentive for insidious creatures. Falin missed their horses very much, hoping the steeds made it safely to Mystica in their return home. Falin wondered where else this journey would take them, and how often they'd be forced to trek on foot. For the amount of strenuous travel, his companions complained little, and for this, he was grateful.

They were unable to see if they approached the mountain at all, as the jungle canopy was so thick they could only catch glimpses of the sky directly above them, and not at all ahead. After miles of walking, Nym stopped and raised her hand. "Do you hear that?" All shook their heads. Her pointed ears twitched. "It's running water. I think it's a river. Come on," she said.

They followed, and in a short hike, arrived at a lazy river, both wide and deep. On the opposite side, a hog slurped water, taking mild notice of the group. Bossador knelt at the water's edge and cupped his hands to splash his face, then again to drink deeply. "This water tastes clean. We should take our fill."

"Look!" Carthon said, pointing over the thicket opposite them. They squinted, and through the haze, they could make out the top of a mountain. "It's Monkey Mountain!"

"We're almost there," Red said. He removed his hat and wiped the sweat from his forehead. "Thank Elsana."

Falin scanned the length of the river as far as he could see. "How do we cross it?"

"I am not swimming in that river," Melquin asserted. "I do not eat animals, but there are many who will eat me. I can promise some of which lurk in that water."

"There's a bridge somewhere along the river, but it's far upstream, I think," Red said.

Falin dipped his staff into the water. "I might be able to hold it back so that we can walk across its bed," he thought aloud. He gripped his staff tighter. "We may need to be fast, though. I'm not sure how long I could hold it."

They lined at the bank's edge and looked over the water. "It's not that far. We can make it," Carthon said confidently.

"Um, guys," Nym said. Falin glanced to see she was not facing the river, but instead, the jungle with a concerned expression. They turned to find twenty monkeys surrounding them, pointing spears, having snuck behind them in silence. Falin and the Champions froze, surprised to discover the unexpected threat.

It was a rainbow of menacing primates, each a different vibrant color within the spectrum. The monkeys stood slightly taller than Nym, but not quite as tall as Melquin. Falin fidgeted with his staff, considering whipping them with river water, but a dark violet monkey to his left grunted, gesturing his rock-tipped spear. "Do not move," he ordered.

"Who are you? Why are you here?" a green monkey asked.

Red raised his hands. "We are Champions to a wizard on his quest for the Gems of Elsana. You may not remember me, but my companion and I passed the mountain some years ago." Red gestured to Jimbuah. "We were hoping to pass again."

The branches above their heads rustled and a light blue monkey—larger than the rest—leapt from the trees and landed in front of the group with a resounding *thud*. He stood straight and puffed his chest. "We do not take kindly to ugly Freelanders and skullies in Suntalla," he said to Red and Jimbuah.

"Tang!" Red yelled, stepping forward in delight. The monkey opened his arms and embraced Red in a hearty hug. The monkeys kept their spears on the rest of the group who waited still.

"As I live and breathe, the great Jimbuah Kah," Tang said, bending to hug Jimbuah.

Jimbuah's voice was muffled, his face buried to the primate's chest. "Mikiso yuka!"

Tang curiously examined Falin and the Champions. "How is it two refugees of the Wildbarrens came to be Champions of a wizard?"

"Lujiko," Jimbuah replied.

"Luck is right. Dumb luck." Red scratched under his hat. "And they promoted you to captain?"

"They did," Tang answered proudly. He beat his icy blue chest once, then looked to his men, still holding spears at the ready. "Lower your weapons, you have nothing to fear." Tang turned back to Red. "Well don't be uncivilized. Introduce me to your friends."

Red gestured to the group who had been standing awkwardly at the riverside. "This is Falin the Wizard, Melquin the Healer, Nym the Assassin, Carthon the Warrior, and Bossador the Bedwetter. They are my companions."

Bossador double-taked at Red and scowled. "Red jests. I am Bossador, heir to the throne of Rodrellan."

Tang chuckled. "I am sure you have grown patient to deal with the humor these two impose. It is an honor to meet you all. I am Tang, Captain of the Guard for Monkey Mountain. I will guide you to the mountain so you can meet our Alpha, Kogg."

Falin stepped forward. "We thank you for your welcome. Any friend of Red and Jimbuah's is a friend of ours. Perhaps you could show us how to cross this river."

"Well it would do you little good to swim," Tang said, "for you would be nothing but bones once reaching the other side. Come this way." He beckoned, walking downstream along the bank.

Falin, the Champions, and the group of colorful monkeys followed the winding river's edge. Falin tried not to stare at the soldiers, but their vibrancy was riveting. They were so distinct, yet wore the colors naturally. A sense of comfort washed over him, finding an innate kindness in Tang's willingness to welcome them. Despite his short time in the world, Falin knew this was a rare occurrence and he greatly valued it.

Tang spoke to Red as they strolled side by side. "What brings you so far south that you wish to enter Stony Valley?"

"We're lookin' for the next Gem of Elsana. It's supposed to be in the southern part of the Wildbarrens," Red answered.

Tang grimaced and shook his head. "Is this Gem worth such a venture? The Wildbarrens have become a Dark place in recent years."

"Well," Red shrugged, "that's why me and Jimbuah are here. To help out since we've been through it."

"I see," Tang said, gazing along the river in thought. "And you chose to forgo Letani because of your past relationship with them?"

Red rubbed his neck in embarrassment. "Pretty much."

Tang threw his head back and laughed. "Well I am glad. It is a rare thing for us to get visitors here at Monkey Mountain. It is rarer that we can call them a friend."

The river curved, and they came upon a sandy bank. Tang searched the river in all directions. "They're never here when you need them," he muttered. Tang moved to stand in a few inches of the water and knelt, smacking the surface with the palm of his hand. *THWAP, THWAP, THWAP, THWAP, THWAP, THWAP, THWAP, THWAP.* He backed away, waiting. A few seconds later, Falin saw great oval shadows gliding underneath the surface in their direction. Eight giant river turtles breached and shimmied halfway onto the bank. Their shells were of ornate patterns, their length more than Bossador's height.

Tang pointed across the river and over the treetops to the mountain and grunted. "*Ah ah ah!*" he demanded of the turtles.

Falin, being the only person able to fully understand the turtle, heard it say to the rest, "Banana-brain wants us to take everyone to the mountain."

Tang turned to his men. "Keep patrolling the shoreline east of here. Return before sundown." The monkey soldiers dutifully nodded and marched off with their spears in hand. "Everyone climb on their backs," Tang ordered, crawling atop a turtle's shell. The group did as told. As Bossador mounted his, Falin heard the turtle curse. The reptiles shimmied their way around and slid into the water.

Falin perched on his turtle's back as it glided downstream over the river, winding and weaving through debris. The turtles floated with their shells just above the surface, and schools of river fish could often be seen scurrying over the bed below. Falin handled his staff and could feel the river flowing as an extension of himself, sensing the creatures living within. He peered left, and saw a gator lazily watch them pass. Little ripples lapped around the turtle's strokes, but for a river of this size, it was mostly calm.

"Can you speak to them?" Melquin called to Falin. "I cannot understand what they say."

Falin tilted his head to better see his turtle's face dip in and out of the water. He didn't know how he sounded to the rest of the group, but spoke to his river-steed. "Why is it you give the monkeys rides on the river?"

The turtled glanced backward, somewhat startled. "You speak like us!"

"I do. I am a beastsayer, and friend to all creatures of Elsana," the wizard said proudly.

"Well now I've seen it all," the turtle answered. "We offer the monkeys service in return for their guardianship of the river. They keep Dark beings, away and we give them travel."

"Very harmonious," Falin said softly.

Nym stood on her turtle's back and took a deep breath with her eyes closed. The sun shined on her skin, and Carthon watched with an expression of extreme affection, something wholly unseen on a drak.

For miles they drifted in leisure, at times moving in a direction away from the mountain, always turning to creep closer. As it came to the late afternoon, the turtles arrived at a bank bordered by more jungle, this time with a dirt path leading through it.

"Thank you all," Falin said to the turtles as they dismounted.

Tang waved the group for the trail leading into the jungle. From over the canopy, the solitary mountain loomed ahead. They began on the path, eager for their destination.

Falin felt a better aura on this side of the river. It was not a sense of Light, but an ancient harmony that he could not explain. No bugs were swarming them, nor noises of sinister sounding creatures. The trail was clear of vines and the brush seemed lush. In a short time, the jungle opened, and they came to the base of the mountain.

As far as mountains go, it was small, but beautiful. The brown terrain that climbed upward was of sparser foliage than the jungle behind them. On the left side of the elevation, a series of waterfalls spilled over the entire mountain, with landings of pools after each. On the right side, scores of huts covered the area, some on the ground and some in trees. Little multi-colored monkey children ran about, chasing one another with sticks. Adults carried baskets of fruit, held infants, or lounged by the waterfall pools. Some napped in hammocks high in the shade of a tree.

Falin couldn't help but chuckle. "What a serene place this is." Tang nodded in appreciation. "It is. I am proud to call it my home. Come, you must meet Kogg."

The group followed Tang as he led them up a winding trail through the monkey village. Inhabitants stopped to watch the visitors pass in curiosity. Some recognized Red and Jimbuah, to which they waved and smiled. The path split three ways, and Tang moved to the left, leading them to the series of waterfalls. Foliage became more abundant as they approached the water, and they took a trail leading to a pool.

By the edge of the water sat a wooden hut built upon rock, larger than those further down the mountain. Its door was covered in long strands of dried vines, making it difficult to see who resided inside.

"Kogg!" Tang called to the hut. "Kogg, we have old and new friends here!"

After a moment, a hand parted the door, and a beastly ape of charcoal fur exited. Kogg's gaze was intense, and when standing upright he was taller than them all. He strutted to them first on two feet, then fell to all four, eye level with Falin. His focus quickly turned to Red and Jimbuah and he smiled. "What mischief brings these two on my mountain?" he said in a voice deep and rich.

Red nodded cordially to the great ape. "We come as Champions to a wizard in his search for the Gems of Elsana. This is Falin and his Champions. Everyone, I would like you to meet Kogg, Alpha of Monkey Mountain."

Before anyone could speak, Kogg laughed heartily and looked to Falin. "You chose these two as your Champions?" He smacked Red on the arm, causing the Freelander to near fall. "Perhaps you should seek some brains to accompany your Gems."

"They have served me as well as the rest. I am honored to have them in my company," Falin replied.

Kogg nodded subtly and examined Falin for a moment with greater seriousness. "It has been a long time since a wizard has visited us on Monkey Mountain. The last was Tani the Wise, and I was but a child."

"It is a difficult trek to get here," Falin replied. "But well worth it. It is a beautiful place, and I am glad to have laid eyes on it."

"You are kind as all wizards are said to be," Kogg said. "What can we offer you in your quest?"

Falin scratched the back of his neck, not expecting to receive such hospitality. "Some shelter for a night or two, and any spare food you might have before we pass into Stony Valley for the Wildbarrens."

Kogg's demeanor darkened. "You wish to pass the mountain?"

Falin nodded. "The next Gem is in the Wildbarrens."

The Alpha sighed deeply and rubbed his chin. "You are aware the Wildbarrens have become a treacherous place in these times, yes?"

"We are," Falin replied, "which is why Red and Jimbuah have come along with us. They will be our guides."

Kogg thought on it more before answering. "So be it. Tang, I believe we have a few unused huts on the western face of the mountain. Should we show our guests there?"

"Yes," Tang answered. "We can have some food gathered for them too. They look hungry."

They departed from Kogg's waterfall home and returned to the main path of the mountain. "How long has Monkey Mountain been here?" Melquin asked.

"Before what you call the Beginning," Kogg answered.

Falin thought on it. "But then what we call the Beginning would not truly be the Beginning."

"A blasphemous statement for many dedicated servants to both Light and Dark," Tang chimed. They veered left on a split in the path, and groups of monkey children scurried past. "Mind yourselves!" Tang yelled as they ran between the legs of the visitors.

Falin inhaled deeply, relishing the fresh air. It was cooler than the heart of the jungle. His lungs were no longer labored. As the sun set on their walk, the sky swathed hues of purple and pink, and the mountain seemed a paradise.

"What is that?" Nym asked, pointing ahead on their left. A cliff face covered in jutting stones and ivy rose high to an open ledge. At its base sat a semi-circle of stone seats on a bed of grass.

"It is the Wall of Faith," Kogg replied. "It is for those who wish to show a sign of commitment to a friendship, and oftentimes, love." Nym stared at the wall as Kogg continued. "Two climbers are tied together by a vine, then scale the wall, having faith in the other to save them if they fall."

They stopped at the bottom of the cliff and craned their necks to see the top. "Has anyone ever fallen?" Nym asked. Falin could see she yearned to climb it, concerning him.

"Not in my lifetime," Kogg replied. "But then again, monkeys are far more adept to climbing than most other races in Elsana."

Nym glanced at Carthon. "May races other than monkeys attempt it?"

"They may," Kogg answered. "But you must have a partner tied to you for it to be a true trial upon the Wall of Faith."

The elf bit her lip in uncertainty, then said, "Will you climb with me, Carthon?"

Falin was surprised to hear her request of the drak. He examined the ivy-covered wall, wishing to halt the endeavor. "I appreciate your gesture of friendship to Carthon, but I am not sure it is the safest idea."

Carthon ignored Falin and turned to the elf with a fiery gaze. "It would be my honor, Nym."

"I will find them a suitable vine," Tang said, stepping off the path into the brush.

Falin raised his upturned palms in confusion. "What is happening right now?" Unsure why this dangerous feat suddenly needed to transpire, he pressed them. "Are you sure you want to do this? A fall from that wall will kill either of you."

"Yes," they answered in unison, seemingly lost in the Wall of Faith.

Tang returned with a lengthy vine, promptly tying one end to Nym's waist and the other to Carthon's. He tugged at the knots to ensure they were tight. "Listen to your fingers and toes," Tang advised. "They will sense weakness in your grip long before your mind does."

Without a word, Nym and Carthon stalked to the base of the ridge and tugged at the ivy. Nym heaved herself up, testing her footing at each new section she climbed. Carthon followed, doing the same, and they crept upwards at a slow and safe pace. Falin and his Champions watched anxiously, but kept silent so as not to ruin their comrades' focus. Up and up they went, little by little.

Two-thirds of the way to the top, Nym tugged at a rock, paused, and tugged again. She opted to move further to her right, with Carthon a body length below her. As she reached for a new spot, her footing gave out and she fell, her arms extending in hopes of catching a grip.

All in the group gasped, while Kogg and Tang watched intently. Carthon grabbed the rope attaching him to Nym and held it tight as she swung beneath. She banged into the rock wall with an awful *smack*. The ivy Carthon clutched strained, as did he, but Nym quickly regained her composure and held place on the wall again. She looked up to Carthon, frightened, then sighed in relief. Falin's heart pounded in his ears.

The drak waited for her to return to his level, and again, they began to climb. Without any further troubles, they pulled themselves over the clifftop and laid at its edge in relief. The group below cheered.

Nym stood, grasping Carthon's hand in hers, raising her arms before dramatically bowing. She gestured to Carthon, and indulging her, he smiled and bowed in their applause.

Carthon peered at Nym, and still holding onto her hand, he pulled her close. He embraced her, and she stood on her toes as he bent his head. They kissed atop the Wall of Faith, their passion for one another evident.

The group fell silent in surprise of the gesture. The drak and elf locked lips, clutching one another beneath a painted sunset. It became suddenly clear to the onlookers, the climb was not only symbolic of friendship, but one of fierce love.

CHAPTER TWELVE:
PRIMITIVE HISTORY

Falin lounged in the hammock of a tree hut, nibbling a green fruit he did not know the name of, but thoroughly fancied. Melquin swung on a hammock of her own, while Nym and Red lazed on mats of moss. Despite their desire to remain on Monkey Mountain for only a couple days, they found themselves savoring their fifth afternoon.

"Why couldn't the second Gem be here?" Nym thought aloud. She lay with her hands cupped behind her head. "It is truly a paradise."

Falin felt guilty for staying so long, but safety, shelter, and food were such a rarity on their journey, finding it in excess made it difficult to relinquish. "We can't stay too much longer. At most another few days."

"You know Red, I'm almost glad we didn't go to Letani now," Melquin admitted. She peeled a long, purple fruit before biting into it. "Why did you wait to tell us about this place?"

Red blew air from his nose. "Y'all never would have come here if I insisted we go to a mountain of monkeys instead of an actual kingdom."

"Well, it worked out for the best," Nym admitted.

Melquin donned a mischievous grin. "Especially since we got to learn you and Carthon are in *love*."

Nym looked at Melquin from the sides of her eyes. "I'm sure it would have come about no matter our route."

Falin swayed on his hammock and thought. "When did you two first admit your feelings?"

Nym thought on it. "We almost shared our first moment in the Oldwoods, but our skully friend ruined that. On our second day in Darva, we explored a tower of the castle where Carthon admitted his love for me, then I for him."

Melquin gushed upon hearing the story. "You are one special elf for a drak to speak so freely of his love."

"Don't tell him I told you this…" Nym paused and singled out Red. "As in, if you repeat what I am about to say, you will find a throwing star in your rump."

Red chuckled. "Scoundrel's oath."

Nym took a breath and continued, a dreamy smile appearing on her face. "Carthon is quite the romantic. When he speaks of his affections for me, it is poetic."

Melquin clamped her hands together in delight. "A poetic drak! How lucky you are!"

Falin smiled, glad that their journey could kindle their romance. "I am happy for you both."

Red looked at the straw hut ceiling, stroking his chin. "How common are romantic relations between different races of the Crown?"

"They are rare, but happen on occasion," Melquin answered. "Sages have been known to mix with elves or madorians, and elves have mixed with draks. Though I have never heard of a drak or elf mixing with a madorian." She looked at Nym. "What beautiful children you and Carthon would make. Of pale beauty and graceful combat skills."

Nym shook her head. "I have many more Dark creatures to kill before I carry a child."

An endearing breeze brushed through the hut. Falin gazed through the window, viewing the path leading to the lower part of the mountain. "Where are the others right now? Does anyone know?"

"They went for a dip in the pools," Red answered.

Falin debated relaxing longer or going for a refreshing swim. Deciding he had the night to sleep, he slid from the hammock and stretched. "I think I may join them. I will see you all tonight come dinner."

Falin grabbed his staff and departed the hut, leading to a ladder made of rope. He descended the tree and followed the path downward, waving to monkeys he passed. Some were mothers with children, others adolescents causing trouble, or the occasional soldier back from patrol, all as brightly colored as the last.

Hearing the shouts of Bossador over a cluster of trees, Falin veered right through a small thicket. On the opposite side, he came to a waterfall with a great pool beneath. Bossador, Jimbuah, and Carthon lounged in the water along its edge of rock, while ten or so monkey children played games, swimming and splashing at its center.

"Falin!" Jimbuah yelled in his skully accent. "Hekalo!"

"Are we all having a good day?" Falin asked his group, undressing to his undergarments and climbing in the water. The chilled pool caressed his skin. He laid his staff beside the edge and watched the monkey children splash.

"I never thought I would enjoy so much sunshine," Carthon admitted. "This is a paradise."

Bossador squatted so the water covered him up to the neck. "We should return here following your discovery of all four Gems. And the defeat of Nyril and Mulgus, of course."

To Falin, it seemed a sin to mention such vile beings in a pure place as this. "I would gladly return. I hope that one day I can repay the monkeys for the hospitality."

Carthon lifted his chin to the sun. "Continue to do wizardly good in all of the world, and I am sure they will be happy."

"Is that all draks expect of wizards?" Falin asked. "Wizardly-good?"

"More or less," Carthon replied. "There is debate among the Drakkish Senate as to when or if we should ever ask the wizards for assistance. Some argue it should only be in dire circumstances, but wizards tend to appear in those times anyway."

Falin thought for a moment. "Were there any wizards assisting Vartulis in the Drakkish Rebellion against Mortulis?"

"Some," Carthon answered. "I believe they were pulling strings in support of us as we were a legion of draks returned to the Light. And Rulo the Peacemaker was instrumental in the creation of the Crown."

Falin smiled. "Amazing to think Rulo is still puttering around on Wizard Island. He's close to a thousand years old now. His time will be over soon."

Bossador, having been listening to their conversation, said, "He was young at the time, was he not? The War of the Crown was near a thousand years ago."

"He was, which is why his name carries such legend," Falin responded. "Most argue the formation of the Crown is one of the most important events to happen in Elsana since the Beginning. If not the most important."

"What is Rulo like? Does he reflect his name of the Peacemaker?" Carthon asked.

Falin couldn't help but chuckle. "He is rather crotchety and has little patience for immature behavior."

Carthon smiled, and his fangs glinted in the sunlight. "A legend no less."

A little red monkey swam to their group, as his friends waited in a cluster on the other side of the pool. "Falin the Wizard," he called.

"What can I do for you?" Falin asked. The primate was young, and half the size of Jimbuah with features of innocence still present.

"My friends said you can move water. Is that true?"

Falin gently tapped the water's surface, and a little splash hit the monkey's face. "Like so?"

The monkey giggled and wiped his eyes. "No! With your staff!"

"Ah! I see, I see," Falin said. He glanced at his Champions and grinned, reaching for the staff. He raised it, and looked to the waterfall pouring into the pool. Much like in the Caves of Isetta, Falin twirled his staff and manipulated the waterfall to form a river in the air. The monkey children gasped, oo-ing and ah-ing as the stream flew over the mountain in fanciful circles. After a moment of showmanship, Falin directed the water to fall atop the heads of the audience. They screamed in surprise and delight, taking cover under the water.

"Will that suffice?" Falin asked the little red monkey.

"Yes!" he answered in glee. "Thank you!"

Jimbuah's eyes scanned the pool in thought, his gaze landing on Bossador. "Upa!" He exclaimed, gesturing a tossing motion. "Upa!"

Bossador tilted his head. "You want me to toss you in the air?"

"Yeh!" Jimbuah exclaimed.

Bossador considered it and said, "I bet I could toss you higher than ever if you were to run first, leaping from my hands."

"Yeh! Yeh!" Jimbuah agreed, climbing from the pool. He walked back to the brush, and Bossador stood at the water's edge, bending and cupping his palms.

"Ready when you are!" Bossador called. The monkey children watched in anticipation.

Jimbuah, with a face of focus, sprinted for the pool, jumping to land his right foot in Bossador's interlocked hands. Bossador tossed him so high he appeared to float for a few seconds. "Boo yattah!" Jimbuah screamed, plunging with a mighty splash. He resurfaced and shook his face, chuckling.

"Toss us! Toss us Prince Bossador!" The children pleaded to the madorian.

Bossador smiled. "Alright. Everyone form a line." Falin watched as ten colorful little monkeys ran to wait their turn. They sprinted to Bossador's arms, and he carefully tossed each into the water. They shrieked in glee as he threw them. Falin, Carthon, and Jimbuah laughed at the display.

As the monkeys scrambled from the pool to return to the tossing line, Kogg emerged from the brush with an amused expression. He walked to Falin and company, sitting beside them at the pool. "I see the children have taken a liking to you." His eyes followed a little yellow monkey flying over their heads.

"They are pure of heart," Falin said. "One would think they are born of the Light."

Kogg chuckled softly. "They are surely Children of Elsana. There is much Light in this place regardless." Droplets if water trickled on them from a sudden splash.

"Where is Tang today?" Carthon asked. "He planned to show me the fighting style of apes before I left."

"He is on patrol on the other side of the river, but should return soon," Kogg replied. "You wish to learn our ways of combat?"

"I do," Carthon admitted. "It must be a unique one. The spears you use are rather…" he searched for an appropriate word.

"Crude," Kogg finished his sentence. "The secret to monkey fighting lies in our strength. A man and monkey of the same size is no competition. Monkeys are far faster and thrice as strong."

Falin examined the alpha ape and believed it. He was the same size as Bossador, with a hidden strength beneath his charcoal fur.

Jimbuah climbed from the water to have Bossador toss him again. "Upa!" he demanded.

Bossador looked to Jimbuah. "Want to show them how high I can really throw?"

"Yeh, yeh," Jimbuah nodded fervently.

"Okay, but really run hard on this one. And put some muscle in your jump," Bossador advised.

Jimbuah took position, and as Bossador cupped his hands, the skully sprinted for the madorian. Jimbuah leapt for his comrade's palms, but in the last second, Bossador grinned and casually stepped away. Jimbuah's eyes bulged and he yelped, hitting the edge of the pool, tripping, and face-planting into the water with a hearty *splat*.

A fit of hysterics befell the monkey children, and Bossador laughed with them. Jimbuah resurfaced and shook his face of water. Bossador pointed at him. "I have returned the favor in our game of tricks, Jimbuah! I warned you!"

Jimbuah muttered, "Prikinsi fujika-fatisu." He fought a grin and stuck his tongue out at the giggling monkeys.

Kogg smiled subtly at the display, then turned to Falin. "I was hoping you had a moment. I would like to share something with you further up the mountain."

"Of course," Falin replied." He lifted himself over the edge of the pool and shook the water from his skin before donning his robes. Kogg departed through the brush and Falin followed with his staff in hand. Not knowing where they went, Falin asked, "Is there something wrong?"

Kogg shook his head. "Not in the slightest." Falin trailed the alpha on the main mountain path past the huts and inhabitants of the village. All nodded to Kogg in respect of his authority, to which he nodded with equal respect in return. Up they went until homes became sparse, and they overlooked most of the mountain. Kogg guided them left onto a tiny trail overgrown with trees and plants, but he brushed them aside for Falin to pass.

Soon, they entered a small opening of grass, and with it, a cave entrance. All else on the mountain below seemed distant. "Does your staff summon light?" Kogg asked.

Falin bumped the bottom of his staff to the ground and it lit aglow. "I assume we are headed into the cave."

"Wizards truly are smart," Kogg teased. "Come, there is something I feel you must see."

Falin walked to the entry behind Kogg, finding the path one of smooth and winding dirt sloping downward inside the mountain. "What is this place?"

"It is where the first apes of Monkey Mountain dwelled some thousands of years ago. Before huts and river guards, they were primal beings of old," Kogg responded.

The sloping trail flattened and they came to a tiny, stone room. Falin's head just brushed the ceiling, and Kogg stooped even though he walked on all fours. "The mountain is filled with these caves, but few as intact as this one. I am glad you are here to see it," Kogg said. "Look," he pointed to the wall.

Falin squinted, realizing there were markings on the rock. He stepped forward with his enlightened staff and peered closer, seeing it was artwork—rough sketches of colorful monkeys carrying fruit, riding turtles, and swinging from vines were shown. The paintings were faded, but it was clear it was an exhibit of the monkey's lives thousands of years ago. Falin slowly moved his staff to inspect the paintings. Images of animals in the jungle and depictions of the mountain were also present. "How old are these?"

Kogg scanned the wall. "No one has ever been certain. But tales of time tell us they were here from the Beginning. I'm inclined to believe so. Look there," Kogg said, pointing to Falin's left.

Falin did as told, then became confused. It appeared to be a clumsy rendition of a monkey holding a stick of fruit. "I don't understand."

"Does it appear familiar? Perhaps to someone in your group?"

Falin blinked, then beamed upon realizing what he saw. "It's a skully!" Kogg smiled wide and nodded. "It has been said skullies were here before even wizards or faeries or giants. This could be proof."

"Maybe," Kogg said, thrilled to see Falin's enthusiasm. "These could have been painted sometime after the Beginning. Look further left, do you see the stonies?"

Falin shined the light and saw a cluster of what seemed to be larger, rounder skullies. "I have never met a stony. I hear they are kind."

"Our friendship with stonies goes back thousands of years," Kogg explained. "I am glad you will be meeting them in your passage to the Wildbarrens."

"Amazing," Falin said. "There are explanations for the existence of most creatures in Elsana," he thought aloud, "but when the question arises of skullies and stonies, the answer is, 'they've just always been there.'"

Kogg chuckled. "I fear we might never know the truth to Elsana's early history."

"Well we know wizards, giants, and faeries came from the God of Light. And from them, the sages, madorians, and elves were born."

Kogg nodded thoughtfully. "And how is it common man came to be?"

Falin replied, "They were created by Elsana... given free will to choose between Light and Dark."

The monkey paused to consider his next words. "That is the reason I brought you here. I may be able to offer you some truth to our world's history. Bring the light here." He pointed to the opposite wall of where Falin stood.

Four parts of a tale were told through images. On the far left, monkeys were portrayed as they existed today; living in trees and swinging from vines with fruit in hand. In the second section to the immediate right, the monkeys appeared duller, standing upright, yet hunched, with less fur and utilizing spears. Falin cocked his head, growing confused by the third image. A creature seeming to be some blend of man and monkey wearing a loincloth, with its colored hair entirely gone, and the posture of a common man. Finally, in the fourth and final section, a primitive man in cloth garb posed with a sword.

Falin ingested all that he saw, then shook his head. "I don't understand… Is this saying man came from… monkeys? That they are related?"

"So it would seem," Kogg said curiously. "It is a conclusion others on this mountain have come to, but for some reason, a history the kingdoms north of here have forgotten."

Falin grappled with what he saw. "Common man was made by Elsana in her own image. As a means to bring balance to the world filled with creatures of Light and Dark. At least that is what we have always been taught…"

Kogg took a seat on the cavern floor and examined the wall. "Tell me, young wizard; why is that man could not come from both monkeys and the hand of a higher power? What you see as separate possibilities may be one event."

Falin thought it through. "I always thought it odd that Elsana would create man and just have them pop from the ground like turnips."

Kogg laughed. "I would agree. This could just be a story made by some imaginative monkey of old, but I am inclined to think otherwise."

Falin sighed deeply, the revelation crumbling his understanding of the world. "But the God of Light made us… so does this mean we came before? Or after?"

"Who knows?" Kogg shrugged.

Falin turned to the alpha. "Why are you showing me this?"

Kogg scanned the paintings. "Is it not a wizard's duty to discover the world's truths? And share your findings for generations to come?"

Falin tapped his staff and nodded, looking to the images depicting half-man, half-ape. "One of our many duties." He examined the artwork. "In my travels south, I never would have thought I would be taught man came from monkey."

Kogg stood and smiled. "Do what you want with these findings. It gives me comfort knowing that those outside the mountain will know of them. Especially a wizard. I trust you will treat my people's histories with respect."

Falin was honored by his words. "Thank you, Kogg. I—"

The bellow of a brash horn carried over the mountain and down the cave. It blew twice, then ceased. By Kogg's sudden alertness, Falin grew concerned. "There are enemies on the mountain," Kogg said. He darted for the cave's exit and Falin followed.

"Should we be prepared to fight?" Falin asked as they hurried up the path. They approached the tunnel entry.

"No," Kogg called behind. "There would have been more calls of the horn. They have captured creatures of the Dark. But that may mean more are in the area."

Falin squinted upon exiting the cave, trying to keep up with Kogg's hasty lope. The alpha ran on all fours, cruising through the brush, panting.

They sprinted on the main path of the mountain, and as they passed the huts, concerned monkeys peered at Falin and Kogg wondering what it meant for them. Mothers ushered their children inside while adult males followed. Near the mountain's base, a circle of soldiers and onlookers stood by, among them Falin's Champions. The crowd parted as Kogg strode forward.

With wrists bound, three gruns and a crag were guarded by soldiers. They sneered as Kogg and Falin approached, careful not to incite the spears held to their heads.

Tang stepped forward to Kogg and said, "We found them prowling the other side of the river. We watched them from the trees for some time until we captured them. It doesn't seem there are any others nearby."

Kogg stood on two feet and lumbered to the crag. They were eye to eye, both towering over the gruns beside them. This particular crag was larger than the ones Falin had seen in the Mortal Caves. At least more muscular, with sharper eyes.

A low growl escaped Kogg as he brought his face close to the crag. "What are you doing near my mountain?" The crag glanced to his smaller comrades then back to Kogg, wearing a subtle smirk. He declined to speak. "I advise you to answer, crag," Kogg rumbled. "I will ask one more time. What are you doing so close to my mountain?"

The crag's lips twitched as he scanned to the colorful monkeys around him. He spoke in a gravelly voice. "Seeking a snack." The monkeys all shifted at the remark. Falin and his Champions watched intently. A sharp breath leapt from Kogg and his nostrils flared. The grun closest to the crag chuckled softly, but the remaining prisoners kept still, fearful of the alpha.

Kogg's gaze turned to the laughing grun, and before it could react, he snatched it by the ankle and lifted it off the ground. The alpha ape swung the screaming grun like a club, slamming it into the crag with a violent *THWACK*.

The crag flew to its back, holding its bound hands in defense of its face. Kogg proceeded to beat the crag with the grun, both creatures wailing. Kogg held tight to the grun's ankle as it flailed, repeatedly being smashed into the crag. The alpha swung the creature as if it were a doll. Falin and company watched in awe, as it was a gruesome sight.

The crag pleaded for mercy, each bash of the grun eliciting more blood and broken bones of each party. Kogg grunted with every swipe. After a moment of clobbering, the grun and crag were covered in blood, their bodies limp. Kogg carelessly tossed aside the grun, breathing heavily. He spit on the dead crag, with specks of blood glistening his darkened fur.

Kogg stalked on all fours to the two remaining gruns. The Dark servants quivered, gulping as the alpha towered over them. From the spectacle, Kogg did not need to speak to receive an answer. The grun to the left spoke first. "We were not looking for monkeys or Monkey Mountain. We were sent to search for someone."

Kogg cocked his head. "Who are you searching for?" Both gruns pointed to Falin. Falin, having been a bystander to the exchange, was surprised to suddenly be yanked into the mix. A jolt of fear struck him as he realized he was the subject of a hunt. "And who is searching for him?"

The grun on the right gulped. "Mulgus the Plague."

Falin grew short of breath to learn the warlock sought him, going as far as ordering scouts to search the jungles of Suntalla. The young wizard stepped forward. "You were sent here to kill me?"

The left grun shook his head. "No. We were ordered to take you and your Champions alive. We had strict orders not to kill, only detain."

"Are there more of you near the river?" Kogg pressed. "You will spend the remainder of your lives in turmoil should I learn you are lying."

"It was only us," the right grun insisted. "We were sent in groups by our captains to search different areas of the Suntalla jungles. They will return to the Varsa borders empty-handed."

"And with four fewer soldiers," Kogg said. He looked between the two gruns, then to Tang. "Imprison them until I decide what we should do."

Tang motioned his soldiers take the prisoners away. The gruns were escorted along the base of the mountain to the other side.

Falin's mind raced, deciding how to proceed. Kogg, Tang, and his Champions walked to him, seeing a great concern on his face. "We can't stay," he said to the Champions. "The longer we do, the more we put Monkey Mountain in danger." He turned to Kogg. "We will leave tonight."

Kogg shook his head. "You will do no such thing. It will be dark soon. Mulgus has no idea you are here. You should take a good night's rest, and we will escort you to the border of Stony Valley come morning."

"Why is Mulgus trying to capture us?" Melquin asked. "Didn't Silas say leaving us alone would help their plan?"

Falin thought on it. "Silas said *killing* us would harm his plan. It was clear Mulgus did not like letting us go, no matter what Silas or Nyril said. He likely wants to take us prisoner."

"What a wretched being," Bossador spat.

"Do not fret," Kogg soothed. "You are safe here for the night. Tang, I want you to double the patrol. Make stealth a priority. Keep to the trees and guard the river. If any more enemies come near, send a signal."

Tang nodded. "I will be ready come morning to escort our friends to the Stony border." The blue monkey departed with a group of soldiers to do as commanded.

"Go to your huts," Kogg insisted. "Get rest."

Falin looked to the dead crag and grun being dragged away. The group marched up the mountain, taking shelter in the same hut. It brought them comfort to share each other's company in such concerning times.

"Now what?" Nym asked, swaying on the edge of a hammock beside Carthon. "We have a warlock hunting us."

"I doubt Mulgus is tracking us himself," Carthon responded. "Didn't Nyril and Mulgus say they were traveling to the Hadrones in the coming weeks? Nyril was opposed to detaining by the counsel of Silas... Something tells me Mulgus would not openly defy Nyril."

"You're right," Falin agreed. "If they parted ways even for just a short period of time in their travels, Mulgus could have easily sent word to servants he has lurking in this part of the world."

"Okay," Nym replied, thinking through it. "But the fact of the matter is, we're still being actively pursued by servants of the Dark. If we are captured, it is a matter of time before Mulgus does get his hands on us."

Bossador sat on the floor with his arms folded. His focus turned to Red and Jimbuah, who casually picked on fruit, half-listening to the conversation. "You two do not seem as concerned as the rest of us. Are you not worried about what has transpired?"

Jimbuah shrugged and waved his hand dismissively. "Bah."

Red carefully peeled an orange and took a bite. "We've been hunted by almost every race in this world. Both Light and Dark.

Some have succeeded by imprisoning us, others have failed. Someone's always going to be after you at one point or another. Best you can do is keep moving forward and glance over your shoulder once in a while."

"Yeh, yeh," Jimbuah agreed.

"Besides," Red started, pausing to wipe his lips with the back of his hand. "We've got bigger things to worry about. Once we're through the Stony Valley, we're headed into the Wildbarrens."

Melquin frowned. "I am not sure that is more concerning than being the target of a warlock's hunt."

Red smirked and bit the fruit again. "The wizards and all of your royals were perfectly happy sending us out into the world, knowing we'd face most of the things we've faced. It was only when they found out we were headed into the Wildbarrens did they start to worry. What's that tell you about what the Wildbarrens have in store?"

A quiet realization hit the rest of the group. For so long, the Wildbarrens seemed like a distant nuisance, one that could be conquered by the aid of the two unexpected Champions. After months of strenuous treks across all sorts of terrain, there seemed little they couldn't accomplish. Now, after being cushioned by the hospitality of Monkey Mountain, they were about to plunge into a harrowing unknown.

Nym spoke with hesitancy. "Is it really that bad there?"

"Yekasa," Jimbuah answered sullenly. "Yeh."

After a few seconds of silence, Falin said, "We should begin getting ready for bed. I believe it is only a day's hike to the Stony Valley from here, and I think it would be in our best interest to only stay there for a night, at most two."

"Before we go," Bossador started. "Could we take a moment to appreciate the sight of Kogg beating a crag to death with a grun."

Carthon nodded intensely. "That was sublime."

"Boo yattah," Jimbuah concurred. The rest murmured agreement.

Falin and his Champions prepared for bed, all departing for their own huts to sleep for the night. As the sun fell, crickets rose and chirped over the mountain. Falin lay in his hammock by the open hut window and stared at the cloudless sky, enamored with the multitude of stars presented over the mountaintop. A gentle breeze caressed his face, and the hammock swayed ever so slightly. The warm air made his eyes heavy, and soon, he drifted off to sleep wishing that he and his group could stay in this wonderful place far longer, unbothered by the nefarious eye of a warlock.

CHAPTER THIRTEEN: INTO THE WILDBARRENS

A day's hike from Monkey Mountain, Falin and company marched into Stony Valley by escort of Kogg, Tang, and four monkey soldiers. The jungles of Suntalla quickly deteriorated into a rocky brown terrain, where all was dry, and arid air stung their throats. Dusty footprints crunched into the sandy path curtained by bouldered hills. Through their hike, Falin often kept glancing behind him, fearing Mulgus would appear to rain terror upon them.

"Ahead," Tang announced. Falin squinted and saw a rock wall built between two hills. It blended into the landscape, cloaked to a casual gaze. They approached, halting at its base, peering at the top three times their height.

"Who goes there?" a stony called.

Falin blinked, having not noticed the creature atop the wall, camouflaged by its color. In an odd sense, it was akin to Jimbuah, as a skully was in many ways similar to a man, and in many ways not. The broad creature loomed overhead, with a muscular frame and skin that appeared of sandy brown rock. With tiny eyes and lack of nose, the stony scanned the newcomers.

"It is Kogg, Alpha of Monkey Mountain, offering passage to a wizard and his Champions."

The stony waved to the left section of the precipice. Surprised yet again, Falin observed three more stonies lumber along the ledge, previously invisible. A crack appeared in the wall, forming a bulky set of doors opening inward by the sound of scraping earth. "You may enter," the stony called.

Kogg confidently led their pack. On the other side, a village of carved homes was built into the sides of hills, chiseled from the earth as entries to caves. Stonies meandered throughout, making casual notice of the newcomers. They seemed not to care.

Stonies wore wide, apathetic mouths, with short legs and rounded backs. Their eyes were tiny and dark, with nostrils set upon noses that were hardly a bump on their face. They had no ears, but a solitary hole on the sides of their heads. Despite stumpy legs, their arms were long and muscular, hands as large as their feet, with only four fingers instead of five.

Wearing nothing but baggy cloth pants, they leisured on rock as one might a cushion. Some leaned against their homes, others carried bales of goods. Stonies sat so still, they blended into the environment, and with every other second examination of an area in the town, Falin found himself noticing a stony gone unseen in a prior glance.

A guard plodded towards Kogg. "You want Dernin?"

"If he is available, it would be much appreciated," Kogg replied. "I understand he is a busy chieftain."

Without another word, the stony departed to retrieve their leader. Kogg muttered in the wizard's ear. "Believe it or not, that was rather polite for a stony."

Falin examined the town. "They seem a lax people."

Tang grinned. "That is until you rustle their rocks the wrong way."

"Do you know any of them?" Melquin asked Red and Jimbuah. "You must've come through Stony Valley, right?"

Red frowned and shook his head. "We stayed near the border of Varsa when we made our way up. We never passed this main portion of Stony Valley."

"Why would you do that?" Bossador asked. "You risked being caught by crags of Varsa instead of stonies?"

"I'd fight anything Varsa has," Red explained. A stony a little shorter than Bossador stomped by, its steps vibrating the pebbles near their feet. "I don't know what I'd do if a stony tried to attack me. They hurl rocks like Jimmy throws berries."

"I'm surprised you two weren't caught," Melquin replied.

"Huh," Red scoffed, offended. "We snuck through without so much as a peep. Not a creature on either side of the border knew we were there."

Tang rolled his eyes. "Your humility is overwhelming."

Falin watched another pack of stonies pass, silent and unspeaking. He sensed no magic in them, but their immense strength and sturdiness was evident. The same stony guard from earlier ambled to them. "Dernin can see you now. Follow me."

They marched through the little valley corridor, flanked by homes set in each hill. Cave openings cut with squares were made to appear like houses. Carthon politely nodded to a stony who leaned against his home, but the stony merely blinked, not to be rude, nor impolite, but watched with a simple contentedness in its existence.

Nym whispered to Carthon. "Do you know how to tell which stonies are girls?"

Carthon shrugged. "Two less pebbles than the men, I suppose."

Coming to a large cave opening sculpted into a hill, the soldier stopped. "Dernin waits for you here."

"Thank you," Kogg said.

They entered a circular room of dim lighting. A tiny fire glowed in the center, and at its opposite side, a stony of grand proportions sat with his legs sprawled like a child. He lifted his head slowly, and said nothing as they entered.

"Dernin," Kogg smiled. "It has been a few years. Thank you for welcoming us on short notice."

"Of course," Dernin answered. He spoke with sluggish wisdom. His gaze turned to the non-monkeys in the group. "You've brought more than monkeys. A wizard."

"Hello," Falin nodded, unsure how best to facilitate a conversation with the stony chieftain. "I am Falin, these are my Champions. We seek the Gems of Elsana. Thank you for meeting us."

Dernin nodded. "You may all sit," he gestured to the earth.

Obliging, they sat around the meager fire. Falin saw that the walls were bare, and there was nothing in the space but a couple of boulders. It was as if the cave had never been entered before.

Well aware of the stony's lack of loquaciousness, Kogg carried the conversation. "Dernin has been Chieftain of the Stonies for near two hundred years. He is revered on Monkey Mountain as an ally and protector from evils in the Wildbarrens."

Dernin made some semblance of a nod. "You do good on your mountain."

"The monkeys and stonies have an ancient alliance," Kogg continued. "We guard the northern passage, and they guard the southern passage."

"It must be difficult to guard the entire valley," Melquin said. "Does Varsa give you trouble from the east?"

"No," Dernin replied simply.

After an awkward pause, Kogg said, "We are here to ask that you offer them passage through your valley. Their journey calls for entry into the Wildbarrens."

Dernin's head moved faster than one would expect a stony could. He looked between Kogg and Falin. "No."

Falin blinked rapidly in surprise of the blunt response. "What do you mean, 'no'? We need to find the next Gem."

"It is a very bad idea," Dernin insisted.

"We don't have much of a choice," Falin responded. He held his staff loosely in his palm and could already feel it tug south. "The second Gem of Elsana is located there." The wizard stood, retrieving the map from his robe. "You see," he pointed to the white dot indicating the Gem in the southern tip of the Wildbarrens. "This is where we must go."

A low rumble of discontent emanated from the chieftain. He stared at the map before looking to the fire. Falin returned to his seat and waited for a response. Dernin said nothing, and did not move in the slightest as he stared at the flames. Jimbuah tapped his fingers on his knees, pursing his lips and glancing around. As Falin opened his mouth to follow up, Dernin finally spoke. "Wildbarrens have become worse. Much worse than ever. No good."

"So we've been told," Falin nodded politely. "But that is why we have brought these two," he gestured to Red and Jimbuah. As Dernin slowly shifted his gaze to the duo, Jimbuah smiled as wide as he could. "The wizards expected my journey to thrust us into the Wildbarrens. Red and Jimbuah have joined my group of Champions as they have ventured through before."

Dernin nodded, already aware. "I know them."

Jimbuah frowned and lifted his chin. "Hotuwi?"

"We didn't come to Stony Valley on the way north," Red responded. "You must have us confused with someone else."

Dernin shook his head, poking his temple. "Few years ago. Varsa border. Scouts tell me man with hat and whip and skully friend pass through. We let them go because they seemed okay."

Melquin covered her mouth and stifled a sharp laugh. Tang pointed at them with a mischievous grin. "They bragged about their subtly not minutes ago," the monkey said.

Red furrowed his brow and glanced sideways at the blue ape. "Big deal. One of their scouts saw us."

"No," Dernin shook his head. "All my scouts saw you. Said you were both noisy and bickered like children." The group, including the monkeys, laughed openly at the duo's expense. Red and Jimbuah crossed their arms.

Despite wanting to enjoy the moment, the underlying anxiety of Dernin's hesitancy to let them pass started to overwhelm Falin. "You must understand that we need to travel into the Wildbarrens. We have guides, and a warlock is hunting us." Falin's tone was aggressive, and the laughter quickly simmered down.

Dernin blinked once and stared at Falin for a few seconds. "I am not stopping you. I am trying to help you. It is a bad place, Falin."

Guilt crept over Falin for showing disrespect in the chieftain's home. "I understand. Your guidance is greatly appreciated."

"You have a warlock chasing you?" Dernin inquired.

Falin nodded. "Mulgus the Plague. He has servants of the Dark searching for us."

"Puh," Dernin said, as if amused. "They will not bother you here. Rest easy tonight. Magic does not hurt stonies."

"Thank you," Falin said. He thought for a moment. "Is there anything you can share with us about the Wildbarrens that might make our journey easier?"

"It will be difficult," Dernin assured. "The area on the map you showed is an oasis. Former home of ancient people. Rumeren's Oasis."

Nym cocked her head. "What people?"

Dernin shrugged. "No one knows."

"Have you been to Rumeren's Oasis?" Falin asked.

The stony nodded. "Once when I was a child, when there were still parts to the Wildbarrens that were not so evil. My grandfather took me. The oasis is quite large. And there is a vast lake at its center." Dernin rubbed his eyebrow in thought and stared off for a moment. "For safety in the Wildbarrens, don't use light at night. Death will find you." Red and Jimbuah nodded glumly, already knowing. "Be quiet, hide when you can," he continued. "There are more servants of the Dark in the Wildbarrens than ever before. Flesh-eaters. Feral gruns. Dragons. Chipcaws. Tarmoths. Evil spirits. Burrow monsters. Eye-snatchers. Poison plants..." As Dernin rattled off the horrors of the land, all listened in terrified awe. He paused for a moment and took a breath. "And now my soldiers tell me a fortress is being built deep in the wilderness."

"A fortress?" Kogg asked. "I have heard nothing of this."

Dernin shrugged. "Didn't matter until now."

"Who controls this fortress?" Bossador asked.

"Dark servants, we think," Dernin replied. "Dark servants of Shadow Kingdoms. Not the tribes of the Wildbarrens. It is likely a stronghold for the Shadows."

Falin rubbed his eyes, wishing the second Gem was hidden on the tropical island with Red's talking lizards. "For what reason could Dark servants have for building a fortress there?"

"It's strange to think about," Red admitted. "The gruns we encountered in the Wildbarrens were barbaric in comparison to those of the Shadow Kingdoms. They were more akin to animals than intelligent beings. I cannot imagine they have mixed with those of the Shadow Kingdoms."

"Bring your map back here." Dernin waved a lethargic hand. "Let me show you the way." Falin held it open for the stony. "Stay headed southwest. The fortress is said to be in this area." His thick finger tapped the parchment in the eastern Wildbarrens. His dark eyes scanned the paper with intense focus. "Avoid the flatlands of this area," he said. "Tribes live there for the springs. And a little south of there is riddled with tragor worms. The earth is soft so they travel freely."

Melquin frowned. "What are tragor worms?"

Dernin peered at the sage. "Giant worms. They have sharp teeth and will chase you, taking you below the surface." Melquin grimaced, and he continued pointing at the map.

"There lies a large canyon in this area," he pointed to a spot a little east of the central Wildbarrens. "It is filled with rock pillars and stretches for as far as the eye can see. It is known to my people as the Canyon of Idolum. You must go around at all costs."

"What lies there?" Falin pressed.

"Torment," Dernin replied.

After a few seconds of silence, Carthon said, "Could you be more specific?"

Dernin looked to the drak as if noticing him for the first time. "Phantoms." The fire sparked, and all but Dernin jumped. "There are endless perils in the Wildbarrens I cannot prepare you for. You must remain vigilant and pray for luck. You may rest here tonight, and in the morning, we can have a wagon ride prepared for your entry across the border with food and water."

"Thank you," Falin nodded. "You have been a gracious host. If you could have one of your men show us where to make camp, we will leave you be."

Dernin tilted his head and stared at Falin blankly. "I said you could rest here."

Falin's jaw dropped a little and glanced around the cave. By the looks on his Champions' and the monkeys' faces, they had misunderstood as well. "Oh, I didn't know you meant in your ca—home. I do not wish to impose."

"No bother. I have plenty of space."

Soon thereafter, the guests of Dernin found their beds upon the rock floor of the cavernous room. Falin resigned to being uncomfortable and laid his head to cool stone. Jimbuah snored softly to his left, with the Rorkshire hat draped over his eyes. After all Dernin warned them of the Wildbarrens, Falin wished not to think of it any further, as more concerning than anything, was the peril his Champions faced. Like an anxious parent, he worried about their safety in the Wildbarrens. To the dying embers of Dernin's fire, he fell asleep with a worried heart.

Come morning, dawn peeked through the cave opening, and Falin sat up, every muscle in his body stiff. Based on the stretches of his companions, he was not alone. Dernin and Kogg were nowhere to be seen. "Where'd they go?" Falin asked Tang, who appeared to have been up longer than the rest.

Tang motioned his head to the cave entrance. "Went to prepare the wagon. Kogg wants to see you off before you leave."

Falin nodded, and seeing no reason to dawdle, gathered his belongings and exited the cave, followed by his group and the monkey soldiers. They squinted in the morning light, shielding their eyes by the palms of their hands. Dernin and Kogg stood by an open wagon while stonies milled about. Falin walked to them, noticing the cart was horseless, with four thick ropes attached to its front. "Are we waiting for steeds?"

"No," Dernin replied.

Falin waited for more explanation, remembering there would be none without prompting. "Alright... then what will be pulling the wagon?"

"Stonies."

Falin peeked to Kogg for assurance. The alpha smiled. "Stonies are faster than you would think." Kogg looked to the surrounding group. "Dernin has had the wagon stocked with jugs of water and food for your journey. Are you all prepared to depart?" With sleepy and anxious eyes, they nodded. "Then I suppose this is goodbye," Kogg said, a bit woefully. Before Falin could react, the alpha enveloped him in a furry hug, squeezing so tight the wizard felt air forced from his body.

Once released, Falin stepped back and couldn't help but smile like a child. "I will miss you, Kogg. I'll be sure to revisit the mountain when I have all of my Gems."

"I would expect nothing less," Kogg grinned.

The monkeys said their goodbyes to the rest of the group, all given hearty and fuzzy hugs.

Tang rested his arms around Red and Jimbuah's shoulders. "I know I often tease these two, but you are guided by good hearts. I have hope for your company."

"Would you like to come with us?" Red asked his monkey friend.

"Not in the slightest," Tang replied.

Falin and his Champions boarded the wagon, and four muscular stonies took hold of the ropes attached to its front. Falin turned to the reserved Dernin and said, "Thank you for your counsel and passage of your land. I hope to see you soon."

"Good luck and goodbye, Falin," Dernin replied. "They are ready," he said to the stony convoy.

With startling force, the wagon lurched as the four stonies darted through the valley, the passengers clutching its wooden sides being jostled about. Falin gazed behind to see the village and monkey friends quickly shrink into the distance, as the stonies sprinted at the speed of a galloping horse.

On occasion, a wheel would catch a rock, bouncing them to land roughly on their bottoms. The hills blurred as their carriers' pounding footsteps kept steady.

Melquin spoke with her voice vibrating. "We should've had stonies take us from the start of the journey."

"I'm not sure my rear could handle it," Bossador admitted, bumping up and down.

Nym yelled over the rickety wagon. "Won't you get tired?!"

"No!" the stonies replied in unison.

The group whizzed on, and in time they became more accustomed to the rickety ride, and the road carried on for miles. Falin looked to the hills, sometimes noticing a stony hidden by the side of the road, blending into the terrain like boulders. The creatures seemed to be peppered throughout the landscape, content with resting unnoticed in the hot sun. After hours of travel, it came to the mid-afternoon, and Falin noticed the stonies begin to slow.

"Ahead!" Carthon announced, pointing further down the road.

They approached a brown rock wall, this one twice as high as the one they entered the valley in. Guards rested along its top and base, watching the wagon roll to a halt. Upon stopping, Falin deboarded, clutching the side of the caravan for balance, sensing his legs wobble. Red and Carthon each carried a sack of food and water on their backs, Bossador opting to take two.

"Thank you for taking us," Falin said to the stonies. They seemed not to exude any strain from their labor.

"You're welcome," they responded, as if completing a simple task. Without further conversation, they turned the carriage around, speeding off with dust clouding their wake.

Falin strode to the wall where a guard stood. He looked to its top, then scanned its length. He knew what was on the other side. It was not something he wanted to experience. Falin peered at his Champions. More than anything, he wished he could send them back to Monkey Mountain, to spend their days in the pools and nights on hammocks.

Falin knew that no matter what he demanded, they would be at his side every step of the journey. It felt a sin for a wizard to bring children of the Light to such a terrible place. His staff seemed to pull towards the barrier, eager to begin their trek. Falin took a deep breath. "We are ready to pass into the Wildbarrens."

The stony nodded without a word and banged the door twice. The wall opened inward by the sound of grinding stone. Falin stared over the threshold. It seemed a portrait of destiny, the final lament in this stage of his journey.

Rolling brown, rocky hills stretched for miles beneath a blue, cloudless sky. He twirled his staff loosely in his palm, staring to the horizon, wishing in a blink of an eye his feet would come upon the next Gem. To his chagrin, they did not, and he stepped through the entrance into the Wildbarrens. The Champions followed, carefully walking over the border. Scraping rock signaled the sealing of the wall's door, and upon its close, they found silence. No wind, no animals, no semblance of existence but for earth and sky.

Without parting his gaze from the landscape, Falin spoke to them. "I do not know what challenges we will face in this part of our quest, but I cannot offer enough thanks for facing them with me."

Speaking for the group, Jimbuah said, "'Tis an honor."

Falin felt a little flame of love spark in his being, turning to the skully with a smile. "The God of Light has blessed me with all of you. Let us venture into the Wildbarrens."

With stoic determination, their journey began on a battered path of hardened earth, the scuffs of their feet the only sound for miles. They kept vigilant and walked in the hot sun for hours, examining their surroundings on a constant basis. Red and Jimbuah appeared the most alert of all, twisting their necks in every direction as if predators were hiding behind every knoll they passed.

For the entire day of their first hike, hills kept them moving up and down. They plodded through tiny valleys, narrowed by steep cliff faces. Sometimes a snake would slither by, or some grotesque bug would dart into a hole, but all else kept quiet. As their first day neared its end, the road flattened, and the hills became less.

As the sun started to dip in the sky, Red whispered to them all. "We should find a place to rest. It will be dark soon, and that's when the Wildbarrens come alive."

"Anywhere you suggest?" Carthon muttered.

Red scanned their path forward. He pointed ahead and to the left. "That cluster of boulders there. We should camp between them. It will keep us out of sight of evil eyes if none already rest there."

In a few moments they came to the boulders, forming a partially enclosed campsite. Red examined every inch of the grounds before deeming it safe. They settled, resting with their backs to the large rocks. They remained still, and the sun fell to an orange sky. A chill set on the air and Falin grew anxious for their first night.

"I'll take first watch," Carthon offered. "But it may be difficult with no fire to see."

"It's brighter than you'd think here at night," Red said quietly. "The stars shine since the clouds are so few." He thought for a moment with a vacant gaze. "Guard with your ears as much as your eyes. Listen for the graze of gentle footsteps overturning pebbles. Don't be afraid to wake us even for a false alarm."

"We should keep our weapons in hand," Falin suggested. He looked to his staff and the solitary blue Water Gem.

Melquin watched his gaze and shot air from her nose in amusement. "It's a little ironic, isn't it?"

"What is?" Falin asked.

"That second Gem resides in a place where the first is most useless. There's not a drop of water here with you to fight with."

Falin grinned. "It seems Elsana has a sense of humor."

Nym rested her head upon Carthon's shoulder, and he wrapped an arm around her. "Is it the God of Light, or Elsana placing the Gems? I always assumed it was the God of Light," she asked.

"You know, I have no idea," Falin admitted. "I always figured it was Elsana since they're named for her."

Bossador carefully rested his sword upon his crossed legs so as not to make too much noise. "How is it they appear where they do? How do they get there?"

Falin yawned, then shrugged with tired eyes. "The wizards aren't even sure. Some divine hand puts them there, I suppose. They say they are placed in a way that is supposed to give purpose to our journeys."

Melquin twirled her dark braid in thought. "Do all wizards have to go to such lengths to find their Gems? Is it always so perilous?"

Falin took a thoughtful breath and remembered the stories Airo told of famous quests for the Gems. "Some do, some don't. Marko the Dragon earned his name because he had to fight an evil dragon for one of his Gems. Then there was Rulo the Peacemaker, who gathered all of his in the north. It was because of his quest he was present to help unite the Crown."

Carthon ran his thumb over Nym's hair. "Why do you think your journey has taken you the places it has?"

Falin searched the ground for an answer. "I've wondered this before. I don't know. I don't know if I'll have that answer for a long time."

Soon, the sun passed the horizon and stars poked through the sky, illuminating the surrounding desert. True to Red's words, night in the Wildbarrens was not quite as dark as other parts of Elsana. All held a dull blue glow, and they were able to see some distance. With Carthon taking first watch and Red agreeing to second, they found uneasy slumber. For hours they slept in the heated terrain, the rocks at their backs a constant nuisance. It was sometime in the early morning they were startled by a horrible scream.

All bolted upright, alert with weapons at the ready, listening intently. In the distance, a soul-wrenching wail flew over the hills, akin to that of a low-toned man shrieking, but not in fear. It howled as if in anger, over and over, causing goosebumps to prickle Falin's skin. It was horrid and inhuman. Red stood by one of the boulders with his fingers loosely fingering the handle of his whip, calmly listening to the sound. The screaming kept on, and with each moan, their ears begged for a reprieve from the awful sound. Nym leaned into Carthon for comfort, and Melquin put her fingers in her ears to soften the noise. Falin could not tell if the sound indicated this creature was being hunted or hunting, but regardless, it was terrible.

As suddenly as the noise started, it ceased, leaving them to the sounds of pounding hearts in their ears. Bossador opened his mouth to speak, but Red quickly raised his hand to stop him, shaking his head ominously. The Freelander placed his finger to his lips and nodded to them, motioning they return to sleep. All laid to rest again with hesitant eyes, but found light slumber until morning broke.

Falin blinked and saw most of his party awake, lifting himself, back aching. His throat stung from the arid air. "Could I get some water?" he said in a hoarse voice.

Bossador dug into the bag provided by the stonies and retrieved a clay jug sealed with a topper. "Here."

Falin took a sip and looked at the bulbous container. "How many of these did they give us?"

"Four," Bossador replied. "We should ration them as much as we can. But if this Rumeren's Oasis exists as they spoke, we should be able to make it without too much of an issue."

Nym frowned as she gazed across the rocky desert. "I don't want to think about what would happen if we ran out of water here."

"Drikino piba," Jimbuah muttered.

Falin cocked his head, usually able to get the gist of what the skully said. He was lost in this instance, as was the rest of the group.

"What did Jimbuah say?" Carthon asked.

Red lifted his hat and wiped the beads of sweat already procuring on his forehead. "Said we'll drink our pee if it comes to it."

Bossador scrunched his nose in disgust. "You jest."

"Nofa," Jimbuah replied with a sigh.

Melquin glanced between their guides. "Did you two drink your own pee last time you were here?"

Jimbuah nodded, "Yeh."

Red pursed his lips. "When you're dying of thirst, pee tastes like the purest spring water you've ever had."

Carthon snorted. "I never thought I'd gain respect for people advocating the consumption of urine."

"Thanks, Carthon," Red replied dryly. He scanned the horizon. "Dernin said we should go southwest, right?"

Falin nodded. "Yes, but we have to be careful to avoid the Tribal Flatlands as well as the Canyon of Idolum."

The Freelander sighed and nodded, gazing across the desert. "Let's go."

They departed southwest for a day of strenuous travel. The terrain changed little, but the further they hiked, the more insidious the Wildbarrens appeared.

Come midday on their third afternoon, Red stopped abruptly, looking ahead. Falin followed his gaze and saw a little white hill in the distance. "What is it?" Falin asked.

"Not sure," Red whispered. Continuing with caution, they quickly discovered it was a pile of bones, stacked tall and tight. The flesh was far gone, the skeletal remains dried and untouched. The group examined the sickening heap.

"What did this?" Nym muttered.

"I think it's tribal," Red said. Jimbuah scanned the hills with fearful eyes, twisting his neck in every direction.

Bossador examined the bones. "What makes you say that?"

Red took a deep breath and crossed his arms. "There are no heads. Do you see any skulls in the pile?" All eyes searched the mass grave, realizing he was right. Not a single skull was kept there. Red explained, "A beast wants the meat. It doesn't have any reason to keep the heads. But the tribes out here…"

"They're trophies," Falin finished his sentence. Red nodded with dismay.

"Are they grun tribes?" Melquin asked. "Dernin mentioned feral gruns that roam these lands."

Red rubbed the scruff of his face in thought. "Maybe. Jimmy and I crossed paths with both gruns and tribes of men here."

"Men do not feast on the flesh of men though," Carthon said. "Many of these bones look like man."

The Freelander peered at the drak with raised eyebrows. "Oh yes they would. Flesh-eaters are very real." Falin's gaze returned to the pile, repulsed. "I'm going to climb to the top of that hill." Red pointed ahead of them. "I want to check the land around us every so often. We should keep an eye out for smoke or any strange noises. If they sense our presence, we're what's for dinner." After surveying the area, Red deemed their trek on the current path safe.

With every step south they trudged, the sun seemed to berate them more intensely. Their skin glistened with sweat, opting to drink their stores of water out of complete necessity. Bossador often scratched his beard in the heat in vigorous and frustrated strokes. Jimbuah donned his green, pointed Rorkshire hat to keep his bald head guarded against the unforgiving sun. For two more days they carried on like this, and the odd occurrences became more frequent the deeper into the Wildbarrens they went.

Bones of strange looking animals littered their path, and there were times where some grotesque reptile would hiss or slither behind a rock before they could catch a glimpse of it. Odd spiky plants sprouted from the earth, with needles long and sharp, and a mucus-like substance that seeped from them. They pressed on, exhausted.

The sounds of the day paled in comparison to the noises of the night, where the Wildbarrens seemed to brag its horrors with bizarre calls of creatures of what kind, Falin had no idea. Multiple times they woke to shrieks, hollers, screams, and wails of monsters with no face. Some sounded to be that of bipedal animals, others hounds, most of nothing they'd ever heard before. Even with the gift of beastsaying, Falin knew not what they spoke, or intended to convey. They were incoherent and bloodthirsty. He merely wished they would not cross paths with whatever beasts lurked in the solemn hours of the night.

On the sixth day, Jimbuah and Bossador led their group. Jimbuah came to a sudden halt and grabbed Bossador by his shirt, pointing at the path ahead. "Spijadu!"

Bossador leaned his head. "I don't see any spiders, Jimmy." Taking another cautious step forward, he put his hand on the hilt of his greatsword.

Jimbuah grabbed him again, tugging him backward so that the madorian stumbled a little. "Spijadu," he insisted.

Bossador's eyes bounced between the empty path and Jimbuah. "I do not think the Wildbarrens is an appropriate place to play our game of tricks." Again, Bossador took a step forward, but this time both Red and Jimbuah held him.

Red tilted his head and examined the ground, crouching with a cautious eye. "He ain't joking."

Carefully, Jimbuah lifted a rock, tossing it underhand to roll twenty feet ahead. Like an illusion, and with blurring speed, a flat flap on the ground lifted, revealing a monstrous spider hidden in a den. A cow-sized, fuzzy brown arachnid lurched from a burrow, its giant pincers clamping on the rock. It hissed and stamped its spindly legs upon realizing it bit an inedible object, darting back inside the den, leaving the earthy flap lifted just enough so that it could watch the group with its multitude of eyes. They backed away, keeping careful watch on it, as it did to them.

Bossador became pale, even evident through his dusty skin and scraggly beard. "What in my grandfather's trousers…"

Red pointed his short-sword to the spider's den. "Look out for those little slits in the earth that seem just a little off-kilter like that."

Falin's skin crawled, imagining the creature taking him into its lair. Nym shivered, and Melquin blessed herself with a sign of the God of Light.

Bossador's eyes remained wide. "How am I ever supposed to sleep soundly again?"

"You won't. You just saw the face of your future nightmares," Red replied, patting his friend on the back.

The madorian prince looked to Jimbuah. "Thanks, buddy."

"Yeh," Jimbuah nodded fervently.

Two more days went on without event. On their eighth morning, covered in the grime of the land, Red trudged on, taking the lead, his head bent, the brim of his hat shielding his eyes of the sun. The earth seemed to sink, forming a trail in which they were surrounded by knolls and sloping cliff faces.

As Falin considered ordering they halt for a rest, the sound of rock tossed on rock echoed across the land. *CRACK*. They jumped, alert, listening intently over their thumping hearts. Falin grew doubly concerned as Red and Jimbuah's eyes bulged in fear. Melquin started to speak, but the duo raised their hands to silence her. They stood statuesque for another few minutes. They appeared as deer in the woods after hearing a twig snap. After the noise failed to repeat, Melquin spoke. "We sh—"

CRACK. It came again, closer this time, behind a hill they already passed. Before Red could speak, a barrage of stones hitting stones flurried over the hilltops. *CRACK. CRACK. CRACK. CRACK. CRACK*. Falin didn't know what it meant, other than trouble. Not bothering to whisper, Red looked to them all with an expression of horror. "*Flesh-eaters. Run.*"

In the same instant, loin-cloth wearing men emerged over the hills, standing above in a sinister presence. As Falin's group took flight, he caught a glimpse of the beings.

They held grim faces and leathery skin, wearing bones as jewelry in the form of necklaces, bracelets, headpieces, hats, and more. Their weaponry consisted of more bones, legs, and arms fashioned into clubs, spears, and crude blades. Falin and his Champions darted through the hills as rocks and sharpened skeletal pieces flew through the air over their heads. Bossador kept watch of incoming objects, using his wooden shield to block those being targeted. CLUNK. CLUNK. Bone spears meant for Nym bounced off his shield.

The flesh-eaters screamed in pursuit, some staying among the hilltops, others descending to take chase. "*JAKAYA! JAKAYA!*" they wailed, hurling their weapons at the prey. Falin and company struggled to keep at a distance, unaccustomed to the rocky terrain as the flesh-eaters were. A rock caught Falin in the back, and he gasped, stumbling, but was caught by Carthon's arm. He kept running, struggling to breathe as his eyes watered. Red led them forward as the flesh-eaters swarmed.

"Should we fight?!" Nym called.

"They'll overwhelm us!" Red responded, ducking a bone that whizzed by his head.

Falin caught his breath, seeing a group of the tribesmen approach from behind, their feet slapping the earth as guttural gasps stained the air. Jimbuah plucked a fireberry and tossed it over his shoulder. They yelped, blown away, one batting at his arm caught on fire. "Draw your weapons!" Bossador demanded.

Falin saw a cluster of ten or so flesh-eaters eager to meet them on the trail. He knew if they slowed to fight, they would be ensnared from behind. "No!" Falin yelled. "Keep running!"

He sprinted ahead of his group, taking the lead. Readying his staff, he bent his head and summoned a swell of magic within his being. A few feet from the troupe of flesh-eaters, he leapt and swatted his staff across them, hitting them with a flare of magic. They barreled head over heels, smashing their heads onto rocks. Despite the taxing cast of magic that fatigued the wizard, Falin and his Champions kept running for their lives.

"*JAKAYA! JAKAYA!*" the flesh-eaters wailed behind them.

Red scanned the hills. "They're swarming from that direction!" he pointed to their right. "This way!" he veered to the left, going off the path between two hills. The land became rockier and the group often stumbled, the flesh-eaters unrelenting.

Ahead, a muscular flesh-eater the height of Bossador trudged down a hill with a bulky bone club. He snarled, running towards the group. As Red prepared his whip, a hidden giant spider leapt from the ground, spewing dust into the air.

The spider bit the flesh-eater's neck, enveloping its captive in its four front arms, yanking the screaming wildman into the hidden underground den. Each member of their party took note to thank the God of Light for the moment of incredible fortune, taking a wide berth around the spider's lair.

Again, Falin peered over his shoulder to assess their situation, feeling his stomach drop. At least a hundred flesh-eating men chased with weaponized bones, eager to feast on the company. "*JAKAYA! JAKAYA!*" they hollered, keen on catching their fleeing meal.

Falin sensed his group was slowing, knowing they would soon tire and be forced to fight. His ribs ached and his legs begged for mercy, feeling limp on the earth in which they fled. His chest burned from the barren, dusty air pumping to and from lungs.

"This way!" Red gasped. The hills leveled off, and Falin saw they came upon a vast canyon, one they could not see the other side of. A steep slope fell into the gorge. It was filled with stone pillars as if a woodland of rock. Without a second thought, Red descended the hill into the canyon, the group following his direction. Upon hitting the bottom, they kept on, running for the cover of the rock columns scattered throughout. At once, Falin noticed many changes in their situation. Foremost, the flesh-eaters fell silent.

A final time, Falin glanced behind, and to his surprise, they were no longer being pursued. "Wait!" he yelled, stopping where the pedestals of rock began to fill the terrain. "Wait!" he shouted again. The Champions slowed in confusion, turning to see what Falin brought attention to. They stood in the canyon, looking up at the top lip of the slope behind them. The hundred flesh-eaters that hunted them seconds earlier stood quiet, lining the edge. His comrades hunched, panting, gasping for breath.

Melquin scanned their formation, gulping air. "Why — did — they stop?" A hundred sets of eyes glared down at them, not daring to chase any further.

Having time to think, Falin realized something else changed in their environment. There was a great Darkness in the place they stood. His gaze turned to their surroundings, examining the tall rock shafts towering over them. He looked again at the savage chasers lining the canyon. "They are afraid of this place," he announced. Falin remembered a warning Dernin offered nights prior. "This is the Canyon of Idolum. Home of phantoms."

The Champions looked to the depths of the canyon, a forest of scattered earthly columns. They could not see farther than a hundred feet ahead through the stone pillars, and despite the bright morning light, the path was shadowy. They faced the choice of flesh-hungry barbarians, or venturing into a Dark-ridden realm said to harbor phantoms of old.

"What do we do?" Nym asked, catching her breath.

Falin examined the line of flesh-eaters, then the canyon. Taking the lead, he passed the first section of pillars. "We have no choice but to move forward." He strode on, chin raised, exuding every bit of Light he could muster, showing the Dark he was unafraid. "We will pass through the Canyon of Idolum."

CHAPTER FOURTEEN:
A REALM OF DARKNESS

Hours after the attack of the flesh-eaters, Falin and company moved with caution through the Canyon of Idolum. To all, the presence of Dark was evident, but no threat could be seen, only felt by the crawling of their skin. Drifting between the pillars, they pressed on, unable to see the horizon or how far they needed to travel to escape.

In the seconds unfettered of footsteps, Falin could hear distant whispers, as if summoning him to depart from the group. None else seemed to notice, and he wished not to plague their already uneasy minds with this information. He didn't know if these were phantoms, or some other evil spirits playing tricks.

"We should rest soon," Falin announced. He examined the unending landscape of columns. "I don't know that we'll find anything better than where we are now. It's all the same."

Melquin bit her lip in thought. "Do you think someone with a light should stay awake at all times? Me, you, or Jimbuah?"

Even as the sun set, Falin could see the shadowy canyon would make it very difficult to see. "I don't know. I don't know what lurks between these stones."

"Dernin said any light would beckon creatures of the night," Bossador argued. "We should continue to follow his counsel."

Falin tapped the base of his staff in thought. "Dernin said there are phantoms in this canyon. If this is true, they already know we're here."

"But what else could be living here?" Carthon pressed. "Could we be luring them by shedding light?"

Not wanting to imagine what monster would find comfort in the home of phantoms, Falin took a deep breath. "One person with the power to summon light will stay on guard these next few nights, only doing so if we sense a threat."

Agreeing with the plan, they all but fell to the ground after a day of mental and physical exhaustion. They bent their heads, silent as the greying sky became darker. A chill set on the air, more so than when they were outside in the upper Wildbarrens. Falin shivered, wishing they could light a fire. Another evil whisper poked from the void, but he ignored it.

"How do we know the flesh-eaters won't come for us in the night?" Nym thought aloud. "Do you think they'll ambush us?"

Red shook his head. "No chance. They wouldn't even step foot in the edge of the Canyon."

Carthon rubbed his eyes and yawned, his fangs poking past his lips as his mouth stretched. "How was it they had so many bones? Are there that many people in the Wildbarrens to kill?"

"I guess so," Red replied. "I'm willing to bet some of the tribes kill and eat each other. Or they kill gruns and gruns kill them. There's always whatever animal they might come across. Then there're the droves of people exiled to the Wildbarrens."

"Are many criminals sent here?" Nym asked. "The Crown doesn't send anyone here as punishment. Only on rare occasions."

"Or as the highest honor," Melquin muttered.

"The Southern Kingdoms will," Red replied. "Letani and Wayili both do. Letani guards their border by a wall and mandatory service of younger soldiers." The Freelander thought more. "Then there are territories in the south and western Freelands who send prisoners to the Valdarian Coast, and from there, they're shipped to be dropped off on the shores of the Wildbarrens."

Melquin twisted her lip. "What a horrible sentence." All nodded glumly.

Falin heard a whisper behind the pillar he leaned against, turning his head to listen, deciding to ignore it. Still, none in his group seemed sensitive to the evil prods, so he left them blissfully ignorant. He would not offer the Dark fear on this night.

"So..." Bossador tapped his sword in thought. "If we come across a phantom, how do we fight it?"

Falin leaned his head on the rock and considered it. "I'm not sure any physical weapon will suffice. Airo taught me most of the phantoms have been scattered to the far ends of the world since the wars of the Beginning. It was mostly wizards who drove them from the mainlands."

"Hotowi?" Jimbuah asked.

Falin sighed with a frown, shaking his head. "The power of Light, I guess."

"It must've been a sight to see," Melquin said. "Wizards exiling phantoms."

"The phantoms left their mark, regardless," Falin admitted. "Many of the evil creatures alive today are spawns of corrupted creatures of Light." The wizard glanced to Carthon, hoping he had not offended his Champion. "And then we have draks, corrupted elves strong enough to return to the Light after thousands of years in the Dark."

Nym looked to her drakkish counterpart. "What is it they teach children of your people's past?"

Carthon shrugged a shoulder. "We are honest. We explain we were once elves taken by phantoms and manipulated into Dark beings, terrorizing lands of old, finding home in Mortulis. We teach about the few draks of Mortulis who were permitted to settle Vartulis on the coast of Elsana. They are taught that these draks sought freedom from the dependence of blood, and once free of the addiction, found Light."

Bossador took a heavy breath. "Makes you wonder what phantoms seek in this day and age."

All shook their heads, not wanting to think of it any further. Yet another haunting whisper echoed to Falin's ears, but none within his group took note.

He examined the faces of his Champions. They were worn, and they no longer hid it. Bags hung heavy under their eyes, with limp limbs resting, wishing not to rise again for some time. The Wildbarrens had taken its toll on them, as had the rest of the journey. They were pure, and such Children of Light deserved better. Falin wished to distract their minds of horrible thoughts as darkness set upon their feeble camp.

"If you could share a meal with *any* person in your race's history, who would it be? And why?" The Champions stared at Falin with surprise, not expecting to be asked such a question. "You go first, Melquin," he prodded.

Taken aback by the request, Melquin played at her long black braid in thought, her eyes darting over the earth. A grin crept across the sage's face. "Likely Zinna the Bountiful, first Queen of Mystica some fourteen-hundred years ago. She not only cemented the queenship as rulers of Mystica for centuries to follow, but she single-handedly saved the Freelands from starvation during her reign. I would love to ask her what ancient magic she used and how she wielded it."

"A good choice," Falin nodded. "And what about you, Bossador? I think I already have a guess."

A bashful smile peeked through the madorian prince's beard. "I feel like it's obvious I would say my ancestor Madrellor. There are so many I'd like to speak to, but to hear the tales of his journey at sea would be incredible."

Carthon scratched at some dirt on his pants and muttered, "Even through our kingdoms' recent distaste for one another, Madrellor is still revered to us. We see him as the ideal madorian."

Bossador beamed at the statement about his ancestor. "Thank you, Carthon. May I ask if you would choose Washborn? Much like Madrellor to your people, Washborn is praised by mine." Falin could feel the tiny bit of happiness shrouding them all in this conversation. He also noticed the Dark whispers increased as the sun disappeared, nudging for his attention, but he would in no way dampen his Champions' moods further. Whatever haunted voices prompted him from the beyond would remain his burden, as he was the only one sensitive to them.

"I'm not sure." Carthon rubbed his neck in thought. "I would love to meet Washborn—learn about what instigated his theory of introducing the Drakkish Senate to Vartulis." The drak smiled. "But I must choose Fex, one of Washborn's inner-circle. He was integral to the Drakkish Rebellion, and is said to be a wild individual."

"I have heard his name, but know little of him," Bossador admitted. "Perhaps some night you could share the tales of Fex."

Carthon nodded in agreement, then peered at his elvish love. "And which elf would you share a meal with?" he asked Nym.

Nym took no time to consider the question. "Tissel the Dragonrider."

Falin couldn't help but chuckle. "Do you need more time to deliberate your answer?"

"No," Nym replied. "She befriended not one, but *four* dragons throughout her life, and they were loyal to her for as long as she lived. Tissel went so far as to ride them to Dragos, being the first person to see a dragon egg hatch."

"That's got to be quite the thrill, riding a dragon," Bossador thought aloud. "I am admittedly envious of your Princess Bloom for getting the experience," he said to Red.

"She's not *my* princess," Red answered. His jaw fell a little, and his eyes glazed over. "Bloom would look real good flying with

Bjorgun though." He shook his head, picturing the sight, taking a deep breath. "Real good," he mumbled.

"What about you, Red?" Falin asked.

Red pried himself from daydreaming. "What?"

"What Freelander of history would you like to share a meal with?"

Red scratched beneath his hat then snapped a finger. "My family was said to have an ancestor who rode from the Valdarian Coast, all the way to the Rodrellan Coast to see which side had better tasting fish." Red chuckled. "I figure him, since he'd know what'd be best to eat."

"Oh, oh," Jimbuah said, eager to offer his answer. They looked to him and he said, "Babadebinko! Babadebinko fikirsti rijadi Buca. Flija Macka Ijales."

Red began to translate right away. "Babadebinko was the first skully to ride a Thunderbird. He flew them and first explored the Magpie Isles before anyone else."

"Yeh, yeh," Jimbuah nodded.

Falin noticed they became sleepy, ready for slumber. The sinister whispers passed through the air multiple times a minute now, growing irate he would not acknowledge them. They were horrible, and Falin's heart grew cold listening to their warped tongues revile his being. He smiled at his group. "All wonderful choices."

"What about you, Falin?" Melquin asked. "You never told us which wizard you would most like to share a meal with."

Falin hadn't considered it, merely playing the game to keep his company preoccupied as it became dark. The sun was near set, and it became difficult to see, but he could tell his Champions were all close to sleep, fighting slumber for a few more moments. Falin wished to settle them into a peaceful night so that he might take an exhausted watch.

He spoke over the evil whispers only he was aware of. "There was a wizard named Osa, thousands of years ago," Falin began, speaking soft and sweet. The Champions listened, taking rest against the rock columns. Melquin laid with her head on her hands and fought droopy eyes. Nym reclined against Carthon's chest.

"Osa wished to discover all the creatures of Elsana, as no one had ever named them. They were just creatures. So Osa went into the wilderness and searched for every animal so that they might have titles."

Falin watched as the group's eyes batted slowly, and their breath became heavy. Night was upon them, and its hold of the canyon was tight. The malevolent murmuring intensified, but Falin kept on. They were voices of pure Darkness, choking him with despair. Falin clung to sanity by offering his children of the Light comfort.

"Osa went to the lakes and named the lily cats, and the otterfoxes, and the turtle hogs. Then he went to the forests, naming the craggon bears, the tree badgers, and the moon skunks." Bossador, Carthon, and Nym drifted off, but Melquin, Red, and Jimbuah remained awake, listening. "And then Osa searched the skies..." Falin said softer. He could barely hear himself over the evil voices now. They were hoarse and hissing taunts, but he would not succumb. "...naming the honey birds, and sparkling canaries, and fleet finches." Melquin fell to slumber, as did Red. Falin looked to Jimbuah who barely kept awake, his eyes remaining closed longer than they were opened when he blinked. The whispers turned to voices of lividity, berating the camp, in an ancient, Dark tongue, but Falin kept speaking to Jimbuah, disregarding them. "And then Osa went to the mountains and named the flying goats, and the leopard bears, and monkey rats." Jimbuah snored soundly, and Falin fell quiet.

The voices yelled through the Canyon, teeming with animosity in Falin's presence. He surmised they were spirits, as a phantom would actually be a threat. These were nefarious gnats with words of scorn. Falin would never know what exact menace they spoke, but he did know they wished him immense pain and torment.

He sat in the shadows, watching the chests of his Champions rise and fall. With stinging eyes, he kept guard, listening to the harsh hatred of his being, focusing on the Light, preventing the

Dark from seeping into his heart. When it came time to wake someone else to keep guard, he remained still, wishing for them all to get
a full night's sleep. Through the night's abyss, the sun snuck over
the horizon, and in time, the voices returned to whispers, depleting
in frequency until morning came to its full might, and his ears were
given a reprieve.

Melquin groggily lifted her head, squinting at the light, seeing
Falin sitting alone, bloodshot in the eyes. "Did you take watch the
whole night?" Falin nodded sleepily without a word. Nym stirred,
as did Red, then the rest woke, climbing from the ground to stretch.
"You should have woken me to take second guard," Melquin insisted. "You should have not stayed up the whole night."

Falin lifted himself, raising his staff by the palm of his hand. It
tilted in the direction of the second Gem. "Let's not delay."

For the day they hiked, it felt more like wandering, at least to
Falin. The air was still hot, but unlike the upper portion of the
Wildbarrens, it felt thick with moistured poison. His head ached
from the night without sleep, and the sun only made the pounding
worse as they went on. He wondered if their exit from the canyon
would even bring them close to the oasis. Their water stores were
already beginning to run low, and in a little time, they would start
reaching a point of crisis.

"Up ahead," Nym pointed between the pillars.

Falin stretched his neck, seeing something lying on the ground
in their path. Bossador put his hand to his hilt and said, "Ready
your weapons."

They approached with caution, and Carthon, walking ahead of
all else, was first to make out what it was. "It looks like bodies. Recently killed."

A chill ran across Falin. Something about the bodies was not
right. "Be careful," he warned. "We don't know what tricks this
canyon has for us."

As the group came upon the grave, a sickening realization battered them all. They stared at themselves. By some Dark magic, the

rotting corpses were that of Falin and his Champions, ghastly pale with flies buzzing around the bodies, brutally mutilated.

Melquin looked away, holding her stomach. "What have I just witnessed?! Is that us?!"

Falin stepped closer and bent over, examining the grave. He looked at his own, half-lidded cadaver, lying motionless. His insides were torn open, with fresh maggots feasting on his organs. His eyes scanned the rest, in a similar fate. They were butchered, their bodies harvested and faces contorted in permanent anguish. It was a horrid sight.

Red stared blankly at his corpse and Jimbuah's. "How is this possible?" Jimbuah shook his head in remorseful awe.

Carthon crouched, and his nose scrunched in fury as he gazed upon Nym's mutilated body. A hiss escaped him as he sprang back up. "Curse the spirits of the canyon who wish this upon us. Let them try!"

Falin looked away from the illusive gravesite to his Champion. "Do not provoke the phantoms, Carthon."

Nym wiped a tear away from her eye and sniffed. "We should keep moving. There is no point in us staying here to look at this atrocity."

"You're right," Falin agreed, staring at the bodies. It was his worst fear, seeing his Champions killed, especially so brutally. If anything, it morphed the fright into determination, promising himself he would never let such a thing happen.

They left the site of the strange massacre, carrying on without event. The stars rose again, and Falin found it odd he was not plagued with whispers as he was the night before. It was silent, and he knew not what to make of it. He fell to the ground with his eyes pleading for slumber. "Melquin, can you take first watch? Jimbuah, you take second. On the off chance we can get out of this canyon tomorrow, we won't need someone with a light. If not, the three of us will share turns tomorrow."

Melquin gulped but nodded dutifully. The Champions muttered amongst themselves, but Falin did not listen, immediately falling to the ground to delve into a much needed slumber. He slept deep and without bother for the first portion of the night until nightmares began to plague him.

Falin woke in the night, and a faceless, shadowy figure of evil aura stood over him, uttering venomous incantations. A phantom.

The wizard moved to spring into action, reaching for his staff, quickly realizing he was paralyzed. He strained to move, remaining immobile. The phantom kept in place, sputtering in a tongue other than this world. It felt like icy daggers plunging into Falin's ears.

From the corners of his eyes, he could see his comrades sleeping soundly. He struggled to scream, but no words came out, and instead, he lay still. He forced every bit of his mind to make some motion, anything to warn them, wishing they could wake and assist, but alas, he remained pinned to the earth with this fiendish presence reaching closer and closer. The phantom placed its hand over Falin's heart, and the moment they came in contact, Falin blinked to sunlight.

He bolted upright, gasping, shocked to see the morning had long been risen. A cold sweat covered him, and he pawed at where the phantom touched his chest. His company looked to him with concern.

"Are you okay?" Melquin asked.

Falin steadied his breath and stood, wishing to hold his staff. "Why did no one wake me?"

"You hadn't slept the night before, we figured we'd let you get some rest," Bossador said. "Were you having a bad dream?"

Falin moved to answer yes, but what happened to him was so vivid. He knew it was not merely a dream. Wiping his face of earthy dust, he sensed there was something concerning their minds. They looked to him fearful, tight-lipped. "What is it?"

Carthon cleared his throat. "I had a poor night's sleep myself." The drak rolled up his sleeves, revealing his arms covered in scratch

marks of a three-clawed creature, the gashes deep and long. He lifted his shirt and showed more across his chest and stomach, and
turned his head to present another along his neck. "Melquin tried to
heal them, but her magic did nothing."

Falin's jaw clenched. "Did you see a shadow being in your
dreams?"

Carthon raised his eyebrows, surprised Falin already knew. "I
did."

Falin lifted his robes to examine his chest, seeing a single claw
mark across his heart, the same as Carthon's. Falin dropped the
robe. "Do you see why you should not incite the violence of phantoms?"

Carthon nodded. "It was out of anger. I apologize."

"You didn't know," Falin soothed.

Falin went to the water jugs and took a sip, squinting in the direction they needed to travel. He looked up to the pillars and back
to their path. He thought to ask Nym if she could climb one and see
if they are close to an exit, but his instinct told him some entity
would cause a slip of her fingers near the top. He shook the jug seeing it was near its empty, leaving only one left for their consumption. The wizard returned the jug to its bag, then started their trek.

As the day went on, Jimbuah hummed a tune to himself, one of
bouncy melody that seemed out of place. Falin sensed it was him
hoping to instill some sort of normalcy, as there was nothing else in
the forsaken place that would.

On occasion, Falin would catch movement from the corner of his
eye, often at the base of one of the pillars, sometimes on their sides,
brushing them off of as tricks of the tired mind. He convinced himself they were shadows, though in time, it became evident there was
something more. Gripping his staff tighter, he carried on, not feeling
he should alert the group until necessary.

"Would you stop humming?" Carthon snapped at Jimbuah. "Do
you want to stir every wretched thing in the Wildbarrens?" Jimbuah
ceased, muttering something under his breath. "What was that?!"

Carthon seethed, stopping to turn and glare at the skully. He panted with clenched teeth, irate. The Champions paused to glance between the two.

Falin examined the drak; he seemed paler than usual, with eyes that flickered a sentiment of hate. The claw marks on his necks seemed to not be healing. It bothered Falin, but he hadn't the energy to say more than, "Enough," in a low voice. "Keep moving."

Yet another day ended with no end in sight to the Canyon of Idolum. Much like the whispers of the first night, Falin noticed the hidden movement increased as the sun dipped. He looked ahead and saw Nym's eyes stuck on a pillar to their left. "Do you see them too?" he called.

The group stopped, and Nym said, "It is the third time I have noticed movement from the corner of my eye in the last few miles, but it appears to be nothing when I look. I assumed it was a trick of the shadows, but now I am not certain."

Falin considered their options. The sky greyed further, and it became strenuous to see too far ahead. Darkness was upon them. "We will rest here for the night." The Champions took their places on the ground, their heads bent in fatigue.

Bossador rubbed his eyes. "Are you certain we are not going in circles?" he asked Falin.

Carthon responded before Falin could. "Of course we're not. Have you not been paying attention to where the sun sets every day?" His words held malice, and Bossador retracted.

"Carthon," Falin said with a warning tone. "Do not let your frustrations pour unto your comrades." The slightest hiss escaped Carthon's mouth as he bent his head and muttered to himself. Nym looked to him in concern.

For just an instant, Falin saw a face behind the pillar where Carthon sat. A white, ghastly face of no emotion, with long, grimy black hair, wide eyes, and wiry lips. Before Falin could react, it slid behind the column again. "No one move," Falin demanded, running to the other side of the pillar. Upon getting there, the creature was gone.

"What was it?" Melquin asked.

"A person. Or some creature that looked like a person," Falin answered. "I saw its face." The image sent chills down his spine. He returned to where they sat, gazing around, as did the rest of the group. They squinted, as the sun was entirely set, and darkness began to envelop them.

Red leapt and pointed in the direction they came. "I saw it! Over there!" His finger trembled at the sight.

They faced where he directed, but as they turned, Nym shouted, "It's over there now!"

Falin quickly realized what was happening. He hit his staff hard to the earth, and it glowed with a bright white light, setting them in a capsule of illumination. "There is more than one."

Upon acknowledging their presence, more than fifty faces crept from the shadows. People of chalky skin peeked around the pillars. Half of them walked to the group, the other half crawling and dragging their bodies along the earth. All had black hair that appeared wet. Their eyes were frozen wide, with black circles underneath, as if sentenced to a life without slumber. The creatures' jaws hung loosely, moving in disjointed rhythm as if trying to speak, causing their teeth to occasionally clack over the constant, subtle hissing noise they made. Some appeared to be women, others men, all horrid.

Falin looked in all directions, seeing they were surrounded, and to his chagrin, even more were above them, clinging to the stone columns upside down. The bloodless creatures stared at the group, each of which halting where Falin's light ended.

"Wh—wh—wh—," Nym stammered. "A—are these—phantoms?"

Falin shook his head, trying to keep his breathing steady. "You cannot see phantoms."

"Bujijis," Jimbuah whispered in a mix of realization and fear.

"What'd he say?" Bossador asked.

Red gulped as a bujiji tilted its head and stared at him, moving its mouth in sporadic clacks as if trying to communicate. "I—I don't know."

"Bujijis," Jimbuah repeated. He shook his staff, and it came to life with an orange glow. He stuck it in the faces of the nearest creatures and they recoiled back to the shadows.

Seeing this happen, Melquin quickly lit her staff causing their isle of light to grow that much larger, keeping the bujijis a little farther at bay. "Anything else we should know about bujijis, Jimmy?"

"Hani mikithi. Hakutu lija…"

Red translated, "They're skully myths. They hate light."

"Ibatu yukari sofali en bebacomi bujiji," Jimbuah said.

Red took a sharp breath of fear and backed closer to Falin in the center of the light.

"What was the last part?" Carthon pressed.

Falin turned to see Red's chin shake. "They eat your spirit, and then you become a bujiji."

The Champions squished together, facing the bujijis in a circle. As the rim of their light tightened, the creatures pressed closer, tilting their heads, unblinking, their mouths dangling with hair flopping about. The monsters crawled over one another, with inhuman stares never breaking from the group. "Can we fight them?" Bossador asked.

"I wouldn't chance it," Falin warned.

Bossador carefully lifted a rock from the ground, shaking it in his palm in consideration. He set his gaze on a bujiji clinging to a pillar near them. He cocked his arm, tossing the stone at the creature, catching it above the eye. They watched its head flinch, then stretch its mouth wider than any human could, blasting a bone-chilling scream unto them. It continued to holler, eyes bulging, over and over until finally settling into groans.

"Bossador," Falin began, "don't do that again." The madorian prince nodded in agreement, staring at the angry bujiji in regret.

Melquin waved her light in an effort to keep them back. "What are we going to do?"

Falin took a tired breath and avoided eye contact with the soul-hungry beings. "We are to stay just as we are for the night, and pray we reach the end of this canyon before dark tomorrow."

The night settled in as did the bujijis. For hours, they stood silent, aside from the hissing and clacks of the monsters. The Champions maintained their positions, stiff and ready to fight or flee if necessary.

Growing as accustomed as he could to their presence, Falin examined a bujiji closest to him. Bujiji eyes remained unblinking, stretched wide, and did not waver when coming to meet their gaze. It was as if they sought it. Falin stared into its eyes, seeing it was indeed soulless, and the longer he looked, the more jittery it became, writhing. Unable to peel his gaze away, it seemed to gasp, trying to communicate.

He could not help but lean forward to listen, and as he did, his staff made part of their circle vulnerable, bringing more shadow into their group. A number of bujijis lunged in that area, and he shined his light on them, casting them back. In doing so, the space behind him became dark, and in that instant, he felt the icy grasp of a hand wrap around his ankle. It tugged, and Falin fell, dropping his staff, being dragged to the darkness.

The bujijis frenzied. He watched as dozens of pale faces swarmed over him. Melquin quickly shined her light over Falin, causing the eager bujijis to recoil. The rest of the group huddled close to Jimbuah. "Come close!" she said to Falin, grabbing him by the scruff of his robes. Falin shook, having seen his existence come to a near end. The bujijis staggered in the shadows, keeping their same expressions.

"Thank you," Falin said. "Thank you, Melquin. I owe you my life." Falin struggled to keep his staff steady in trembling hands.

Melquin's voice tremored as she spoke. "You owe me nothing. I took an oath."

Another few hours went by, and Falin's group fought exhaustion in the constant company of the bujijis. Their heads would at times nod, but they held strong, not giving the entities any chance at attacking again. In the early hours of the morning, Falin thought his ears started to play tricks on them. He heard a man's voice yell 'no!' from around them. As he searched the dark for the source of the voice, Red asked, "Did y'all hear that?"

"Yes," Nym nodded. "It was—"

A woman's sobs came from the shadows. "Please! No! Please! Please!"

Falin's eyes searched the creatures. "Is that the bujijis?" His neck twisted in all directions.

"Yekasa," Jimbuah whispered.

As if by a chain reaction, a flurry of voices sprang from the crowd of bujijis, not of their own. They continued to make the same faux-speaking motion with their mouths, as the voices of pleading people resonated through the air. The words the creatures spoke did not match the movement of their lips. "Not my child! Not my child!" a woman screamed from a male bujiji's mouth.

"I'll do anything! Please!" an old man's voice begged from a female bujiji. Mismatched shouts imploring for mercy filled the air, near incoherent in their multitude. Falin guessed they were the voices of the victims of the bujijis, seeking sympathy in their final moments. He stared at a white bujiji in front of him, crawling closer to the light in her brazen attitude. Her eyes bulged behind strands of hair, her mouth resonating the cry of a toddler. His stomach turned as they locked eyes. The group clustered closer together.

Then in an instant, the cries ceased. Falin saw one of the most beautiful things in his life—the crack of dawn. The sky seemed a hair lighter, and the bujijis became less bold in their intrusion upon them. Falin and his Champions remained firm, keeping a careful watch. As the sun rose, ever so slowly, the bujijis slinked away behind the columns, one by one, out of sight. Rays of morning shined on the Champion's faces, and finally, they were free of their night's tormentors. They fell to the earth in overwhelming fatigue.

Melquin held her head in her hands. "That was the worst night of my life."

Falin blinked, wiping his stinging eyes. "It was for all of us." The faces of the bujijis were burned in his mind. He noticed Jimbuah lay on his back, quickly finding sleep. "Jimmy, we must travel today. We can't stay here."

Jimbuah slowly nodded and stood, scratching his head. "Yeh."

"We would have been better off fighting the flesh-eaters," Carthon scowled. "It was foolish of us to come here."

"We have no choice but to move forward," Falin said. "I sense we are coming to an end."

"How would *you* know?" Carthon spat.

Falin examined the drak, still not himself. The Canyon of Idolum had taken its toll. "Wizard's Instinct. Let's go."

Through grunts, they stood, trekking on, with eyelids weighing like stones of their faces. Falin would often check their surroundings. He no longer saw movement in the shadows, nor heard whispers of infernal voices taunting him. He sensed much of the evils of this canyon were behind them, yet a final Darkness plagued their group, one he could not shake. He figured it would soon disappear in their exit of the gorge. The sun rose high in the sky, and they kept quiet, though every so often, Carthon would mutter angrily to himself. Nym watched him from the sides of her eyes in concern, but said nothing. Their focus was to make their exit.

Come noon, Bossador bellowed excitement. "Look!"

Falin lifted his gaze to where Bossador pointed, standing on his toes. A couple hundred yards ahead, the pillars appeared to come to an end at a hill that climbed from the Canyon of Idolum. Relief swept across them.

"We're almost out!" Melquin cried. "I thought we'd never see the end!"

Falin scanned the columns around him. He still sensed some hovering Darkness, but could not place where. "Let's not delay. We might even be able to find shelter before nightfall." Needing no encouragement, they hurried, hiking at a fast pace in the final stretch of their journey through the canyon. Falin hoped the oasis they sought would not be far on the other side.

In no time at all, they came to the bottom of the slope climbing from Idolum, free of the forest of pillars. To Falin's comfort, he felt the Dark aura suddenly fall behind them, assuming it was merely the canyon's energy. Red began to eagerly scale the hill, as did Bossador, Melquin, and Jimbuah.

Nym did not, turning around. "Where is Carthon?"

Dread spilled over Falin. He turned, seeing the drakkish Champion at the edge of the thicket of rock columns. Carthon crawled on all fours, his head bent.

"Carthon!" Nym screamed, darting towards him.

Fearful for her safety, Falin ran after, the Champions descending the hill to follow. Coming to the drak, Nym crouched and placed a hand on his back, stooping to examine his bent face. "Carthon, are you alright? What happened?"

Carthon choked, struggling to breathe. Falin saw Carthon's sleeves appeared wet, and blood dripped down them onto his hands. The wizard knelt, lifting a sleeve to find the phantom's claw marks pulsing, oozing a sickly dark blood. Falin felt his own claw mark burn. An undeniable Darkness shrouded his friend. Carthon batted Falin's hand away as if the wizard's touch hurt, muttering something none could understand.

Surprised by the gesture, Falin and company gave Carthon space, except for Nym, who kept close. "Carthon," she said softly. "What is wrong?"

Without warning, Carthon leapt up, grasping Nym by the throat, lifting the tiny elf off the ground. She choked and clutched his wrist, eyes bulging in terror. The rest gasped and recoiled before taking action, shocked at what they saw.

Carthon's eyes were black, and his face was covered in throbbing purple veins. He snarled, squeezing the neck of his beloved.

Falin hit the drak with magic, causing him to drop Nym and fly into a stone pillar. Jimbuah ran to assist Nym who clutched her windpipe, gasping for air, red in the face. The rest circled Carthon, weapons prepared. Carthon pulled himself upward, removing his swords and hissing at his comrades. He seemed savage and out of control of his body.

"What has happened to him?" Bossador said, holding his greatsword and shield at the ready.

Falin peered into Carthon's black eyes, sensing the same dread from his encounters with the warlocks Nyril and Mulgus. "He is possessed by a phantom." Falin recalled the drak's aggressive mood from the previous days, having assumed it was frustration with the canyon. "It must've been corrupting him for days. It has finally taken control."

Phantom Carthon wildly swung at Red, who parried the attack with his sword. "We can't hurt him!" he exclaimed. "What do we do?!"

"Keep him surrounded," Falin said, biding time to think.

Melquin dodged a blow from Carthon, tossing him backward with magic. Carthon landed on his feet, hissing. Fear fled Falin, and he became enraged; enraged some phantom would be brazen enough to corrupt the Champion of a wizard. Falin confidently walked to Carthon. As the bedeviled drak lunged, Falin hit him in the face with magic again. Carthon tumbled to the dirt, disoriented. "Hold him!" Falin demanded of his Champions.

Before Carthon could stand, Bossador took hold of his ankles. Melquin held one arm and Red the other. They struggled as the drak thrashed, hissing and gasping. Jimbuah and Nym came closer. Jimbuah put his arm around his elven friend as she watched in shock, tears streaming down her face.

Falin stood over Carthon, lowering the head of his staff to the drak's face. "Release him!" he ordered. "The Light demands it!"

Still, Carthon flailed, moaning and clawing for escape. He nearly broke free of Red's grasp, but the Freelander kept him pinned. Falin yelled louder, pressing his staff onto Carthon's chest. The staff's head began to glow a white light. "Release him! I demand it as a servant of Light! Release him!"

Carthon's chest arched, writhing, desperate, his mouth foaming. "By the God of Light, I demand you release him!" Falin growled. Carthon's black eyes began to weep blood, and the cuts on his arms and legs oozed, making them difficult to grip. Falin channeled all the Light he could. "Be gone phantom! Release him! Release him! I demand it in the name of the Light!"

Carthon choked, his face turning purple, the veins pulsing on his pale cheeks. Nym cried, "You're killing him!" she leapt forward to stop Falin, but Jimbuah held her tightly. She fell to the ground, watching Carthon sputter.

"*Release him!*" Falin yelled, his staff glowing so bright all present squinted. Falin would not yield. "*The Light demands it! He is not yours to take!*" he bellowed. His proclamation echoed over the Canyon of Idolum for miles. Carthon convulsed, no longer breathing, his mouth stretched, face streaked with black, bloody tears.

Nym sobbed, watching the event from Jimbuah's arms. The Champions did all they could to maintain their grasp on Carthon. Falin drove every bit of Light he could through Carthon, his voice booming. "RELEASE HIM! THE LIGHT DEMANDS IT!" The head of Falin's staff shined like an earthly star, emboldened by his tenacity to free his Champion. "RELEASE HIM!"

Carthon jerked, his lips stretched, and a cloud of black smoke poured from his mouth, nostrils, and eyes. Falin heard some otherworldly tongue murmur in the dark mist exiting his Champion. It rose over their heads and fled for the canyon.

Falin fell to the ground, depleted of energy. His head pounded in severe exhaustion, but he sensed his work was done.

Carthon lay unconscious, soaked in blood, but the veins on his face were gone. Jimbuah released Nym, and she ran to him, carefully lifting his head into her lap. He seemed not to breathe. "Carthon," she said feebly. She brushed his forehead. "Carthon, please," she squeaked.

The drak suddenly inhaled, and his eyes fluttered. He looked to Nym and his mouth fell open, gasping, shocked to be alive. "I fell into Darkness. I have seen true Darkness!" he proclaimed, horrified. "I have seen the Darkness!"

"You are free now," Nym wept. "You have returned to the Light." The Champions watched in extreme relief. Falin rested on the ground, so fatigued it felt a struggle to keep his head lifted. Nym wiped the blood that streaked Carthon's face. She bent and pecked her lips to his forehead.

Carthon clasped Nym's hand. "I was lost." His breathing returned to normal. He rolled to his side, struggling to stand, even with Nym's assistance. Bossador hoisted him from under the arm. Carthon looked to Falin, who remained on the ground. "I owe you everything. You saved me from an eternity of unspeakable suffering."

Falin nodded half-heartedly, lifting himself with his staff, leaning heavily on it as his knees wobbled. "No problem." He looked to his Champions. "It is time we leave this Light-forsaken place."

Agreeing with every fiber of their beings, the Champions assisted Falin and Carthon up the slope. Once at the top, Falin gazed over the edge of Idolum, praying he would never return. He looked ahead to the remainder of the Wildbarrens, seeing no sign of the oasis. A cluster of rocks formed a makeshift shelter some hundred yards away, and Falin pointed to it. "We will take rest there for the remainder of this day." Battered in every way, Falin and the Champions made for some semblance of safety, grateful to live another day.

CHAPTER FIFTEEN:
VUG-RHAL

"For how long does this wretched land go on for?" Bossador moaned. "Are we even close to Rumeren's Oasis?"

Falin felt his staff tug south, but had no idea where they were. Three days passed since their exit of the Canyon of Idolum, and they traveled still, deprived of energy in their endless trek. The evening prior, their final jug of water was depleted to a final swig, and none wanted to claim the sips for themselves.

Red wiped the dust from his eyes, waving away a fly with his hat. "Couldn't tell you, your highness." He fanned himself of the relentless heat, squinting across the rocky landscape. Tilting his head, he pointed to a cluster of hills. "You see that, Jimmy?"

Jimbuah lifted his gaze to where he directed, shrugging. "Ah?"

"Those plants?"

Jimbuah peered closer. "Yeh!"

"Is it the oasis?!" Melquin exclaimed.

"Shhh!" Red demanded. "We're still in the Wildbarrens." He peered at the hills. "I don't think so. I figured we're lookin' for something bigger. But those plants indicate there could be some water feeding them."

"Well then let's go!" Bossador urged, hustling on.

"Step lightly," Carthon warned. "We do not know what hides on the other side."

Bossador ignored him, hurrying to the hills, the rest trailing. Falin's head pounded from dehydration, and he prayed their luck had changed.

Once circling the hill, an immaculate sight met their eyes. A modest spring of water bubbled gently, forming a tiny pool, tightly surrounded by cliff faces.

"Thank the Light," Nym praised.

Falin thought it too good to be true considering their past Wildbarrens experiences. "Wait," he commanded. "How do we know that it's safe to drink?"

They crouched at the lip of the pool and stared, desperate to quench their thirst. "Are you afraid it's poisonous?" Bossador asked.

Falin shrugged, entertaining the possibility. "Everything else here has tried to kill us, why would the water be any different?"

Melquin blinked slowly, impatient for a decision. "Falin, we're a couple of hours away from filling our water jugs with pee. I'm ready to take the chance."

"I'll do it," Carthon volunteered. "You all rescued me from the phantom. It is the least I could do to repay you." Nym moved to argue, but Carthon dipped his hand before she could.

"You don't have to, Carthon," Falin said. "It should be me who tries it."

Carthon played at the water with his fingers. "Don't be ridiculous. I took an oath."

Cupping his hand, he lifted some water, sniffing it. He pressed the liquid to his parched lips and slurped, focusing on his body's reaction. "It tastes fine to me. I feel nothing. I feel better."

"That's good enough for me," Bossador said, thrusting his hands to the pool. The madorian scooped from the spring, taking a heaping gulp. Water dripped down his beard, little sprinkles rippling the water as they fell. He groaned in pleasure. "By Elsana, that is incredible."

Carthon drank again, then turned to them all. "I think it is safe to say we may consume this without harm." Needing no further encouragement, Falin and Champions began to guzzle water by cupped hands, splashing their faces like birds at a bath. They couldn't help but laugh at their luck.

"I'm so glad we're not drinking pee," Melquin said.

Jimbuah nodded whole-heartedly. "Yeh, yeh."

Falin sat crosslegged, examining the hills around them. They were completely surrounded. "We should stay here for the day, fill up our jugs, and leave tomorrow. We have enough food."

"I think that is a splendid idea," Bossador concurred. He fell to his rear, having drunk his fill. "I was certain we would die."

"We still had a ways to go before that happened," Red replied. "You'd be surprised how tough you get when you're on your last few strings."

A harrowing thought crossed Falin's mind. "We need to worry about getting back after the second Gem."

The group became somber at the thought. Nym pursed her lips. "What's the next Gem supposed to be?"

"I think its air," Falin responded. "The Water Gem was blue on the map, and this little dot appears white. I'd be surprised if it were the Earth or Fire Gem."

"Well if it's the Air Gem…" Nym pondered. "You should figure out how to just fly us back."

Falin chuckled, shaking his head. "Unfortunately, wizards cannot fly, even when in control of the Air Gem."

"So then how are we going to get back across the Wildbarrens?" Carthon asked. "Even if we can fill our canteens in the oasis, we must still journey back with all the troubles we've already passed. We've barely made it this far."

Bossador watched the rippling spring water with a ponderous stare. "In the event we believe the journey back will be too treacherous..." He hesitated before starting again. "Could we hug the coast up to Letani? Fishing for food?" Bossador's gaze flipped to Red and Jimbuah. "With Falin at a greater power, you would be safer if they tried to capture you. We would fight for you if they did."

Red and Jimbuah glanced at one another. "Bah," Jimbuah shrugged.

"I'm not sure," Red shook his head. "It ain't a bad idea, but I don't know if I want y'all fightin' for us."

"We would," Nym assured. "Wouldn't we Falin?"

Falin nodded. "I would die before I let something bad happen to any of you."

A mocking voice called from above. "Glad to hear it."

The group jumped, twisting their necks, examining the hilltops. To their shock, they were surrounded by twenty gruns, half of which aimed bows and arrows at them.

The voice came from a creature Falin did not recognize. Their taunter was lanky, with ashen skin and gaunt features, taller than the gruns, yet not quite the height of a crag. Its eyes were bulbous, with a tiny pointed nose and ears, wearing a smirk that insinuated a cunning mind. "Cast aside your staff and the others will live, wizard."

"An augur," Red seethed.

Falin glared at the augur. It clutched a short black baton the length of a short-sword. Falin knew it could harness magic, but had no idea as to what extent.

"I will not ask twice," the augur warned. Falin cast aside his staff in repudiation. "The rest of your weapons. Drop them," the augur ordered.

Falin examined the circle of gruns. Begrudgingly, the Champions disarmed. The augur twirled his baton between its spindly fingers in amusement, speaking to his soldiers. "Chain them and take their weapons. We have a long trek ahead of us."

Red stood, raising his hand. "Wait!" The gruns tensed their bowstrings. He stared at the augur. "I only ask where you take us."

The augur's grin dissolved to a scowl. "And why should I offer you such knowledge?"

"Is it not good luck to announce a destination's journey so you might not falter on the path?"

The augur's nostrils flared above small, clenched teeth. "We go to the Prison of Vug-Rhal. Miles east of here." He motioned at the gruns. "Now take them!"

Red pondered the information, nodded to himself, then Jimbuah, who also appeared content with the predicament. They met each other's gaze, and subtly signed approval. Falin could not ascertain what the Freelander and skully planned, but trusted them regardless.

The gruns chained their captives' hands and feet. Falin watched as a grun collected their weapons into a large burlap spoils bag, slinging it over his shoulder.

Shoved from the spring, their bound legs were forced to shuffle, often tripping on the uneven earth. The augur watched like a hawk, toying with his baton as if desperate to wield it. They were escorted a mile away behind a dune, finding a meager camp of gruns, including wagons hitched to belg.

Falin examined the belg, a beast akin to a bison, except these animals had a mouth of razor teeth and dotted yellow pupils.

"Get in the wagon," a grun nudged. A second grun sat behind the intimidating steed, with reins in his grimy hands. They awkwardly climbed into the wagon's hold, searching for an escape.

"Should I knock them unconscious, Felicus?" a grun asked the augur.

"Let them appreciate their shackles," Felicus jeered, riding a belg as others might a horse. "Come!" he decreed. "We have captured a wizard! We will be praised at Vug-Rhal on this night!" The augur snapped his reins, ordering the belg to lead their departure.

The wagon carrying the captives followed, as did the horde of gruns, gawking at their prisoners. Falin scanned a trailing cart, noticing their bag of weapons within.

Nym leaned across to Red and whispered, "What do we do?"

Red inhaled, assessing their situation. "We wait."

This answer would not suffice for Carthon. He spoke soft, yet harsh. "What do you mean we should wait? We followed your lead as it seemed you prepared a plan."

Red craned his neck to ensure Felicus the Augur was not listening, huddling to his companions. "You heard he was taking us to some prison east of here, right?"

Bossador nodded. "A prison called Vug-Rhal. But how do we know he isn't lying?"

"Let me give you one piece of advice about augurs. They're smart, cunning, and wicked. They wield magic like a sage, and live to make you suffer." He glanced again at Felicus. "But their biggest weakness is they're superstitious. It's good luck to announce where their journeys are headed, so I made him tell us."

"But how does knowing where we are going help us?" Falin pressed. "Should we have fought?"

"Nofa," Jimbuah shook his head adamantly.

The augur peered over his shoulder, and they reclined, pretending to be miserable. When the augur turned to the road, they began conversing again.

"If he said we were goin' to Cadryl or somethin' I would've fought," Red assured. "But we're staying in the Wildbarrens. We're better off letting 'em imprison us now, and trying to escape later."

Carthon grew frustrated. "That is your plan? Allow our imprisonment with the hope of escape?"

"Silence!" Felicus yelled over his shoulder. "Or I shall feed one of your limbs to my belg." Red stopped speaking, accepting the augur's threat as genuine.

Their caravan limped beneath the beating sun for hours. Fatigue consumed Falin, and for the time they traveled, he slipped into disheartened slumber, jostling within the rickety ride. When he woke, he scanned the lagging gruns from the corners of his eyes. Some rode in wagons, and others were atop belg. Their gnarled faces appeared darker than the gruns he had encountered further north, leaner, less fattened by the plethora of food available elsewhere in Elsana.

Falin examined Felicus, realizing how terribly emaciated the creature was. Despite standing taller than the wizard, its back appeared narrower than Nym's, as if it'd snap from a tumble. The black baton dangled from its belt, shiny and made of material other than metal, too bright for wood. Falin wondered what magic an augur possessed.

Soon, a red sunset veiled the Wildbarrens sky, and in the distance, Falin noticed a structure. Assuming it was the prison, he nudged the rest of the group with his feet, motioning his eyes. They craned their necks, viewing their destination. An apprehension moved through them, unsettled by their new home.

The Prison of Vug-Rhal stood a crude construction of charcoal siding, exotic to the beige landscape. With massive walls, it stretched some twenty feet high, near a thousand feet long.

In their approach of a metal gate, it sluggishly rose to allow their entry. Falin sensed Darkness seep into his heart, attempting to remain positive, instead burdened by the fate of his Champions. They were carried into a courtyard where gruns fulfilled duties, overseen by augurs. Past the yard waited the central prison, where guards were posted by its front. Falin followed Red's gaze, noticing the gate was controlled by a lever atop the wall.

The wagon let up, and Felicus dismounted, proclaiming to the courtyard, "We have captured Falin the Wizard!" The other augurs and gruns turned their attention to Falin's company. Instead of cheering, they glared at the Light prisoners. "Remove them from the wagon," the augur demanded. "We must take them to Qarza." As the group was gathered, a grun carried the burlap bags of spoils, weapons included, to a corner of the courtyard. The items were tossed to a pile of other, similar sacks.

Shackled and straggling, the company was escorted from the courtyard to the prison's main gate. Upon entry, a reeking smell swatted their nostrils, and a more awful sight met their eyes.

An endless row of cells confined prisoners, crammed into puny quarters within the sweltering building. A central corridor was curtained with metal bars to the front cells, the cages separated by ragged stone walls, impenetrable to those brazen enough to attempt freedom. The row stretched so far the other side was invisible. Augurs and gruns patrolled the penitentiary with glowering frowns. Thousands of inmates were incarcerated, mostly common men, packed in living tombs.

"This way," Felicus demanded, waving his baton. Their chains tugged in unison with the motion of his device. Falin stumbled, peering between the chains and the baton in surprise. They marched into a dim stone hall lit by torches, trailed by two gruns. Felicus strolled in pride of his prizes, with pomp in his gangly traipse. The odors of the central prison faded, as they passed chambers, workrooms, and bunks of guards. Augurs walked by, some gruns, all glaring at Falin.

At the end of the hall, Felicus came to a crudely built wooden door, rapping his bony knuckles on it. "Enter," a deep voice called from within.

Felicus strode in, beckoning their chains by command of his baton. "I come bearing gifts, Qarza."

Falin squinted through the gloomy space, realizing it was a working chamber, containing a table covered in maps, chairs, and barrels of water. A broad and tall being standing over the charts turned. He appeared to be a cross of an augur and a crag, wearing both an augur's baton at his waist and a longsword on his belt.

"Kneel for General Qarza," Felicus demanded, swishing his baton, forcing them to their knees.

Qarza scanned the group with intense malice, his gaze locking on Falin. "Is this who we seek?" His voice was low, speaking with slow confidence.

"It is," Felicus said proudly. "We found them at a spring west of here. Drinking like beasts."

General Qarza's eyes flitted to Bossador, and a glottal growl emanated from his throat. "Good work. Mulgus will be pleased." Terror struck the group; they glanced at one another, learning of their captor's employer.

Qarza snorted, and a smile-less amusement passed across his leathery face. "Oh, yes. Our warlock friend has been very eager to detain this group." He strolled towards them, resting his wrist atop his baton. His frame was muscular, but slightly shorter and far leaner than the average crag, with a broad face holding sharp features. "Do not fret, Mulgus has given me strict orders to keep you alive. That is, until he comes to collect his belongings." Qarza's attention locked on Bossador, frowning, sauntering to tower over the prince. "I take it you are Bossador, heir to the Rodrellan throne."

Bossador raised his chin. "I am."

Qarza stared in consideration. In a violent motion, he drove his knee into Bossador's mouth, causing blood to spurt from the madorian's lips. Rattled, Bossador lay on his back, groaning, trying to blink through watery eyes. "I hate madorians," Qarza seethed, removing the baton from his waist to twirl it over his victim. Bossador's chains jerked, and he screamed, his bones being twisted by the general's magic. "They are arrogant, land infringing creatures who think that every act of warfare is one of valor."

"Enough!" Falin yelled.

Qarza glanced at Falin, but did not cease. Instead, he twisted his wrist, and Bossador wailed louder. "I do not take orders from a wizard, boy," Qarza scoffed. He dropped his baton and Bossador fell limp, panting in agony. "But luckily for your royal scum, I cannot kill him by the orders of a warlock. Yet."

Falin glared at Qarza. "Let us go, or the full wrath of the wizards will dismantle you."

Qarza chuckled softly, lumbering to his desk of maps, leaning against it with folded arms. "I may carry some features of my crag grandfather, wizard, but I am not so stupid as his kind. Your people don't know where you are. They wouldn't know where to look, even if they knew you were taken. When you walk a path of Darkness, you should not be surprised to lose your way."

Falin's teeth clenched. Bossador lifted himself to his knees, blood dripping over his beard. Qarza tapped his fingers on the table in thought. "Did you happen to see the wizard's staff, Felicus? How many Gems were there?"

"Only one," Felicus replied. "Same as what Mulgus saw. The second must be in the Wildbarrens."

Qarza breathed deeply. "Rumeren's Oasis. It is an ancient place of Light. It must be hidden there." He clicked his tongue, scanning the group again. He tilted his head. "I know a wizard's Champions belong to the Crown, so why is it this group travels with a common man and a skully?"

"They are my Champions as much as the other four," Falin replied.

Qarza's eyes darted to Red's arm, and they fluttered in surprise. "You carry the mark of my home." He approached the Freelander, crouched, and lifted Red's arm, examining the runes of Cadryl. Red met the general's gaze with a cool calmness. He shook Red's wrist so the chains rattled. "You have known shackles for much of your life, haven't you, Freelander? Did the augurs of Cadryl treat you well? Digging the mines for precious metal?"

Red considered his response. "It was a bit glum, so I left."

Qarza stared at Red for a moment before responding. "It is rare for someone to escape Cadryl, despite all being eager to." He stood, walking with his hands behind his back. Falin noticed how sharp Qarza's nails were. "There is an abundance of slaves there now, you would be amazed, Freelander. I hope that this prison will one day be the capital of a new Cadryl."

"This is a place of slaves?" Falin asked.

"Soon to be slaves, yes," Qarza answered. "There are many valuable metals ready to be harvested from the earth here. Our excavations will begin soon."

Falin glanced at the maps covering the table. He remembered Nyril and Mulgus indicating they had greater, insidious plans. "For what purpose? An invasion of the Crown?"

Qarza furrowed his brow. "What in Elsana gives you that idea?"

Falin wasn't sure he should respond, but did anyway. "I assumed Nyril and Mulgus were planning some sort of attack on the Crown."

Qarza scoffed. "The Light is riddled with such arrogance. They assume all revolves around them. What would we want with grotesque places like Rodrellan?" He stepped towards Nym, kicking her in the stomach with his boot. "Or Lelyalis."

Carthon hissed, lunging for the general, but Felicus slammed him to the ground by control of the chains. Nym buckled over, the wind blown from her. Qarza snorted in sly pleasure. "I hate elves almost as much as I hate madorians," he muttered. He returned focus to Falin. "I suppose it doesn't matter that I tell you; you won't be able to do anything about it." Qarza spoke with determination to the entire group. "Nyril and Mulgus intend to take control of the *Freelands* by force. They view it as wasted potential, infested with the way of the Light. I am inclined to agree, so I have been recruited to aid them in this journey."

A stunned silence hovered until Falin finally responded. "The Freelands hold more people than the Crown and the Shadow Kingdoms combined. They would never be able to invade. And the wizards would never allow it."

"All valid concerns," Qarza said. "All of which Nyril and Mulgus have taken into account. They are not fools, marching into battles like your madorian friend might." Qarza peered at Bossador with hatred. "But I do know this: sooner than you expect, the Freelands will know new masters, and they will be of the Dark." General Qarza strolled the room, imagining aloud. "And perhaps one day

I may be fortunate enough to lead an invasion of Rodrellan." He turned to Bossador. "I would keep you until that day, prince. I would keep you chained, and wheel you in a cage all the way to the north so you may watch your madorian forests burn. And when every person of your kingdom has been slaughtered, only then will I cut your throat."

Bossador breathed heavily, his nostrils flaring, fists clenched in rage. Before he could respond, Qarza said, "Take them away, Felicus. I must send word to Mulgus that we have his wizard. I'm sure he will come to collect him in the coming weeks."

Felicus motioned his baton, and the chains lifted, yanking them from the room. Falin glanced over his shoulder to see Qarza already placing focus on the maps.

They plodded through the hall, ingesting all that was said to them. Falin could not fathom an invasion of the Freelands, for so many reasons.

Returned to the main prison, they were paraded by the rows of cells, often ten prisoners to a space, crammed together, mostly men sickly and scrawny. Some rested in fetal positions in corners, and others hung on the bars to assess the passing newcomers. The prison stench settled into their nostrils, the air thick with human excrement. Groans of misery bellowed from all around, and on occasion, a guard would demand their silence. Near the end of the long-stretching row, Felicus halted at the front of a cell, a sleeping elderly man its only occupant.

The augur swung his baton, and the barred door flew open. He flicked his wrist and their chains unclasped, falling to the ground. "In," Felicus demanded. Two gruns pointed spears at them. Falin and the Champions filed inside, standing beside the slumbering old man in the corner, who did not stir in their entry. With a final swish of the augur's baton, the cell door slammed shut. Felicus examined them in approval. "They shall remember me for generations to come," the augur thought aloud. "Felicus, Entrapper of Wizards."

They said nothing in response, and the augur stalked off in a daydream.

With resigned acceptance, both Red and Jimbuah took seats on the stone floor. Red crossed his legs and inspected the ground around him. Jimbuah pulled his knees to his chest and rested his chin on them. The skully sighed deeply, lost in thought.

The other Champions and Falin watched, not understanding their indifference. Carthon stared, agitated. "Are you two not concerned for our current predicament?"

Red scanned a few hand-sized stones that had fallen from the rock wall. He lifted them individually in examination, tossing them to the corner "'Course we are."

"What do we do?!" Nym whispered urgently. "Mulgus could come for us any day. We need to escape to warn the wizards of their plans to invade the Freelands. What do we do?" Red didn't seem to be listening, chucking aside another rock.

"Wato," Jimbuah replied lethargically.

Melquin blinked rapidly. "Wait for what? What do we wait for?"

"You are our guides in this place," Carthon seethed. "You are supposed to offer us better counsel than this."

Red turned a rock over in his hand, nodding to himself. He began to scrape it along the floor, back and forth, creating a little white line in the stone. "Carthon, do you remember in the Mortal Caves, you asked me how I escaped Cadryl? Do you recall my response?"

The drak thought back to the conversation. "Patience."

"Patience," Red repeated, grinding the stone. "Patience," he said softer, a frown forming on his face. "I know it's the most difficult thing to do when you're sittin' idle, but let me warn you: an impatient mind will wander, and often miss the opportunities a patient mind may catch." Red sighed deeply, grinding the rock to stone. "And in a place like this, those opportunities are far and few between. So sit with me as we wait for our moment to ensnare freedom."

Carthon rubbed his tired eyes, deciding to sit against the wall. The rest followed suit. Falin felt lost without his staff, incomplete and not at all a wizard. He stared over the prison row, amazed at the multitude of captives within Vug-Rhal. All these men who would soon face enslavement to forcibly support a war meant to take the Freelands. The elderly man beside him snored gently, not at all aware of their presence.

"How are two warlocks going to take the Freelands?" Nym mused. "They would need the support of the Shadow Kingdoms, and Airo told us there wasn't any inkling of preparation for war there."

Falin shook his head, trying to make sense of it all. "Maybe they don't have the support of the Shadow Kingdoms yet. They don't answer to warlocks the same way the Crown doesn't answer to wizards. They are merely advisors and provide spiritual guidance."

"I think the Shadow Kingdoms would listen to them," Nym argued.

"Kifen the Morbid," Bossador said, the first time he'd spoken since before Qarza's chambers.

Nym tilted her head. "Who?"

Bossador gingerly touched his split lips, speaking carefully. "Some seven hundred years ago, Kifen the Morbid, a warlock, tried to convince the Shadow Kingdoms to rally their navies and attack the coast of Rodrellan. They declined, knowing they'd face the Crown if they did. It's happened before."

Melquin tapped her legs, chewing on her cheek. "Well if they don't have command of the Shadow Kingdoms now, I'm willing to bet they're working on it. It seems they've been scheming. They already have Qarza and a number of other Dark servants doing their bidding."

"What would the Crown do in the event of an attack on the Freelands?" Nym wondered aloud. "Should we fight to protect the Freelands?" The old man snored heavily, stirred, then settled again.

"Rodrellan would," Bossador replied without a second thought. "They would be there to drive back the Dark."

"If Rodrellan fights, I think it's safe to say Mystica and Lelyalis will as well," Melquin surmised. "They all have close connections with the Freelands."

Carthon bent his head, scratching the edge of his dirty boot. "I am afraid Vartulis may not come to the defense of the Freelands."

Nym raised her eyebrows in surprise. "How can you be so certain? A Freelands controlled by warlocks is undoubtedly a threat to the Crown."

Carthon shrugged. "The Drakkish Senate has taken an increasingly isolationist attitude every decade. Plus, the Vartulian Charter will not allow it."

"I find it hard to believe they would not fight for the Freelands," Bossador muttered.

"Believe what you want," Carthon replied. "Vartulis' stance on war has remained law for near a thousand years. The Drakkish Senate cannot and *will not* wage war unless the Crown or Vartulian blood is at risk."

The elderly man rolled over, waking. The group turned to him, having not given him much attention since their arrival in the cell. He opened his eyes, then jumped, promptly sitting up, startled by the foreigners. He pressed himself against the wall farthest from them. This was the first instance Falin had taken a good look at the man. He was bald, and the grey hair on the sides of his head hung in all directions. With a pointed chin, he sneered, revealing only a few, yellow teeth. "What are you doing here?"

Melquin blinked slowly. "Taking in the view."

"How long have you been here?" the old man growled.

Red stopped grinding his rock, placing it carefully on the ground so he would not mistake it with another. "Only a few minutes. How long have you been here?"

Surprised by the question, the prisoner said, "Why do you care?"

"Because we are in this together now," Red responded. The Freelander reached into his shirt and retrieved a chunk of dried fruit from Monkey Mountain. He extended the snack. "It's fruit. From Suntalla."

The old man examined it with scrutiny. "What is it?"

"I don't know what it's called, but it's sweet, and better than anythin' you've ever had in here. Scoundrel's oath." Red shook the fruit. The group watched as the old man considered it.

Glancing to the outside row to ensure there were no guards watching, the old man snatched the fruit, taking a bite. Relief fell across his pale, wrinkled face upon tasting a bit of the outside world. "Thank you," he muttered.

"What's your name?" Red asked.

"Harven," he replied, gnawing the dried fruit.

Melquin pointed to the old man's hand. "What is that gash?"

Lifting his arm, Harven examined a deep cut across his palm. "One of the guards hit me with their blade a couple days ago. They didn't like that I had my arms outside the bars." Melquin moved to reach for his hand, but he recoiled. "What are you doing?" he asked the sage.

"I can help heal it," she replied. Melquin took hold of his forearm. Harven sat rigid and suspecting. She ran her hands over the wound and whispered a series of incantations, and in a moment, it appeared as if being healed for a week.

Harven looked at the cut in amazement. "I... thank you." Bashfulness swept across his wrinkly face.

"Of course," Melquin nodded.

Harven scanned the newcomers with more openness than before. "You're a motley bunch. Why're you here?"

Falin introduced the group as he had countless times, but in this instance, it came across rather depressing. "I am Falin. The wizard. These are my Champions. I'm on a quest for the Gems of Elsana."

Harven stopped chewing and nodded slowly. "Yes. I see. And I am Harven, Faerie Goddess of Butt-Licker Forest."

After an unamused silence from them all, Jimbuah replied, "'Tis an honor."

Falin scratched over his eyebrow. "We're um...I'm actually a wizard."

Harven ate the last bit of fruit and stared at him with a cocked eye. "What sort of wizard gets himself captured by augurs?"

"We were ambushed," Falin replied. "But I'm confident my Champions will help me escape."

A glimmer of light caught Harven's gaze, and he sat up straighter. "You're really a wizard?" Falin nodded sullenly, near ashamed to admit it. Harven scooted forward and whispered, "You really think you can get out of here?"

Nym nodded. "Well we don't plan on staying."

Harven scratched his white, coarse beard. "I want in. I want out of here. I'll do whatever you need."

Falin saw his desperation. "Of course. We don't have a plan yet." He glanced at Red. "We are waiting for the right opportunity."

"You let me know when," Harven nodded.

A grun guard sauntered by, and they hushed, gazing at the ground conveying a sight absent of conspiring. Once unsupervised again, Red lifted his rock and began to scrape it to the floor. "Settle in," he said to his group. "It may be a long time before we see that opportunity."

Days passed, and Falin lost the ability to estimate how much time they'd spent in the Vug-Rhal. There were no windows, thus no light. Guards kept on constant patrol, and the gag-inducing meals they were served came at odd times, cast into their cage like one might feed a piggish nuisance.

Food consisted of stale bread, raw meats, snakes, insects, and bitter fruit. They slept at odd hours, becoming numb to the distressing sounds and putrid smells of the prison. Their bodies ached and minds ran fraught with the possibility they might never leave. Not once was their door opened by the magic switches held by augurs.

Perhaps it had only been a few days, maybe ten, there was no telling.

Red spent most of his time rubbing his rock to the stone, its sides now flat. There were moments he would inspect it, blow the dust off, then continue grinding. The Freelander seemed to have a sixth sense as to when a guard would pass, because each time he tucked the rock away, soon enough, a grun or augur would appear. His wariness in their presence was well deserved. Multiple times they were audience to a prisoner's beating for some arbitrary reason.

For two days straight, they were served belg meat, and Melquin refused to consume it despite their pressing that she needed sustenance. In a quiet portion of the guards' watch, presumably night, the sage seemed unable to hold her head up she had grown so weak. Falin feared they might need to force her to eat the belg if she continued her stubbornness. "Are you going to be okay?" Nym asked her friend. Without response, Melquin nodded. Her debilitated demeanor said otherwise.

Examining the sage from the sides of his eyes, Harven stood with a grunt, shuffling to the bars. He clutched the metal and peered in all directions to ensure no guards were in sight. "*Pst*," he signaled to the cells across the way. "Anyone got anything non-meat?" he half-whispered. "Maybe some sour fruit?"

A prisoner to the left stood, peeking around before responding. "I've got some bread."

"How much?" Harven asked. The prisoner retrieved a small loaf from his robes. "That'll do," Harven replied. "I'll trade you my next helping of belg for it."

The prisoner mulled it over. "Two helpings."

Harven tapped the bars in consideration. "Fine. Toss it here. No belg if you miss."

Taking another chance to examine the row, the prisoner pressed his face to the bars. Seeing it was clear, he tossed the bread underhand across the way. Harven stretched his arms and caught the loaf, yanking it inside, scurrying to Melquin. "Hey, eat this," he demanded.

Melquin peered at the bread with heavy-lidded surprise. "Is that for me?"

"It's for the Duchess of Dumb Questions," Harven replied. "So yes, it's for you. Eat it before the guards see." Harven crouched and positioned himself in front of Melquin. She slowly began to break off pieces and eat. Falin and his Champions were relieved to see her pep up upon completion of the loaf.

"Why did you do that?" Melquin asked. "You could've gotten in trouble."

Harven shrugged, returning to his seat. "Because I felt like it."

Red wiped the dust from his stone's edge with a subtle smirk. "Harven's got a soft spot."

"Shut it, cowboy," Harven grumbled.

"You still haven't told us, Harven," Nym began. "Why are you here? Where are you from?"

The old man ran his thumb over his nose. "I was a sailor for most of my life. Lived off of the Valdarian Coast as a crab fisherman. But, err…" He furrowed his brow as if struggling to remember the story. "I was out at sea and our crew kept pressing south, down towards the coast of Letani. That's when an augur ship picked us up, sent us here."

Nym frowned. "How long ago was that? Where is your crew?"

"I couldn't tell you how long," Harven said with mournful eyes. "And they're dead. They didn't last in this place as I have."

"We're sorry that it happened to you," Falin comforted.

Harven avoided their gaze. "They were the lucky ones," he muttered, turning to sleep with his back to them. The group exchanged glances of pity.

Days more slinked by, and the meals changed from belg to cactus. They were forced to remove needles from the plants before consumption. Prisoners throughout the block would yelp from missing a spine in their meal preparation.

The impending threat of Mulgus the Plague suffocated their minds with every hour passed, and each time footsteps echoed the floor outside their cell, Falin feared it would be the warlock, turning the corner, rotted smile and all. To their luck, the warlock remained unseen. Their knowledge of the Freeland invasion also weighed on them, unable to act in a way that might save the lives of innocent people.

Seeing his Champions lose bits of life with each passing minute, Falin sought a way to lift their spirits. He remembered a conversation in the Canyon of Idolum that brought them some joy in a moment of misery. He considered something similar, forming his question. "Would you rather..." he began, gaining their unexpected attention. "Eat half of Bossador's beard, or lick each one of Jimbuah's toes? Nym, you answer."

The elf blinked rapidly as the rest gaped in disgust. "Excuse me?"

Falin pressed her as if asking a valid question. "Would you rather eat half of Bossador's beard, or lick all of Jimbuah's toes?"

"In what scenario would that ever happen?" Nym argued.

Falin shrugged. "A pretend one. Pick."

Nym grimaced, and her eyes darted between Bossador's face and Jimbuah's bare feet. "I guess Bossador's beard. We have been all over Elsana, and not once have I seen Jimbuah wash his feet."

Jimbuah wiggled his grey toes and chuckled. "Yeh."

The group laughed softly in response. Falin examined them. "Alright. New question for Carthon." Falin tapped his chin in thought. "Would you rather kiss Nym right after she ate rotten belg *or* kiss Red dressed up as Nym." As they snickered at the question, Falin added, "And Red is in a red wig like Nym's hair, with fake pointy ears and the utility belt. Everything."

Carthon's face contorted and he rubbed his forehead. "I would still choose Nym. I will always be glad to kiss her no matter the state of her mouth."

Harven covered his mouth and giggled like a child. "Let's see you say that after you taste rotten belg."

Falin saw the game appeared to do as he hoped, most of all for Harven, gleefully grinning with all four of his teeth. The wizard hid a smile and worked at his next proposition. "Alright," he started, landing one. They leaned forward, eager for the following hypothetical situation. "Red..." He held back a laugh. "Would you rather share a bath with Carthon or a bath with Princess Bloom?" As the listeners moved to say that was not a difficult decision, Falin raised a finger and added, "But the tub with Princess Bloom is filled with soured milk. And you can't hold your nose."

Another ripple of revolted laughter cut across the cell and they peered at Red, eager for his verdict. The Freelander opened his mouth twice, unable to decide which would be worse. He threw his hands up. "I gotta take the milk."

Scrunched noses and chortles were had all around. Bossador threw his head back and held his chest, laughing with a closed mouth so as not to stir the guards. "You are a dog among men."

"Don't laugh so fast," Falin warned the prince. "You're next." The wizard needed little time to cultivate a dilemma for Bossador. "Would you rather eat a bowl of normal sized, non-poisonous spiders..." At once Bossador's face fell in revulsion. "Or would you rather spend a night cuddling a giant spider of the Wildbarrens in its lair." Bossador's shoulders lifted as he cringed at the thought, shivering. Jimbuah bounced in delight upon seeing the expression of nausea pass his comrade's face.

"I—I—" The prince shook his head, not knowing what to pick. "I'd eat the bowl of spiders. I would never sleep again having spent the night in the arms of such a monster."

When the reaction to his choice settled, Falin turned to Melquin. "Mel..." he thought. When deciding what to ask, he stopped to laugh, shaking his head. "Would you rather that each time you speak to an animal, it sounds like belching to everyone else..." he was stopped by a billow of chuckles. "Or, would you rather that every time you wield magic with your staff, it makes the noise of someone passing wind."

Nym covered her eyes and shook from laughing so hard, and Harven doubled over with tears streaming down his face. Carthon's smile was wide, and his fangs were bared in delight. Melquin's eyes bulged and she toyed at her braid, not knowing which would be worse. "I think the belching. How would I ever seem a threat to an enemy when my staff sounded like…"

Carthon completed her sentence. "Jimbuah after eating beans."

Jimbuah laughed sharply at the remark, looking to Falin. "Miba," he said, asking to be next. "Miba."

Falin gazed up at the ceiling in thought. "Jimmy, Jimmy, Jimmy… Would you rather have to act like a chicken every time Red says, 'y'all', or wet yourself every time Melquin reminds us she doesn't eat meat?"

"Ah!" Jimbuah beamed, imagining each. "Chikini!" he replied, leaping up and clucking as if a chicken, wagging his elbow like wings.

Harven fell back and held his stomach in hysterical glee. With a red face, he said, "You have not yet done me, wizard! Ask me a question!"

"Alright," Falin nodded, wishing he knew more about the old man. He bobbed his head about in thought. "Would you rather sniff a grun's rear end, or pick an augur's nose?"

Harven threw his head back and cackled, kicking his feet. He did so loudly and his voice rang over the row. "I do not know! What an awful decision!"

Nym's brow scrunched and ears twitched. She began to snap her fingers, "Hey, hey!" she whispered to them urgently. "Guards."

They became silent in an instant, and a few seconds later, two gruns and Felicus the augur turned the corner. "What is the meaning of this ruckus?" Felicus asked. His wiry frame loomed over them like a master would a pet. "Answer me," the augur seethed. Its eyes searched the cage, landing on Harven. "It was him," he told the gruns. "I know his voice, the old man has been here long enough. Bring him out here."

Harven trembled as he backed to the wall, hands raised in defense. As a grun entered, Red leapt up and punched him in the face. The grun growled, and its counterpart nabbed Red by the arm, tossing him outside the cell. Felicus scowled. "Striking a guard is a severe offense. Did you think that because you are a wizard's Champion, we would show leniency?"

Red lifted himself and spit at the feet of the augur. Falin wished his friend had not done that.

Raising his baton over his head, Felicus brought it down upon Red's cheek with a *smack* so loud, all prisoners watching averted their gaze. The augur proceeded to beat Red, and despite the baton not having sharp edges, cuts formed across the Freelander's body.

Red took the punishment in stride, merely grunting, clenching his fists with eyes closed. Helplessness taunted Falin's group, wishing they could do anything to stop the horrific battery of their companion. Instead, they kept silent for fear their pleas for mercy would incite further lashing. With a final swing of his arm, Felicus struck Red in the cheek. He lay barely conscious and bloody.

"Get him back to his cell," Felicus demanded. The augur waved his baton and the door opened again. They tossed Red into the arms of his comrades who laid him down gently. Felicus slammed the gate shut, striding off with the guards in tow.

Red lay half-conscious with his head rested in Bossador's lap. They crowded over him as Melquin began to mutter into his flesh. The bleeding slowed, but the wounds remained fresh. "These are the wounds of Dark magic. They will be difficult to heal."

"He should have let them hurt me," Harven said over the group. A transparent cloak of disapproval covered his guilt. "It was foolish what he did." Harven peered over Melquin and frowned. "Please don't let him die." The old man's voice fell. "My life is not worth his."

Melquin nodded, pressing her hands over the wounds and whispering. Falin walked away to the bars not wishing to view his injured Champion any longer. He clutched the barrier that detained them, examining the endless row of prisoners who kept crammed in their own little spaces. Melquin's healing of Red would matter little if they were not able to escape before the arrival of Mulgus the Plague.

CHAPTER SIXTEEN:
PATIENCE

With more than a week gone by in their dreadful state of existence, the group's hope began to falter, certain Mulgus would collect them at any moment. Red's wounds from Felicus' beating began to diminish under the healing hands of Melquin, but he still wore faded cuts and bruises from his effort to spare Harven. Their skin was pale, and faces were drawn from lack of proper nourishment, food, and sunlight.

They often rested with their backs to the walls, other times pacing the cell like trapped animals. Red spent most of his imprisonment grinding his rock to the floor, and in his efforts, it sharpened like a handheld spearhead. Falin didn't know what the Freelander intended to do with it, assuming it was meant for some act of defense.

A parade of footsteps ushered from down the row, and they lazily turned their heads to listen, hoping it was not a warlock. Falin could sense it wasn't.

General Qarza and Felicus walked in front of the cell, accompanied by a group of gruns. The part-augur, part-crag general towered over them, examining each with a frown. "I came to take one last look at you before I left," he rumbled. "I am glad to see you in such misery." He gripped the bars. "Especially you, prince," he said to Bossador. Bossador glared at Qarza.

"Are you going somewhere?" Falin asked, his voice hoarse from the lack of water.

Qarza's eyes flitted to the wizard, and his jaw clenched. "We have word of a Letani battalion traveling through the Wildbarrens, why, I do not know. I am taking forces from Vug-Rhal to capture them. They will make good slaves. Felicus will be in command until we return."

As Qarza relayed the news, Falin noticed Red shift ever so slightly. "I hope that I can return before Mulgus takes you," the general continued. "I intended to convince him to let me keep the prince." A minuscule smirk appeared on his lips, staring at Bossador. "My threat was not idle. I fully intend to make you watch your kingdom burn."

Despite his fatigue, a parental urge to protect Bossador jolted Falin. He rose slowly, strolling to the edge of the cell, raising his chin to meet Qarza's gaze. The wizard examined him for a moment before speaking. "You are insignificant."

Qarza clutched the bars tighter. He snarled, and air shot from his nostrils.

Falin went on. "A pawn to a warlock, and a mutt-breed of two deplorable races." Falin noticed Qarza's hands reach for his baton. "I wouldn't do that if I were you," he warned the general.

Qarza clutched his baton but kept it on his belt. "And why is that?"

Falin's tone dropped and he spoke so softly, all in proximity leaned forward to listen. His aura was sinister, more than one would expect a wizard could be. "In my travels across Elsana, so many races of the Dark seem to have a false understanding of the Light. That we are passive, and averse to violence." Falin blinked slowly and shook his head. "No," he whispered, looking away from Qarza in thought. "We are kind by nature, and what is perceived as weakness is in reality mercy." Falin bit his cheek, looking off in a vacant stare. "That mercy has its limits." His gaze darted back to Qarza's, alive with a fiery Light. Falin stood on his toes, placing his hands over the bars where Qarza's rested, half-rasping, half-snarling. "Harm any member of this cell today, you best pray to the God of Darkness for the rest of your existence. Because if I escape, I will spend the rest of *your* life hunting you. And when I find whatever hole you cower inside of, I will subject you to a merciless life of torment at the hands of the Light."

Qarza breathed heavily, glowering. Reluctantly, he removed his hand from the baton and spoke to the rest. "We have too much to prepare. We waste our time conversing with these vermin." The general turned swiftly, Felicus and the guards following. Falin returned to his seat and rested his head against the stone.

Bossador rubbed his eyebrow and took a breath before speaking. "You did not have to threaten him on my behalf," the prince said softly.

Falin gazed across the row. "It was less so a threat and more of a vow."

Another day passed, and from the noises through the prison and sudden lack of guards, the group assumed Qarza departed in his operation to capture the Letani soldiers. The row became quiet as the occasional guard strolled past, and soon, they slumbered. Sometime during their sleep, Falin stirred, hearing voices outside their cage. By the brashness of the first, and ooze of the second, he surmised it was a grun and an augur. He kept his eyes closed to listen.

"A sage's braid will give you an eternity of luck," the augur explained. "My cousin gained all his wealth by taking one."

"Can we share it?" the grun asked. "If I lie for you, will you give me half?"

The augur thought on it. "I don't see why not. Her braid is plenty long. But we need a believable story as to why she is dead. Her braid will not give us any luck if she is not killed."

Falin resisted the urge to move, but kept eavesdropping, steadying his breath. The grun spoke next. "We'll blame it on one of the others in her cage. We'll say they were fighting and one had a knife and did it. That she already bled out by the time we were here."

The augur sighed. "I suppose that could work. But Felicus cannot find out. He will have our heads."

The grun chuckled softly. "He may spare us if we have the luck of a sage's braid."

"That is a rather intelligent point," the augur admitted.

"Well, are we going to do it?" the grun pressed. "If you open the cell with your baton, I'll go in and get it. I'll kill her quick-like and take the braid."

Falin heard the cell door open. "Go quickly," the augur demanded.

As the footsteps of the grun entered, Falin leapt up to defend Melquin and wake the others. To his surprise, Harven, who also faked slumber, stood first, lunging at the entering guard while shouting, "You will not harm her!"

The pair tussled for a moment as the rest woke. Before anyone could assist, the grun plunged a knife into Harven's chest before retreating. The augur swung his baton and the door slammed shut. The rest of the block stirred from Harven's scream, and the old man fell to the floor, moaning in pain.

"What happened?!" Carthon shouted.

"He was stabbed!" Falin said. "Melquin heal him!"

Harven gasped, struggling to breathe from the wound in his chest. His mouth filled with blood. Melquin frantically hunched over him and pressed on the wound, rapidly spewing spells. They held Harven still as he wriggled and made incoherent gurgling noises. A frantic sadness crept over his face as he examined his cellmates. "The cut is too deep," Melquin said, tears welling in her eyes. "I can't heal it fast enough." Her hands were crimson, and she continued praying, tears streaking her dusty face.

Harven's breathing slowed and his eyelids grew heavy. A light escaped his eyes and he fell still, staring at the ceiling. "The wound was too deep," Melquin whispered. "I'm sorry," she said to Harven's body. "I'm sorry," she repeated, chin trembling.

Nym put a hand on her shoulder. "You did all you could."

Falin turned to the guards with venom, standing and pressing his face to the bars. "You will regret this moment," he growled. They backed away in fear.

Another group of gruns and augur guards rushed to the scene, finding Harven stabbed. "What happened?" an augur asked.

The initial grun and augur looked to each other. The grun replied, "We heard shouting, and when we came to the cell, the old man was rabid. I feared he would hurt Qarza's prisoners, so I stabbed him through the cage when I had the chance."

"You lie," Falin seethed.

"Get him out of there," an augur demanded of gruns. "He won't be the only dead one if anyone tries anything," he warned the prisoners. He waved his baton and the door opened. Quickly and quietly, the gruns lifted Harven from the cell and away down the row. Melquin fell back to the wall with bloodstained hands covering her face. Nym comforted her with a gentle arm.

Falin and his Champions sat against the wall, staring at the puddle of blood at the center of their cell. It reeked of misery. A person they had welcomed into their family was now dead. Melquin wept. "Why do the people I try to help keep dying?"

Carthon looked to her with sorrow. "What do you mean?"

Melquin's eyes streamed, and she nervously clutched at her braid, staining it with Harven's blood. "First Tula, and now I try to help Harven, and he is killed."

"Their deaths are not on your conscious," Bossador soothed. "You did all you could for both."

"But it wasn't enough," Melquin replied, growing despondent. "I am a fraud."

"No," Nym said, stroking her friend's arm. "You are a wonderful soul who places too much burden on yourself. You cannot save everyone." Melquin sniffed, shaking her head.

Another day went by and they kept quiet, mourning the loss of their friend. Red no longer ground his stone, but instead, twirled it in his hand, his eyes locked on the drying stain of Harven's murder. "That could've been me," he said suddenly, calling their attention.

Nym raised her palms as if to say 'Who knows.' "They likely would not have stabbed you, as Mulgus wants us."

Red shook his head. "No, I mean that could've been me had I not escaped Cadryl. Or every other prison I've been locked up in. Nothing but an imprisoned old man until someone put me out of my misery." He looked at the stone in his hand, then peered at the outside row.

As there was earlier, a diminished amount of guards were on patrol. As far as they could tell, only about twenty or so guarded the row, and they assumed far less were in the rest of the fortress. It was the quietest it had been since their arrival. "It's time," he announced.

"For what?" Falin asked.

Red stood, running his thumb over the sharpened tip of the stone. "This is the best opportunity we're gonna get. I wished we had done it sooner before they killed Harven." He turned to Jimbuah. "Can you do what you did in Krattle's Cove? When we first became partners? See if you can draw Felicus out."

Jimbuah nodded dutifully and wiped the dust from his pants, standing and stretching. Red stepped back to the wall, hiding the stone behind his back. Falin scanned them. "What are you doing? Should we be prepared to fight?"

Red frowned and shook his head. "Nope. Just hang tight and look confused. It'll help sell it."

Jimbuah cleared his throat, taking a wide stance, then began to chant in a loud, monotone voice, swinging his arms in random, fluid motions. "*Felicus isi dujimo fujiko... Felicus isi dujimo fujiko...*" The skully's eyes rolled back, and his head trembled as if in a trance. Guards started to investigate, peering into the cage. "*Felicus isi dujimo fujiko... Felicus isi dujimo fujiko...*"

A grun rapped at the cell with his sword. "That's enough!" he growled.

Jimbuah's voice loudened, ignoring the order. He waved his arms in a sporadic and dramatic fashion, keeping his wide-set stance. "*Felicus isi dujimo fujiko! Felicus isi dujimo fujiko!*" All guard eyes were glued to the skully, baffled by the display. Prisoners craned their necks to see what the commotion was. "*Felicus isi dujimo fujiko! Felicus isi dujimo fujiko!*"

A frantic set of footsteps hurried down the row, and Felicus appeared, shocked upon finding Jimbuah, white-eyed and in a seemingly hypnotic state. The lanky augur's jaw dropped. "What is— enough! I demand you to stop!" The augur smacked the bars with his baton.

Jimbuah began to shout, his gravelly voice reverberating across the prison in ominously clattering echoes. "*FELICUS ISI DUJIMO FUJIKO! FELICUS ISI DUJIMO FUJIKO!*" He upturned his palms and let his face vibrate wildly.

Another augur shouted and pointed. "He is placing a skully curse on Felicus!"

Felicus' lips grew tight as his eyes bulged. He waved his baton and the door whipped open, to which he charged in, wanting to halt whatever jinx was being cast.

It was in this instant, Red grabbed the baton-wielding arm of the augur with one hand, pressing the sharp end of his stone to Felicus's neck with the other. Before Felicus could wave his wrist, Jimbuah stopped chanting and ripped the baton from the hands of the prison captain.

Red lowered Felicus to his height, holding him close, the weaponized rock pressed into the hostage's throat, testing the strength of the augur's skin. "Tell them to drop their weapons," Red demanded. "Or die."

Felicus took no time to consider it. "Drop your weapons," he ordered the guards. "Do it!"

Carefully, the augurs and gruns did as told, raising their hands. Red held Felicus as a living shield, shuffling from the cell to stand in front of the guards. Jimbuah followed, clutching the augur's baton. Felicus pleaded in Red's grasp. "I am sorry I beat you. We will let you leave if you spare my life. I swear it by the God of Darkne—"

"Shut up," Red rasped. "I'm thinking." He quickly glanced at Jimbuah. "Can you work that thing?"

Jimbuah examined the baton then shook it, causing their cell door to close and open. A few more times of waving it, the doors of all the prison cells began to shudder. "Yeh," Jimbuah answered.

Red scanned the row, filled with thousands of prisoners. The inmates crowded together, eager to see what the hostage situation meant for them. Red's focus landed on the meager number of guards.

An expression of mischievous animosity crept across Red's face as he came to a decision. "Open them, Jimmy," he sneered. "Open them all."

Jimbuah smirked. "Yeh." He twirled the baton with deep concentration, causing the row to rattle with the sounds of jimmying cell doors. Felicus struggled in Red's grasp and the guards looked in all directions, not knowing what to do. The skully grunted, and simultaneously, the gates to every cage flew open with a crash. A hanging silence trailed the echo of metal slamming stone.

Red inhaled and screamed a call to action. "RIOT!"

Mayhem reigned supreme. Prisoners poured from their cages, some attacking the guards, others running for the exit, a few taking the weapons of their captors. All shouted, and guards from outside the main row entered, beating back the escapees.

Red plunged the stone into Felicus' throat, casting the augur to the ground. Dark red blood poured across the floor as Felicus clutched his neck.

Falin and the Champions sprinted from the cell, following Red and Jimbuah in the thicket of prisoners. Gruns and augurs were beaten to death, many trampled by those desperate for freedom. They ran across the row, coming to the exit.

The doors to the prison were forced open, and a hammer of desert sunlight blinded them, causing them to squint as they ran into the walled yard of the fortress. Guards fought with the run-aways, overpowered in a matter of minutes. The group was bumped and jostled in the crowd, struggling to stay together.

"My staff!" Falin yelled. "We cannot leave without my staff!"

"This way!" Carthon called, running to a corner of the courtyard where bags of spoils were kept. Prisoners wrestled with guards, and the screams of every race present were heard.

They came to the pile of sacks and began to inspect each, tossing them away as pandemonium swarmed behind them. Falin reached deep into the pile, and upon his fingers touching a specific bag, a jolt in his arm signaled he found his staff. He clutched the sack and yanked it to the surface, distributing their weapons. By some divine glory, they were once again Champions of the Light.

Falin raised his staff and pointed, "To the gate!", dashing across the yard. Dust spewed in the air as the rebellion raged, some prisoners struggling to scale the dark stone wall. As they darted for the exit, Falin saw a major dilemma: the front gate to the prison was securely closed, guarded by a final horde of twenty armed guards.

"That lever above the gate!" Red called, pointing to a ledge on the wall. "We need to open it!"

Jimbuah nudged Bossador as they ran. "Upa!" he said, pointing to the lever. "Upa! Upa!"

Bossador looked between the skully and wall's top, nodding in understanding. "I'm sending Jimmy atop. When he gets up there, we charge!" The madorian rushed ahead of the group, stopping a safe distance from the guards at the gate. The gruns watched, deliberating whether or not to leave their post to attack him. He cupped his hands low, prepared to toss Jimbuah.

"Run with Jimbuah," Carthon called. "We will charge when Bossador sends him up."

"Now!" Falin yelled.

In a flash, they rushed the final stretch of the yard. Jimbuah aimed for Bossador with fierce focus. He leapt, landing his foot in the madorian's palm. Bossador roared, exerting his entire body into launching Jimbuah over the heads of the blockade to the top of the wall.

Falin and the Champions barreled into the enemies. Jimbuah flew overhead, tongue extended and body twirling. As their weapons clashed, Jimbuah caught the lip of the wall and yanked himself up, tugging the lever. The gate rose, and a rush of prisoners lurched for the exit.

The final fleet of guards was trampled, and Red bolted for a wagon beneath the wall, already hitched to a belg. He hopped into the driver's seat, the rest piling in. Jimbuah dropped from above and landed beside Red with a heavy *thud*, grinning at his counterpart.

Red thrashed the reins, demanding the belg haul them from Vug-Rhal. As the commotion of the prison choked on the dust spewed in their departure, the escapees took pleasure in the fresh air and sunlight. Their wagon bounced over the desert terrain, and Red urged the belg faster as they flew south across the Wildbarrens, free to pursue the second Gem of Elsana.

CHAPTER SEVENTEEN:
A STORM AWAKENS

Two days since their escape of Vug-Rhal, the travelers pressed further south in the barren terrain. The belg lugging them hobbled. They roamed in the excruciating heat, gone without food and drink in their hasty departure. Their heads pounded from dehydration and skin burned bright red from the ruthless Wildbarrens sun. Falin clung to his staff in a physical form of hope, as he felt it tug south. They were close to the second Gem.

Red sat with the reins of the belg loosely in his hand, dipping his head so the brim of his hat shielded his eyes. It was then that the belg stumbled, plunging to the ground, halting their travel. It lay unconscious in the dirt. In their apathetic misery, they stared at the dying animal from the wagon. Red lethargically snapped the reins. "Hyah."

"Now what?" Falin rasped.

"We eat it," Red replied. "And drink its blood." Melquin opened her mouth to speak, but Red raised his hand to silence her. "And before you argue, I think you should consider the oath you took to protect Falin."

Melquin scowled. "That is not what I was going to say. Look," she pointed ahead of them.

They squinted, and over the heat waves of the landscape, they saw a bit of brown turned green. Bossador leapt up in the wagon and shielded his eyes. "Is that what I think it is?!"

Nym stood, craning her neck. "Rumeren's Oasis!"

"We've made it," Carthon said in disbelief. "Let us not waste anymore time!"

"Do we take the belg?" Melquin asked.

Red examined the nearly dead animal. "He's dinner if there's no food at the oasis."

Without a word, Falin led the charge in the final stretch of the Wildbarrens. His staff hurried him forward, yearning for the placement of the second Gem. His legs were weak and throat stung, and above all, an emotional tiredness plagued him. He'd experienced so much Darkness and so many vile creatures in the first stint of his journey. He thirsted for the power to do good in the Elsana, to drive back all the evils that hindered the land.

In their final hike, sprouts of plants developed, and a great line of green met their gaze. They bore witness to an immaculate sight.

Rumeren's Oasis was not just an isolated patch of foliage, but instead, wondrous ruins of brown stone surrounding a majestic lake. Palm trees and bushes were plentiful, and the shore of the water was circled by lush grass so vibrant it seemed impossible to have survived in a desert. Streams of water ran over the ruins and fed the lake so that its lapping ripples sparkled like jewels. The desert earth quickly became grass beneath their feet.

The travelers ran to the lake, falling to their knees at its edge, cupping their hands for deep gulps of water. As they did, Falin sensed overwhelming Light as he had in the Pools of Isetta. Breathing heavily from the sudden intake of water, Falin fell back, running his fingers through the cool grass. Rumeren's Oasis seemed twenty degrees cooler than the outside desert.

Falin scanned the place, and on the other side of the lake was a line of stone homes, standing three stories tall, with windows and entrances at each. In the center, was a tower with a single, steep rock staircase climbing to its top. He wiped his mouth of droplets and stood, reinvigorated. "Wait here," he told the Champions.

Falin walked the lakeside, letting the bottom of his staff graze the water's edge. The pool was massive, and he could hardly see the other side from where he stood. He circled it, taking note of the buildings he passed, searching for statues or artwork that hinted what people resided here so many years ago, but there were none. All that remained were the beige stone homes they'd built, overgrown with ivy. It surprised Falin there were no other creatures present, but perhaps it was because those dwelling in the Wildbarrens saw no need for the oasis. Perhaps those Dark creatures feared the Light of the place, so they stayed away.

Reaching the opposite side of the lake, he scanned the tower and its single, thin staircase leading to its top. He started the ascent, his climb one of urgency, and with every step passed his staff trembled with excitement. The Water Gem was soon to have a friend.

At the top of the tower, Falin came to a landing. A thin pedestal stood at the height of his chest. A white Gem floated freely in the air above the podium, hovering with the slightest bounce and radiant sparkle. It hung midair like nothing he had ever seen before.

Falin approached, gently reaching his hand to touch the Gem. As his fingers grasped it, he felt a lightness come over him, as if he'd truly inhaled for the first time. Lifting the Gem from its place, Falin tucked it in the slot beside the Water Gem. At once, the Gem locked in, and he became one with the air in Elsana.

A gust of wind swirled around Rumeren's Oasis, causing the lake to ripple and palm trees to flutter, all applauding his collection of the Air Gem. Falin turned to gaze over the ruins, high above the Wildbarrens. In an inexplicable way, he knew the air as an extension of himself, the same as he felt one with the water. His Champions watched from the opposite side of the lake, no more than tiny figures at this distance.

Wishing to send them a sign of joy, he raised his staff, causing a gale to brush the top of the water and caress their faces. Falin saw them react and wave. He noticed in his message to them, there was a strange harmony in the water and the air. He raised his newly gemmed staff, this time concentrating on combining the lake and the wind, and to his surprise, a little cloud lifted from the lake, rising above its surface. The wizard toyed with it, feeling the water within the cloud before letting it spill as rain.

Wanting to share the recent success with his group, he plodded down the steps, hurrying around the lake to return to their camp. They waited, standing, proud to have witnessed the event.

Bossador raised his chin and beamed. "We take it you have found the Air Gem."

Falin nodded and smiled, waving his staff to let a breeze tickle their faces. "Indeed I have. Thanks to all of you."

"Look what Jimbuah found," Nym said, pointing to the skully.

Jimbuah's arms were filled with a bushel of orange fruits ready for consumption. "Ibato?"

"Yes," Melquin nodded. "I am starving and do not wish to feast on belg."

Jimbuah quickly distributed the fruit, and the group dined, taking great bliss in their meal. They'd gone so long in the Wildbarrens without any semblance of happiness outside each other, it was refreshing to experience a reminder there was still good in the world, as hidden as it might be.

Carthon wiped juice from his lips and tossed aside a fruit pit. "So where do we go from here? Do we rest before we travel back?"

"It depends," Falin thought. "Bossador had the idea we hug the coast to Letani if Red and Jimbuah are okay with it. If they decide to take you in as fugitives, we will flee."

Red chewed his lip nervously, then looked to Jimbuah. They exchanged a thought before nodding subtly. "Alright," Red replied. "We'll do it. But I'm done with prisons for a bit. So if it looks like they're gonna take us, I'm out."

"Yeh," Jimbuah agreed.

"How do we know if we're even near the coast?" Melquin asked.

Carthon pointed to the sky. "I think we are. Look at the clouds." The group turned their heads to see streaks of clouds further south from where they were. "Those are the first clouds we've seen since coming to the Wildbarrens. They must be accumulating from the Sea of Eternal Fire."

Falin toyed with his staff. "I think he's right. I can feel it."

"So then it's settled," Bossador said. "We will find the coast, then follow that path until we make our way to Letani. Falin will have the power of the water at his back to protect us in the event we are attacked again."

Red scratched under his hat and nodded. "It's a solid plan."

The sun began to set over the Wildbarrens, and their eyelids grew heavy, comfortable in the soft grass of Rumeren's Oasis. Nym stretched and yawned. "Who even lived here before, anyway?"

Falin shrugged. "Your guess is as good as mine. Could've been the talking lizards Red mentioned for all I know."

The group chuckled, and Red fought a smile. "You know what, it very well could've been," the Freelander said.

"We should sleep," Melquin suggested, a yawn of her own triggered from Nym's. "Should one of us take watch?"

"I will take first watch," Carthon offered.

"I'll take second," Bossador added. "Don't be afraid to wake me when you grow tired."

Carthon nodded. "Thank you."

As the sky darkened, the group fell to sleep, the air in the oasis a refreshing blanket protecting them from the desert heat. They slept unbothered and unafraid for the first time in weeks.

In time, the sun rose again, and they stirred, splashing their faces in the lake and drinking until their bellies were full. Melquin and Jimbuah gathered another batch of fruit, and they ate breakfast, seeing no need to hurry from the oasis. They savored their morning with silly amusements, not wanting to return to the desert. Red tried to teach Bossador to juggle fruit, and Jimbuah and Nym challenged one another to handstand contest.

Come early afternoon, when the sun was high and they were at their most relaxed, they heard a distant rumbling from the desert. "Do you hear that?" Melquin asked.

"It sounds like thunder," Bossador said.

Nym looked to the desert. "Something approaches." In an instant, their hearts dropped. She walked to the edge of the oasis, listening intently. Her elvish eyes stared across the barren landscape.

"What is it, Nym?" Carthon asked.

Nym shook her head, not knowing what it could be. "I see a dust cloud. And it sounds like a stampede." The rest rose, standing beside her, viewing the sandy mist in the distance. The earthly grumbling loudened, drifting across the open desert. Nym tensed upon realizing what approached. "It is the soldiers of Vug-Rhal! Riding belg! Qarza must be coming for us!"

"Get your belongings! We have to run!" Red yelled.

"Should we hide?!" Melquin asked.

"We should fight," Bossador demanded, unsheathing his greatsword and holding his shield.

Carthon put his hand on Falin's shoulder. "What do you want us to do? We go where you demand."

As an endless drove of gruns and augurs came into sight, some riding belg, others sprinting chaotically, an impassioned fury rose within Falin. "Stay in the oasis," he demanded of his Champions. "I will protect you."

"Falin, we—" Melquin began, but the wizard stalked from the edge of the oasis into the desert in a trance-like state.

Falin raised his staff to the sky and closed his eyes. He knew bountiful rage at that moment—rage fueled by the Dark's insistence that his Champion's must run, fight, and flee for their lives on a constant basis. His kind, forgiving, and wonderful Champions would fear no more, as he would show the Dark what it meant to face the power of the Light.

Upon opening his eyes, he saw the horde closing in. Storm clouds rolled over the oasis, summoned by Falin's furor. A grumble of thunder responded as a warning to the oncoming enemies, a warning they did not heed. The sky grew darker, quickly blocking the sun, and soon, all was shadowed, covered by blackened clouds.

Gusts of wind began to rush across the desert, and Falin felt an overflow of force at his fingertips, desperate to burst. The patter of rain spotted the dusty earth. A clatter of thunder crashed so violently it muffled the oncoming charge. Falin felt the clouds swell. Upon seeing the whites of his enemies' eyes, the snarls of their insidious mouths, and sensing the hatred in their hearts, he released the storm.

With a mighty wave of his staff, the sky broke, and a terrible rain plummeted across the desert. A howling wind reamed so ferociously his Champions clung to palm trees so as not to fly off the ground.

As the first line of belg-ridden enemies came near, Falin swung his staff, and from it, a blast of wind tossed them hundreds of feet back into the Wildbarrens. He welcomed anyone brazen enough to attack a wizard's Champions, as he was glad to see their demise. With every swoosh of his staff, another gust of wind would fling augurs, gruns, and belg like a hurricane would leaves.

Rain poured like a ceaseless waterfall, choking the assailants. Another boom of thunder warned the attackers, but they drove on, and Falin could see more approaching in the distance. His acrimony for the Dark surged, and lightning began to spike to the earth all around. Servants of warlocks would not harm them on this day. Beneath the cracks of thunder, the turbulent downpour, and whooshing gales, the shrieks of enemies could be heard as they were thrown across the desert.

It seemed the more assailants he cast away, twice the number pressed forward. A caravan of gruns ushered by belg charged. To Falin's surprise, a bolt of lightning struck the caravan leaving it a smoldering pile of filth.

Falin shouted, and the rain plummeted harder. Muddied streams of water formed around his feet as the oasis lake behind him started to flood. Seeing at a distance became difficult, and the wizard's Champions squinted to view the fight, hugging the trees so as not to fly from the earth. This constant hiss of the rain meshed with stampeding attackers was deafening.

On and on Falin fought, waving his staff, harnessing the wind and summoning endless rain upon his enemies. Another clatter of thunder punched the eardrums of those present, but still, the onslaught of assailants was relentless, sweeping across the desert in droves.

Falin began to tire, panting, drenched from his own storm. The barreling rain faltered to a steady pour, and every boom of thunder seemed less imposing with seconds passed. He whirled his staff, throwing the onslaught back, each time less powerful than the last. His body was becoming depleted of magic, but still, the enemies came.

Gruns and augurs soon surrounded, blitzing for a chance to maim the wizard. The wind of Falin's staff became no more than a brash gust, holding them at bay. When Falin was certain the blades of his foes would impale him, the sound of clashing metal met his ears at all sides.

The wizard's Champion's circled him, holding back the overwhelming swarm, and through the deluge they fought, with battlecries of Light.

Melquin bludgeoned an augur with a quick swipe of her staff, and Red cracked his whip to the eye of a grun, impaling another with his sword. Nym tossed stars with one hand, slicing the throats of enemies with her blade, and Carthon stood by her, swinging his swords in a frenzy. Jimbuah threw fireberries that seemed impervious to the rain, causing bright bursts of violet flame on the skin of those attacking.

Falin looked over his shoulder, seeing General Qarza break through the fray, holding both his baton and longsword, roaring in hideous terror. As Qarza raised his weapon to strike Red, it was blocked by the greatsword of Bossador. Their eyes locked in mutual hatred.

Bossador swung his blade, cutting the baton hand of Qarza so the magical weapon fell. The two became embroiled in a mighty sparring match, hitting one another's blades so loudly the clang of metal pierced the ears of those too close.

The Champions' glimmer of hope quickly faded upon realizing a fresh reinforcement of assailants dashed across the desert. Beaten and exhausted, fatigue settled into their company. They would not be able to hold them off for much longer.

It was then that a sound unlike anything heard in the battle thus far met their ears. Over the thunder, rain, stampede, and screams, a noise came from above, hidden in the clouds. *FWOOM. FWOOM. FWOOM.*

Falin turned his attention to the sky. His heart leapt upon recognizing the sound. *FWOOM. FWOOM. FWOOM.* Bjorgun the Dragon emerged from the clouds, ridden by Princess Bloom, swooping over the new line of attackers. The dragon breathed a mighty flame across the oncoming battalion, scorching them to ash in an instant.

Princess Bloom pointed to the Champions, calling Bjorgun to turn to the frenzy. The dragon dove to the earth and landed atop enemies, crushing them beneath his scaled claws, blowing another breath of fire to those nearby. "Get on!" Bloom called, beckoning them to take hold of Bjorgun's bony spines as she was.

Nym, Carthon, Red, Jimbuah, then Melquin leapt atop Bjorgun. Falin turned, seeing Bossador remained in a bitter fight with Qarza. Before he could call for his Champion to flee, Bjorgun whipped his tail, flinging Qarza to tumble across the earth like a doll. "Come Prince Bossador!" Bjorgun called. "Your wizard needs you for another day!"

Falin and Bossador climbed onto Bjorgun, and the dragon breathed another dose of flame upon those still brazen enough to attack. Getting a running start, Bjorgun flapped his wings, and they took flight. The dragon panted, as it was evident the group was a burdensome one in all of their weight. With the remaining energy Falin had left, he blew air beneath Bjorgun's wings to give his friend a greater lift. Soon, Bjorgun soared, and they left the battlefield behind.

The clouds quickly faded, and they overlooked the Wildbarrens. "Boo yattah!" Jimbuah screamed. "Boo yattah!"

Weightlessness brought smiles to each of their faces, eternally grateful for their incredible luck to be saved by Princess Bloom and Bjorgun. Falin and his Champions flew over the Wildbarrens, alive another day to continue their quest.

CHAPTER EIGHTEEN:
ONWARD AND ONWARD

Exhausted from carrying eight people atop his scaly back, Bjorgun landed on the shore of an empty beach. They climbed off, and Princess Bloom neatened her hair as she turned to the travelers, having not been able to speak during the flight. "We were so lucky to have found you all."

Falin nodded. "I don't know that there will ever be enough thanks we can offer you for rescuing us."

Red stared at Bloom in awe. "What were you doing in the Wildbarrens?"

Princess Bloom smirked, cocksure, glancing at Bjorgun. "I convinced a certain someone to take me."

Bjorgun laid in the sand, sighing a hot breath. "She wouldn't shut up for weeks about it. I think she just missed the Freela—"

Bloom cut him off. "Anyway, we saw the storm clouds in the distance. Bjorgun thought it was strange, and thought it could be Falin."

"Only a wizard could conjure such a storm in a place so dry," the dragon added. "I was right."

"We owe you our lives," Falin stated. His Champions nodded in agreement.

"Do good in the world, Falin," Bjorgun responded. "That is all we ask."

One by one, Falin and the Champions fell to the sand. They sat in silence for a moment, listening to the crashes of waves upon the unending coastline. Melquin spoke first. "Well, we're halfway done."

All let out an exasperated laugh. Carthon shook his head. "And we still have warlocks to worry about."

"And invasions," Bossador added.

Bloom looked between them. "What's all this about warlocks and invasions?"

Nym rubbed her eyes. "We'll tell you later. I think we just need a minute." The elf unclasped her utility belt and cast it side, laying back, propped up by her elbows. She stared over the ocean, where a setting sun seemed to call them to the water. "So what now?"

"I figured we would camp here for the night," Bossador replied. "Take flight for Letani in the morning?" He glanced at Bjorgun, hoping no argument came from the dragon.

"No, I mean where are we going next?" Nym corrected. "Where is the next Gem?"

Falin sighed, not sure he wanted to know. He removed the map from his robes and pressed the head of his staff to the parchment. A glowing green dot appeared on the north end of the island known as Hadrones. "We go to Hadrones. Across the Magpie Isles."

They thought about it for a moment. Carthon said, "I know little of Hadrones. Does anyone know what is there?"

Melquin shook her head. "No one really knows what goes on in the Magpie Isles at all. It is a land far different from mainland Elsana."

"Maybe the talking lizards can give us directions," Bossador teased Red.

Falin stared across the water. "Well then I hope Letani can give us a nice boat. Does anyone know how to sail?"

"Yeh, yeh," Jimbuah nodded.

"I can as well," Carthon replied.

"Wait a minute," Melquin said, turning to Red and Jimbuah. "You were brought to help us through the Wildbarrens, which you have done. You are free from this quest if you choose."

The duo scowled at the sage. Red spoke for both of them. "We're seeing this thing through. You're not going anywhere without us until Falin has a staff that's twice as shiny."

Falin looked to the head of his staff and smiled at the sparkling Gems. "I am very glad Queen Martana released you two from prison."

Bloom furrowed her brow at Red. "You were in prison? In Mystica? You did not tell me this."

Red shrugged. "Your family thinks you got eaten by a dragon. Sometimes we leave details out."

"Fair enough," Bloom muttered.

Bossador took a deep breath, then held his stomach as it grumbled. "I am very hungry. I wonder if there is anything edible in that water."

"Maybe some type of seaweed," Melquin thought aloud.

Bjorgun stood. "There may be Lava Seals along the coast south of here. I would be happy to find some as I am famished myself."

Bloom leapt up, eager for any chance to ride atop her dragon friend. "I'll come with you!" She stopped, looking over her shoulder. "Do you want to join us, Red?"

Before Red could answer, Bjorgun did. "I am not a steed, Princess. I only carry you because you're more akin to a feather than a lady."

"Alright, alright," Bloom sighed, climbing atop his back. "We'll be back soon." She stared at Red as the two took flight over the beach, sending sand spewing into the air. The flapping of Bjorgun's wings faded as he glided gently on the ocean air.

Falin and his Champions sat in a row, gazing across the water at the sunset, painting the sky purple and crimson with the Wildbarrens at their backs. Nothing but the crashing of waves met their ears for some time, and they took comfort in the peace. "We've been through much," Falin said. "And we'll go through more. We need to stop Nyril and Mulgus from invading the Freelands. The best way we can assist is finding all the Gems."

"'Tis an honor," Jimbuah replied.

"He's right." Bossador nodded. "It is."

Falin wished to wash away the hanging threats of tomorrow that plagued them. They deserved a mental reprieve. One more time, he proposed a question. "If you could pick any moment in our quest so far..." The Champions turned to him, ready for whatever game he posed. "If you could pick any moment as your most joyful in this quest, what would it be? Bossador, you first."

The prince raised his eyebrows and sighed. "There were many great moments we've shared." He paused and considered it. "But I would have to say when we were announced as Champions after we swore the oath to my father. Everything in my life had been leading up to that moment."

Falin nodded, remembering how innocent the world seemed before embarking on the journey. "Carthon, what about you?"

Carthon played at the sand, letting it run over his fingers until scooping it again. "The Siren of the Oldwoods. Rila was it?"

Melquin scrunched her nose. "That was *joyful*?"

"Yes," Carthon replied with confidence. "It is the moment I first realized I loved Nym. Her grace in battle was like nothing I'd ever seen. When she killed the siren, I was smitten."

"Draks are weird," Red mumbled.

"My most memorable moment was also in the Oldwoods, shortly after that," Nym said. "When Carthon and I found the rupela tree. It was beautiful; a little island of beauty in a dreary place. It was very romantic until Jimbuah joined us." Jimbuah chuckled upon hearing the story.

"What's yours, Jimmy?" Falin asked.

The skully scratched his chin in thought, snapping his finger when coming to an answer. "Pukali Isetta. Jofayo fakumili."

Red translated, "He said the Pools of Isetta. We were a happy family."

Falin thought back to the night spent together after they had found the first Gem in the Mortal Caves. "That was one of my favorites too, Jimmy." He turned to Red. "And your favorite moment would be?"

Red gazed down the southern shoreline. "Meetin' Bloom." He offered no further details, but his longing stare said all it needed.

Falin nodded, unsurprised. He looked to Melquin and gestured that she take a turn. "I liked Monkey Mountain," she said. "It was paradise, and the type of place I hoped to visit at the start of this journey." The sage took a deep breath. "Are you going to share your favorite moment with us?"

Falin thought through all they'd experienced, shoving aside the fearful and tragic moments, seeking the seconds of Light. For some reason, one of the more mundane nights stuck out. "Our dinner in Rorkshire," he replied.

"Really?" Red asked. "Out of it all we've done, that Rorkshire dinner did it for you?"

"Yes," Falin answered. "I don't know why, but in that moment, having us all gathered around the same table, I knew my purpose as a wizard. Seeing my Champions, children of the Light, enjoying one another's presence—the spirit of that dinner is what all wizards want for Elsana, and I caught a tiny glimpse that night."

"I hope for many more of them to come," Bossador said.

"Yeh," Jimbuah nodded. "En pija," he added.

Falin chuckled. "Yes, and more pie."

The wizard and his Champions sat together on the shores of the Wildbarrens, basking in the sunset. Falin raised his chin to the ocean breeze. He felt hope. There were many adventures to come, but for now, this family brought together by the Gems of Elsana could rest, taking comfort in each other's company.

THE END

A NOTE FROM THE AUTHOR

Let me start off by saying thank you. Your support to an author is most appreciated, as it is a reader like you who allows me to cultivate the work I do.

If you enjoyed my book please leave review Goodreads or Amazon. You can find more information about the world of Elsana on:

Elsana.net

To stay up to date on latest works, or speak to me on social media, you can follow me on Instagram here:

Instagram: @christiansterlingg

To sign up for my email list to be the first to receive the next installment of *Gems of Elsana* and other works, go to:

christiansterlingauthor.com

Again, I thank you for reading. See you on the next adventure!

Works by Christian Sterling

The Gems of Elsana Series:
Into the Wildbarrens (The Gems of Elsana #1)
The Magpie Isles (The Gems of Elsana #2)
For the Freelands (The Gems of Elsana #3)

American Parable Series:
Ashes and Embers (American Parable #1)
Breaking Chains (American Parable #2)
One At War (American Parable #3)

Bandits Series
Of Saints and Sinners (Bandits #1)

Death Row: A Novella

Made in the USA
Middletown, DE
07 June 2020